SWEET SEDUCTION

The surging power of Bart's presence was spellbinding. Bending his head, he kissed Sheila demandingly, urgently, his lips overpowering hers with compelling persuasion. Then he released her with reluctance.

Sheila asked tremulously, "Bart, is something wrong?" Had she somehow disappointed him?

He smiled a little shakily. "Sheila, I wonder if you have any idea how much I want you."

"Yes, I think I do," she replied. "And I want you, Bart. I want you with all my heart."

"It wouldn't be right," he said. "I won't take advantage of you."

His chivalry didn't surprise her; his kindness was one of the reasons she loved him. A twinkle, as bright as it was seductive, shone in her eyes. "Bart Chandler, if you won't take advantage of me, then I shall take advantage of you." She slid her arms about his neck and pressed her body to his.

He claimed her lips in a captive caress, his rekindled passion blazing hotly.

Explosive sensations ruled Sheila's heart and mind, sending reality soaring into space. Forgotten was the perilous situation surrounding her. She was conscious of nothing except Bart's lips on hers . . .

ROCHELLE WAYNE

CAPTIVE SPLENDOR

PINNACLE BOOKS
WINDSOR PUBLISHING CORP.

For Aunt Loretta and Uncle Roger—with love and thanks for their loyal support

PINNACLE BOOKS

are published by

Windsor Publishing Corp.
475 Park Avenue South
New York, NY 10016

First Printing: April, 1993

Printed in the United States of America

Prologue

1

The Sioux village, nestled in a lush green valley, was quiet, for the warriors, along with several women and children, were gone to hunt buffalo. The area surrounding the village was serene and breathtakingly beautiful. A backdrop of rugged cliffs overflowing with aspen and blue spruce loomed in the west, and a waterfall cascading over deep ravines emptied into a clear stream that meandered through the fertile valley. Overhead, interlocking clouds moved weightlessly in a pewter sky as the sun slowly climbed its meridian.

The Indian village consisted of conical-shaped tepees, which were arranged methodically in a large circle. By Sioux custom, they were set up according to family prestige. Cooking smoke from the tepees' open flaps swirled upward to disappear into the billowing clouds, and savory aromas permeated the air.

Inside one of the tepees, which was located in the heart of the village, a young boy slept fitfully. Yesterday he had returned home after seeking his vision, and he was still weak from having gone four days and nights without food or water. The medicine man, Loping Elk, had taken him to the vision pit, a deep hole dug into the hill, and had left him there. The boy, somewhat frightened, had watched the old man walk away until he was only a moving mote on the horizon, and was soon gone altogether. It had been an experience that would stay with him always . . .

Truly alone for the first time in his life, the fourteen-year-old lad remained crouched in the pit trying desperately to conquer his fear. He was shivering, but not from the cold. Despite all his efforts to be brave, he was scared. The village was several miles away, and the four days and nights he would spend alone in this deep pit seemed a very long time. He had never been so completely separated from others, for Indian children were never left alone but were always surrounded by relatives and friends.

Fighting his fear, the boy reminded himself that Sioux warriors were never afraid to endure hunger, thirst, and loneliness, and as soon as his present ordeal was over, he would emerge a man. Someday soon he planned to become a fearless warrior and make his family proud. The thought gave him courage, and with a brave lift to his chin, he mentally prepared himself to face his vision, suffer the elements, and close his mind to thoughts of food and water.

He wrapped his blanket tightly about his nakedness, and its warmth was comforting. His grandmother had made it especially for his first vision-seeking. It was a heavy quilt woven with colorful designs. The medicine man had left him a peace pipe along with a bag of *kinnick-nnick*—tobacco made of red willow bark. The boy hadn't yet smoked a pipe, but leaving it in the vision pit was a ritual. The pipe was even more of a comfort than the quilt, for it had belonged to his father, and to *his* father before him. The boy believed it would someday pass to his own son, and through him, to his grandchildren. He suddenly felt that his fore-fathers who had smoked the pipe were now with him in the vision pit, and that he was no longer alone. He wasn't afraid any more, and a feeling of peacefulness came over him. The whistling winds, the whispering treetops, and the sounds of wild animals became a constant and lulling presence.

As time passed, the boy seemed to lose all sense of his surroundings, and he drifted into a dreamlike state. He couldn't tell the difference between day and night, he was asleep, yet he was awake.

Finally, his vision came to him in the form of a white butterfly that flew down and landed on his shoulder. As it flapped its wings, it told him that he would soon embark on a long journey that would take him far away. The butterfly then flew away immediately, as though anxious to embark on its own long journey. Sometime thereafter, the shape of a white man rose from the darkness to stand before the lad. The man's features were obscured by a dark shadow, but the boy somehow knew that tears were

7

flooding the man's eyes and rolling down his face. Unashamed of his grief, he made no attempt to brush them away. Though he spoke in the white man's tongue, the boy understood, for his grandmother had taught him to speak English. The white man lamented for his daughter, who years ago had been abducted by the Sioux. He called her name, which was Elizabeth, but it meant nothing to the boy. Then, suddenly, the man disappeared like a puff of smoke.

A short time later, a large fluffy cloud descended from the heavens to hover above the pit, causing a dense fog to envelop the lad in a shroud of white mist. What seemed like an eternity later—but had it only been minutes?—a hand touched the boy's shoulder. He looked up to find the medicine man gazing down at him. The fog was now gone, and the sun was shining brightly.

Loping Elk helped the boy from the pit, looked him over carefully, then told him he would give him food and water. Afterward, the boy should tell him of his vision and the medicine man would interpret what the lad had seen and heard.

When Loping Elk at last heard the boy's vision, he was deeply troubled, for he knew Wakan Tanka—the Great Spirit—had sent a sorrowful message. Loping Elk told the lad that his man's name was White Cloud. Then, as gently as possible, he explained the vision. The white butterfly represented a journey with the *Washechu*— white men—and the butterfly's flapping wings meant they were coming in great numbers. The white man who had appeared before him was of his blood, for the Great Spirit would only allow a relative to visit the sacred pit. This white man who cried for his daughter was good and

8

could be trusted. Loping Elk told the boy that if he ever encountered this man, he must trust him completely. The white cloud that descended from the heavens represented the white man's world, he continued, and someday he would be enveloped into the white man's life as surely as the white mist had shrouded the pit.

Although the boy didn't question Loping Elk's interpretation, for he knew the medicine man was never wrong; anger flamed inside him. He could not stand the thought of leaving the Sioux, nor could he imagine never seeing his father, stepmother, brother, sister, and grandmother. They were his family, and he loved them with all his heart. He felt he would rather die than leave them to live in the white man's world.

Now, sleeping restlessly, White Cloud tossed and turned on his bed as his grandmother watched over him. Earlier, as the boy slept, Loping Elk had come to the tepee and told her of her grandson's vision. The woman had listened with mixed emotions. She dreaded losing her grandson, yet there was a part of her that was happy to hear that he would soon live in the white man's world. At one time it had been her own world, but that had been thirty-three years ago. She had no desire ever to return, for the Sioux way of life was now hers.

She sat beside White Cloud's bed, which had a headpiece made from willow rods laid parallel and woven together by means of a strong warp. Padded with pelts and a thick pile of blankets, the bed was indeed a comfortable place to rest. The boy moaned in his sleep, and the woman placed a gentle hand on his brow.

"Do not fret, my grandson," she murmured to the sleeping boy. "The life that awaits you will be much better than the one you leave behind." She sighed heavily, and a wistful smile touched her lips. If White Cloud had been awake she would not have dared to say such a thing. Her words would certainly have provoked his anger, for despite his white blood, in his heart he was Sioux. She had often spoken to him of the white man's way of life, and the boy always listened attentively, but his interest stemmed from curiosity, not from any wish ever to leave the Sioux to live with the whites.

Now, as she continued to watch over her grandson, the woman's thoughts moved back in time, and memories rippled through her mind like gentle wind on water. She saw herself as a young woman in a gingham dress. Her hair was not streaked with gray but rather the color of ripe wheat, and the thick tresses cascaded to her waist in full, silky waves. She was once again sixteen years old, and her name was Margaret Latham. Her blue eyes turned misty as she continued remembering.

Thirty-three years ago Margaret had come westward. Her father, hoping to better their lives in Oregon, had sold his farm in Ohio, gathered his family, and packed their meager belongings. They had all joined a wagon train leaving from St. Joseph, Missouri.

The train had traveled deep into the Wyoming Territory, and the wagon master had advised everyone to stay close to their wagons, for a small party of Sioux warriors had been spotted. But Margaret had disobeyed, and had wandered away to meet a young man she had met on the trip. The pair hadn't dared to tell their parents that they had fallen in love, for she was Protestant and he was

10

Catholic. They knew their headstrong fathers would have forbidden them from seeing each other. Margaret waited until her parents and her two younger brothers were asleep, then had slipped from the wagon to meet her young man. As she crept stealthily past the other wagons that night, she couldn't possibly have imagined that she would never see her family again. Nor could she have known that her life would change forever.

Margaret was the first to arrive at the prearranged rendezvous spot, but she was there only a minute or so when, hearing footsteps, she turned about expecting to see her beau. Instead, she was confronted by a young Sioux warrior. Before she could scream he clamped a hand over her mouth. He then knocked her unconscious, and flung her over his pony. Joining the rest of his party, he fled into the night taking his captive with him.

Days of strenuous travel followed. The warrior took her to his village, where he planned to make her his wife. He delivered her to his uncle's tepee, which was to be her home until they married. Several months passed before Margaret learned the Sioux's language and their customs. For the first few weeks, she didn't even try, for she was certain that her father and the other travelers would rescue her. Finally, though, she gave up hope, and, needing to communicate with those people around her, she began to try to learn their language. Her captor's name was High Hawk she discovered, and his father was Chief Big Thunder. As the weeks became months, she found herself falling in love with High Hawk, who was a handsome and fearless warrior. The day before their marriage, the medicine man named her Golden Dove, and Margaret accepted the name as she had now accepted her new life.

11

She married High Hawk, and one year later, she gave him a son. She longed for more children, but fate had blessed them with only the one.

Golden Dove's memories faded and her mind returned to the present. She studied her sleeping grandson, her eyes filled with love. Yes, she had learned to accept her life as High Hawk's wife, but deep in her heart, she had never forgotten that she was white. Her son, Iron Star, had followed in his father's footsteps and had stolen himself a white bride. Her name had been Elizabeth, and like Golden Dove, she had finally accepted her captivity and had fallen in love with her captor. Elizabeth had died giving birth to White Cloud, and Golden Dove had raised the boy until he was two years old. At that time, Iron Star had taken himself another wife, a young Indian woman named Red Blanket. He now had two children from his second wife, a son and a daughter. Red Blanket and the children were on the buffalo hunt with Iron Star.

Golden Dove continued to study her grandson. His white heritage was so obvious that he actually bore little resemblance to the Sioux. This was understandable, as his father was half white and his mother had been *fully* white. The boy was only one-fourth Sioux. His hair was coal black and his complexion was dark, but there his physical likeness to the Sioux ended. His eyes were charcoal gray, and even at the age of fourteen, it was apparent that he would grow much taller than most Indians. His physique was lean but tightly muscled, and his facial features were finely sculpted.

White Cloud, leaving his worrisome dreams behind, came awake suddenly. He wasn't surprised to find his grandmother watching over him.

She smiled tenderly. "You were sleeping very restlessly."

He sat up and brushed a hand across his perspiring brow. "I wish I had never gone into the vision pit!" A deep frown wrinkled his forehead. "I should have gone hunting with Father and the others!"

"It would not matter when you had your vision, it would still have been the same."

"But if I had waited, at least Father would have been here."

Golden Dove sighed wearily. "Iron Star cannot help you. He cannot make the vision go away. The Great Spirit has spoken. Your future is already set and it cannot be altered." Golden Dove believed what she said, for she had lived with the Sioux too many years to question their rituals. She had never known the Great Spirit to be wrong.

"But I do not want to live with the whites!" the boy said stubbornly, as though mouthing the words would somehow change everything.

"You are now a man, White Cloud, and you must start acting like one. A warrior does not whine like a child."

He flinched as if Golden Dove's words had struck him physically. He looked away from his grandmother, for he was suddenly ashamed. She was right; he *was* behaving childishly.

"I will get you some food," she said.

He watched her as she went to the lodge fire to dish up a bowl of venison stew. The cooking pit, outlined with cobblestones, was in a circular shape. Above, where the lodge poles crossed, the smoke drifted upward through an opening. White Cloud watched his grandmother with admiration. She was still attractive, and with

13

her tall, slender frame, was as firm as a woman years younger.

She brought him his food, and although he managed to eat most of it, he was still weak. He gave her back the bowl, lay down, and tried to go back to sleep. His young body was completely drained. He felt a little lightheaded and dizzy, as he had felt after leaving his first sweat bath. Before going to the vision pit, he had gone to the sweat lodge to be purified. He had sat there, covered with blankets, in a beehive-shaped hut made of bent willow branches. Loping Elk and three other medicine men had been in the lodge with him. With his back against the wall, the lad had stared wondrously at the red-hot stones glowing in the center. Loping Elk had poured water over the rocks, and hissing steam had enveloped White Cloud. The heat was intense, and it burned as it filled his lungs. Afterward, he was totally drained and his mind was blank, which meant he was ready to seek his vision.

White Cloud slowly drifted back into slumber, and Golden Dove covered him with a blanket. She knew it would take a few days for him to get back his strength. The sweat bath, followed by four days and nights without food and water, was physically exhausting.

She went to her own bed, where she tried in vain to take a short nap. But her mind was too occupied with White Cloud's vision for her to relax and fall asleep. Her grandson would leave the Sioux to live with the whites! It seemed too miraculous to be true. She smiled and her heart filled with joy. Yes, she would miss her grandson, but she was well pleased with his vision. A better life awaited him. Golden Dove was certain that the Sioux, and all Plains Indians, were doomed. Many battles would take place between the Indians and the soldiers, and, in time, the Indians' way of life would be destroyed. A stab of pain took away the joy in Golden Dove's heart as she thought of all the brave warriors who would die fighting for their lands. At least White Cloud would be spared, for he would no longer be one of them.

She closed her eyes and imagined White Cloud living in civilization, and growing into a handsome, polished gentleman. The vision brought her peace.

Captain Charles Dwyer stood impatiently beside his horse. A deep frown furrowed his brow as he waited for his two scouts to return. His mounted troops were tense but silent. Only the musical chirping of birds and the periodic snorting of a trooper's horse broke the silence.

The sun sinking in the west cast a golden glow over the verdant area, and a gentle breeze stirred the aspen and spruce that grew in abundance. Large, fluffy clouds skimmed across the azure sky as though they were bent on following the setting sun's trip over the horizon.

Nature's exquisite painting made no impression on Captain Dwyer. At the moment, his thoughts prevented appreciation of such serenity. Revenge alone was on his mind, and it would take spilled blood to appease it.

He had recently lost his wife, who had been on her way to Fort Laramie to join him. She was traveling with the payroll wagon, which was escorted by over forty troopers. There had not been any recent trouble between the Army and the Sioux, and there was no reason for anyone to expect an attack, but a Sioux war party comprised of over a hundred warriors had struck suddenly, killing everyone, including the captain's wife.

Now, Captain Dwyer was out for blood.

The scouts, who had been looking over the area ahead, returned quietly. The two men were dressed in buckskins and sported full beards. They were at home in the wilderness, for they used to be trappers.

"Captain," the one named Luke said. "There's a village up ahead, but it ain't the one you're lookin' for. The Indians you're awantin' skirted this area and headed farther into the mountains."

Dwyer sighed.

"We might as well head back to the fort," Luke continued. "It's impossible to track them Indians across the mountains."

The captain's eyes widened. "Are you telling me that the warriors who killed my wife cannot be apprehended?"

"Yep, that's exactly what I'm sayin'. Them Indians are long gone, and you ain't gonna find 'em. If you take your soldiers up into the mountains, you ain't gonna accomplish nothin' 'cept to run out of rations. Believe me, Captain, you might as well turn around and go back to the fort."

Dwyer was bitterly disappointed. He couldn't imagine terminating his mission without gaining some satisfaction. He thought about the village that lay ahead.

"Well, if I can't attack the Indians I'm hunting, then I'll simply set an example that will keep all these murdering savages cowering in their beds."

Luke's friend, Daniel, looked questioningly at the captain. "Example? What do you mean by that?"

Dwyer didn't explain. Instead, he asked, "How large is this village?"

"Pretty big," Daniel answered. "Luke and me, we stayed hid and watched it for a while. Considerin' what we saw, I'd say that most of the warriors are out huntin' buffalo."

A malicious gleam shone in the captain's eyes, and a determined expression hardened his face. "We're going to attack that village and kill every male, regardless of his age! I'll teach these heathens to murder my wife!"

"Captain, you can't be serious!" Luke exclaimed.

"I'm dead serious! If you don't want to come along, then stay behind! I don't give a damn!"

He mounted his horse, then looked down at the trappers. "Well?" he demanded. "Are you coming or not?"

The men glanced at each other.

"Are you goin' or stayin', Luke?" Daniel asked.

"I ain't takin' no part in a massacre." He glared disdainfully at the captain. "When I get back to the fort, I'm gonna report you to your commanding officer, and then I'm gonna find me some new kinda work!"

Dwyer smiled coldly. He didn't fear a court-martial; the fort's commanding officer hated Indians as much as he did. Furthermore, there wasn't a soldier in the area who didn't long for revenge. The Sioux had killed over forty of their comrades!

Daniel went to his horse and swung into the saddle. He had decided to ride along.

Charles Dwyer spoke crisply to his sergeant. "Pass the

word that I want every male in that village killed! By God, no little bastard there will grow up to murder a white woman!''

"Yes, sir!" the sergeant replied.

Luke, finding it difficult to keep his emotions under control, stepped to his horse, took its reins, and walked a short distance away. He wrapped the reins about a tree limb, then sat down and leaned back against the wide trunk. He considered warning the residents of the village, but the outcome would still be the same, except that he would be dead, for the captain would certainly have him shot. No, a warning would solve nothing. The village was without the majority of its warriors now, so even if they knew an attack was imminent, the massacre would still take place. Captain Dwyer had a hundred armed soldiers under his command.

Luke watched sadly as the calvary moved on. An ache filled his entire being, and a sickening sensation found its way to the pit of his stomach. For a moment, he thought he might actually be sick, but in time the nausea passed, only to be replaced by an empty, sodden dullness.

He had never felt so helpless, and his inability to save the Sioux children who would certainly die caused him suddenly to feel a terrible anger toward himself. Why in God's name was he sitting here like a spineless coward when perhaps he could save lives? He didn't question how he could achieve such a feat—after all, he was only one man against a hundred.

But Luke Thomas was a man of integrity, and that was the driving force that sent him mounting his horse and following the path the soldiers had taken. A lonely tear moistened the corner of his eye, but he quickly brushed it aside. Against his own volition, a picture of children being slaughtered had flashed horribly in his mind.

2

Golden Dove was about to start on her afternoon chores when a sudden barrage of gunshots, the pounding of horses' hooves, and then a scream, soon followed by other screams sent a streak of terror coursing through her. She was so frightened that her body grew limp and her knees trembled. She was dangerously close to fainting, but fighting back the blackness threatening to engulf her, she willed herself to move across to the tepee. She swung the flap open, stepped outside, and felt as though she had stepped straight into Armageddon. Her face turned deathly pale, her eyes widened with horror, and a blood-chilling tremor shook her entire frame. She watched, frozen, as her people—men, women, and children— scurried for their tepees, only to be shot down on the way by marauding soldiers.

She sensed a movement behind her, and turned about to find White Cloud stumbling toward her. The attack had awakened him, but he was still dizzy and lightheaded, and was perspiring heavily. He moved outside, placed a weak arm about his grandmother's shoulders for support, and stared at the massacre taking place before his eyes.

Captain Dwyer, charging on his white stallion, had discarded his pistol and was swinging his sabre, unmercifully hacking at any Indian, regardless of age or sex, who crossed his path. That his order to kill only males had been disregarded in the chaos didn't seem to matter; he was gleefully murdering his own share of women, young girls, and babies.

White Cloud caught sight of Loping Elk. The old man had his rifle and was squatting to take aim at the man on the white horse. He never got a chance to fire his weapon, for a young soldier had spotted him. He rode up to the medicine man, pointed his pistol, and shot him in the head.

The sight drove White Cloud across the line from boyhood to manhood, and taking sudden charge, he shoved Golden Dove back into the tepee.

"Stay in here and out of sight!" he ordered. He looked around the dwelling, searching frantically for a weapon. Iron Star owned two rifles but had taken the guns with him to hunt buffalo.

He decided to make a run for Loping Elk's rifle, as it still lay where the medicine man had fallen. He hurried to the open flap, but before he could dart through, three soldiers barged inside.

Golden Dove moved shakily to her grandson. She stood in front of him, sheltering him with her own body.

The boy was not about to hide behind a woman, and grasping her shoulders, he moved her firmly aside, staring unflinchingly at the three intruders. He recognized the man standing in the middle; he was the one who rode the white stallion.

Charles Dwyer gave the boy and the woman a mere cursory glance. He was disappointed, for he had hoped to find the village's chief. He knew this tepee belonged to someone important, for it was situated in the heart of the encampment. Dwyer was familiar with the Sioux custom of setting up dwellings according to a family's importance.

"Kill them!" he commanded his soldiers, gesturing toward Golden Dove and White Cloud. He whirled about to leave then, but was halted by Golden Dove's desperate cry.

"No! You cannot kill us! We're white!"

The woman's perfect English hit the captain's ears unexpectedly, and he turned around quickly. Now, taking time really to see the woman and boy, he could tell that she spoke the truth.

White Cloud speaking in the Sioux tongue, said sharply to Golden Dove, "I do not want my white blood to save me! I would rather die than live because I am white!" He spit on the dirt floor to emphasize his disgust. The deaths he had witnessed kept flashing before him, and he longed to break down and cry like a child. But he had visited the vision pit and was no longer a boy. He was now a man, and he would not show weakness before the enemy. The fact he shared the same blood that flowed through the enemies' veins repulsed him. An animallike snarl curled his lips, and turning to his grandmother, he said viciously, "I curse this white blood that flows through my veins!"

"No! You must not feel that way!" Golden Dove said desperately. "Not all whites are like these soldiers!"

"Silence!" Captain Dwyer told them. He didn't want the two speaking words he couldn't understand. He eyed Golden Dove stoically and asked, "Who are you?"

"My name is Golden Dove, and I was married to Chief High Hawk. He died five years ago." She waved a hand toward White Cloud. "This boy is my grandson. His father, Chief Iron Star, is my son. The boy's mother was a white woman."

Dwyer started to question her further, but was interrupted by Luke's coming into the tepee. His face was haggard, and he moved lethargically. However, there was a fiery anger in his eyes that gave the captain a start. Dwyer suspected that the mountaineer was itching to wrap his fingers about his neck and squeeze until he stopped breathing.

Dwyer's suspicions were right. Luke did want to kill him, but he knew that wouldn't bring back the innocents who had died; it would only bring about his own death. And Dwyer wasn't worth dying over!

When Luke had ridden through the village, the slaughter was still in process. He had attempted to stop the bloodthirsty soldiers, but they were like a pack of wild animals. Not all the soldiers were involved, however, quite a few hadn't taken part in the massacre. They, along with Lieutenant Evans, had refused to enter the village.

Luke's eyes bore into the captain's. "You murderin' sonofabitch! You goddamned cold-hearted bastard! How does it feel to be a murderer of children and women?"

"That's enough!" Dwyer bellowed. "One more outburst and I'll have you restrained!"

Luke looked away from the captain; he couldn't stand the sight of him. The gunshots outside had ceased, and an eerie silence now prevailed. For the first time since entering the tepee, Luke took notice of Golden Dove and White Cloud. He could see that they were both white. "Do you remember any English?" he asked Golden Dove.

22

"Yes," she replied, taking an instant liking to the man. She repeated everything she had told the captain.

"What was your white name?" Luke asked.

"Margaret Latham. Sir, I have lived with the Sioux over thirty years, and I doubt if I have any family left who would care if I was dead or alive." She touched White Cloud's arm. "But my grandson must still have relatives who would take him in. His mother's name was Elizabeth Chandler, and my son abducted her fifteen years ago."

White Cloud stared at his grandmother with surprise. She had never told him his mother's white name, but then, he had never bothered to ask. Recalling his vision, he remembered the white man crying for a daughter whose name was Elizabeth. Could this man be his grandfather?

Luke found the Chandler name familiar. He mulled it over for a moment, then suddenly remembered. "Chandler!" he exclaimed. "This boy's grandfather must be J.W. Chandler! His daughter was kidnapped by the Sioux. He spent years tryin' to find her; hired every man he could to search for her. I'm sure *her* name was Elizabeth."

"J.W. Chandler?" Dwyer pondered. "Are you referring to the same man who is a cattle baron in Texas?"

"Yep, I sure am. He used to live in the Wyoming Territory, but after he lost his daughter, he left Wyoming and moved to Texas. He bought himself a good spread of grazin' land and became rich."

The captain was amazed. "You mean, this young savage is his grandson? Good God!"

Luke's eyes raked over White Cloud. "This is his

grandson, all right. I've met J.W. a few times, and I can see a resemblance between him and this boy."

Golden Dove spoke up. "Elizabeth told me that her father's name was James West but that he was called J.W."

Luke shook his head with wonder. "J.W.'s gonna be mighty shocked to see his grandson."

"He will not see me!" White Cloud remarked angrily. "This is my home and I will not leave!"

"So you speak English," Luke said.

"Yes, Golden Dove taught me to speak your tongue."

"It's your language, too, son."

"No!" he hissed. "I do not claim kin to the whites! I am Sioux!"

"You're more white than Indian," Luke pointed out.

White Cloud placed a hand over his heart. "In here, I am Sioux!"

Charles Dwyer was in no mood to listen to the boy's protestations. "You're leaving with us whether you want to or not! When we get to the fort, your grandfather will be notified. If he wants you, he can come get you. Otherwise, there are places for young half-breeds like you."

"There ain't no reason for that," Luke said. "I'll take 'im to his grandfather."

"Are you crazy? He's a savage! He'll kill you in your sleep!"

"I don't think so," Luke replied confidently.

Dwyer raised an eyebrow and said, as though he was amused, "I thought you were determined to report my conduct to Colonel Fleming and testify at my court-martial."

"I won't have to. Lieutenant Evans will talk to the colonel."

"Yes, I'm sure he will." Captain Dwyer wasn't worried. He knew the colonel well, and was certain he would disregard the lieutenant's complaint.

"Open your ears and hear me!" White Cloud ordered sharply. "I am not leaving!"

The captain chuckled. "Well, Luke, it seems you'll have to hogtie that heathen to get him to his grandfather."

"No," Golden Dove said. "That won't be necessary. My grandson will leave willingly." She turned to White Cloud. "Have you already forgotten your vision? Wakan Tanka has made his intentions clear. He wants you to live in the white man's world. You cannot go against his wish. To do so would anger him, and our people will suffer his wrath. A terrible plague will befall all the Sioux."

Luke watched the woman closely. He wondered if she really believed her own words, or was she using the Great Spirit as an excuse to get the boy to leave?

White Cloud felt as though a heavy burden had been placed on his shoulders. If he stayed, the Sioux might pay for his rebellion, but if he left, he'd be doomed to the white man's world. Deep in his heart, he knew there was no choice. The people's welfare was more important than his own desires. His chin lifted, he met Luke's eyes and said calmly, "I will leave with you. There is no reason to tie me up, or to fear for your life. I will go peacefully."

"What about you?" Luke asked Golden Dove. "Don't you want to come with us?"

She shook her head. "My place is here."

25

Luke understood. She had been with the Sioux too many years to return to her other life. He spoke to the boy. "Get your things together. We'll leave immediately." In a tone that sounded apologetic, he added, "We'll have to ride to the fort with the soldiers so I can buy supplies." Luke could well imagine how much it would gall the boy to travel with Dwyer and the others. He motioned to the captain and the two soldiers. "Let's leave so they can say goodbye in private."

They stepped outside, and, looking around, Luke was relieved to find that the soldiers hadn't massacred the entire village; the number of people surviving the attack was a pleasant surprise.

Inside the tepee, White Cloud turned to Golden Dove and said firmly, "Someday I will come back. Tell my father I will see him again."

Golden Dove nodded, but she didn't believe her grandson would ever return. Once he became adjusted to the white man's way of life, he was certain to lose all desire to come back to the Sioux. She smiled tenderly. "White Cloud, you cannot imagine the life that awaits you. It will be filled with many wonders. Your grandfather is rich and lives on a big ranch. It will be a fine place to grow into manhood. Also, you will learn to read and write. Promise me you will read many books. Through them, you will learn everything there is to know."

"These books, are they as wise as our medicine men?"

"Yes, they are."

"Then I will read as many as I can find."

She brought him into her arms, and clung tightly. "I love you, White Cloud."

He drew her closer, and she could already feel a man's

strength in his arms. "I love you, too, Grandmother. When the time is right, I will return. I promise you."

Golden Dove, wanting only the best for her grandson, hoped he would never come back. She believed the life awaiting him was much better than the one he was leaving behind.

For several days White Cloud remained withdrawn and sullen. Luke, understanding his feelings, didn't pressure him. He was sure, in time, the boy would come around. Luke was right; they were about halfway to Texas when White Cloud let down his guard and accepted Luke as a friend.

A warm camaraderie developed between them. Luke found the youngster good company, and he spent many hours around the campfire talking about his life. White Cloud always listened raptly, for he found the mountaineer's adventures intriguing.

Chandler's ranch was located in central Texas, outside the small town of Pleasant Hope. As Luke and White Cloud rode through the town, the citizens stared curiously. An Indian was a rare sight in Pleasant Hope.

White Cloud was aware of their stares, but he wasn't bothered by them. His attention was centered mostly on the town itself. As they traveled from Wyoming, Luke had avoided any towns or else had left White Cloud safely concealed on the outskirts. He had worried about the boy's welfare, for he knew a lot of whites hated Indians. He had considered buying clothes for the boy; that way he wouldn't look like an Indian. But when he had mentioned doing so, White Cloud had seemed offended. So, Luke went alone into these towns to buy supplies. But he saw no reason to avoid Pleasant Hope, where the people might as well get used to seeing White Cloud. He was J.W. Chandler's grandson after all. The boy would soon be living on his grandfather's ranch, and Luke didn't doubt that Chandler was the most influential and prosperous man in these parts. The citizens of Pleasant Hope would have to accept White Cloud, whether they liked it or not.

White Cloud found the town a curious attraction. He had never seen a white man's settlement. As he and Luke rode past clapboard buildings that lined both sides of the street, Luke pointed out a few of them and explained what they were. White Cloud paid close attention, and he stared inquisitively as they passed a livery, barber shop, mercantile, a doctor's home and office, and the most curious attraction of all—a large building with swinging doors, where music could be heard. Luke told him the place was a saloon, and he identified the strange music as a piano. White Cloud listened closely to the lively melody. He liked the sound of it, and wondered what a piano looked like. He asked Luke to describe it to him. Luke explained the musical instrument as best he could. White Cloud was intrigued, and he wondered if he could learn to play one. He had never heard such beautiful magic! He began to understand what Golden Dove meant when she told him his new life would be filled with wonders.

The town's sheriff was sitting outside his office in a rocker. He had been watching the pair, and as they rode toward him, he got to his feet.

"Howdy," Luke said.

The sheriff nodded tersely.

"I need directions to J.W. Chandler's ranch."

The lawman's interest was aroused. What did this man and Indian boy want with J.W.? He suppressed the need to ask, though, since he supposed it wasn't any of his business. "When you leave town, ride straight south. You can't miss the Triangle-C. In fact, you'll be on Chandler's land way before you see his house."

"Thanks," Luke replied, and he and White Cloud went on their way.

The sheriff watched the pair until they had ridden out of sight.

It took two hours to reach Chandler's home. The journey had taken them across a green tapestry of rolling hills; they, periodically, spotted cattle grazing leisurely and spotted cowhands in the distance. Luke waved a hello to them but didn't attempt to make contact.

When Chandler's impressive home loomed into sight, White Cloud could hardly believe his eyes. He had never imagined that such a dwelling existed. It was certainly a far cry from a tepee. The two-story house sitting atop a hill, was constructed of white clapboard with black shutters bordering the windows. Six towering columns ran the length of the front porch. A white picket fence surrounded the house and its several out buildings, and a huge, intricately curved arch was erected over the open gates. A sign was affixed to the arch; Luke told White Cloud that the letters painted on it said Welcome To The Triangle-C. A meandering drive lined with large shade trees led up to the front porch and a wrangler sat there in a wicker chair smoking a cigarette. Getting to his feet, he looked the two strangers over cautiously.

Luke dismounted, gesturing for White Cloud to do likewise. He sauntered up the porch steps, the boy at his heels. "I need to see Mr. Chandler," he said to the wrangler.

"What's your business with Mr. Chandler?" the man asked curtly.

"That don't concern you. Just tell your boss I'm here."

The cowhand eyed White Cloud with hostility. "Whatcha doin' with that Indian boy?"

Luke's expression was suddenly far from friendly. "Mister, you ask too many questions."

The intimidating aura of the brawny mountaineer quickly persuaded the wrangler to mind his own business. "Wait here; I'll tell the boss you need to see him. In case he should ask, who's callin'?"

"Luke Thomas."

The man went into the house, returned quickly, and gestured Luke and White Cloud inside. He led them down a hall to Chandler's study. White Cloud, staying close behind Luke, bumped into him. He wasn't looking where he was going; his full attention was riveted on the grandeur all about him! Never in his wildest dreams could he have envisioned a home such as this one. The foyer itself had taken his breath away. It had a highly polished floor, a crystal chandelier, and three framed paintings on the walls. A marble stairway with carpeted steps led upstairs. White Cloud had merely caught a glimpse of the parlor as the wrangler guided them down the hall; he had turned his head to look back, which had caused him to run smack into Luke. He was certain he had seen the instrument Luke had described earlier as a piano. Could it be possible that his grandfather actually owned such magic?

They reached the study. The wrangler opened the door, waved them inside, then went on his way.

Chandler was sitting at his desk, but got to his feet as his visitors came into the room. He went to Luke and shook his hand. "Mr. Thomas, it's good to see you again. What brings you to these parts?" He gave White Cloud a curious glance.

Luke didn't know how to begin. Learning about White Cloud was bound to shock the man. Also, he would have to know that his daughter was dead. A large liquor cabinet occupied one corner of the room. Luke nodded toward it. "I sure could use a drink."

"Of course," J.W. replied. "Brandy?"

"Whiskey."

Chandler poured his guest a drink and handed it to him.

Luke took a big swallow. "Is it all right if the boy waits in the hall for a few minutes? We need to talk alone."

Chandler had no objections.

Luke sent White Cloud out of the room.

"Who is that Indian boy?" J.W. asked. "And why are you traveling with him?" That Luke Thomas would have an Indian for a companion didn't especially surprise Chandler. When he lived in the Wyoming Territory, he hadn't known Thomas very well, but he was familiar with his reputation and knew he often traded with Indians.

He wondered if he had adopted this boy, or maybe the boy was even his son.

"Mr. Chandler," Luke began. "That boy ain't got much Indian blood in him." He quaffed down another generous swallow of whiskey. Luke wasn't one to beat around the bush, he believed in saying things outright. "That boy is your grandson."

J.W. gasped. "My grandson! Are you out of your mind?"

"I was ridin' with the soldiers who attacked his village. It was a goddamned massacre!" Luke controlled his anger. Later, he would tell Chandler about Captain Dwyer, but at the moment he didn't want to veer away from White Cloud. "The boy's grandmother is a white woman. She told me that the boy's mother was Elizabeth Chandler."

"My God!" J.W. cried. "Elizabeth! Was she in that village?" His heart hammered. After all these years, was he about to find his daughter?

"The woman told me that Elizabeth died in childbirth."

A moan rose from deep in J.W.'s throat; otherwise, his expression didn't change. He turned about and went to sit on the sofa. He leaned forward, bowed his head in his hands, and remained that way for quite some time. Then, looking up at Luke, he said hopefully, "Maybe she wasn't my Elizabeth."

"She told the boy's grandmother that her father's name was James West, but that he was called J.W."

"Oh, God!" the man lamented. "Then she *was* my Elizabeth!"

32

"That boy in the hall is Elizabeth's son. He's only one-fourth Sioux. He belongs here with you."

"But . . . but he's been raised as a Sioux. He'd never be happy here, and he might even be too old to adjust to this life."

"I don't think so. You see, the boy already had his vision." White Cloud had told Luke about his four days in the vision pit. "It told him that he would leave the Sioux to live in the white man's world. He even saw you. He said you were cryin' for your daughter, whose name was Elizabeth. White Cloud believes in his vision, and he's willin' to accept his fate."

J.W. got to his feet slowly. "Tell the boy to come in. And by the way, does he speak English?"

"Speaks it real good. His grandmother taught him." Luke stepped to the door, opened it, and gestured White Cloud inside.

J.W. studied White Cloud and found himself gazing into a pair of eyes as gray as his own. As he continued his scrutiny of the boy, he suddenly felt as though he were seeing a younger version of himself.

White Cloud returned J.W.'s scrutiny. Although the man was much older and sported a thick mustache, he could still see the resemblance between them. It was there in the eyes, the high forehead, and the strong square chin. Their kinship could not be denied.

Chandler's eyes hazed over with tears. He knew this boy was his own flesh and blood.

White Cloud remembered Loping Elk telling him that this man could be trusted completely. But even if the old medicine man hadn't foretold it, he would have sensed his grandfather's integrity. He knew J.W. Chandler was a good person.

J.W. moved slowly to White Cloud. He longed to embrace the lad, but wasn't sure if he should. Instead, he took the boy's hand, shook it firmly, and said sincerely, "Welcome home."

Chapter One

TEN YEARS LATER

Sheila Langstord watched the soldiers and civilians pile out of the log-constructed building that had temporarily served as a courtroom. She stood across the way, searching the crowd for Lieutenant Donald Dwyer. Winter was ebbing, but a slight chill still lingered and Sheila drew her shawl more snugly about her shoulders. She could hardly wait for spring, she disliked winter, especially here in Wyoming, for the bitter cold forced one to stay indoors, and Sheila found confinement boring. She had grown up in Kentucky, raised by an aunt and uncle who bred and sold the finest thoroughbred horses in the country. Sheila loved the horses and helped care for them, so she was used to spending her days outdoors. For a moment, she grew wistful as she thought about the home

35

she had left behind. But then, it hadn't really been her home, she had simply been allowed to live there. Her aunt and uncle had always treated her kindly, but she nevertheless felt like an outsider. Her five cousins had vied for their parents' love and attention, leaving the couple little time for Sheila. However, she didn't harbor resentment toward her foster family, she knew she had been taken into their home like a stray puppy that nobody else had wanted.

If she were to feel resentment toward anyone, it should be toward her father. After all, he was the one who had failed her. Her mother had died giving her birth, and shortly thereafter, Sheila's father had handed his daughter's care over to his wife's sister. He paid for her keep and came to visit every two or three years. He always apologized for his long absences, explaining that the Army kept him busy. As Sheila matured, she realized the Army always came first with him. He lived and breathed it!

Last year, on Sheila's eighteenth birthday, she received a letter from her father, asking her to come live with him. She wrote back at once, telling him she would be delighted. She was hopeful that, at last, she and Colonel Langsford would build a relationship. The colonel made preparations for her trip, and she was soon on her way to Fort Laramie.

Now, she had been at the fort almost a year. She and her father got along well, but they hadn't grown as close, as she had hoped. A short time after her arrival, Lieutenant Dwyer had asked the colonel's permission to court his daughter. Langsford granted it—he liked the young lieutenant and encouraged Sheila to see him. Wanting to please her father, she accepted Dwyer's attentions.

Spending time with the lieutenant certainly wasn't a chore, for the young man was dashingly handsome and treated her with the utmost respect. Before asking Sheila to marry him, Dwyer sought the colonel's permission. He not only received his consent, but his blessings as well! The night Lieutenant Dwyer proposed to Sheila, he pointed out to her that their marriage would delight the colonel. But Sheila wasn't certain of her feelings. Was she in love with the lieutenant? She wasn't sure. She liked him, and his kisses were wonderfully romantic. But was she in love? Wasn't love supposed to make one's heart ache with sweet torment? Dwyer didn't make her feel that way at all! She decided she was behaving foolishly and like a naive schoolgirl. Sweet torment, indeed! That only happened in books, never in real life!

For days, the lieutenant pressured Sheila for an answer, and her father was just as persistent. Finally she told Dwyer she would marry him.

They had been engaged a couple of weeks when the lieutenant received a transfer to Fort Swafford. It was farther north, located in the wilderness, and much smaller than Fort Laramie. Sheila wasn't anxious to move there; she had heard that it was quite crude. Dwyer, on the other hand, was eager to leave, for his older brother, Major Charles Dwyer, was stationed at Swafford.

Sheila and the lieutenant planned to marry at Fort Laramie, then make the journey to his new post. The marriage date was set for April the twentieth, exactly two weeks away.

Now, as a brisk breeze ruffled Sheila's chestnut-colored hair, she absently brushed the silky locks away from her face. She continued to search the crowd, but failed to spot Lieutenant Dwyer. Apparently, he was going to be one of the last to come out of the courtroom.

Suddenly, a tall, dark-haired man caught her eye. He was new to Fort Laramie, she had gotten her first glimpse of him three days ago. She had been coming out of the traders' store as he had been riding into the fort. That day, he had gotten her full attention, and he was doing so again. There was an aura of masculinity surrounding the stranger that held her riveted. He was strikingly handsome, but she was mesmerized by more than his good looks. The man moved proudly, like an aristocrat, yet he seemed to glide across the ground as lithely as a panther. He was dressed in tan buckskins that fit his frame flawlessly. A gun was strapped low on his hip, and the leather thongs were tied securely around his right thigh. She didn't think he was a gunslinger, the day she had seen him ride into the fort he'd had pelts to trade. He was obviously a trapper, but he certainly didn't resemble one. So far, every trapper Sheila had encountered was unkempt, loud, and had a mouth full of chewing tobacco. This man's clothes were clean, she'd never seen him speak unless spoken to, and in lieu of chewing tobacco, he clenched a burned-out cheroot between his teeth.

Sheila watched, entranced, as the stranger struck a match and lit his half-smoked cheroot. He was making his way through the throng of people, and Sheila noticed that he towered over the others. She supposed he had attended the trial, otherwise, he wouldn't be caught in the middle of the dispersing spectators.

Her eyes never wavered from the dark stranger as he brushed his way free of the crowd. He was walking in her direction, and she told herself to look away. But he was upon her before she could.

For a heartbeat, he gazed down into her face, then he touched the brim of his hat, smiled, murmured "good day" and passed her by. The man's closeness had caused Sheila's breath to lodge in her lungs, and she now released it in one long sigh. The stranger's image lingered in her mind. His short-trimmed beard was as black as his hair, which grew past collar length, and his smile had revealed straight white teeth. His greeting had taken only seconds, and now, as she tried to recall the color of his eyes, she wasn't sure if she had even looked into them.

She thrust the stranger from her thoughts and again scanned the crowd. Seeing the lieutenant, she called out to him and waved.

Meanwhile, the stranger, who hadn't walked very far, turned around and looked back at Sheila. He wasn't surprised to find that she was waiting for the lieutenant, he knew they were engaged. He had been at the fort only three days, but during that time, he had kept his ears open and had learned a lot.

An icy coldness came to his eyes as he watched Lieutenant Dwyer walk to Sheila, embrace her, and kiss her on the cheek. He didn't like Dwyer, he was familiar with the man's reputation. Evidently, he was very much like the Dwyer who had attacked Iron Star's village. He had heard that the two Dwyers were brothers, and in his opinion, neither one was worth a damn! Now, as he continued to watch the lieutenant and Sheila, he wondered if the young lady shared her fiancé's loathing for Indians.

From the first moment he had set eyes on Sheila, he hadn't been able to get her out of his mind. Her pretty face plagued his thoughts and entered his dreams. He was determined, however, to remain strong and not be swayed by her beauty. He had a job to do, and he wasn't about to let anything or anybody stand in his way. He wasn't looking forward to using Miss Langsford to accomplish his goal, but after much consideration, he had decided that kidnapping her was his best course of action. He glanced at his pocket watch, he had to hurry, for she and the lieutenant would be taking their customary ride in a few hours, and he had much to do to get ready. He headed for the stables to get his horse and pack mule. A wave of uncertainty passed over him, he knew there was always the possibility that Dwyer and Miss Langsford might decide not to go for a ride today. If that were to happen, what would he do? Nothing! he thought bitterly. There would be nothing he could do to save Yellow Bear.

He uttered a silent prayer that the pair would not change their daily routine. He had been at the fort three days, and every afternoon, Dwyer and Sheila went horseback riding. Yesterday, he had followed them, he now knew where they went and what they did. He had certainly been surprised to find that the lieutenant was teaching his fiancée to shoot a rifle. He admired Miss Langsford for wanting to learn; in these parts, a woman should know how to defend herself. Apparently, her lessons had been going on for some time, for she was already a good shot.

He hoped—prayed—that they would leave again this afternoon. If for some reason they changed their minds, then tomorrow morning Yellow Bear would hang. Dear God, after all these years, had he come back home only to see his brother die at the end of a rope? The possibility sent a sickening shudder through him.

Lieutenant Dwyer slipped Sheila's arm into his as they began walking toward Colonel Langsford's quarters.

"What happened at the trial?" Sheila asked him.

"Yellow Bear was found guilty, of course. He'll hang in the morning."

Sheila gasped. "How horrible!"

"Horrible? The savage is a cold-hearted murderer! Hanging's too good for him! He should be shot down like a mad dog!"

Sheila's steps slowed as she looked up into her fiancé's face. She had heard him speak this way before, and such callousness bothered her. "Donald, sometimes I think you loathe Indians and wish they were all dead."

"They're heathens," he replied. "The whole lot of them are uncivilized and ignorant."

"But that isn't true. I've talked to some of the Indian women who come to the fort to trade and they seem very nice."

"Nice?" he ridiculed. "These women would very *nicely* slit your throat if they could get away with it."

Sheila let the subject drop. "Are you going to call for me at the usual time?"

"Darling, do you mind if we don't ride today? I have a lot of paperwork to take care of."

"That's all right; you don't have to come along. I'll go by myself."

41

"You'll do no such thing! If you're that determined, then I'll go with you. I'll start my paperwork now, then finish it when we get back."

"Thank you, Donald. The shooting lessons mean a lot to me, and I also love riding again. Back home in Kentucky, I rode every day."

As they reached the colonel's quarters and stopped, Donald bent and kissed her hand. His thoughts turned to their marriage and caused him to murmur thickly, "Darling, I can hardly believe our wedding is only two weeks away. I'm very eager to marry you." He was also eagerly awaiting their wedding night, but that expectation he didn't voice.

Dwyer gazed deeply into Sheila's soft brown eyes. Their pupils were the color of chocolate. He admired her long dark lashes and perfectly arched brows. He found her beautiful beyond compare. And her every features was indeed lovely. Her nose was delicately formed, and her high cheekbones enhanced her beauty. Her lips were sensually shaped; and Donald, finding them tempting, pressed his mouth to hers and kissed her fervently.

She responded, wishing the touch of his lips would make her heart pound erratically. However, she was disappointed, his kiss was pleasant, but that was all.

Sheila gazed thoughtfully into his face. He was indeed dashingly attractive. His well-clipped mustache was as flaxen as his hair, and his eyes were a luminous shade of blue. He was average height, his uniform fit his slim frame perfectly, and he wore it proudly. She knew that, like her father, he was a military man through and through.

42

He kissed her again, and then he was on his way with a reminder that he'd come for her at three o'clock.

Sheila watched him leave, then opened the door and went into her home. She was a little downhearted, but she shrugged the feeling aside. After all, these should be happy days. She was engaged to be married and would soon embark on a brand-new life. Feeling melancholy was unwarranted.

She went into the parlor and sat on the sofa. The colonel's home wasn't elaborate, but it was nonetheless comfortable and cozy. The clapboard house had a parlor, two bedrooms, a dining room, kitchen, and an extra room that Colonel Langsford used as his study. The home was adequately furnished, there were several paintings on the walls, and colorful curtains bordered the windows.

The front door opened, and Sheila watched as her father stepped inside, removed his hat, and hung it on the rack beside the door. He went into the parlor and straight to his liquor cabinet, where he poured himself a tumbler of brandy. He swallowed a generous amount and then dropped into his favorite chair. The soft chair enveloped his tired body, which ached with rheumatism.

"You look fatigued," Sheila told him.

"Do I? Well, it was a trying morning. I'm glad the trial is finished. At daybreak Yellow Bear will be executed, then this whole ordeal will be over." He didn't mention his rheumatism, his aching joints were a complaint he kept to himself. He was a colonel in the U.S. Army and had high expectations of making general. He feared he'd never receive the promotion if the Army knew he wasn't still in good physical condition.

43

"Father, are you certain that Yellow Bear is guilty of murder?"

Her question startled him. "Why would you ask such a thing?"

"Well . . ." she began hesitantly, "Yellow Bear is a Sioux warrior, and the men who found him guilty are white. Are you sure he received a fair hearing?"

"Good God, girl!" he bellowed angrily. "I hope you never make a remark like that outside these walls! Are you implying that the Army's judicial system is unjust? Why, Yellow Bear is a savage, yet we gave him an honest trial! If it were the other way around, do you think the Sioux would be as civilized?" He answered his own question. "No, of course not!"

Sheila didn't say anything, she knew it would be pointless. With her father everything was black or white, good or bad, and the Army was always right.

"Do you and Donald plan to go riding this afternoon?"

"Yes, we do."

"Well, I suppose today is safe enough, but starting tomorrow everyone will be confined to the fort. After Yellow Bear is hanged, we might have trouble from the Sioux. Even the ones on reservations might decide to start an uprising. But don't worry, dear. The troops will be on full alert, and we will quickly squelch any attempts to retaliate."

He finished his brandy, put the empty glass on the table beside his chair, then smiled at Sheila. "I've enjoyed having you with me this past year, but your engagement to Donald pleases me very much. He's a fine and ambitious young man. He'll go places in this army. You couldn't have made a better choice.

"I suppose I should have remarried and had sons."
He chuckled softly. "Well, I'm too damned old now to
think about starting a family. But I'm so fond of Donald
that it's almost like having a son. I hope you two will
give me grandsons who will grow up to become military
men. But of course they will, it'll be in their blood."

"Father, there's more to life than the Army."

"Not for me there isn't! And, mark my words, your
future husband feels the same way. That's why he'll
succeed!"

Sheila didn't doubt it. "I'll fix lunch," she said, getting up.

"Thank you, dear. But first, pour me another brandy,
please." He didn't want to leave his comfortable chair,
his joints were still bothering him.

She did as he asked, then went into the kitchen. Her
earlier dejection had returned, and it hung over her like
a dark cloud. Something was pulling her down, but she
couldn't isolate the cause. Maybe it was tomorrow's
hanging. Outside, in the distance, she heard the pounding
of hammers. The soldiers were building a crude gallows.

In an effort to block out the constant hammering and
what it represented, she began to hum a lively melody as
she prepared lunch. The execution soon fled her thoughts.

A group of warriors, gathered about a campfire, got
quickly to their feet as the white man rode into their
midst. More warriors, who had been away from the fire,
hurried over. The one called Three Moons waited for the
white man to dismount, then asked urgently, "Is the trial
over?"

"Yes, it is," the man answered, speaking the Sioux tongue fluently. "Yellow Bear was found guilty and will hang at daybreak."

Three Moons was livid. "If he dies, many whites will pay with their lives! My lance will be heavy with fresh scalps!"

Three Moon's fervor was contagious, and the other warriors hurled similar threats. They were hungry for blood.

The white man was apprehensive, he knew the situation here was precarious and that he must tread cautiously. These warriors had accepted his presence, but he wasn't really one of them. He had no authority, and very little influence.

"Three Moons," he began carefully. "I have a plan. If it works, Yellow Bear will be free and no one will die."

The young warrior viewed him skeptically. "What is this plan?"

"As you know, I stayed at the fort three days, and I learned a lot in that short time. Colonel Langsford's daughter and Lieutenant Dwyer ride every afternoon. I plan to kidnap the woman, then trade her for Yellow Bear. As soon as the trade is made, we will head into the mountains and to my father's village."

Three Moons considered the plan. "Yes, it might work. We will help you kidnap the woman."

"No!" the man said firmly. "I go alone."

"You do not trust me, White Cloud?" The warrior's gaze was tinged with anger.

The white man spoke cautiously. "It does not take more than one warrior to kidnap a woman."

Three Moon's vanity couldn't argue with that. He frowned harshly. "But you are not a warrior." He spit onto the ground, then said with repulsion, "You are a white man!"

"I am Chief Iron Star's son, and Yellow Bear's brother."

"Yes, that is true. And that is why I do not kill you! Go; kidnap the woman, then bring her here. If you do not return by sunset, we will find you." His dark eyes narrowed maliciously. "I do not trust you, White Cloud, but I honor your father and brother. Still, I swear before the Great Spirit that I will kill you if I think it is necessary."

"You might not find me that easy to kill," the man replied calmly. He moved away to unsaddle his horse. He planned to ride an Indian pony. Opening his carpetbag, he withdrew borrowed Indian garb, then removed his own clothes and slipped into the other apparel. He could feel the warriors' eyes on him, but he simply ignored their stares as he delved back into his bag for his shaving paraphernalia.

He wanted the lieutenant and Miss Langsford to see him as an Indian. It was vital that he keep his true identity a secret. He didn't intend to become a bounty on a wanted poster; also, in a few weeks he'd be on his way back to Texas and would need to stop at Fort Laramie for supplies. Dressed in his own clothes, and again sporting a beard, no one would recognize him as White Cloud—the warrior who by then would be notorious for kidnapping the colonel's daughter.

The man laughed under his breath. He was Bart Chandler, and his grandfather was the richest cattle baron in

Texas. That Bart Chandler and White Cloud were one and the same was so phenomenal, it was difficult for him to accept himself. Yes, he had changed a lot in ten years, but Yellow Bear was still his brother, and he didn't deserve to hang. Bart was determined to try to save him.

Chapter Two

Bart dismounted, tethered his Indian pony, then, taking his Winchester with him, he started up the hillside. He climbed agilely, his moccasins treading silently as he made his way to the top. The verdant rise was filled with pines and spruces. He sat beneath a tree's shade, placed his rifle at his side, and scanned the sun-splashed countryside. He was facing west, for he knew Dwyer and Miss Langsford would come from that direction. From his lofty vantage point, he'd spot them long before they arrived. Yesterday, when he had followed the couple, they had stopped in this area for Miss Langsford's shooting lessons. The surrounding landscape, rich with trees and shrubbery, had afforded him a place to hide, and he had watched the couple undetected. Now, Bart could only hope they would choose this spot again.

He leaned back against the tree trunk and stretched his

legs. His gaze traveled over his tan leggings and down to the beaded moccasins covering his feet. He hadn't worn such garb for ten years; the clothes seemed strange to his eyes but comfortable to his body. He had forgotten how free one felt in Indian apparel, forgotten the softness of tanned leather against the skin. He lifted a hand and touched the leather band about his head; wearing it had been a last-minute decision. He hoped this final touch to his disguise would fool Dwyer and Miss Langsford. It was vital that they take him for a Sioux warrior. He was fairly confident that they would; after all, he was dark complected, almost as brown as Three Moons, in fact, and Three Moons was a full-blooded Sioux. But then, he was one-fourth Sioux himself, and he bore a slight resemblance to his Indian forefathers. Bart didn't plan to get too close to Lieutenant Dwyer, but he and Miss Langsford would be spending time together. She would undoubtedly notice that his eyes were gray, but he wasn't concerned. She'd most likely assume that he was a half-breed.

The afternoon sun shone in Bart's face, and he closed his eyes against the glaring rays. A gentle breeze stirring the treetops and the musical chirping of birds had a lulling effect, sending Bart's thoughts floating back into time.

It hadn't taken the young boy known as White Cloud very long to adjust to his new life. He was naturally inquisitive, and his mind was hungry for knowledge. J.W. had hired a tutor for his grandson, and White Cloud absorbed his lessons like an sponge soaking up spilled water. J.W., knowing how much White Cloud liked Luke Thomas, asked the man to stay on. Luke needed a job and agreed to remain. He wasn't experienced as a cow-hand, but he learned quickly.

J.W. named his grandson Bart James, after himself and his father. White Cloud had no objections; he accepted his new name as easily as he was accepting his changed lifestyle. He often thought about his Sioux family, and especially missed Golden Dove. In the beginning, he considered leaving Texas and returning to his former home several times. But he never got any farther than mulling it over. His white heritage was dominant, and it dictated that he remain. It soon became apparent to him that he belonged in the white man's world, and he adjusted perfectly to living at the Triangle-C with his grandfather and Luke.

He had been with J.W. only a short time before his inquisitive mind demanded that he achieve more than an education. He asked his grandfather to teach him all there was to know about running a ranch. J.W. was pleased and eager to cooperate. In due time, Bart was as adept at roping and branding cattle as an experienced cowhand. J.W. allowed him to help with all the paperwork involved in running the large spread; and Bart, a natural with figures, was soon adding columns faster than J.W.

But the boy craved to learn more in this white man's world. He admired Luke's Colt revolver, and pleaded with the man to teach him to use one. Luke received J.W.'s permission, and taught Bart how to draw and fire a handgun. Bart caught on so quickly that before too much time had passed, he was faster and more accurate than his instructor.

Bart's need to learn wasn't yet appeased; he remained

secretly fascinated with the instrument called a piano. J.W.'s piano sat silent in the huge home, for no one knew how to play it. J.W. had bought it for his wife and daughter. His wife died a year after Elizabeth's abduction, and when he moved to Texas, he brought the piano with him. It reminded him of his wife and daughter, and he couldn't bear to part with it. One day, when J.W. caught Bart sitting at the piano tinkering with the keys, he asked him if he'd like to take lessons. The boy wasn't sure if playing a piano was manly, and he was hesitant to reveal how much he longed to play. But J.W. read his mind, and convinced him it was acceptable for a man to play an instrument. J.W. had the piano tuned, then hired the reverend's wife to teach Bart to play. Having his mother's gift for music, he was a talented pupil.

Bart's days were full and rewarding, but there were times when vivid memories came crowding back. He couldn't forget the first fourteen years of his life. He missed Iron Star and Golden Dove, and he often thought about his younger brother and sister. He had promised his grandmother that he would someday return. It was a promise he intended to keep.

The years passed quickly and pleasantly, though. Bart left his boyhood behind and grew into a tall, handsome man. He became a much sought-after bachelor. Yet, although the countryside had its share of young, unmarried ladies, not one of them captured Bart Chandler's heart. He escorted various women to various festive occasions, but, the courtships failed to blossom into love. He wasn't discouraged, however; he was still young and had plenty of time to find the right woman.

Although Bart courted proper young ladies, he also on

occasion visited the town's saloon to enjoy a harlot's lustful charms. He learned to play a good game of poker, and could hold his liquor like a gentleman. Bart Chandler sowed his wild oats to the fullest, but he was also a hard worker, and his grandfather came to depend on him more and more to operate the Triangle-C.

The citizens of Pleasant Hope and the neighboring ranchers accepted J.W.'s grandson into their fold. His bloodline to the Sioux was so slight that they disregarded it altogether.

J.W. gave a large barbecue to celebrate his grandson's twenty-fourth birthday. The festivities lasted well into the night, and by the time Bart went to bed, he was exhausted. He thought he'd sleep like a log, but that night he dreamt of the massacre led by Captain Charles Dwyer. The dream was so real that he woke up trembling, and had perspired so heavily that the bed sheets were damp. Memories of his Sioux family filled his mind and pulled at his heartstrings. Guilt, like a jolt of lightning, hit him with a terrible force. He threw off the covers, got dressed, and went outside. For a long time he sat alone on the front porch, remembering his former life. His heart began to ache to see the loved ones he had left behind. He decided then to find them. He didn't plan to make his home with them, for he no longer belonged in their world. But he longed to see them again, and was ashamed of himself for waiting so long. Ten years! The time had flown by so quickly.

J.W. watched his grandson leave with grave reservations. He didn't fear that Bart would decide to stay with the Sioux; he knew how much Bart loved the Triangle-C. Also, his grandson was no longer an Indian in heart, body, or soul. J.W.'s reservations were for Bart's safety. Much hostility existed between the Sioux and the whites, and Bart could very well get caught in the middle. The desire to visit his Sioux family could possibly cost him his life.

Luke's feelings coincided with J.W.'s, and he offered to ride along, but Bart refused his offer. He felt he should go alone.

Bart wasn't sure where to start looking for his family, and his search took him to several Sioux villages. The Indians in these villages were at peace with the soldiers and lived on reservations. There were still thousands of Sioux living in the mountains who considered themselves at war with the Army, and Bart knew he couldn't possibly infiltrate their territory. He would probably be killed before he could explain who he was and what he was doing there.

As he visited the villages on the reservations, Bart often got the feeling that some of these people knew where his family lived, but wouldn't tell him because they saw him as a white man.

Bart began to grow discouraged and contemplated giving up his search when he entered another village and found Chief Flying Feather. The old chief was Iron Star's uncle, which made him Bart's granduncle. Flying Feather remembered Bart as a boy, and he welcomed him into his village. Through Flying Feather, Bart learned that his father was living in the mountains. Iron Star, along with several other chiefs, had signed a peace treaty with the soldiers. Iron Star had asked the Army's permission to leave the reservation to hunt buffalo. The Army had given him its word that he could hunt in peace. Apparently, the agreement was never made official; quite the contrary, for at the same time, the military received orders to treat any Indians found hunting off the reservations as hostiles.

Iron Star, believing he could hunt in peace, packed up his village and left to find buffalo. The hunt was bountiful, and his people's tepees were filled with meat and hides. They were about to pack up and return to the reservation when soldiers were seen in the distance. Iron Star wasn't alarmed; he had permission to be where he was. Any fool could see that he wasn't about to make war, for he had women and children with him.

Unfortunately for Iron Star and his people, the troops were led by Major Charles Dwyer, and the major didn't care if the village was peaceful or not. He had his orders. The soldiers came tearing into the village, shooting, yelling, stampeding the horses, and riding down the people. Several Indians, including children, were killed or injured. Major Dwyer and his soldiers quickly took command, plundering the tepees, taking what they wanted and destroying the rest. Iron Star and his people were escorted back to the reservation, their weapons confiscated and their meat gone.

Shortly thereafter, Iron Star gathered up his people and anyone else who wanted to come along, left the reservation, and journeyed into the hills. He now considered himself at war with the soldiers, and he swore never to surrender.

Chief Flying Feather invited Bart to stay in his village, and he sent runners to Iron Star to let him know that his son had returned. Bart settled in, and in a short time, all the Sioux language and customs came back to him as though he had never been away.

When the runners returned, Yellow Bear and several warriors were with them. Yellow Bear and Bart's reunion was warm, joyful, and filled with emotion. As a young-ster, Yellow Bear had looked up to his older brother and loved him very much. The passing years hadn't changed his feelings. Bart was indeed happy to learn that Iron Star, his sister, and Golden Dove were well.

Bart planned to go back into the hills with Yellow Bear and his warriors, for he was determined to see his family. The day before they were to leave, Yellow Bear and two of his friends left to visit a nearby village. They planned to return before dark. As they were nearing this village, they heard a woman's scream. They hurried over to see what was happening and were enraged to find three drunken trappers molesting a young Sioux maiden. The trappers had their rifles close, and they fired their weapons at the three braves. Yellow Bear's companions were fa-tally wounded and their bodies toppled from their ponies and onto the ground. Yellow Bear, returning the men's fire, sent a bullet into a trapper's heart, killing him in-stantly. The young girl panicked and ran away.

Yellow Bear was heading for cover when a bullet grazed his head, knocking him off his horse and into oblivion. When he awoke later, it was to find himself tied and gagged. The trappers slung him facedown across his pony, then tied their dead friend on a horse and quickly left the area. They went to Fort Laramie, where they turned Yellow Bear over to the Army. They told the officer in charge that they had crossed the reservation on their way to the fort. They swore that Yellow Bear and his braves attacked them for no apparent reason. Yellow Bear was arrested and placed in the stockade. He could peak English, and he tried to tell his side of the story, but no one would listen.

The Indians who came to the fort to trade soon heard that Yellow Bear had been arrested, and word spread rapidly from one village to another. When Bart learned what had happened, he knew he had to find a way to talk to Yellow Bear. He couldn't imagine Yellow Bear attacking three trappers without provocation; he wanted to hear his brother's side of the story. He also knew that he might decide to help Yellow Bear escape, which would be no easy feat. But Bart thrust that worry aside; he had to take this one step at a time.

Since arriving at Flying Feather's village, Bart hadn't shaved or cut his hair, and, deciding to disguise himself as a trapper, he borrowed some pelts and rode to Fort Laramie. Later, under the cover of night, he slipped into the stockade, went around to the side of the building, and talked to Yellow Bear through a barred window. After learning exactly what had happened, he returned to Flying Feather's village and repeated what Yellow Bear had told him. Three Moons, who had traveled to Flying Feather's village with Yellow Bear, took several braves with him and rode to the Sioux camp where the girl was attacked. They returned disheartened; no girl from that village had been molested. She had been Yellow Bear's only hope, and now she seemed to have vanished from the face of the earth.

That was when Bart made his decision to go back to the fort and look for a way to help Yellow Bear escape. Time was short, however, for Yellow Bear's trial was only three days away. Bart didn't wonder about the verdict; Yellow Bear would certainly be found guilty. Three

Moons and his warriors rode part of the way with Bart then set up camp to await his return.

Again, Bart entered Fort Laramie, his pack mule loaded with borrowed pelts. This time as he cantered into the fort, he caught a glimpse of Miss Langsford. She was coming out of the traders' store; for a moment she looked his way, then headed down the wooden walkway. Bart noticed that she moved lithely, with a graceful sway to her hips. He watched her for a minute or so, then went on his way.

The fort had a hotel of sorts; it was crude and lacked several conveniences. Bart had checked in under the name of Smith, and during his three-day stay there he kept his ears and eyes open. He learned that Sheila was the colonel's daughter and that she was engaged to Lieutenant Dwyer. He saw the couple leave on horseback, and when they left the same time the next day, he followed. That was when he began plotting to kidnap Miss Langsford.

Bart brought his thoughts back to the present. The sun's rays still glared, and as he looked into the distance, he shaded his eyes with his hand. He saw two figures on horseback. They weren't very close, and he knew they couldn't see him. He grabbed his rifle and swiftly got to his feet. Concealing himself behind the tree's broad trunk, he kept the riders in sight.

Sheila and Donald rode at a leisurely pace. The month's pleasant temperatures had turned the prairie a rich green; the grass was high and thick, the distant slopes were overflowing with wild flowers, and the songs of birds filled the air.

Sheila was thoroughly enjoying her ride across nature's

58

beauty. Her hat was attached with leather ties, and, wanting to feel the wind in her hair, she removed it and let it hang down her back.

Donald looked over at her. His fiancée's windblown tresses presented such a sensuous vision that he became aroused. He had desired Sheila from the day he met her, and curbing his passion all these months hadn't been easy. Their daily outings had tempted him to try to seduce her; here, on the plains, they were alone and no one would know if they became lovers. However, Donald continued to control his passion; Sheila Langsford was a lady. Furthermore, he wanted her to be a virgin on their wedding night. That way, if his lovemaking didn't please her, there would be nothing she could do about it—they would already be married! Donald liked to love a woman roughly; such treatment always intensified his desire. If he were to take Sheila before she was his wife, she might find his passion too harsh and refuse to marry him.

Now, as she rode at his side, his eyes raked her. Her riding apparel, which she had bought in Kentucky, was practical yet feminine. The orchid-colored blouse had long sleeves, French, cuffs, and buttoned in front. She had left the top two buttons undone, and the effect was provocative. Her long skirt, divided so she could ride astride, was a deep purple, and it adhered smoothly to her slim hips. Gloves, their color matching the skirt, protected her hands, and black, high-topped boots covered her feet. The outfit was made to conceal most of her flesh; nevertheless, Sheila Langsford projected an alluring picture.

They reached the area where Donald habitually took Sheila to practice with his rifle. Dwyer helped her dismount, then went to his horse to draw his Remington from its scabbard, but before he could, a voice called out.

"Do not touch gun, Bluecoat!"

The voice had come from the top of the hill, and Dwyer looked up to find an Indian holding him at rifle point.

"Move back away from horse," Bart told him, speaking in broken English. He hoped his uneven speech would make him sound more like a warrior.

Carefully, Dwyer stepped back.

Bart descended the hill gracefully, keeping his rifle pointed at the lieutenant. He stepped to Dwyer's horse, removed the Remington, and placed it at his feet. He then said forcefully to Sheila, "Woman; come here!"

She didn't move.

"You come, or I shoot bluecoat!"

"For God's sake, Sheila, do as he says!" Donald said sharply. If she didn't cooperate, this wild savage would kill him!

Sheila looked at her fiancé and saw fear in his eyes. She had believed him brave, and was terribly disillusioned. She had a sudden feeling that Donald was only brave when he had troops to back him up. She turned away from him, and set her gaze upon the warrior.

"Move!" Bart demanded harshly.

She walked slowly to his side. She was frightened, but she hid it well. "What do you want with me?" she asked. Although she tried to keep her voice even, it was a little shaky.

"You no talk!" Bart demanded. He looked at Dwyer. "Return to fort and tell your chief I have woman. Tomorrow when sun is in middle of sky, I trade woman for

Yellow Bear. I wait here for you. You come alone with Yellow Bear, or I kill woman." He gestured toward Sheila's horse. "Take horse with you."

"So that's what this is all about," Dwyer replied. "You aim to save Yellow Bear from the gallows!"

"Go!" Bart yelled. "Now, or I shoot leg, then other leg!"

The lieutenant wasted no time going to his horse and mounting. He turned to Sheila. "Don't worry, darling. You'll be all right. I'll hand Yellow Bear over to this savage personally."

Bart raised his rifle as though he were about to shoot. The lieutenant caught his movement, slapped the reins against his steed, and, taking Sheila's horse with him, he rode away quickly.

As Chandler watched Dwyer hightail it across the plains, Sheila decided to make a move for the Remington, which still lay at the warrior's feet. She dropped to her knees, but as she touched the rifle, Bart's moccasined foot pinned the weapon to the ground. He reached down, clutched her arm, and drew her upright. He glowered down into her upturned face. "You do as I say, you no get hurt! You understand, white woman?" Bart found it difficult to play the role of an angry warrior. The face looking up at him was lovely, frightened, and vulnerable. He fought back the sudden, overwhelming urge to kiss her.

"Yes, I understand," she replied. Despite her fear, her eyes shot daggers at him.

"Come," he said, grasping her arm firmly. Leaving the Remington where it lay, he forced Sheila to climb the hill with him, then descend the other side.

He went to his pony, untethered it, then lifted her onto the horse. He swung up behind her, slipped his rifle into its sheath, and then his arms went about Sheila as he picked up the reins.

Bart urged the pony into a steady gallop. He could detect the fragrance of Sheila's perfume, and the smell of soap that lingered in her hair. Such feminine scents reminded him that he had been without a woman for a long time. Sheila's closeness aroused his passion; with effort he managed to suppress it.

Bart would have been shocked to know that Sheila's feelings were very close to his own. She was frightened, true, but she was nevertheless aware of the warrior's body pressed close to hers. She studied the arms encircling her, and was amazed by their strength. If he had a wife or sweetheart, she must feel wonderfully safe in his embrace. Suddenly, aghast at her own thoughts, she chastised herself. This Indian was her enemy and would think nothing of killing her, then displaying her scalp on his lance!

A chill ran up her spine, and her fear peaked. She might not come out of this alive! The thought made her stomach churn and sent her heart pounding. She made an effort to control her fear and calm her shattered nerves. If she did as this Indian said, he would have no reason to harm her. Somehow, she would make it through this day and night, then tomorrow Donald would bring Yellow Bear. The exchange would take place and she would return safely to the fort.

Sheila's spirits improved, but deep down inside she was afraid she might never see Fort Laramie again.

Chapter Three

Bart would have preferred not to return to Three Moons and his warriors, but he didn't have a choice. There was no place he and Miss Langsford could hide where Three Moons couldn't find them. Bart held the pony to a steady gallop, and headed straight toward the warrior's camp.

Sheila had gotten some control of her emotions, but she was still shaky. Her heart was pounding and, fear, like an icy snake, was coiled deep in her stomach.

Bart, sensing her fright, said gently, "Do not be afraid."

His gentle tone did little to ease her anxieties. "Where are you taking me?" she asked.

"Three Moons's camp," he replied.

"Then you aren't alone?"

God, how he wished he were! Three Moons, however,

was determined to become involved. "No, I not alone," he answered softly.

Sheila thought she detected a note of regret, but she didn't pursue it. "Are you from Yellow Bear's village?"

"Yellow Bear is my brother."

"Colonel Langsford will make the exchange. But that won't be the end of it, you know. The Army will hunt you down—you and your brother."

"The bluecoats not find us."

"This country isn't big enough," she replied firmly.

Bart smiled. The woman had courage. He had believed his captive would cry, plead for her life, and might even become hysterical. But he had certainly misjudged Sheila Langsford!

Three Moons's camp came into sight, and the warriors gathered around Bart's horse as they rode in. Bart dismounted, then reached up and lifted Sheila from the pony.

"You did good, White Cloud," Three Moons remarked, speaking in his own language. His dark gaze traveled over the prisoner, and he responded to her exceptional beauty. He quickly smothered such desire. This woman was white, and he hated all whites passionately.

"The trade will take place tomorrow at midday," Bart told him. "I will give the woman back, then return with Yellow Bear."

"We will go with you," Three Moons said firmly.

Anger sparked in Bart's eyes. "I will handle this alone!"

Sheila, wished she could understand what they were saying. She could tell that the warrior who had abducted her was upset.

"The bluecoats cannot be trusted," Three Moons replied. "They will trick you. Alone, you will be helpless to save Yellow Bear or yourself. My warriors and I will stay out of sight, but we will be close by."

Bart shrugged as though he didn't care one way or another. "Do what you want, Three Moons." Staring unflinchingly into the warrior's eyes, he continued in a voice as hard as steel. "The exchange will take place peacefully. If you or your men harm this woman or anyone else, I will kill you."

Three Moons didn't doubt that, but he wasn't perturbed, for he wasn't planning on killing anyone. He only wanted Yellow Bear back safe and well. If he didn't get what he wanted, however, then the soldiers would pay dearly. He would take many scalps before returning to Iron Star's village.

Grasping Sheila's arm, Bart led her to the edge of camp and ordered her to sit in the shade of a tree. He then stepped to his pony, removed his rifle, returned to Sheila, and sat beside her. He intended to stay very close to his captive; she was his responsibility and he wasn't going to let anything happen to her.

Sheila studied his profile; she could see that his face was set in deep thought. She found herself admiring his handsomely sculpted features. She had seen enough Indians to know that he wasn't full-blooded. Bart, feeling her scrutiny, turned his gaze to hers, and, for the first time, she noticed the color of his eyes. Indians didn't have eyes as gray as charcoal; this man had white blood in him!

"You aren't a full-blooded Sioux," she remarked, as though they had been discussing the possibility. "Which of your relatives is white? Your mother—your grandmother?"

"It does not matter."

"What is your name?"

There was no reason to keep his name a secret. Too many Indians knew that White Cloud had returned to the Sioux. After the exchange, the Army would interrogate villagers and would hear the name of White Cloud several times. Even so, he would be safe because the Indians didn't know his true identity—not even Flying Feather. Only Yellow Bear knew his name was Bart Chandler.

"I am called White Cloud," he told Sheila. He rested his rifle across his lap, leaned back against the tree trunk, and said firmly, "No more talk." He thought it prudent to keep their conversations at a minimum. Miss Langsford had a keen mind; if he were to slip and say too much, she would certainly want to pursue it.

His refusal to communicate didn't upset Sheila; she didn't really have anything to say. Except, perhaps to plead for her life! But she had heard that Indians admired courage; she didn't think she could bring herself to beg. Pride had been instilled in her since she was a child; living with relatives instead of her blood father had made her self-reliant. Her father had paid for her keep, and she had worked hard with her uncle's thoroughbreds; she certainly hadn't taken charity from anyone. In the process, she had built a wall around her emotions to protect herself from feeling like an unwanted waif. Now, drawing upon that strength, she suppressed the temptation to plead for her life.

Sheila's thoughts went to Donald, and she recalled the look in his eyes. He had been afraid of White Cloud. She supposed she shouldn't see that as a weakness; after all, there was nothing wrong with being scared. No, it wasn't his fear that bothered her; she was disillusioned to read in his eyes that he only feared for himself. But maybe she had been mistaken; Donald loved her and wanted to marry her, so surely her life was as important to him as his own! Sheila sighed deeply, but she couldn't quite convince herself that he felt that way. She dismissed Donald from her thoughts; tomorrow, when she was safely back at the fort, she'd give his behavior more consideration.

Three Moons and his warriors had settled about the campfire. They were talking in low, amiable tones. Sheila watched them closely, particularly the Indian who had argued with White Cloud. She had a feeling that he didn't especially like White Cloud, and she wondered if White Cloud's mixed blood had anything to do with it.

She looked away from the Indians, held back a weary sigh, and leaned against the tree trunk. Her shoulder touched White Cloud's, and she moved over an inch.

Bart smiled. Apparently, Miss Langeford preferred to avoid personal contact. Well, he couldn't really blame her. He cast her a sidelong glance. Her eyes were closed and he noticed the way her long lashes curled on the ends. He couldn't recall ever seeing a woman more beautiful. But he admired more than her beauty; she was impressive—brave, and very likable. He wished he had met her under different circumstances and before her engagement to Lieutenant Dwyer. He wondered why she had fallen in love with Dwyer; he didn't seem a good match for her. Bart didn't ponder the question for long, though; love and war made strange bedfellows.

"You hungry?" he asked her. "You want food?"

Her eyelids fluttered open, and she gazed at him from

67

under thick, sooty lashes. Her expression was defiant. "No, I don't want any food," she said coldly.

Bart didn't try to persuade her to eat. He figured if she got hungry enough, she'd change her mind.

Sheila was mentally preparing herself to face the evening ahead. She had a feeling it would be a long night. At least she was being treated kindly. She supposed she had White Cloud to thank for that; if it were left to the other warriors, she suspected they wouldn't be quite so considerate.

She thought about her father and wondered how he was. She knew he loved her; he just wasn't the kind of person who showed much affection. More than likely, he was terribly worried. He probably believed she was being treated cruelly, for she couldn't recall the colonel ever saying anything complimentary about the Sioux; in his opinion, they were all savages.

Sheila stole a quick look at White Cloud. He certainly didn't seem like a savage. But, of course, she could be mistaken. After all, she didn't know very much about Indians. Her father and Donald were the experts! Sheila decided to stay alert. White Cloud could at any moment turn on her with a vengeance.

The night ahead suddenly looked menacing.

Colonel Langsford, pacing his office restlessly, talked with wide sweeps of his arms, "My God, I can't believe my daughter is at the mercy of some bloodthirsty savage! There's no telling what he'll do to her!"

Lieutenant Dwyer was only half listening. Langsford had been carrying on in such a manner for nearly an hour, mouthing the same worries and threats over and over again. Dwyer was sick and tired of hearing them. He wanted to leave, have dinner at the offices' mess, then go to his own quarters and retire with a bottle of whiskey. The colonel's tirade kept hitting him where it was the most painful: Sheila was at the mercy of that savage! What if he were to force himself on her? The thought alone was repulsive to Donald. If that were to actually happen, he knew he wouldn't marry her. Marry a woman who had been used by a warrior? He couldn't imagine himself even considering it.

"Lieutenant!" the colonel suddenly bellowed. "Are you listening to me?"

Donald was caught off guard; he had been completely ignoring the man's ranting. "I'm sorry, sir. What were you saying?"

"I asked you if you think that warrior will honor his part of the trade?"

Dwyer wanted to say "How the hell should I know?" but he didn't dare. That would be insubordination. "I don't know, sir."

"What do you mean, you don't know?" Langsford complained. "You must have formed some kind of opinion. Did the warrior seem sincere?"

"Yes, sir. I think so."

"Good! Then we'll do as he says. Tomorrow, you'll take Yellow Bear to the area where the warrior kidnapped Sheila."

"Alone?" Dwyer asked. Was the colonel mad? The warrior might have others with him! What would keep them from taking Yellow Bear, then killing him?

"Yes, alone!" Colonel Langsford snapped. "Unless

69

you're afraid." The colonel considered making the exchange himself, but was afraid Sheila's life might depend on his moving quickly, and his rheumatism would slow him down. He looked closely at the lieutenant. Would the man risk his life to save his fiancée? Was Lieutenant Dwyer not the soldier he had believed him to be?

Donald sensed the colonel's misgivings and answered firmly, "No, sir. I'm not afraid. I'd give my life to save Sheila." He calculated his next words quickly. "My concern is not for myself, but for Sheila. Alone, I can't protect her if the warrior has others with him and they decide to keep her."

"You're right. I should have thought of that myself. I'll send troops with you, but, during the exchange, they will stay behind and out of rifle range. If trouble erupts, they'll be ordered to charge and attack."

"Will you accompany them, sir?"

Langsford thought about his rheumatism again; riding horseback aggravated it. "No, I'll stay here. Major Evans will lead the troops. I'm sure I can depend on the two of you to bring my daughter home safely."

"Yes, sir," Dwyer replied respectfully, though he considered the colonel a jackass. After all, Sheila was his daughter—his responsibility; he should be the one making the trade. But hell no, he wasn't about to put his life on the line! Yes, rank certainly had its privileges! Dwyer was angry to the core. He was also scared; he would be a sitting duck during the trade!

The colonel moved to Dwyer, who had been standing since the time he entered the colonel's office. Langsford put a hand on the lieutenant's shoulder. "I apologize for talking so long. I'm sure you're tired, as well as hungry.

Get something to eat and a good night's sleep, then report to me in the morning. You're excused, Lieutenant.''

"Thank you, sir. Good night.''

Dwyer left the office on tired legs. He moved stiffly; his brand-new boots pinched his toes and his back ached. He was starved, fatigued, and upset. By this time tomorrow, he might be dead and already cold. Not that Colonel Langsford gave a damn! Dwyer's brows knitted into a deep frown. Did the colonel think sending troops along would save his life? Of course he didn't. Otherwise, he wouldn't order them to stay behind and out of rifle range. The colonel was only worried about Sheila's life! Dwyer chuckled harshly. Hell, he wasn't too damned worried, or he'd make the exchange himself!

Dwyer headed toward the officers' mess. He was in a foul mood when the two trappers who had brought in Yellow Bear caught up to him. They had been standing outside the colonel's office, waiting for the lieutenant to leave.

"Lieutenant Dwyer?'' the one named Jesse called.

Donald turned around. "Yes?''

"There's a rumor goin' round that Colonel Langsford's daughter was kidnapped by a warrior.''

"So?'' Dwyer was impatient. He was anxious to have dinner, then go to sleep.

"It's also rumored that Yellow Bear's gonna be traded for the woman.''

"It's no rumor. It's the truth.''

Jesse turned to his companion. "Can you believe that, Nathan? The Army's gonna turn that Indian loose?''

Nathan scowled viciously. "You soldiers ain't got no right to set that murderer free!''

71

"I'm sorry you feel that way. However, the matter is entirely out of my hands. Colonel Langsford is in charge. If you have a complaint, take it to him."

"Helluva lot a good that'll do!" Nathan muttered.

"Who's makin' the trade?" Jesse asked Dwyer.

"I am."

Jesse's eyes bore into the lieutenant's. "If I get me a chance, I'm gonna shoot that Indian, and I don't give a damn if you're protectin' him or not! He killed Willie, and Willie was my cousin. Him and me was not only kin, but we was friends, too!"

"Is that so?" Dwyer said bored by the whole exchange. "As I said before, talk to the colonel. I'm merely carrying out orders." He whirled around to leave, but had taken only a couple of steps when he was suddenly struck with an idea. He halted abruptly, turned back around, and stared thoughtfully at the two trappers. The men were unkempt, burly, and scraggly beards covered their faces. They were a loathsome pair, and as a brisk breeze blew their scent in Dwyer's direction, his nose wrinkled with disgust; their body odor was overwhelming.

"You got somethin' else to say, Lieutenant?" Jesse asked.

"Yes, I do. But what I'm about to say is confidential. If you confront me with it publicly, I will deny it."

"Go ahead, Lieutenant. Tell us what's on your mind," Jesse coaxed. He was indeed interested.

"I make the trade tomorrow at noon. Colonel Langsford plans to send troops with me; however, their orders will be to stay behind and out of rifle range, which means, when I make the exchange, I'll be totally vulnerable. If the warrior who is holding Miss Langsford isn't alone, I might be shot down in cold blood. But if you two were hiding close by, you could draw the warriors' fire. That would give me time to take shelter and would also give the troops time to arrive. Naturally, when you draw the warriors' fire, your first shot will kill Yellow Bear. That way, you'll get your revenge and I'll gain time to get away."

"What if there ain't no other warriors?" Nathan asked. "Maybe that redskin who got Miss Langsford is alone."

"In that case, the moment the trade is carried out, what's to keep you from shooting Yellow Bear and his friend?"

"Won't the Army arrest us?" Jesse questioned.

"As soon as you kill them, disappear! I'll swear that I didn't recognize the men who fired the shots. I'll say you were too far away from me to see you clearly."

"What about Miss Langsford? She might recognize us."

Dwyer spoke testily. "She's a woman! She'll be so hysterical during the shooting that she won't know what's happening."

"Yeah," Nathan agreed. "You're right." He looked at his companion. "Well, Jesse? What do you think?"

Jesse's wide smile revealed yellowed, decayed teeth. "I think we're gonna kill us some Indians."

"Splendid!" Dwyer replied. He quickly told the men where the exchange was to take place and they assured him that they'd arrive there early and take cover.

The threesome conspired a few minutes longer, then Dwyer went on his way. His spirits were greatly improved. If the warrior who had apprehended Sheila tried to trick him, the trappers would be there to help out.

When they opened fire, he would take Sheila and run for cover. The troops would hear the shots and arrive quickly. Dwyer hoped Jesse and Nathan would either escape or get killed, but if they didn't, he'd certainly deny any involvement with them. It would simply be their word against his, and the Army would believe him.

Dwyer's stomach growled, reminding him again that it was dinnertime. He hurried to the officers' mess and went inside.

Bart spread a blanket for Sheila beneath the tree; the grass underneath was thick and served as padding. He laid out a second blanket for himself, placing it beside hers. He still intended to stay protectively close to his captive.

Sheila, standing, watched as he prepared the bedrolls. That she and the warrior would spend the night in such close proximity was unnerving. A part of her was afraid of White Cloud; he was her enemy! But there was another part of Sheila that responded to his masculinity, for she found him disturbingly attractive. She was entirely in awe of him, but it was a mixture of fear and desire. She couldn't understand these feelings; she was engaged to Donald, yet this warrior excited her in a way that was undeniably sensual. An engaged woman shouldn't feel such attraction for another man! Moreover, engaged or not, the primitive hunger White Cloud provoked in her was shameful!

"Sleep!" Bart said suddenly, pointing at Sheila's blanket.

Sleep! she thought. She wasn't sure if that was possible, not with him lying so close! She didn't say anything, she simply did as he ordered.

He stretched out on his own blanket, folded his arms behind his head, and rested against his hands. He gazed up at the myriad of stars glittering in the heavens. Tomorrow's trade had his nerves on edge. God, he prayed nothing would go wrong! If anything happened to Miss Langsford, he'd never forgive himself. He set his jaw firmly. He'd make damned sure nothing happened! She would come out of this unharmed, even if it meant Yellow Bear's life—or his own!

He rolled to his side, raised his head, and looked down into her face. Her gaze met his, and he stared deeply into her coffee-brown eyes. She was the first to glance away.

"What do you want?" she asked uncertainly. "Why are you staring at me?"

"You very beautiful," he murmured, wishing he could speak English naturally. Expressing himself in this forced way was not only difficult but also aggravating.

"Thank you," Sheila said softly. Considering the circumstances, such amenities sounded ridiculous, but she didn't know what else to say.

"Do you have man?" he asked, hoping to draw her into talking about Lieutenant Dwyer. He wasn't sure why he wanted to know about her relationship with him. It certainly wasn't any of his business.

"Yes, I do," she answered. "We're getting married in two weeks."

"The bluecoat you with, he the man you marry?"

She nodded. "His name is Lieutenant Dwyer."

"You love him?"

The question surprised her. "But . . . but of course I

do! Otherwise I wouldn't marry him." She realized she didn't sound too convincing.

Bart grinned knowingly. "Maybe you better put off marriage. Give yourself more time."

"I can do without your advice, thank you!" she remarked petulantly. She wasn't about to tell him that he had hit a sensitive chord. The idea of postponing her marriage had been skirting the back of her mind. It had been there even before she met White Cloud; she just hadn't brought it forth. She wasn't sure why she hadn't done anything about it; maybe she dreaded disappointing her father.

"The lieutenant not worthy of you," Bart murmured.

She stared into his face, and wished instantly that she hadn't. His sensual good looks held her mesmerized. She told herself to glance away, but she couldn't

Bart was also captivated, but his feelings of responsibility for their situation were such that he turned his face away. God, how badly he wanted to kiss her! He grimaced. Damn it, he had to take control of himself! His purpose was to save Yellow Bear, not to fall in love with Sheila Langsford. She was not only engaged to another man, but if she knew the truth about him, she'd undoubtedly despise him.

His resolve holding firm, Bart rolled to his other side and turned his back to Sheila. Drawing his rifle close, he muttered abruptly. "Time to sleep, white woman!"

A folded blanket lay at Sheila's feet; she reached down and drew it over her. She closed her eyes and waited for sleep. The campsite was quiet, for the other warriors, except for the two standing guard, had retired to their own blankets.

Sheila was worried that she would lie awake for hours, but fatigue took over and she gradually drifted into slumber.

Dwyer had eaten a hearty dinner, then, taking a bottle of whiskey with him, he had gone to his own quarters. He now lay in bed; an arm dangling over the side held the half-empty bottle. He was drunk, but he didn't care. The liquor was soothing, and made tomorrow's mission seem less threatening.

His whiskey-laced thoughts went to Sheila. A grimace of disgust crossed his face. Right this minute that damned warrior could be using her for his own pleasure! That a savage was enjoying what was rightfully his enraged Dwyer. After the trappers killed the bastard, he'd personally castrate his dead body! The stinking sonofabitch would enter the happy hunting ground minus his manhood!

If Sheila had been molested, Dwyer hoped she'd have the decency to call off their marriage. If she expected him to still marry her, then she was in for a big disappointment! He'd break their engagement himself, and he didn't give a damn if the colonel liked it or not! Furthermore, in two weeks he would transfer to Fort Swafford, and Langsford would no longer be his commanding officer. His brother was Fort Swafford's commander.

A gleeful smile curled Donald's lips. Together, with troops under their command, he and his brother would scour this territory with Sioux blood!

Chapter Four

The sun's morning rays slanted across Sheila's face, bringing her out of a deep sleep. Awakening slowly, she was too drowsy to remember where she was and what had happened. She was lying so close to Bart that her body was almost touching his. He was awake, and he watched as she stretched cat-like, then rolled to her side, her face turned to his. Her eyes opened sleepily, and her lethargic gaze met his.

A smile flickered across Bart's lips. "Good morning," he murmured.

She sat up instantly, and stared wide-eyed around the campsite. The Indians were sitting around the fire, eating their morning meal. She turned back to Bart, who was still watching her. Waking to captivity had frightened her, but seeing only kindness in White Cloud's eyes calmed her fear.

"You hungry?" he asked.

She was famished. She hadn't eaten since noon yesterday. "Yes," she said softly. "I'm very hungry."

He rose gracefully, went to the fire and filled two bowls. He then returned to sit beside Sheila and offer her the food.

She accepted the proffered fare a little hesitantly, for she wasn't sure what she was about to eat.

Reading her thoughts, Bart said with a smile, "Rabbit stew, left from last night."

She took a tentative bite, and discovered it was quite savory. Appeasing her hunger, she began to eat with relish. Bart, famished himself, devoured his meal quickly. He uncapped his canteen and took a generous swallow. Waiting for Sheila to finish her food he then offered her a drink of water.

"Thank you," she murmured, taking the canteen.

"Come; I take you to bushes," Bart said after she had helped herself to a drink.

A blush colored Sheila's cheeks. Last night before retiring, White Cloud had escorted her into the shrubbery and had stood nearby as she took care of her personal needs. She had found the incident embarrassing, and this morning was no better.

Bart stood, helped her up, then, with a firm hold on her arm, he led her away from camp. He took her to an area dense with overgrown shrubbery.

Sheila made her way into the thicket, where the prickly bushes snagged at her riding skirt. The material was completely ripped through in places. The skirt was also dust covered, and her blouse was just as dirty. She longed desperately for a bath and fresh clothes. She ran her fingers through her long tresses; the dark locks were mussed and tangled. What she wouldn't give for a hairbrush!

When she emerged from the shrubbery, Bart was waiting for her. She wished she wasn't attracted to him; he was her enemy and she should find him threatening. But the longer she was with White Cloud the less dangerous he seemed. It was very hard for her to imagine him hurting her. She sensed a gentleness in him that contrasted starkly with his abduction of her. He had told Donald that he would kill her if he didn't get Yellow Bear, but Sheila somehow knew that White Cloud was not capable of such a thing. This man was not a murderer!

As she moved slowly toward him, her gaze traveled over his tall, manly frame. He was handsome beyond compare. His tan leggings seemed molded to his strong physique, and his fringed buckskin shirt fit tightly across his wide chest. Her eyes dropped to his soft-soled moccasins, which were decorated with beads. With such shoes, he could certainly slip up on his prey undetected. She raised her scrutiny to his face. His charcoal-eyes were staring into hers. She wasn't intimidated and continued to study him intently, finding his pronounced cheekbones and strong, square chin impressive. Her gaze rested on his full lips as she wondered how it would feel to have him kiss her. She knew it would be thrilling, yet she was aghast at herself for thinking such a thing! What had come over her? How could she even imagine something so outrageous? White Cloud was not only her enemy, but his world was completely alien from hers. She was suddenly struck with a sharp pang of guilt. If her father knew she had found a warrior attractive, he would be ashamed of her! More than ashamed—he would be enraged.

As Sheila was battling with her conscience, Bart was totally immersed in her beguiling beauty. Her disheveled hair and dust-coated attire didn't detract from her sensuality; quite the contrary, her tousled locks falling about her face were arousing. In intense perusal, his eyes raked over her tall, slender frame: her blouse, the top two buttons undone, barely revealed the fullness of her breasts, and her skirt adhered smoothly to her hips before draping down to touch the tops of her boots. He noticed how elegantly she moved, her head held high, her shoulders straight, and her steps gracefully light.

She came to his side, paused, and looked up into his face. He gazed deeply into the brown eyes watching him without fear. Bart found her an exciting challenge. She was more than just a pretty young woman, she was brave, daring, and self-confident. He suspected she was also warm-hearted and sensible. There was a delicate vulnerability about her that touched a tender chord inside him. He wished he could take her into his arms and spend the rest of his life protecting her. The wish, however, was fleeting; she wasn't his to claim, she was in love with Lieutenant Dwyer. His eyes revealed a quick flare of anger as he thought about Sheila marrying Dwyer. In his opinion, the man didn't deserve Sheila—she was too damned good for him!

Sheila saw his flicker of anger. "Is something wrong?" she asked.

He reached out and grasped her shoulders. "Wait; and give more thought before you marry Lieutenant Dwyer."

Sheila was stunned. Whatever prompted White Cloud to say such a thing?

Realizing he had spoken rashly, Bart dropped his hands from her shoulders and stepped back. He must stop speaking impulsively. He again reminded himself that his only aim was to save Yellow Bear. Miss Langsford's engagement to Dwyer was not his concern.

He gestured in the direction of camp. "We go back."

Sheila was still puzzled. "White Cloud, why do you think I should postpone my marriage?"

Bart was now against discussing the matter. The less communication he had with Sheila the better. After all, he would soon resume his true identity. If their paths were to cross and she got to know him too well, she would certainly realize that White Cloud and Bart Chandler were one and the same.

He gave her a gentle shove toward camp. "We go!" he said gruffly.

She resented his treatment and flashed him an angry scowl before starting back. He walked closely behind.

"Excuse me, Colonel," the sentry said, entering Langsford's office. "An Indian is at the fort, and he's askin' to speak to you. He has an Indian girl with him."

The colonel got up from behind his desk and went outside with the soldier.

"He's over there," the trooper said, pointing toward the fort's gates.

A Sioux warrior, mounted on a pinto, sat regally. He wore a yellow feather in his hair, and his apparel was made from buckskin. Beside him was a young woman astride a white pony. Her long black hair was braided, and she was wearing a fringed dress that softly hugged her ripe curves.

Langsford, with the sentry trailing at his heels, walked over to greet the warrior. Several other soldiers had gathered about the visitors. The warrior was unarmed, and the troopers were there more out of curiosity than to protect the colonel.

"I called Crow Dog," the warrior said to Langsford. He waved a terse hand at the woman. "She my daughter—called Dream Dancer." He spoke firmly to his daughter in his own tongue, then turned back to the colonel. "Dream Dancer speaks to you."

Langsford gave the young woman his attention.

She was nervous, and, for a moment, the English she had learned seemed to take wings and fly. She swallowed heavily, wiped a hand across her sweat-laden brow, as she concentrated on the white man's language, and said in a meek tone, "I the woman the white men attack. Yellow Bear and others find me. The white men shoot at them, they shoot back. I scared, and I run away. I got to my village. I tell no one what happened. I too ashamed." She bowed her head for just a moment, then lifted tear-filled eyes to the colonel. "My heart hurt for Yellow Bear. I know I must tell truth. I go to mother, she tell me to go to father. He bring me here."

"Are you saying that you were molested by these trappers?" Langsford had heard the story before; during the trial, Yellow Bear had testified in his own behalf.

Dream Dancer was confused! she didn't understand the colonel's question.

"Molested!" Langsford repeated. "Attacked? Did they force themselves on you?"

Crow Dog answered in place of his daughter. "She no longer maiden. She supposed to marry Black Elk. Now, Black Elk not want her."

Langsford frowned irritably. Damn those trappers for endangering an already precarious truce between the Army and the Sioux! Well, there was nothing he could do about it! Yellow Bear was gone, and so were the trappers! Besides, the girl might be lying.

"I thank you, Crow Dog, for bringing Dream Dancer here. But Yellow Bear is no longer my prisoner. He is being released today in exchange for my daughter. The trappers who attacked Dream Dancer are not at the fort. I guess they returned to the mountains."

Crow Dog, his expression inscrutable, turned his horse around. With his daughter riding close behind, he galloped through the open gates.

The colonel watched them leave, then, glancing at his pocket watch, he saw that it was almost noon. The exchange between Sheila and Yellow Bear would soon take place. He prayed all would go well.

"Colonel, sir?" the sentry said.

"Yes, what is it?" He spoke a little testily, for his mind was on Sheila, and he resented the soldier's intrusion.

"Did you believe what that Indian gal said?"

Langsford shrugged. "She could be telling the truth, I suppose. Who knows?"

"Does this mean when Yellow Bear is rounded up, he won't hang?"

"Oh, he'll hang, all right! Him and the warrior who stole my daughter! I'll see them both swing at the end of a rope!"

Dream Dancer kept her pony behind her father's. She didn't want to see his face. Those white men had disgraced her, and her shame was almost more than Crow Dog could bear. She was his youngest child, and only daughter, and he had been pleased that Black Elk wanted to marry her. Black Elk's father was chief, and Black Elk's choosing her as his bride had been a great honor for her family. He had also promised her father many horses; now, of course, he would pick another maiden, and the horses would go to that girl's father.

Tears filled Dream Dancer's eyes and rolled steadily down her pretty face. Now, no young warrior would want her; she would remain unmarried or else her father would marry her to a old man who craved a young wife. Her future looked bleak. She seriously considered death. Dead she would no longer be a disgrace to her family. Nor would she be forced to live with her shame.

She kneed her horse and rode up alongside Crow Dog. "Father, tonight I will say goodbye to you, my mother, and brothers. Then I will leave our village and never see any of you again."

"Where will you go, my daughter?"

"I will go to the spirit world. I leave without water or food, and I will not find water, nor will I search for food."

Crow Dog, holding back a sob that had risen in his

throat, made no attempt to dissuade her. He could understand why Dream Dancer had chosen death over life.

"I will miss you, Dream Dancer."

He coaxed his pony into a fast gallop and took the lead. He didn't want his daughter to see that his eyes were filled with tears.

Bart dismounted, helped Sheila down, then, leading the pony, they climbed the steep hillside. The horse's agile hooves scaled the grassy slope without a slip. Reaching the top, Bart suggested that Sheila sit beneath a tree. He tied the pony, then moved to the edge of the rise and scanned the land stretching before him. Yellow Bear and Dwyer were not in sight. Shading his eyes with his hand, he glanced up at the sun; it had reached its zenith—the lieutenant and Yellow Bear should arrive any moment. Bart's nerves were tightly strung and anxiety gnawed at his stomach. He prayed the exchange would take place without a mishap!

Sheila, resting under the tree's canopied branches, stared thoughtfully at Bart's back. She could tell that he was troubled. She wondered if his concern was for her as well as for Yellow Bear. Like Bart, she was anxious, and she nibbled at her bottom lip. Three Moons and his warriors were close by; if they should decide to intervene, their interference could put her life in jeopardy. If a full-fledged attack erupted, bullets would fly randomly and she could get killed in the cross fire.

Bart turned and looked back at her, and their eyes met. Inexplicably, Sheila felt as though she had seen him somewhere before. The feeling passed quickly, and she didn't examine it. If she had seen White Cloud before this, she would certainly remember him. Such a handsome warrior would be unforgettable.

"Do you see Lieutenant Dwyer and Yellow Bear?" she asked him.

He shook his head. "They not come yet."

Sheila swallowed nervously. She hoped nothing had happened to prevent the exchange. She didn't think White Cloud would harm her, but she wasn't sure about Three Moons and his warriors. White Cloud might try to protect her, but he was outnumbered. Three Moons and the others could easily overpower him.

Bart, moving with as much agility as a forest creature, came to her side, gazed down tenderly into her eyes, and murmured, "Do not be afraid. Yellow Bear no come, you still go home." He had held her captive long enough and wasn't about to further endanger her.

She was grateful. "Thank you, White Cloud."

A smile crossed his face; it was so sensual that Sheila was taken aback. "You think long before marrying lieutenant?" he asked. Bart silently berated himself. Why couldn't he let Sheila's relationship with Dwyer rest?

Sheila found his persistence flattering. "Yes, White Cloud. I will think long and hard. In fact, I've been considering postponing my marriage for some time now. You see, I'm not sure that I'm in love with Lieutenant Dwyer." A tiny frown furrowed her brow. "For weeks I've been downhearted, and I now realize that my upcoming marriage is the reason why."

Sheila was suddenly embarrassed. She could hardly

believe that she had confided her deepest thoughts to a Sioux warrior.

Bart moved away, stood at the hill's edge, and once again scanned the landscape. That Sheila planned to postpone her wedding pleased him. He hoped she would eventually cancel it altogether.

Riders in the distance suddenly caught his attention, and he watched closely as they drew nearer. He recognized Yellow Bear and Dwyer.

Bart hurried to Sheila, helped her to her feet, and said, "They come." He untied the pony, and with Sheila a step in front, they descended the hill to await Dwyer and Yellow Bear.

"Sir," the sentry said, entering Langsford's office. "There's a man here to see you."

The colonel glowered. This seemed to be his day for visitors. He was in no mood to see anyone; his mind was too preoccupied with Sheila. The trade was probably taking place this very moment.

"Did he give a name?" the colonel asked the sentry.

"Yes, sir. Luke Thomas."

Langsford mulled the name over; it didn't sound familiar. "Very well, show him in."

The soldier opened the door, waved Thomas inside, then returned to his post.

"I'm sorry to barge in on you like this, Colonel," Luke said, shaking the officer's hand. "But I'm lookin' for a friend of mine. I thought he might be stayin' here at the fort. His name is Bart Chandler."

"Did you ask at the hotel?"

"Yep, but no one by that name checked in."

"I'm afraid I can't help you, Mr. Thomas."

"Colonel, I just heard talk that your daughter was abducted by a Sioux warrior who plans to exchange her for Yellow Bear."

"Yes, that is true."

"What is this warrior's name?"

"I don't know."

"Can you describe 'im to me?"

"I've never seen him, but Lieutenant Dwyer said he's very tall for an Indian, and also appears to be a half-breed."

Thomas was worried. Could this warrior be Bart? He certainly hoped not! Thomas had never heard of Yellow Bear; when Bart had left the Sioux, his brother hadn't yet received his man's name. Luke knew it was a long shot, but he nonetheless pursued it. "What village does Yellow Bear belong to?"

"His father is Chief Iron Star."

Luke grimaced. Damn, Yellow Bear was Bart's brother!

"Mr. Thomas, why are you so interested in Yellow Bear and the warrior who abducted my daughter? If you have information I should know about—"

"I don't know nothin'," Luke cut in. "I was just curious. I won't keep you no longer, Colonel. Good day, and thanks for seein' me."

Luke made his departure hastily. Outside, he paused to gather his thoughts. He had a visceral feeling that Bart was the warrior who had kidnapped the colonel's daughter. He had been afraid that something like this would happen. That was why he had decided to come look for Bart.

He headed for the stables to get his horse and pack mule. He was an experienced tracker and was confident that he'd find Bart. When he did, he'd give him a piece of his mind! Passing himself off as a warrior and abducting the colonel's daughter— Damn it to hell, had he gone mad? He never dreamed that Bart would do something so foolhardy. The stubborn cuss was gonna mess around and get himself killed! Luke loved Bart like a brother, and the chance that he could die quickened Luke's steps. He had to find Bart before it was too late!

Jesse and Nathan were well hidden in the shrubbery, and they watched as Lieutenant Dwyer and Yellow Bear rode to meet the warrior and Miss Langsford.

"You reckon we're close enough to get off an accurate shot?" Nathan asked.

Jesse's rifle sported a rear sight for greater accuracy, and he was sure he wouldn't miss. The weapon was cradled in his arms; he ran a hand over it as though he were caressing a woman. "I won't miss," he mumbled. "Not with this here rifle. I'm gonna kill Yellow Bear, then if I get me a chance, I'm gonna shoot that other Indian."

"Goddamn it, Jesse! Don't I get to shoot one of 'em?"

"What with?" he asked gruffly. He pointed at Nathan's shotgun. "That thing ain't no good 'less you're right up on a man." He grinned expectantly. "I reckon both them Indians is mine!"

Nathan withdrew into a sullen pout. Jesse was gonna have all the fun!

Chapter Five

Dwyer reined in his horse, gesturing for Yellow Bear to do the same; they stopped a couple of yards from Bart and Sheila. Dwyer glanced nervously around and noticed an area thick with shrubbery. He wondered if the trappers had taken cover there. It was the ideal spot, for it was dense and within rifle range. His eyes searched farther, and he was relieved not to spot a band of warriors. Thank God, the Indian with Sheila was apparently alone, he thought. Then a feeling of uneasiness crept over him, for the warrior might have others waiting out of sight; after all, Captain Evans and his troops were not very far away. He and this warrior might be using the same strategy.

"Lieutenant Dwyer!" Bart called. "Send Yellow Bear to me, and I give back woman!"

Dwyer looked at Yellow Bear and ordered gruffly for him to dismount. The horse he was riding belonged to the Army, and Dwyer wasn't about to let him ride off with it.

Yellow Bear slid from the horse's back; it wasn't saddled, the warrior had ridden bareback. He stood still and stared up at the lieutenant with an expression filled with loathing. He despised Dwyer, but he hated his brother even more. It had been Charles Dwyer who had attacked his father's village ten years ago. He had also led troops against Iron Star and his people during their buffalo hunt. It was Charles Dwyer's evilness that had finally driven Iron Star from the reservation and into the mountains.

Yellow Bear's hostile expression unnerved Donald; he felt the man would relish taking his scalp. He looked away from the warrior, and yelled to Bart. "I'll release Yellow Bear; you send the woman at the same time!"

"I do as you say!" Bart called back. He turned to Sheila, smiled gently, and said, "You go now."

She returned his smile. "Goodbye, White Cloud."

Bart was touched by her kindness. She had good cause to despise him, yet he saw only understanding in her gaze. She turned away, and he watched as she began a slow, steady walk toward the lieutenant. Meanwhile, Yellow Bear was coming toward Bart, his strides unhurried.

Sheila was seeing Yellow Bear for the first time. Some people at the fort had found him a curious attraction and had gone out of their way to catch a glimpse of him. But Sheila hadn't wanted to look upon the face of a man who would most likely be executed. The possibility of a hanging had excited the fort, and several soldiers and civilians had been looking forward to the event; Sheila had found the whole matter depressing.

Now, as she approached Yellow Bear, she looked closely at him. She couldn't see a resemblance to White Cloud. Both men were impressive looking, but Yellow Bear's Sioux blood was more apparent. Sheila had a feeling that the brothers didn't share the same mother. Yellow Bear's straight black hair was shoulder length, and his high cheekbones accentuated coal-black eyes.

The warrior was now so close that she could reach out and touch him. As his gaze met hers, she tried to read his expression, but his black eyes curtained his thoughts.

She turned her face away; at that moment, she saw a flash come from the nearby shrubbery. The sun's bright rays had fallen across the barrel of Jesse's rifle. Sheila, realizing what she had seen, stopped abruptly, turned to Yellow Bear, and cried, "Watch out!"

Reacting instantly, he dove to the ground, and in doing so collided with Sheila and knocked her off her feet. Unable to break her fall, she fell with a force so hard that it nearly drove the air from her lungs.

A rifle shot rang out thunderously, but the bullet whizzed harmlessly in the air, missing Sheila and Yellow Bear. Jesse, afraid he might hit the colonel's daughter, held his fire.

The shot not only alerted Captain Evans, but was heard by Three Moons as well. The warriors were closer, and as they appeared over the rise, yelling and whooping vociferously, Bart was racing toward Sheila and Yellow Bear. Dwyer, protecting his own skin, slapped the reins against his horse and headed for the shrubbery to take cover.

The horse Yellow Bear had ridden was left behind. The warrior, leaving Sheila where she lay, scrambled to his feet. He was swinging up onto the horse's back when the soldiers arrived. He pressed his knees into the animal's sides, and as it took off with a bolt, a bullet slammed into Yellow Bear's side. Concealed in the shrubbery, Jesse grinned with satisfaction. He hadn't missed! However, when Yellow Bear didn't fall, his smiled vanished. He was about to shoot again, but the advancing Indians changed his mind. He quickly ducked his head, and crouched behind the bushes.

Three Moons and his warriors opened fire, which was quickly returned by the troopers. Sheila was caught in the cross fire. She remained flat on the ground. If she stood up, a bullet would certainly find her, but if she stayed where she was, she'd undoubtedly be trampled by the Indians' ponies. They were racing toward her, and the ground beneath trembled with the pounding of horses' hooves.

Sheila was about to take her chances, get up, and run for safe ground when Bart reined in beside her. He brought his horse to a stop so suddenly that it whinnied and stood up on its back legs. He quickly calmed the steed and offered Sheila his arm. "Come on!" he said anxiously.

She leapt to her feet, clutched his arm, and helped as he swung her up behind him. She grabbed him about the waist, and with a barrage of gunfire exploding all about them, she held on for dear life as Bart sent his pony into a breakneck run. They soon caught up with Yellow Bear, who raced beside them as they headed away from the battle. Sheila dared to glance over at Yellow Bear and was startled to see blood oozing from his wound.

Bart and Yellow Bear kept their horses at a fast run

until they were so far away that the sounds of gunshots could no longer be heard.

They drew up, and Bart looked at his brother with concern. "How badly are you wounded?" he asked in the Sioux tongue.

"I can get to Flying Feather's village. We must go there so the medicine man, Lame Wolf, can take out the bullet."

Bart's thoughts went to Sheila. Should he take her with them, or leave her here and hope the Army would find her? But if he left her behind, Three Moons and his warriors might find her. He didn't trust Three Moons and wouldn't put it past him to harm her. For now, it was in Sheila's best interest that he keep her with him. Besides, it was his fault that she was in this predicament, which made her his responsibility. And furthermore, he could spend more time with her this way. That last thought skimmed across his mind almost without him knowing it.

He spoke gently to Sheila. "We go to Flying Feather's village."

She didn't protest. Like Bart, she had already considered her options and didn't want to be left behind. She could well imagine what might happen to her if she were found by Three Moons.

"The trade was ruined," Bart told her bitterly. "Dwyer try to trick us."

"Maybe he didn't know about the ambush."

"He knew," Bart said harshly. "Now, Three Moons fight with bluecoats. Maybe big war will start, many people die!"

Yellow Bear, despite his pain, stared curiously at his

97

brother. Why was White Cloud speaking the white man's words in such a strange way? His brother knew English fluently; in fact, it was now his own language.

Bart, seeing his confusion, said in the Sioux tongue, "I will explain everything at a later time. Now, we must get you to Lame Wolf."

They coaxed their horses into a steady canter, and Sheila's arms returned to Bart's waist. She glanced cautiously over her shoulder, but no Indians or soldiers were in sight. She wondered why she wasn't disappointed not to see soldiers. She should want to be rescued as soon as possible. Her conscience sent a stab of guilt through her, making her feel as though she had betrayed her own people. White Cloud was the enemy, and she must stop thinking of him as a friend. Friend! her mind intervened. What she felt for White Cloud was much more intense than friendship. She was attracted to him, and was probably falling in love. She made a vow to fight these feelings and remain loyal to her own kind; especially to her father!

Three Moons and his warriors were outnumbered, and leaving two dead, they turned their ponies about and retreated. The soldiers, led by Captain Evans, gave chase.

Dwyer, still hidden in the bushes with Jesse and Nathan, waited until the troops were out of sight before saying briskly, "You two make tracks! I'll tell the captain that when I got here you were gone." When they didn't obey, he shouted harshly, "Move, damn it!"

They rushed to where their horses were concealed, mounted, and rode away.

Dwyer stepped to his own horse, swung up into the

saddle, and galloped away from the shrubbery and into the open. He wasn't sure if he should start back to the fort or wait here for the captain. He decided to wait, but not for very long.

Sheila's image came to mind, and he recalled the way in which she had walked toward him. She hadn't moved like a woman who had been physically or even mentally misused. Could it be possible that she hadn't been molested? That a warrior wouldn't use Sheila to satisfy his lust was hard for Dwyer to comprehend. After all, they were a race of uncivilized savages, and Sheila was very beautiful. He simply could not imagine a warrior treating Sheila, or any white woman, with courtesy and respect. That was more than his prejudiced mind could accept. Sheila had certainly been molested, and he came to the conclusion that she didn't appear abused because she had liked it! A cold, demonic sneer crossed Dwyer's face. She was worse than a trollop, she was the scum of the earth! A murderous rage filled the lieutenant as he pictured Sheila coupling with the warrior and enjoying it! He was so angry that his eyes widened and his features twisted into a leer. His anger intensified as he thought about all the months he had denied himself Sheila's body. And now this warrior had stolen what was supposed to be his! He would kill him if it was the last thing he did in his life! And if Sheila tried to stop him, he'd kill her, too!

The sounds of horses pushed Sheila and the warrior out of Donald's thoughts. He looked on as Captain Evans and his soldiers rode into sight.

"What went wrong?" Evans asked, stopping alongside Dwyer.

"The exchange was in process when a shot came from those bushes." He pointed in the general direction. "After that, all hell broke lose. A band of Indians came charging over the hill, and the warrior who kidnapped Miss Langsford grabbed her again."

"What were you doing when all this was going on?"

"Well, sir, I couldn't get to Miss Langsford, so I rode into the shrubbery to apprehend whoever fired the shot. There was no one there; he got away. I was trapped into staying where I was, for by then those damned Indians were all around."

"Was Miss Langsford harmed?"

"No, sir, I don't think so."

"The Indians have hightailed it toward the mountains, but they didn't have the woman, so I didn't see any reason to continue pursuit." The captain looked worried. "The colonel's going to be mighty upset."

Dwyer dreaded facing Langsford. "Believe me, Captain, there was nothing I could do to save Sheila."

Evans had his doubts. He didn't like Dwyer, nor did he like his older brother. Ten years ago when Charles had attacked Iron Star's village, Evans had been under his command. Back then he had been a lieutenant. He and several other soldiers had refused to take part in the massacre. Later, Evans had tried to bring charges against Charles Dwyer, but their commanding officer had turned a deaf ear to his complaint.

Evans shrugged. "It doesn't matter whether or not I believe you, Lieutenant. It's what the colonel thinks that matters." With that, he rode to his corporal and told him to pass the order to pull out.

Dwyer fell into formation. He was apprehensive—

Colonel Langsford would no doubt be upset. He mentally braced himself to face the man's anger. Thank God he had only two more weeks at Fort Laramie. He was indeed looking forward to his transfer, and could hardly wait to report to his brother at Fort Swafford.

It took over two hours to reach Flying Feather's village. Yellow Bear had lost a lot of blood and was terribly weak. He stayed on his pony by sheer willpower.

The people watched the visitors ride into their encampment with misgivings. Yellow Bear was now an outlaw, and the white man's army forbade them to harbor a fugitive. Their sympathies lay with Yellow Bear, but if the bluecoats should learn that Flying Feather had given Yellow Bear refuge, the entire village would pay the price.

Sheila noticed that the people didn't appear very friendly, but she assumed it was because of her. She was partly right; they were strongly against having a white captive in their village.

But two warriors hurried to Yellow Bear and helped him down from his horse. He was too weak to stand, and they carried him to the medicine man's tepee.

Bart, with Sheila's arms still wrapped tightly about his waist, continued on to Flying Feather's lodge. The old chief was standing outside waiting for him, and he invited White Cloud and the woman into his home.

Sheila had never been inside a tepee, and she looked around her with interest. The interior resembled a hollow cone, and the lodge poles were covered with leather painted with picture writing. The fireplace, set in a little depression, was encircled with cobblestones. Beds made

101

with pelts and blankets occupied the north and south sides of the tepee. Clothing and personal items were neatly tucked behind these beds; nothing was left scattered about.

Bart touched her arm, pointed at a spot close to the fire, and told her to sit. He sat to the front of her, and Flying Feather, his legs crossed Indian-style, sat across from them.

Sheila looked closely at the old chief. His skin was wrinkled and weather-worn. His snow-white hair was braided, and a leather band, adorned with beads, was wrapped about his head. His dark eyes were alert; they were also penetrating. He gazed intently at Sheila, and she felt as though his eyes could see through to her very soul.

Flying Feather, turning his attention to Bart, said gently, "White Cloud, you must take Yellow Bear and leave."

Bart was surprised. "Leave? But why?"

"The soldiers will search for him. If he is found here, my people will suffer their anger. Also, I will be arrested. The bluecoats have warned us not to hide anyone who is wanted by them." He had seen the two warriors carry Yellow Bear to the medicine man's tepee. "How badly is Yellow Bear wounded?"

"I don't think his injury is too serious."

"As soon as the bullet is removed, you must leave."

Bart understood Flying Feather's hesitancy to offer aid. The people in this village were his responsibility, and they had to come first. "Is it all right if I leave the woman here? You can send a runner to the fort to let the colonel know where she is."

"You must take her with you!" the chief said firmly. "If she is here, the bluecoats will know I helped you and Yellow Bear." He got quickly to his feet, stared unflinchingly at Bart, and asserted with authority, "All three of you must leave at once. I will see that you have supplies, and a travois for Yellow Bear. While I assemble these things, you and the woman may stay here and rest."

Sheila watched as he left the tepee. It wasn't necessary to understand the Sioux language to know he was upset. "Is Flying Feather angry because you brought me here?" she asked Bart.

"He does not want *any* of us here."

"Why is he against having you and Yellow Bear?"

"If soldiers find us here, it will bring much trouble to him and his people." Bart frowned. He was sick and tired of speaking in broken English. To his ears, it sounded ridiculous! And, he was fed up with this damned charade he was playing. He curbed his impatience, however; it was still imperative that he protect his true identity.

"If you can't stay here," Sheila began, "where will you and Yellow Bear go? And what do you plan to do with me?"

"Yellow Bear and I travel to mountains and to my father's village."

When he didn't say anything more, Sheila questioned again, "What will happen to me? Are you taking me with you?"

Bart sank into serious thought. If Flying Feather were to give her a horse, could she make it back to the fort safely? Uneasiness settled in the pit of his stomach. There was no guarantee that Flying Feather wouldn't send warriors after her to silence her. He'd be opposed to Sheila returning to the fort and telling her father that he had helped Yellow Bear. Suddenly, Bart had a terrible feeling that by bringing Sheila here, he had placed her life in jeopardy. He grew anxious to put Yellow Bear on a travois and leave without further delay.

Bart drew a deep breath, turned to Sheila, and said with a calm he didn't truly feel, "I take you to mountains with me. I do so to protect you."

"Protect me?" she repeated. "Am I in danger?"

"Maybe."

"From Three Moons?"

"There are many who might harm you."

Sheila's heart pounded. She didn't want to travel into the mountains. The Sioux who had taken refuge in the Dakotas were warlike, and they hated anyone who was white.

Bart stood up. "I go check on Yellow Bear. I be back soon."

He hurried outside and was on his way to Lame Wolf's tepee when Three Moons and his warriors rode in. They were leading Bart's horse and pack mule. The horse was saddled, and Bart's belongings were stored on the mule. Although Bart wasn't pleased to see Three Moons, he was glad to have his horse and belongings back.

Three Moons dismounted and went to Bart. "Where is Yellow Bear?" He asked.

"He is with Lame Wolf. He was wounded."

"I will take him to Iron Star's village."

"He is traveling with me," Bart said firmly. "We're leaving right away. Flying Feather doesn't want us here."

"Then we will ride with you."

104

"No!" Bart said. "If we all travel together, it will make it that much easier for the soldiers to track us."

"You are right, White Cloud. Alone, you and Yellow Bear stand a better chance of eluding the soldiers. Tell Yellow Bear that we will take the south pass up into the mountains and draw the bluecoats away from you. That way, you and Yellow Bear can take the north route, which is shorter and less hazardous. You will reach Iron Star's village about two days ahead of us." Three Moons paused, eyed Bart with hostility, and said with disdain, "You dress like a warrior, but you are not really Sioux. You are a white man, and there are many, including myself, who do not want you living among us. I do not kill you because you are Yellow Bear's brother and Iron Star's son. You are also Spotted Wing's brother, and she is the woman I plan to marry—"

"You are marrying my sister?" Bart cut in, surprised.

"We will marry very soon. But I will never accept you as one of my family. I do not like you, White Cloud."

"I do not care if you like me or not."

A smile more like a sneer, crossed Three Moons's face. "Be careful, White Cloud. I am your enemy, and I will be watching you." He whirled about and walked away.

Bart didn't take Three Moons's words lightly. He knew the warrior could cause trouble. He went to his horse and patted its neck. He wondered if Sheila could handle the stallion; it was spirited but obedient. He knew she would be more at ease riding a horse that was broken to a saddle. He decided to give it a try. If she couldn't control the stallion, then she'd have to ride an Indian pony. He led the horse to Flying Feather's tepee, secured it, and headed for Lame Wolf's tepee.

He deeply regretted getting Sheila involved in all this, but there was nothing he could do about it now.

Chapter Six

Dream Dancer walked slowly, keeping her watchful eyes on the mountain range that stretched across the horizon. Between her and the foothills, the plains spread out in a perfect tapestry as the sun, sinking westward, cast an orange glow across the quiet landscape.

Dream Dancer wasn't sure how long it would take to walk to the mountains; the towering peaks were probably farther away than they appeared. Regardless of the distance, the mountains were her destination. She wanted to die among the trees and the wooded bluffs. There, surrounded by nature's beauty, her spirit would leave her body and journey to meet her ancestors.

Death wasn't depressing; quite the contrary, compared to life, it was a blessing. Living filled Dream Dancer with despair. She could no longer bear her shame, nor could she bear witnessing her family's disgrace.

Her face hardened into a bitter frown. The white trappers had destroyed her dreams. Now, it almost seemed unreal that she had once been so happy. It was such a short time ago, yet it seemed like eons.

Dream Dancer was seventeen years old. Her slender, graceful frame was softly contoured, and long black hair, as dark as a raven, fell past her waist. She had an arresting face, liquid brown eyes, and high cheekbones broadly spaced but delicate.

Her gait remained unhurried, and her moccasins moved soundlessly through the tall blades of grass. The tiny metal cones embellishing her dress jingled musically with her slow, steady strides. She had chosen her finest garment, for she wanted to enter the spirit world looking her best. The dress was made entirely of deerskin. Fringe adorned the neckline, shoulders, and the hem, which fell just below her knees. The cones were attached in clusters at the garment's side seams and yoke.

A trickle of fear suddenly slid through Dream Dancer's veins. Behind her had come the sounds of speeding horses. She whirled around quickly, and the sight awaiting her was worse than any nightmare she could imagine.

Jesse and Nathan were racing toward her. After leaving Dwyer, they had decided to go to their cabin, which was located at the foot of the mountains. They were shocked to find an Indian woman alone on the plains. As they drew nearer, they were pleased to see that she was young and pretty.

Dream Dancer turned away and began running as fast as she could, her heart pounding with fright.

The trappers quickly shortened the distance, and Jesse

brought his horse alongside the fleeing woman. He gave the reins a sudden jerk, which caused his horse's flank to brush against Dream Dancer, and the contact sent her tumbling to the ground.

Laughing, Jesse dismounted. He went to Dream Dancer, grabbed her arm, and brought her roughly to her feet. "Well, I'll be damned!" he said, surprised. He turned to his companion. "Look here, Nathan. Ain't this the same gal me, you, and Willie done pleasured?"

"She sure looks like the same one," he answered.

Jesse turned back to Dream Dancer. "Well . . . well! Did you enjoy us so much that you been wanderin' around alone hopin' we'd find you again?" Jesse, having no idea she understood them, was merely mouthing words for his and Nathan's amusement.

Dream Dancer responded by spitting into his face.

"You damned slut!" he raved, wiping the spittle from his scraggly beard. He drew back his arm and slapped her so viciously that she was knocked off her feet.

Dream Dancer stayed on the ground. She lay on her stomach, and hid her face in her folded arms. She didn't want the men to see the tears in her eyes. That she was about to be molested twice by the same trappers seemed too horrible to be true. Why was the Great Spirit punishing her so severely? She wished she had brought a knife so she could plunge it into her own heart! Knowing these men would again touch her and invade her body was enough to drive her over the brink into insanity.

Jesse and Nathan dropped to their knees beside her. "You hold her arms while I take her," Jesse said.

"How come you get her first?" Nathan whined.

" 'Cause I can whip your butt, that's why!"

Nathan didn't argue; Jesse was bigger and stronger.

The trappers, totally involved in their assault, didn't detect the sound of a horse's hooves, which were muffled by the prairie's thick turf.

The men forced Dream Dancer onto her back, then Jesse's strong hands spread her legs. He knelt between them, pushing her skirt up to her waist. She wore no undergarments, and was exposed to his lustful gaze. Jesse's manhood grew erect and throbbed uncomfortably inside his confining trousers. He was about to undo his buttons and free his hard member when a rifle shot blasted thunderously. The boom carried to the mountains and echoed ominously across the open plains.

Jesse and Nathan leapt to their feet and stared apprehensively at the man holding them at rifle point. He remained on his horse and made no move to get down.

Dream Dancer drew down her dress and stood shakily. She stared wide-eyed at the intruder.

"Whatcha want, mister?" Jesse asked. He gestured toward Dream Dancer. "If you want some of her, we ain't got no objections. Do we, Nathan?"

"Hell no! There's plenty for all of us."

A cold, murderous glint shone in the man's eyes. He spoke softly, but his voice was nonetheless threatening. "Get on your horses and get the hell out of here. If you backtrack, you're gonna be tonight's supper for the vultures."

Jesse and Nathan didn't want to tangle with the stranger; there was an intimidating aura about him that was chilling, and they weren't about to risk their lives. They hurried to their horses and rode away quickly.

Dream Dancer looked on warily as the man dismounted. She was afraid he had saved her only to enjoy her himself.

He smiled kindly. "Do you speak English?"

"A little," she murmured. The man had a nice smile, and it put her somewhat at ease.

"My name is Luke Thomas. What are you called?"

"Dream Dancer," she said so softly that he barely heard.

"Why are you out here alone?"

"I go to mountains."

"Where are your people—your family?"

"I have no people, no family. I tell them goodbye."

"I don't understand."

"I go to mountains to die."

Luke was astounded. "Why do you want to die?"

"I was shamed. The men you chase away, they attack me before. I was to marry Black Elk, but he no longer want me. My father, Crow Dog, his heart heavy with my shame. I no want to live. I go to spirit world."

Luke hoped to change her mind, but he knew it was too soon to try to persuade her. First, he had to become her friend. "I'm lookin' for Yellow Bear and his brother."

"Brother? You mean, White Cloud?"

He sighed heavily. Apparently, his suspicions were right. Bart had resumed his Sioux identity. "Yes, White Cloud. Have you seen him?"

She shook her head. "No, but I hear White Cloud come back to Sioux. He ask about his family."

"Dream Dancer, it's very important that I find White Cloud. He's a good friend of mine. But I'm not sure if I can do it alone. Will you help me?"

She gazed toward the mountains, longing for death. But this man had saved her from a dreadful experience, and she was in his debt. She decided death could wait.

"You help me. Now, I help you. What can I do?"

Luke smiled inwardly. She felt she owed him a favor. He had hoped she'd feel that way. With time, he'd surely convince her to go on living.

"I'm kinda helpless out here in Sioux territory. If I come across a band of warriors and they don't speak English, you can tell 'em why I'm here. And explain that I don't mean 'em no harm. Let 'em know I'm just lookin' for White Cloud." Truthfully, Luke didn't feel helpless at all. Furthermore he could speak the Sioux tongue fairly well, and was familiar with the Indians' sign language. He could certainly make himself understood, but helplessness was the only excuse he could conjure up to coax Dream Dancer into accompanying him. He wasn't about to let the young woman go to the mountains to die.

"I help you," she replied. "But when you find White Cloud, I leave you and go to my death."

"All right," Luke said, determined it wouldn't come to that. "Since you ain't got a horse, we're gonna have to ride double."

"I walk beside horse. Sioux women travel many miles that way."

"Well, I ain't ridin' while a woman's walkin'. We ride double or we both walk."

Dream Dancer studied Luke with wonder. His manners were strange but pleasant. She had heard that some white men treated women as though they were delicate and precious, but, until this moment, she hadn't believed it.

"We both ride," she murmured.

He waved her to his horse, followed, and offered her a hand up. For a moment, she gazed into his face, trying to judge his age, but his beard, which was well groomed, camouflaged the years. His smoky-blue eyes were set under prominent brows; they were watchful eyes that missed nothing.

When she didn't take his hand, Luke grasped her around the waist and lifted her onto the horse's back. He mounted behind her, and his brawny arms encircled her as he took the reins into his hands.

Dream Dancer felt as though she had suddenly slipped into a world of unreality. That she had entrusted herself to this man was more than she could fathom. One minute she had been walking to the mountains, her fate sealed, and the next minute, she was riding to parts unknown with a man who was not only a stranger, but was also white.

Bart and Sheila were forced to travel slowly. Yellow Bear was on a travois, which was attached to his horse. But Sheila, having spent years working with her uncle's spirited horses, had no problem controlling Bart's powerful stallion. She was a skilled rider and knew how to take charge. From the moment she had swung up onto the stallion's back, Bart's doubts that she could handle the steed had evaporated. He was impressed and wondered where she had learned to ride with such confidence.

Now, as they rode over the quiet landscape, Bart's curiosity rose. "Where you learn to ride as good as warrior?"

His question put a smile on her face. "I used to live

in Kentucky. I was raised by an aunt and uncle who owned horses that were bred for racing. I worked with these horses, groomed them, fed them, and rode them. They're called thoroughbreds, and such horses are high-spirited.''

"You learn to control these horses?''

"Yes, I did. I have no fear of them, and I also know a well-bred horse when I see one. This stallion is a superb animal. Where did he come from, and who does he belong to? He certainly isn't an Indian pony. He's shod and broken to a saddle.''

"He belong to white man.''

"That's obvious,'' she replied impatiently. "But what happened to his owner?''

"It does not matter.'' Bart grimaced. He was getting tired of avoiding the truth!

"This horse carries a brand, a triangle with a C. I noticed it at Flying Feather's village. Whoever owns this stallion lives on a ranch.''

Bart didn't say anything, he was too busy silently cursing his own negligence. He should have known she would see the brand. Why hadn't he thought of that? She had now found a link between White Cloud and Bart Chandler. When she was back at the fort, she'd tell her father about the brand; he would investigate and would learn who owned the Triangle-C. He would also learn that J.W. Chandler's grandson had lived with the Sioux. After that, the pieces would fall into place. The Army would certainly put a bounty on his head. Bart sighed inwardly. There was only one thing to do. He must tell Sheila the truth, hope she would understand, and ask her to keep his identity a secret. Bart had a sinking feeling he would

114

be asking too much of her, but, he had no other choice than to be perfectly honest; his fate was now in Sheila Langsford's hands. He wondered when he should confess. He thought about it for a long moment, then decided to wait until they had reached Iron Stars' village.

It was getting late. The sun had already descended over the horizon. They made camp in a area surrounded by trees and shrubbery. As Bart tended to the horses and the pack mule, Sheila changed Yellow Bear's bandage.

The warrior watched her face closely as she cleaned his wound and put on a fresh bandage. His scrutiny was intense, and she grew uncomfortable under his unwavering stare.

"Why do you keep looking at me?" she finally asked.

"I wonder if you are as pretty inside as outside." His English was flawless.

"I don't understand."

"I think you have a good heart. During the trade, you warned me. Why did you do that?"

"To save your life, of course."

"Why did you want to save me? Why should you care if a Sioux warrior lived or died?"

"Why shouldn't I care?" she murmured softly.

A faint smile touched his lips. "I am grateful for what you did. You are a good woman."

Bart had finished with the horses and was starting a fire. Sheila moved over and sat beside him.

"How Yellow Bear?" he asked.

"He's fine," she replied. She eyed Bart thoughtfully. "Your brother's English is superb—much better than yours."

"Maybe he much smarter."

115

She didn't say anything, but she had a feeling that he was toying with her. She sighed wearily.

"You tired?"

"Yes, I am. I'm very tired." She glanced down at her dust-covered apparel. "What I wouldn't give for clean clothes and a bath." Her fingers brushed through her tangled tresses. "A hair brush would be nice, too." A teasing twinkle shone in her eyes. "The next time you decide to kidnap a woman, do her a favor and pack her grooming items and some changes of clothing for her beforehand."

Bart chuckled. "No next time. You only woman I kidnap." He had stored his belongings close to the mule. He left the fire, moved to his bag, delved inside, then returned with a brush. He handed it to Sheila. "Here; use this for hair. Tomorrow, we cross river. We stop there so you can take bath and wash clothes."

"Where did you get this?" Sheila asked, indicating the brush.

"Sioux often trade with whites. We exchange pelts for white man's trinkets."

"How many pelts did this cost?"

He shrugged. "It does not matter." Actually, he had bought the brush at the mercantile in Pleasant Hope.

"That seems to be a favorite reply of yours. When you don't want to answer a question, you always say it doesn't matter." She watched him intently. "Why do you keep evading the truth? You're keeping something from me, aren't you?"

"Later, you know everything. Now, we must fix something to eat. Then we sleep."

Her eyes remained on him as he filled a coffeepot with

116

water and dropped in a sprinkle of grounds. This man was indeed a mystery. She had encountered Indians at the fort, but White Cloud was somehow unique. He was obviously part white; maybe his mixed blood made him different. But, no, it was more than that. She couldn't pinpoint exactly what it was, but there was something about him that set him apart from other Sioux braves.

She looked at him not as a warrior, but as a man. His wide chest and strong arms strained against his tight-fitting shirt, and his tan leggings adhered smoothly to his muscular frame. Though he was powerfully built, he was slim and moved with an innate litheness. His hair, as black as ebony, was thick and grew to collar length. His features were classically handsome, with dark brows arching over charcoal-gray eyes and sensual lips that blended into a strong chin. His rakish good looks were irresistible, and Sheila couldn't help but fall victim to him.

Bart knew she was looking him over; he wondered what was going through her mind. His eyes met hers. "You try to see if I more white than Sioux?"

"Are you?" she came back.

"Would it make difference to you?"

She looked away, and shrugged a reply. "It doesn't make any difference to me."

"Could you love Sioux warrior?" he wasn't sure why he asked the question, nor did he understand why he was so anxious to hear the answer.

Her eyes flew to his; her expression was obviously startled.

"Can you not answer?"

"I've never really thought about it. Why do you ask?"

"It does not matter."

"You evade my question again." She frowned petulantly.

"Soon, I no longer evade questions. I will tell you everything."

"Why can't you tell me now?"

"It better if I wait. I tell you when we reach Iron Star's village."

She sensed it would be useless to try to change his mind. She'd simply have to curb her curiosity and wait until he was ready to confide in her. She gazed deeply into his gray eyes, and, recognizing desire in their depths, a thrill raced through her. Her heart pounded as she controlled a sudden urge to fling herself into his arms. She longed to feel his sinewy body pressed against hers, and imagined the feel of his lips ravishing hers with unbridled passion.

"Where your thoughts?" he asked softly, his eyes looking intently into hers.

A blush rose to her cheeks. She couldn't possibly tell him her thoughts! She turned away, dropped her gaze to her lap, and mumbled Bart's own words, "It does not matter."

Bart laughed. It was hearty and infectious.

Sheila's own laugh was touched with embarrassment. "You see, White Cloud, I also know how to evade questions."

Her lovely smile reached clear to Bart's heart. That he was falling in love with Sheila hit him with a sudden jolt. It was a disturbing revelation. When he told her the truth, she might very well resent him. She had accepted her abduction because she believed he was a Sioux warrior who had no other way to save his brother. When she learned he was really a white man, would she turn on him with a vengeance? Would she despise him for taking her away from her father and forcing her to travel into the mountains and to a Sioux village? There were no answers to these questions yet; he'd have to wait to find out. He willfully wiped all doubts and anxieties from his mind. Thinking about these things was too upsetting.

Sheila, sitting silently, wished she knew what he was thinking about. She could see that he was troubled. She reached over and gently touched his arm. "Try not to worry, White Cloud. Once you're back home in your own village, everything will seem brighter."

Her kindness amazed him. "You should hate me. I abduct you, make you go into mountains. I do this to save Yellow Bear. Why you nice to me and to my brother?"

"I heard rumors at the fort. Everyone was talking about Yellow Bear. These people had him guilty before he was even tried. The trappers who testified against Yellow Bear are known to be unsavory characters, yet the Army accepted their testimony, but disregarded Yellow Bear's. I don't think your brother received a fair trial, and I said as much to my father."

"Yellow Bear not murder trapper, but shoot back in self-defense. The trappers attack Indian girl, Yellow Bear try to help her."

Sheila sighed sympathetically. "I'm sorry this had to happen to your brother." She paused a moment, then asked, "White Cloud, how do you intend to get me back to the fort? If you take me yourself, my father will have you arrested."

His plan was to take her back as Bart Chandler, with

the explanation that he had found her traveling alone. He could only hope that she would agree to support his story. "Later, I tell you how I get you home. I give my word that you will soon be back at fort."

She was still touching his arm, and he placed his hand over hers. The contact quickened her pulse and triggered her desire. She quickly slid her hand out from under his. She must remain strong and restrain her amorous feelings. If she were to fall in love with a Sioux warrior, it would totally destroy her father.

Chapter Seven

The next day, Bart, Sheila, and Yellow Bear hadn't traveled very far before spotting a horse in the distance. Two people appeared to be riding it. As they drew closer, Bart could make out a man and a woman. A deep frown suddenly crossed his face—the man looking very familiar. Telling Sheila to stay behind with Yellow Bear, he rode out to intercept the pair.

Despite Bart's Indian attire, Luke, recognized him immediately. He reined in, dismounted, and moving away from Dream Dancer, he left to greet Chandler. When he had walked far enough to ensure a private conversation, he stopped and waited.

Riding up, Bart brought his pony to a halt, swung to the ground, and asked testily, "What the hell are you doing here?"

"Lookin' for you," Luke replied, his own tone irritable.

"You want to get yourself scalped?"

"Not especially, no! I'm kinda fond of my hair."

"Don't you realize you're in Sioux territory?"

"Hell, yes, I know where I am! I was travelin' these parts 'fore you were born. I know this countryside like the back of my hand."

"Damn it, Luke! Why didn't you stay home?"

"I was worried 'bout you." His gaze meandered over Bart's Indian apparel. "By the looks of you, I'd say I was right to be worried. Have you got Yellow Bear?"

Bart nodded, affirmatively.

"Did you trade the colonel's daughter for 'im?"

Bart, fearing Luke's response, answered haltingly. "Well . . . not exactly. We were ambushed. The woman's still with me."

Luke's temper snapped. "Bart, you crazy fool! Do you know what you're doin'? Why, the whole damned army's gonna be lookin' for you."

"Yes, but they think I'm a Sioux warrior."

"What about the woman? Does she think you're Sioux?"

"So far," he replied.

"What does that mean?"

"When we get to Iron Star's village, I plan to tell her the truth."

Luke was confused. "Why do you wanna do that?"

"She saw the brand on my horse. I have to confess everything. I hope she'll understand."

"You're hopin' for an awful lot, ain't you?"

Bart grinned warmly. "I suppose, but Sheila . . . she's

122

special. She just might understand." He glanced over at Dream Dancer, who was still sitting on Luke's horse. "What are you doing with her?"

Luke explained about the trappers and why he and Dream Dancer were traveling together.

Bart's brow furrowed. "You say these trappers attacked her once before?"

"Yep, that's what she told me."

"Then she must be the woman Yellow Bear and the others tried to save. I wonder why she didn't come forth and testify in Yellow Bear's behalf."

"Would it had made any difference?"

"Probably not," Bart replied flatly.

"Are you on your way to Iron Star's village?"

"Yes."

"Then Dream Dancer and I will ride along. But you better make your visit a short one. Trouble's brewin' and you don't need to get caught up in the middle. If Miss Langsford agrees to protect you, we'll take her back to the fort. If she won't agree, then you hightail it home, and I'll take her to the fort."

"How's J.W.?" Bart asked, changing the subject abruptly.

"He's fine, but he's mighty worried 'bout you. He had a feelin' you'd get yourself in trouble, and I reckon his feelin' was right."

"I had to help Yellow Bear. He isn't guilty of murder."

"I understand, Bart. I really do. But just the same you're knee deep in manure."

Bart chuckled. "I'll get out of it somehow."

"Then you'd better be real nice to Miss Langsford,

'cause you're only gonna come out of this if she lets you.'' He turned around, mumbling, "I'll go get my horse and Dream Dancer.''

Bart mounted his pony and waited.

"You find White Cloud?'' Dream Dancer asked as Luke walked up to her.

"Yep, that's him,'' he replied, waving an arm in Bart's direction. He placed his horse's blanket so that it covered the Triangle-C brand.

"You find White Cloud. Now I leave for mountains,'' Dream Dancer said.

"Not yet,'' Luke responded firmly, swinging up and taking his place behind her. "I still might need you.''

"Why you need me now?''

Luke thought quickly. "You see, White Cloud's on his way to his father's village. I might not be welcome there. If I have to leave, I'll need you to travel with me. Once we get back to where I found you, we can go our separate ways.''

A faint smile touched her lips. "I not fool, Luke. You not want me to die. But you good man, I stay with you. Death will wait.''

Considering Dream Dancer's tender years, Luke hoped death would wait a long, long time. He kneed his horse into a gallop, then along with Bart, they rode back to Sheila and Yellow Bear.

Sheila looked the pair over curiously. She wondered why the white man was traveling with an Indian girl.

Bart, cleared his throat uneasily. "The white man friend,'' he said to Sheila. "He ride with us.''

"Oh?'' she questioned. "Does he know what's going on?''

124

"He know about Yellow Bear. He also know you colonel's daughter."

"Don't worry, ma'am," Luke spoke up. "All we wanna do is get Yellow Bear to his father, then we'll take you safely back to the fort. Nothin's gonna happen to you. I give you my word."

The man's word didn't impress Sheila in the least; she knew nothing about him. Her suspicions were, however, aroused. There was more going on here than White Cloud would admit. He was obviously keeping something from her. But what? She felt as though she were part of a puzzle put together with irregular pieces. Nothing seemed to fit.

"Put Dream Dancer there," Bart told Luke, pointing at the horse pulling Yellow Bear's travois.

Luke started to assist Dream Dancer, but she was instantly off his horse's back and on her way.

Sheila was pleased to note that the girl evidently understood English. Later, she would question her. Maybe through her she'd learn why the pieces didn't fit.

When they reached the river, they stopped and made camp. Late-afternoon shadows were blanketing the landscape and a warm breeze was stirring the air. The rippling water was a welcome sight to Sheila, for she was longing for a bath and a chance to wash her dust-covered clothes.

She wanted to go downstream, strip away her apparel, and jump into the river immediately, but she didn't have clean clothes to change into. She supposed she would have to dismiss the idea of washing her attire and put it back on after she bathed. Also, she wasn't sure if White

125

Cloud would allow her to leave the campsite; and she certainly wasn't about to bathe where he and the other men could see her.

Bart tended to the horses, then, carrying his carpetbag, he went to Sheila, who was sitting at the fire. He reached inside the bag, brought out a bar of soap, and handed it to her. "You can take bath now."

"Not here," she said firmly.

Bart hid a smile.

"I'll go downstream," she continued.

"Take Dream Dancer with you. It not safe you go alone."

"All right," she agreed. She glanced down at her dusty apparel. "I guess I'll just have to put these same clothes back on," she said heavily.

"You take blanket, wrap it about you. In morning, your clothes be dry."

Sheila blushed. She couldn't imagine herself wrapped in a blanket, and totally naked underneath. But she knew it was either that or wear dirty clothes.

"I get Dream Dancer," Bart said, getting to his feet.

Sheila watched as he walked over to the Indian girl and spoke to her.

The women soon left camp and walked a short distance down the river's bank. They stopped at an area bordered with thick shrubbery. Dream Dancer started to undress.

"Wait," Sheila said suddenly. She knew this was a good time to question Dream Dancer. "How well do you know White Cloud?"

"I not know White Cloud."

"You mean, you never met him before today?"

126

"No, but I hear of White Cloud. He come back to Sioux."

Sheila was confused. "He came back to the Sioux? I don't understand. Where has he been?"

"Many years ago, White Cloud leave Sioux to live in white man's world. I hear he live with grandfather."

"He's been living with his grandfather who is white?" Sheila exclaimed in surprise.

"Many of my people say White Cloud no longer Sioux, he now white man."

"Exactly how long has White Cloud been away from the Sioux?"

"He still young boy when he leave."

Sheila's anger built slowly, like a burning ember growing hotter and hotter until it suddenly burst into flame. Oh, the contemptible cad! How dare he pretend to be a Sioux warrior when all along he had been raised by a white grandfather! She thought about his broken English—her fury rose a few degrees. The man was undoubtedly schooled!

Dream Dancer, seeing the rage in Sheila's eyes, asked hesitantly, "You upset? I say something wrong?"

With effort, Sheila managed to control her anger. "No, you didn't say anything wrong. Let's bathe and wash our clothes before it gets dark." She touched Dream Dancer's arm, her fingers gripping tightly. "Please don't let White Cloud know that I questioned you. Please!"

Dream Dancer didn't really understand the need for secrecy, but she instinctively liked this white woman and wanted to be her friend. "I not tell him."

"Thank you very much." Sheila's feelings coincided

127

with her companion's; she had taken an instant liking to Dream Dancer.

The pair, anxious to bathe, undressed hastily, then hurried into the sun-warmed river. As they washed, Dream Dancer told Sheila why she wanted to die, and the way in which she had met up with Luke.

Sheila's heart ached for Dream Dancer, and she could only imagine all she had suffered at the hands of her attackers. But death wasn't the answer, and she tried to convey this to Dream Dancer, who listened attentively. Her mind, however, was set, and nothing Sheila said changed it.

Dream Dancer helped Sheila wash her clothes; her own apparel, made of doeskin, merely needed a good dusting off. It was then suitable to wear again.

Sheila had brought Bart's hairbrush, and Dream Dancer groomed Sheila's long, chestnut-colored hair. She drew the hair back from Sheila's face and weaved the heavy tresses into one long braid. She then removed a strip of fringe from her dress and used it to bind the end of Sheila's braid.

Back in camp, Bart was sitting at the fire drinking coffee. Luke, having a cup himself, remarked, "I wonder what's takin' so long. Don't you reckon the women oughta be back by now?"

"If they aren't here by the time I finish this coffee, I'll check on them."

Amusement flickered in Luke's eyes. "Miss Langsford's probably questioning Dream Dancer."

"About what?"

"About you, of course. She ain't no fool, you know. She's gotta suspect things ain't how they appear."

128

"Damn!" Bart cursed, leaping to his feet. "Sheila might not be a fool, but I am! I can't believe I actually sent her off alone with Dream Dancer!"

Luke couldn't help but chuckle. "If you're gonna be a liar and a cheat, you gotta start thinkin' like one."

"Thank you," he replied sarcastically. "But I didn't know I was a liar and a cheat."

"I don't reckon Miss Langsford's gonna see it that way." Luke's expression was firm.

Bart turned away.

"Where are you goin'?" Luke asked.

"To check on Sheila and Dream Dancer," Bart replied over his shoulder.

As he headed downstream, his moccasins moved silently over the grassy bank. Dusk was falling rapidly, and gray shadows were stalking the land. It would soon be full dark. Bart glanced up at the darkening sky; not a cloud was in sight, the night ahead would be clear and filled with stars. He watched as the sun sank below the horizon, leaving a glowing red rim in its wake. A balmy breeze ruffled his hair; twilight had brought a slight chill to the air. He continued on, with long strides and an innate grace inherited from his Sioux forefathers.

He soon came upon Sheila and Dream Dancer. They had gathered up the wet clothes and were about to start back when Bart arrived. Sheila was wrapped in a blanket. Her hair, still damp, was braided neatly.

Bart spoke to Dream Dancer. "Take clothes to camp. We be there soon."

Seeing Bart refueled Sheila's fury, but she managed to conceal it. Apparently, the man liked to play at games! Well, two could play this one!

129

Bart waited until they were alone before asking Sheila warily "what she and Dream Dancer had talk about."

Sheila suppressed a bitter smile. "What do you mean?"

He moved to stand before her and gazed down into her dark eyes, which revealed nothing. "Tell me what you and Dream Dancer talk about!" He purposefully raised his voice as though he were threatening her.

"We discussed a lot of things," she said nonchalantly. "But I don't think we talked about anything that would interest you." She managed to look perplexed. "Why do you ask?"

"It does not matter," Bart replied, evading the answer in his usual way. Relieved, he sighed inwardly. He wanted Sheila to learn the truth, but from him and not someone else. She would never agree to help him if she didn't know everything from beginning to end. He knew she must be told slowly and carefully; otherwise, she would certainly turn on him with a vengeance.

Sheila watched him thoughtfully. She pictured him with a haircut and wearing white man's clothing. His resemblance to the Sioux would be almost undetectable. Suddenly, she once again sensed that she had seen him somewhere before. The memory flashed across her mind like a bolt from the blue. She had seen him at Fort Laramie dressed as a trapper! She was certain he was the same man. She quickly imagined him in buckskins and sporting a beard. The image fit White Cloud!

Her anger escalated. She had believed he was a warrior, and his plight had gained her sympathy. She had even understood the desperation that led him to kidnap her. How could an Indian brave truly understand the hardships he had forced upon her by taking her away from the fort and her father? But this man was not really an Indian. He was perfectly aware of what he was doing.

She controlled her anger, but it wasn't easy. She didn't want to confront the lying rake, she wanted to leave him! She would stay on guard and find a way to escape before they traveled much farther into the mountains. She knew she must make her move soon, for once they were deep in the hills, turning back alone would be too dangerous.

Watching her, Bart wondered what she was thinking about. Her expression was inscrutable, but he could tell she was deep in thought. Although he was tempted to question her, he decided not to do so. He waved a hand toward camp. "We go back now."

Sheila was more than ready to oblige. She didn't want to be alone with him—he still attracted her physically, and she didn't trust herself.

She took a step to leave, but her foot got tangled in the folds of the blanket, which draped to the ground. The mishap sent her stumbling into Bart's arms.

He drew her so close that her body was fused to his. Finding her in his embrace was a temptation he couldn't overcome, and their sudden physical intimacy sent his better judgment fleeing. His hand swept to the back of her neck, and bending his head, his mouth claimed hers feverishly. Her nudity, covered simply by a blanket, intensified his passion. He longed to fling it aside and feast his eyes upon her flesh.

Bart's demanding kiss stole Sheila's senses, and for a wonderful, ecstatic moment, she forgot his deceit and the way in which he had used her.

But as Bart's lips left hers to touch the soft hollow of

131

her throat, Sheila's senses suddenly came back to her. Anger ruthlessly destroyed her passion, and she pushed out of his arms. "How dare you!" she said with fury. Don't ever do anything like that again!"

She was fuming; however, she was more upset with herself. Had she no pride at all? She knew this man for the lying scoundrel that he was; still, she had responded to his kiss! She gathered the blanket tightly about her as though its folds could protect her from herself.

Her fierce retort surprised Bart. Why had she rejected his kiss so vehemently? He could think of only one reason: She believed he was a Sioux warrior, and that made him repulsive to her. She claimed she had no grievance against Indians and felt sorry for them, but she still considered them inferior.

Bart was disappointed in Sheila. Apparently, he had placed her on too high a pedestal. Concealing his feelings, he said evenly, "I not kiss you again." He wasn't sure, however, if he could keep his word. He couldn't deny that Sheila Langsford held some kind of power over him. He had never wanted a woman so desperately.

He gestured tersely toward camp. "We go!"

Sheila bit back a retort. His clipped English flamed her fury. He was playing her for such a fool. She wanted to lash out and tell him exactly what she thought, but willfully, she suppressed the desire. She planned to escape, and if he knew she was aware of his deception he would certainly start watching her more closely. So far his vigil was lax—she intended to keep it that way.

With a defiant tilt to her chin, she brushed past him and started back to camp.

Chapter Eight

Yellow Bear was lying on his blanket, watching Dream Dancer as she draped Sheila's wet clothes over a bush to dry. Earlier, Luke had told him why she hadn't come forth to testify in court. Yellow Bear harbored no resentment; he knew that her testimony would not have made a difference. The soldiers would have taken the trappers' word over hers.

As Dream Dancer moved about the campfire, Yellow Bear called to her. She went to him hesitantly, for she was certain he resented her.

His wound was still painful, and he sat up with a grimace, gesturing for her to sit beside him.

She did so reluctantly.

Understanding her hesitancy, he said kindly, "Dream Dancer, if you had come to the white man's court, it would not have made a difference."

She regarded him with surprise. "You do not hate me?"

He smiled handsomely. "No, I do not."

The shame she had suffered at the trappers' hands caused her to look away from Yellow Bear. She didn't think she would ever be able to look any young warrior in the eye.

Yellow Bear placed a hand under her chin and turned her face back to his. Her eyes were downcast. "Look at me, Dream Dancer," he murmured tenderly.

She gazed up at him through long, thick lashes.

"I am your friend. Do not be ashamed to look into my face." He waited, but she didn't say anything. "Why did you leave your people?" he asked.

"Luke did not tell you why?"

"No, he said very little about you."

"I left my village to go to the mountains. There, I plan to enter the spirit world. I can no longer live with my shame, nor can I bear to see my family live with it. I was to marry Black Elk, but he no longer wants me." She shrugged. "I do not blame him."

"There is no reason for you to go to the mountains. You can live in my village. You will be welcome in my father's home."

"No young warrior will want me. Iron Star will have to ask an old man to marry me. Otherwise, I will only be a burden."

Yellow Bear couldn't argue with that. Anger fumed within him. The white trappers had destroyed this young woman's life! It would have been more merciful if they had killed her.

"Dream Dancer, I am sorry. But if you decide not to

134

go to the mountains, I promise you that my village will be your home.''

She rose to her feet. ''I am grateful. But, Yellow Bear, why are you so kind?''

''Because I care about you. You are Sioux, and I care about all our people.''

''Your grandmother is white, but I can see that the white man's blood flows weakly in your veins.''

Yellow Bear scowled. ''I am Sioux, and I will kill any man who says I am not!''

A tiny smile curled Dream Dancer's lips. ''That is good.'' She turned around gracefully and went to the campfire, where she sat beside Luke. She considered the whites her enemies, but she knew there were exceptions. She certainly felt no animosity toward Luke or Sheila. And although White Cloud was more white than Sioux, she liked and trusted *him*.

''What did Yellow Bear have to say?'' Luke asked her.

A warm twinkle lit her eyes. ''He not angry at me.''

''He knows your testimony wouldn't have made any difference—''

Sheila and Bart's return broke into their discussion. Sheila promptly set about making herself a bed, and Bart, saying he'd take the first watch, grabbed his rifle and walked off into the distance.

''If I was makin' a guess,'' Luke mumbled, ''I'd say those two just had a squabble.''

''Squabble?'' Dream Dancer questioned, not understanding the word.

''An argument,'' Luke explained. ''Probably a lovers' quarrel.''

"You think White Cloud and Sheila are lovers?" She was amazed at the idea.

"Well, I think they're fallin' in love."

"Why you think that?"

"Just a feelin' I got."

"You married, Luke?"

He shook his head.

"You ever been married?"

"Nope," he murmured. "But I came close to it once."

"Did woman die?"

He smiled wistfully. "She didn't die; she married someone else."

"You still carry love in your heart," she remarked.

"Dream Dancer, I knew her years ago, 'fore you was even born. A man doesn't carry a torch for twenty years."

"I not understand what carry torch mean."

"Never mind," he replied. "You'd better get some sleep. Tomorrow's gonna be a long day."

She stood up. "You need sleep, too."

Dream Dancer left to make her bed beside Sheila, and Luke stayed by the fire, staring into the flickering flames. He hadn't thought of Amanda in a long time, but memories of her now moved through his mind like a gentle breeze drifting through the treetops. He hadn't loved a woman since Amanda; he wasn't sure why. He supposed for some men love only came around once in a lifetime. Or maybe he was just unlucky and had never met anyone he could love the way he had loved Amanda. She had broken his heart, destroyed his dreams, and had caused him to be embittered. Still, he had never truly stopped loving her.

He shook the memories aside. After twenty years, it was foolish to waste time thinking about a lost love.

Dawn was only minutes away when Sheila awoke, and keeping her blanket wrapped tightly about her, she got to her feet. The campsite was starkly quiet, for everyone, except Luke, who was standing guard, was asleep. She glanced at Bart; his bed was close to Yellow Bear's. His back was turned and she could only hope that he was sleeping soundly, for she planned to run away now. She didn't think a better opportunity would present itself.

Moving furtively, she gathered up her clothes. Luke was in the distance, but in clear view of the camp. Stepping quietly, she went to him and told him that she was planning to go into the bushes to get dressed. She returned to camp, took an extra rifle, then made her way to the shrubbery that grew thickly in the background. There, the horses were hobbled and protected from predators. She dressed hastily, then carefully saddled Bart's stallion. Holding the reins, she led the horse through the shrubbery and down to the river's bank. She mounted quickly, then guided the stallion into the water. Staying close to the bank where the river was shallow, she kneed the horse into a steady gallop.

That she was leaving without supplies didn't bother her, for she knew of a trader's post that wasn't too far away. She had once ridden there with her father and his soldiers.

Sheila was tense, but she wasn't afraid. She had a rifle and knew how to use it. Also, she was a superb rider, and with the stallion beneath her, she should make it to the trader's post by noon.

She wondered if White Cloud would pursue her. White Cloud! she thought peevishly. Did he really consider that his name? She seriously doubted it. He certainly had another name that he went by—a white man's name!

She grew angrier as she thought about the way in which he had deceived her. What nerve, to pretend to be a warrior when he was really a white man! Well, he obviously wasn't fully white, but he was a far cry from a Sioux warrior. The cad's effrontery infuriated her. He actually planned to take her into the mountains where she would be surrounded by hostile Indians. Considering that he had been away from the Sioux for so many years, she seriously doubted he had any influence among them. If they decided to kill her, she didn't think White Cloud could stop them. Fury flamed in her. White Cloud apparently didn't care whether or not he put her life in jeopardy!

Sheila kept to the river, placing more and more distance between herself and the camp; meanwhile, Luke, wondering why she hadn't returned, vacated his post to check on her.

He called her name softly, but Bart still heard him. He awoke instantly, leapt to his feet, and hurried to Luke. "What's wrong?" he asked.

"Miss Langsford's supposed to be in there gettin' dressed," Luke replied, pointing at the shrubbery.

"How long has she been there?"

"Too long," Luke replied.

Bart tramped into the foliage, his arms shoving the shrubs aside. He realized at once that his horse was missing. He was angry, but he was also worried. He had thought Sheila was too shrewd to try something so dangerous! A woman alone in the wilderness was easy prey.

He went to his Indian pony, and was untying it when Luke came up to him. Seeing that Bart's stallion was gone, he said lamely, "I'm sorry, Bart but I didn't think Miss Langsford would run away."

"It's not your fault. Don't worry, I'll find her. She can't have gone very far."

"She took to the river. Otherwise, I'd have seen her leave."

Bart swung up onto the pony's back. "You and the others stay here."

Luke returned to camp and built up the fire. He prepared a pot of coffee, then set it on the fire to brew. He admired Miss Langsford's spunk and courage; nevertheless, he knew she had acted recklessly. He hoped nothing would happen to her before Bart could find her.

Sheila was now on dry land, and was riding south toward the trader's post. The sun had fully crested the horizon, and its warmth was spreading over the verdant landscape. Wildlife began to emerge from their dens, nests, and places of concealment. She saw a deer standing in the distance, but as it picked up her scent, it loped gracefully into the surrounding thicket. An eagle soared overhead, and birds of various sizes chirped musically as they flew from treetop to treetop. Two rabbits hopped across her path before taking cover in the tall grass. Behind Sheila, the mountain range rose majestically, its towering peaks almost touching the cottony clouds skimming across the turquoise sky. The unblemished countryside was breathtakingly beautiful, its splendor unsurpassed. Sheila, impressed, suddenly understood why the Indians were willing to fight so hard to keep it. She didn't blame them; if this land was *her* birthright, she certainly would fight to hold on to it.

A steep hill awaited ahead. Sheila was wary about crossing it, but she had no other recourse, not if she intended to follow the route to the trader's post. She hoped, prayed, that danger wasn't lurking on the other side.

She held the stallion to a steady canter and had almost reached the grass-covered hill when a small band of warriors crested the rise. Spotting her, they pulled up their ponies and gaped at her as though she were an apparition. They certainly hadn't expected to find a white woman alone in the wilderness.

Sheila had never been so frightened. For a split second she considered making a run for it, but she knew the act would be futile. The Indians had rifles and she was within their range. They would undoubtedly shoot her or the stallion.

Dear God, leaving the others had been a terrible mistake, maybe even a fatal one! Tears smarted her eyes but she held them back. It was too late for tears!

She watched fearfully as the warriors came toward her. If they were hostile, and she had a feeling they were, she hoped they would kill her quickly. At the fort, she had heard that Indians often tortured their victims and she feared such treatment more than death itself.

The warriors were six in number, and they circled their ponies around her horse. One man reached out and drew her rifle from its sheath, then jerked the reins from her hands and mumbled something in his own language.

Sheila, despite her fear, looked the warriors over as though she were undaunted. They wore no war paint, but were nonetheless threatening. Although they regarded her with animosity, she could tell that her presence had astounded them.

The Indian holding her reins spoke briefly again to his companions, then kneed his pinto into a gallop; taking his captive with him, he rode back up the hill. The others followed close behind.

Sheila wondered where they were taking her, but she didn't have to wonder very long. On the other side of the hill, situated in dense foliage and trees, other warriors were camped. As her captors took her into the concealed area, she was startled to find three white captives tied to a covered wagon, their arms bound to the large wheels.

She was suddenly jerked from her horse by a warrior who quickly tied her hands behind her. Grasping her arm, he then took her to the wagon and shoved her roughly to the ground. She landed, facedown, beside an attractive woman not much older than herself. Sheila's bound hands made it awkward for her to rise to a sitting position, but she somehow managed it. She looked curiously at the other captives; there were two women and a man. The women were tethered to the same wheel, but the man was tied alone. He was sitting slumped over, and his head dangled forward causing his chin to rest on his chest. Dried blood was caked on the front of his shirt, he was so still that Sheila wondered if he was alive.

She studied the two women. The one beside her didn't appear to be injured, but the other woman had a deep gash on her forehead. At one time the cut had apparently bled quite badly, but now it was covered with coagulated blood that had turned brownish in color.

"My name is Sheila Langsford," Sheila said to the woman at her side.

"I'm Janice Gilbert," she replied. Nodding toward the other woman, she said, "She's Mrs. Wilson."

"The gentleman?" Sheila questioned.

"That . . . that man . . . is my husband."

Sheila had never heard the word "man" spoken with such disdain.

"Were you alone when you were captured?" Janice asked her.

"Yes, I was."

She was apparently shocked. "You were by yourself out here in the middle of nowhere?"

"Well, actually I was with other people, but I left them." The hope that White Cloud would rescue her skimmed fleetingly across her mind. The hope was quickly dashed, however; how could he possibly save her? She and the others were held captive by over a dozen Sioux warriors.

"Were you three traveling alone?" Sheila asked.

"No, there were others with us." She sighed, then added flatly, "They're all dead."

"What happened?"

Janice frowned with bitterness. "My husband and Mrs. Wilson's husband wanted to prospect for gold in the Black Hills. Disregarding the Army's advice to stay out of the mountains, they hired three men as guides." She

142

moaned, but it sounded more like a grunt. "We never even made it to the mountains. These Indians attacked us yesterday. Everyone, except for the three of us, died during the assault."

Although Mrs. Wilson hadn't said anything, Sheila could see that she was listening. She spoke gently to her. "I'm sorry about your husband, Mrs. Wilson."

The woman who appeared to be in her late thirties, smiled sadly. "Thank you, Miss Langsford. I appreciate your kindness."

"Where do you suppose the Indians are taking us?" Janice asked Sheila.

"Probably to their village."

"Whatever for?"

"They might want to make slaves of us." A shudder ran through her. "Or maybe they want to wait and kill us where their people can watch."

"They'll torture us, won't they?" Janice asked, her voice raspy.

"Of course they will," Mrs. Wilson remarked. "Otherwise, they'd kill us now and get it over with." She sounded more resigned than frightened.

Sheila studied Mrs. Wilson with renewed interest. Her golden-brown hair was disheveled, and her face was flawed with dirt and dried blood; still, Sheila could see that she was very attractive, too. As a younger woman, she had no doubt been strikingly beautiful, and the years hadn't marred her beauty; her looks had matured with grace and elegance.

Farther down the wagon, Janice's husband groaned and asked weakly for water. If the Indians heard, they were content to ignore him.

"How badly is your husband wounded?" Sheila asked Janice.

"I'm not sure. More than likely, he's dying." Her voice lacked compassion.

"You sound as though you don't care if he lives or dies," Sheila said, wondering how the woman could be so unfeeling.

"She *doesn't* care!" Mrs. Wilson intervened. "She blames him for getting her in this predicament."

"Predicament?" Janice snapped. "Is that what you call this? I'd call it losing our lives! And God only knows what atrocities we'll suffer before we actually die."

Sheila leaned back against the wagon wheel and withdrew into silence. She berated her foolishness, for she knew she was caught in a web of her own weaving. She had been safe with White Cloud and the others, but she had let resentment get the better of her. She had acted recklessly and was now paying the price—the ultimate price, most likely!

"Miss Langsford?" Mrs. Wilson called softly.

Sheila emerged from her reverie. "Yes?"

"You said you were traveling with others, but left them. Is there a chance that the people you were with will try to find you? Is there any hope, regardless of how small, that they might rescue us?"

"Yes, we can always hope," Sheila murmured.

Bart, lying flat at the top of the hill, looked down at the camp located in the dense foliage. Although the site was mostly hidden by shrubbery and trees, he could see his stallion and could also distinguish what was taking place. From his position, however, he couldn't see the prisoners, so he wasn't aware that the Indians had three other captives. He watched with apprehension as the Indians prepared to leave. He estimated at least a dozen warriors, and he wondered how he could save Sheila from so many. He would be one man against twelve or more; the odds seemed insurmountable. He'd certainly fail if he tried to rescue her alone. He decided his best alternative was to return for Yellow Bear. His brother was highly respected among the Sioux, and he might be able to convince these warriors to release their captive.

Bart moved soundlessly down the hill and to his pony. The warriors would soon finish breaking camp and move on, but he and the others could pick up their trail.

As he swung up onto the pony's back, he tried to imagine how frightened Sheila must be. He blamed himself for getting her involved in such a dangerous situation. If it hadn't been for him, she'd still be at Fort Laramie, safe in her father's home.

Chapter Nine

The warriors broke camp, and, discarding the wagon, they put their prisoners on horses. Janice's husband was slung facedown across his mount, Mrs. Wilson and Janice rode double, and Sheila was allowed to ride Bart's stallion.

They headed toward the distant mountain range, and as the passing minutes lengthened into an hour, then two, Sheila's hopes began to dwindle. Apparently, White Cloud wasn't planning to pursue her; or if he had, he had seen the danger and decided not to risk his life to save hers. Could she really blame him? In a way, she supposed she did. After all, if he hadn't kidnapped her, she wouldn't be in this situation. And, there were the other captives to consider; surely White Cloud wouldn't turn his back on them. If he followed her, he must certainly know that she wasn't alone. Although he was born of the

Sioux, he hadn't grown up with them. Her fellow prisoners were White Cloud's own people. How could he leave them at the mercy of their captors?

She was suddenly gripped with anxiety. Even if White Cloud did try to rescue them, he would most likely fail. She couldn't imagine these Indians handing over their captives to a half-breed who had been raised by a white grandfather.

Logical thinking told her that she and the others must plot their own escape. But how? The man was obviously badly wounded, and she and the other women couldn't very well threaten the warriors. Sheila could think of only one means of escape; somehow she must get her hands on a rifle. That, of course, would be no easy task; quite the contrary, it would probably be impossible. But, in her opinion, it was better than giving up. There was a force in Sheila Langsford that defied submission, and surrendering meekly was not something she would ever do.

She glanced over her shoulder, scanning the sun-dappled landscape for a sign of White Cloud and the others. She saw no one, evidently they were not in pursuit. She was certain now that escape would be up to her and the other captives. The women were riding at her side; she studied them out of the corner of her eye. She didn't think Janice Gilbert would be much help; she sensed weakness in her. She had a feeling, however, that Mrs. Wilson was dependable and courageous. Sheila was quite certain that she would assist in their escape.

As Sheila was contemplating escape, Bart and the others were waiting up ahead. They had picked up the warriors' trail, circled them, and had now taken shelter in the foothills. From their vantage point, they could see the riders as they steadily approached.

Bart was crouched behind a boulder with Luke on one side and Yellow Bear on the other. Dream Dancer was standing behind them, holding the reins to the horses.

Bart was surprised to see that the warriors had three other captives besides Sheila. He shifted uneasily; he hadn't counted on this turn of events.

Luke, watching him, mumbled irritably, "I suppose you're gonna pretend you're an Indian in front of them people, too."

Bart didn't say anything. Luke went on. "Damn it! You'll never get away with it! Miss Langsford's ridin' your horse, which means those people have seen the Triangle-C brand. She might as well be carryin' a banner with your name on it. You ain't got no choice now but to stop playin' Indian!"

"Playing?" Bart questioned. "You talk as though I have no connections with the Sioux at all."

"You got damned little," Luke grumbled. "Well, at least them people don't know you was masqueradin' as White Cloud. If Miss Langsford don't give you away, maybe the Army won't learn that it was you who kidnapped her."

Bart smiled dryly. "Considering Sheila escaped to get away from me, I seriously doubt she'll protect me."

"I suppose you're right," Luke said, obviously worried. "Hell, Bart, what are you goin' to do?"

"Change my clothes, resume my white identity, and take a chance." He shrugged. "What other choice do I have?"

"None, I reckon."

149

Bart turned to Yellow Bear. "Do you know the warriors with Sheila?"

He nodded. "They belong to Chief Running Bull's village. Like our father, Running Bull fled to the mountains."

"Do you think you can convince them to give you their captives?"

"I think so."

Bart was relieved.

"I will go first and talk to them." Yellow Bear went to his horse, and, mindful of his wound, mounted gingerly.

Bart waited until he had left, then, taking his packed bag from the mule, he stepped into a thick patch of shrubbery. There, he discarded his Indian attire and changed into a pair of brown trousers and a tan shirt. His moccasins were replaced by leather boots, and a Colt .45 was strapped about his hips. His hat had become somewhat mashed inside the bag, but it was pliable, and Bart molded it back into shape. He put it on, and adjusted it so that the wide brim shaded his eyes.

As he emerged from the thicket, Dream Dancer gaped at him with wonder. His likeness to the Sioux was now so small that she could barely spot it.

Bart, noticing her surprise, said softly, "I'm still the same inside."

"If I not know you have Sioux blood, I think you only white."

Bart smiled, then walked over to Luke. He knelt beside him and looked over the boulder. Yellow Bear had reached the warriors and Sheila.

* * *

Yellow Bear's arrival filled Sheila with hope. Surely he intended to ask these warriors to set her and the others free. She wondered about the whereabouts of White Cloud, Luke, and Dream Dancer. She supposed they were somewhere close by.

As the Indians reined in to talk with Yellow Bear, Sheila grasped the opportunity to tell the women that Yellow Bear was her friend.

Janice was appalled. "You're friends with that savage?" she exclaimed.

"For heaven's sake, Janice!" Mrs. Wilson remarked testily. "You should be grateful that she has an Indian for a friend. 'That savage,' as you call him, might be your salvation!"

Janice withdrew into a sulking silence. She didn't trust Yellow Bear; in any case, he probably was Sheila's lover, not her friend. When he tired of Sheila, he most likely would force his intentions on her!

"You have to forgive Janice," Mrs. Wilson told Sheila. "She usually isn't this ungrateful."

Janice, offended, said peevishly, "You don't need to apologize for me."

"Sheila . . ." Mrs. Wilson began, ignoring Janice's retort. "Was this Indian traveling with you?"

"Yes, he was."

"Weren't there others?"

She nodded. "I suppose they're close by."

"Dear God!" the woman prayed. "Please help this Indian set us free!"

"Try not to worry, Mrs. Wilson," Sheila murmured. "I'm sure Yellow Bear will convince the warriors to let us go."

151

"Please call me Amanda."

Sheila smiled. "We'll be all right, Amanda. Just wait and see."

At that moment, Yellow Bear signaled for Bart and the others to ride in. Sheila watched as they rode out of the foothills and onto open ground. As they drew closer, she was astounded to see that Bart had discarded his Indian apparel. She wondered why.

Arriving, the riders reined in. At that same moment, Janice's husband, passing out, fell off his horse. Luke dismounted, and, paying no attention to anyone, rushed to help the fallen man.

Amanda was aware that the stranger had gone to Tom Gilbert's aid, but she didn't look closely at him. Luke's full beard camouflaged his face, and there was no reason for her to suspect that she had once known him.

Sheila dismounted and hurried to help Luke with Janice's husband. As she knelt beside the wounded man, she cast Janice an angry look. This man was her husband, how could she treat him so impersonally? Didn't she care about him at all?

Luke's brow knitted with consternation as he examined the man's wound. "Looks like the arrow penetrated deep," he said to Sheila. "But I don't know if it punctured any vital organs." He touched Gilbert's forehead. "He's burnin' up with fever. He'll die if he don't get medicine to fight off the infection."

"If these Indians set us free, we'll take him to the nearest doctor."

"The nearest doctor is days from here. This man will be dead by then. We'll have to take him to the closest Indian village."

For the first time since her capture, Sheila looked carefully at Janice's husband. He was young and quite handsome. His sandy-colored hair was thick and curly, and a thatch falling across his brow lent him a boyish look that was touching.

Sounds of movement attracted Sheila's attention, and, standing, she watched with joy as the warriors told Yellow Bear goodbye and rode away, leaving their captives behind. Thank God, Yellow Bear had been successful! Sheila's joy, however, quickly turned into apprehension as Bart got down from his horse and headed toward her. With a defiant lift to her chin, she mentally braced herself to face his reproach.

Taking her unawares, he grasped her arm in a viselike grip and forced her to walk at his side. When they were far enough away from the others not to be heard, he released his grip, folded his arms across his chest, and eyed her testily.

She met his stare unflinchingly.

"I didn't know you were so foolhardy," he grumbled. "This countryside is no place for a woman alone. But then, I guess you found that out, didn't you?" That he was suddenly facing Sheila as Bart Chandler temporarily slipped his mind; at the moment, anger alone controlled his thoughts.

"My goodness, White Cloud," she said caustically, "I'm impressed with your English! I'm also quite taken with your new attire! A few hours can make such a difference. When I saw you last, you were a Sioux warrior, and now you're a white man! I do wonder what you'll become next!"

"Sheila, I can explain . . ."

"Why don't I explain for you!" she snapped. "You were born in a Sioux village, but raised by a white grand father."

"How did you know?"

"Dream Dancer."

"So you did question her."

"Yes, I certainly did!"

"Is that why you ran away?"

"Of course!"

"Then you rejected my kiss because you were angry and not because you believed I was an Indian?"

His question took her off guard. "Wh-what has tha got to do with what we're discussing?"

"Never mind," he murmured. He was glad that he had misjudged her. She had turned away from him ou of anger; his Sioux blood had nothing to do with it!

Sheila's fury flamed back to life, and, placing he hands on her hips, she snapped at him. "What is you real name?"

He arched a brow. "White Cloud is my name."

"You know what I mean! You must have anothe name!"

"Bart Chandler."

"Mr. Chandler, you are a deceitful, obnoxious cad How dare you kidnap me under false pretenses! Who d you think you are to take such liberties? Your gall i infuriating!"

Bart sighed heavily. "I'm sorry; but when I abducted you, I never intended to keep you this long." A tint o anger came to his eyes. "I didn't count on your fiance plotting an ambush."

"Don't you dare blame Donald! If you hadn't kidnapped me in the first place, none of this would have happened!"

"That's true," Bart said quietly. "And Yellow Bear would be dead."

His words, like a douse of cold water, extinguished Sheila's fiery temper. "Yes, he would have died," she murmured. A horrifying vision of Yellow Bear swinging at the end of a rope flashed before her eyes. "Your brother's life is the only reason I don't completely despise you. I can understand the desperation that drove you to save him. However, I don't understand why you didn't tell me the truth. You're a liar and a cheat, and, for that, I can never respect you!"

He hoped she was speaking out of anger again and not from the heart. "I promise I'll deliver you safely back to Fort Laramie. But first I want to see my family."

"If you take me to the fort, my father will have you arrested."

"Not if you don't tell him that I kidnapped you. I plan to take you back as Bart Chandler."

"What if I refuse to back up your story?"

He shrugged as though he didn't really care. "I'll still take you home."

"I'll think about it," she replied. Deep inside she knew she didn't really need to consider the matter. She was very angry, true, but she certainly didn't want Bart to be arrested.

Bart changed the subject. "The other captives, who are they?"

"Mr. and Mrs. Gilbert, and Amanda Wilson." She

quickly told him what little she knew about all of them. "Luke, said the man will die if he doesn't get medical care," she added.

"We're days away from a doctor."

"Yes, that's what Luke said. He thinks we should take Mr. Gilbert to the closest Sioux village."

"Chief Red Owl's village is near."

"Did he sign the peace treaty with the Army?"

"Yes, he did, and his village is located in the foothills. After we leave there and head into the mountains, we won't find any more villages at peace."

"Including your father's," she remarked softly.

"He, like the others, went into the mountains to get away from the Army."

"When did you last see your father?"

"I was fourteen when I was taken away."

"You must be very anxious to see him again."

"I am, and I'm also anxious to see my sister and grandmother."

"Is your mother dead?"

"Yes, she died when I was born."

"Was she white?"

"Yes. And so is my grandmother."

Sheila was amazed. "Then you aren't a half-breed. Actually, you're only a quarter Sioux."

"Does it matter?" His eyes bore intensely into hers.

"Well, it certainly doesn't matter to me," she replied coldly, her anger suddenly reborn. For a little while she had forgotten his deceit, and the way in which he had used her.

"Let's go back to the others. We need to get Mr.

Gilbert to Red Owl's village.'' Sheila's sudden coldness was chilling, but Bart hadn't expected her to forgive him immediately. Still he hoped, with time, she would.

He gently grasped her arm to escort her back, but she drew away and cast him a look that said clearly that she did not welcome his touch.

Her behavior sparked his own anger, and he grasped her arm again; but this time his hold was firm. "I would appreciate,'' he began, "if you didn't tell the Gilberts and Amanda Wilson that I was the Indian who abducted you.''

"You needn't worry, Mr. Chandler,'' she replied tartly. "Your secret is safe with me!''

"Thank you,'' he murmured.

Her response was to wrest free of his grip, and walk ahead of him.

Earlier, when Bart had forced Sheila to leave with him, Amanda had watched the pair for a moment. She had seen the anger in the man's eyes, and the resentment in Sheila's. Evidently, there was some kind of rift between them.

Her thoughts turned to Tom Gilbert, and she told Janice to dismount and help care for her husband.

Janice did so reluctantly. That her husband might die didn't really matter to her. She certainly didn't love him; in fact, she didn't especially *like* him. She glared indignantly at Amanda as she, too, dismounted. Janice's feelings weren't very amiable toward her; Amanda Wilson always irritated her.

157

Amanda was perfectly aware that Janice resented her, but she didn't care. There was no love lost between them. She did, however, like and respect Mr. Gilbert. Now, she met Janice's peevish stare. "Why are you just standing here? Help take care of your husband!" She knew how much the man loved his wife, which compelled her to add, "Tom needs you."

Janice whirled about huffily and went to Luke, who was still kneeling beside her husband. Yellow Bear and Dream Dancer were standing close by, watching. The warrior's presence unnerved Janice. He had gained their freedom, true, but she feared and disliked all Indians, whether they were friendly are not. She considered them savages and would relish their extinction.

"How is my husband?" she asked Luke.

"His wound's bad, and he's runnin' a high fever. We need to take 'im to the nearest village."

"That would be Red Owl's," Yellow Bear told him.

"What?" Janice butted in, glowering at Luke. "If you think I'm going to an Indian village, then you're out of your mind! I demand you take me to the closest white settlement!"

Her tirade didn't unsettle Luke in the least. "I'm sorry, ma'am. But we're takin' your husband to Red Owl's village. He needs care, and he needs it now. If you don't want to come along, then you can stay here by yourself; the rest of us are leavin'."

"How dare you talk to me like that!"

Luke ignored her and looked at Yellow Bear. "We left the travois behind. I'll get it and be back in a few minutes." He turned to Janice then. "If your husband regains consciousness while I'm gone, give him a drink of water.''

Her reply was a petulant glare.

Luke stood up, and began walking toward his horse. As he passed Amanda, who was sitting in the grass resting, he nodded cordially but didn't really look at her. She, however, looked closely at him.

Luke had already walked by Amanda before her heartbeat suddenly increased and a tingly excitement filled her whole being. All at once, she leapt to her feet. ''Luke!'' she burst out. ''My God, Luke, is it really you?'' Were her eyes deceiving her? Could this possibly be the man she had once loved with all her heart? *Once* loved? God help her, she had never stopped loving him!

Luke halted abruptly. He knew who this woman was, for he had never forgotten the sound of her voice. He turned around as though moving in slow motion and gazed incredulously at Amanda. Despite her disheveled appearance, he could see that she was still beautiful.

She came closer and gazed up lovingly into his face. She tried to imagine what he looked like beneath the heavy beard. She had a feeling he hadn't changed all that much.

''I can't believe it's you,'' Luke murmured.

She smiled tremulously. ''When I agreed to make this trip, I never dreamed our paths would cross. I knew this countryside was your home, but our meeting is a miracle I couldn't . . .'' She hesitated. ''I *wouldn't* let myself imagine.''

''It ain't, no miracle, Amanda. Just a rare coincidence.''

His voice was emotionless, and Amanda controlled the urge to beg him not to distance himself! Surely the past twenty years had mellowed his bitterness.

Luke looked closely at the cut on her forehead. "Are you all right?"

"Yes, I'm fine," she murmured.

"What are you doin' in these parts? How come you left St. Louis?"

"It's a long story."

"Make it short, and tell me why you're here."

"My husband wanted to prospect for gold in the Black Hills."

"Was he killed?"

"Yes, he died when we were attacked."

"Why did he want to look for gold? I can't imagine you two needin' the money."

She sighed heavily. "We were almost destitute."

"Destitute?" Luke questioned. "How could that be? You married one of the richest men in St. Louis."

"My husband lost his fortune during the war. He backed the Confederacy."

"He wasn't too smart, was he?" Luke's bitterness was apparent.

"No, he was a very foolish man," Amanda admitted sadly.

"Well, I reckon things don't always turn out the way we think they will. When you married 'im, I'm sure you believed you'd never want for anything."

"Luke, you make it sound as though I married Norman for his money."

"Didn't you?"

"There was more to it than that."

"Were you in love with him?"

"You know I loved you!" she cried.

"Nope, I don't know that," he replied acridly. He suddenly shrugged as though he didn't care. "It happened a long time ago, Amanda. It just don't matter anymore."

She thought it did still matter, but she didn't say so.

"I gotta get a travois. We'll talk later, okay?"

She nodded as she held back tears, and watched Luke walk to his horse. Her gaze took in his every movement as he mounted, then galloped toward the foothills. The tears welling up in her eyes finally overflowed and rolled steadily down her face. He was still such a good-looking man, and so impressively masculine!

Amanda had been eighteen when she met Luke Thomas; he had been twenty-four. There was a dynamic aura about Luke that had completely overwhelmed her. In spite of his impressive self-confidence and strong demeanor, he could be gentle and sensitive. Amanda, raised as a genteel young lady, had little in common with Luke, who had grown up in the wilderness. But in spite of their different backgrounds, they had fallen in love. Fate, however, came cruelly between them, destroying their dreams and breaking their young hearts.

Now, as Amanda watched Luke ride away, she wondered if she should tell him why she had married another man. Should she open the door to the past, or leave it closed? She wasn't even sure if Luke cared enough to hear what she had to say. After such a long time, he probably never gave her a thought; that is, until today. He was more than likely happily married and had a family who loved him very much. That she had once jilted him certainly no longer mattered.

161

She rubbed an arm over her eyes, drying her tears with her dress sleeve. She would keep the past where it belonged, behind life's closed doors. She resolved to keep it there, unless . . . unless Luke wanted it otherwise. For an ecstatic moment, the possibility lifted her spirits, but they quickly took a downward plunge. She was grasping at straws. After twenty years, Luke Thomas surely couldn't care less.

Luke, riding speedily toward the hills, felt as though he were living a dream. Never in his wildest thoughts had he imagined that his path would again cross with Amanda's. Seeing her again had opened the flood gates to painful memories, and they now poured forth like a bursting dam. His love for Amanda had always been inescapably locked in his heart, but he thought he had thrown away the key.

Luke chuckled bitterly. Thrown away the key, hell! All these years Amanda had held the key, and damn her for coming back into his life and unlocking memories that still had the power to wound!

Chapter Ten

Bart decided not to ride into Red Owl's village unannounced; he sent Yellow Bear ahead to let the chief know they were coming. Bart remembered Red Owl from the time he was living with the Sioux; he knew him to be a kind, generous, and fair leader. He was also a man of peace, so Bart wasn't surprised that he had signed the peace treaty with the Army.

Luke was at Bart's side, the women were behind them, and Dream Dancer, riding the horse pulling the travois, was bringing up the rear.

Silence, so complete it was almost tangible, hung over the travelers, for everyone was deep in their own thoughts. Bart's mind was on the journey ahead. He was wondering if he should take Sheila and the others with him to Iron Star's village. He was certain Iron Star wouldn't object if it was only Sheila and Luke, but now he had three other people. Bart was also a little wary; he didn't really know the Gilberts and Amanda Wilson. He wondered if he could convince Luke to take them to Fort Laramie, but even then, such a trip could be dangerous, for Luke would be wholly responsible for two women and a wounded man. Furthermore, if he sent the others back to the fort, Sheila might insist on leaving with them. The truth was, he didn't want to let her go. If she returned to the fort, she'd probably marry Dwyer. Bart's thoughts remained unsettled.

Meanwhile, Luke's mind was on Amanda. The shock of seeing her again was beginning to wane, and he was able to sort his thoughts more rationally. It was vital that he keep a distance between them, otherwise, he might fall in love with her all over again. Such a love would probably be disastrous. Twenty years had separated them, and those years couldn't be washed away like debris on a swift current. Twenty years! He had changed a lot, and she had no doubt changed as well. They were no longer two young star-crossed lovers. Moreover, she had shared her life with a husband, and he had lived his in his own way. It would be foolish even to imagine that they could go back twenty years and pick up the pieces. She had chosen another man over him; he still hadn't forgotten that pain! He deliberately put Amanda from his thoughts. She belonged in the past, and he intended to keep her there.

Sheila's reverie was completely focused on Bart. She was still perturbed that he had deceived her, but her feelings were beginning to mellow. However, should he use her again, or lie to her, she would deal with him firmly, cast him out of her life, and never see him again.

If he wanted her alliance, then he had better well earn it! Yet she felt a moment of weakness even as she made this pledge to herself. Could she really forget Bart so easily? She wasn't sure. She strongly suspected she was falling in love with him. Nevertheless, she told herself stubbornly, if he couldn't maintain an honest relationship, then she would dismiss him from her life; one way or another!

Amanda, riding beside Sheila, was immersed in memories. In her mind, she was again seeing Luke Thomas for the first time. They had met quite by accident. He was visiting St. Louis, and she was in town shopping. Crossing a street, her arms laden with packages, she didn't see a runaway buggy charging in her direction. By the time she heard the horses' pounding hooves, they were almost upon her. Frozen with fear, she stood riveted. Suddenly, a pair of strong arms went around her waist and swept her from the horses' deadly path. When she was out of danger, she looked into her rescuer's face to thank him; he was young, handsome, and his masculinity was overpowering. Entranced, she gazed deeply into his smoky-blue eyes and fell instantly in love. Now, recalling the incident in vivid detail caused Amanda to smile wistfully. Yes, she had fallen in love with Luke at first sight. She wondered if finding him after twenty years was a coincidence, or was it fate? Luke had called it a rare coincidence, but Amanda wanted to believe otherwise. Did she dare hope that they might renew their love? Renew? she questioned. Her love didn't need to be revived, it had never stopped. Despair suddenly swayed through her mind. Luke had probably stopped caring a long time ago. Hoping they might get back together again was foolish, she was thinking like a silly schoolgirl. The chance that Luke might be married crossed her mind again. It was certainly likely. A man as handsome and as warm-hearted as Luke wouldn't have remained a bachelor all these years.

Janice had thoughts of her own. She was angry, bitter, and miserable. She could hardly believe she was actually traveling to an Indian village. The savages would most likely take them all prisoners! She was afraid the man called Bart Chandler was leading them into a trap. As her musings shifted to Bart, however, her resentment took a backseat. She was very impressed with Bart's good looks, and he had also piqued her curiosity. She wondered exactly who he was, and why he was traveling with Sheila and the others. But most of all, she wondered if he was romantically involved with Sheila. At first she had thought Sheila was Yellow Bear's lover, but now she wasn't so sure. She hoped Bart had no interest in Sheila, for she was considering pursuing him. Her husband was already an obstacle—she didn't need Miss Langsford as one, too! Well, regardless, she would pursue Bart Chandler, for she was certain he would fall prey to her irresistible charms. Wrapping a man around her little finger was always easy for her, and she didn't think Bart would be an exception. Her amorous mood changed abruptly as her thoughts returned to the matter at hand. Was Bart Chandler blindly leading them into a trap? But the man certainly did seem to know what he was doing, and his self-confidence was apparent—maybe she was worrying unnecessarily.

Dream Dancer glanced over her shoulder to check on

Tom Gilbert. He was still unconscious. She hoped he would live to reach Red Owl's village. That the man's wife was so uncaring was hard for Dream Dancer to fathom. Sioux women loved and respected their husbands. The whites were certainly a strange breed of people. Her thoughts moved unwillingly to Yellow Bear. She had been trying desperately not to think about him, but her willpower had weakened. Did she dare dream that he might desire her? Was his consideration simply kindness, or did it stem from something much stronger? She quickly chastised herself for such fantasy. Dream Dancer! *Yes*, she thought, *my name most assuredly fits. Foolish dreams are always dancing through my mind*! She forcefully cleared her head of such wishful thinking. Yellow Bear's kindness was just that: kindness!

The travelers crested a steep hill, and Red Owl's village came into view. The encampment was bordered on one side by a narrow river, the other side was bounded by a tapestry of rolling hills filled with trees and wild flowers. Behind the village, the rugged mountains loomed like an impenetrable fortress.

The Indians looked on with misgivings as the visitors entered their peaceful camp. Whites often brought trouble with them, and they hoped these people wouldn't stay very long.

Yellow Bear, standing in front of Red Owl's tepee, waved to Bart and got his attention. Two braves were standing beside him, and they moved to Gilbert, lifted him from the travois, and carried him to the medicine man.

As Bart dismounted, the chief pushed aside the flap on

his tepee and stepped outside. His gaze quickly settled on Bart, and he smiled warmly. He spoke in the Sioux tongue. "It is good to see you again, White Cloud."

"And I am happy to see you, Red Owl. I am also grateful for your hospitality."

The chief suddenly looked worried. "Come inside; we will talk." He turned around and went back into his tepee.

"Go with him," Yellow Bear told Bart. "I will see to the others."

Sheila, still on horseback, watched as Bart disappeared into the chief's home. In Bart's presence she felt safe, but now that she could no longer see him, she began to feel uneasy.

Yellow Bear, speaking to the ladies, gestured toward an elderly woman standing close by. "She is called Laughs-With-Birds. Go with her, she will make you comfortable in her home."

The women dismounted, and with Dream Dancer leading the way, they followed Laughs-With-Birds to a nearby tepee. She waved her guests inside. The woman's home was neat and orderly; everything seemed in its place.

In preparation for her visitors, Laughs-With-Birds had placed blankets beside the fire pit. She pointed to them and spoke in her own language.

"She ask you to sit down," Dream Dancer interpreted.

Tired, the others gladly complied. A pot of coffee was brewing, and their hostess poured cups for everyone.

Dream Dancer sat beside Laughs-With-Birds, and they began a discussion in their own language.

"Sheila?" Amanda said softly.

"Yes?"

"Is Luke married?" Amanda held her breath, hoping for the answer she so desperately wanted.

"I don't know," Sheila replied. "I barely know Luke."

The woman's disappointment was evident.

"Why are you so interested in him?" Sheila asked.

"I knew him years ago. I met Luke before I was married to Norman."

"I wish I could help you, Amanda. But I don't know anything about Luke. I've just met him. He was with Dream Dancer when we came across him."

"Are he and Dream Dancer . . . ?"

"No, of course not," Sheila was quick to reply. She told Amanda why Luke had been traveling with Dream Dancer.

Amanda looked over at Dream Dancer, her eyes filled with sympathy. "That poor child!" Her tone deepened with anger. "Luke should have shot those two trappers right between their legs!"

Janice, listening, said peevishly, "Honestly, Amanda! Why, everyone knows Indian women rut like animals. She probably wanted those trappers to take her."

Sheila's temper snapped. "Janice, you're either the most cold-hearted woman I ever met, or the most ignorant!"

"How dare you!" she hissed.

"For heaven's sake, Janice!" Amanda protested. "Have you no feelings at all?"

"Not for Indians!" she retorted. "In case you don't know it, they are our enemies!"

Sheila was about to make an angry reply but was

169

stopped by Bart and Luke's entrance. Bart asked Laughs-With-Birds and Dream Dancer to let him talk alone with the other ladies. They nodded and left the tepee.

"Is anything wrong?" Sheila asked him.

"We can't stay here," Bart replied as he and Luke sat down. "We have to leave at once. Red Owl will give us medicine for Gilbert, but then we must go. Much unrest exists among his young warriors. They want to break the peace treaty and go into the mountains. These warriors feel such animosity toward whites that Red Owl is concerned for our safety. That is why he wants us to leave. We'll go back to Fort Laramie," he added.

Sheila detected regret in his voice. "Back to Fort Laramie? But what about your family? You were so anxious to see them."

"I still plan to see them. Once Luke and I get you and the others to the fort, we'll start the trip all over again."

"And what will happen to Dream Dancer? My God, Bart! We can't let her go to the mountains to die!"

"Yellow Bear will insist that she travel with him to Iron Star's village. He thinks he can help her."

Sheila prayed Yellow Bear was right.

It hadn't been easy for Bart to make the decision to turn back, but he couldn't very well force the Gilberts and Amanda Wilson to accompany him to Iron Star's village. Sending everyone to the fort with only Luke for protection was too risky. Besides, he had a feeling Luke would be hesitant to leave him—Luke was too worried that Bart might get himself in trouble, or worse.

Yellow Bear suddenly entered the tepee. Speaking English, he said excitedly, "Three warriors just rode in.

They went into the mountains to attend a big meeting of many tribes. They visited Iron Star's village, and they say our father is very ill.''

"Dear God!" Bart groaned.

"If we want to see our father before he goes to the spirit world, we must hurry.''

"Bart, Yellow Bear is right," Sheila said firmly. "You don't have time to take us back to the fort.''

Bart sighed heavily. "But how can I ask the Gilberts and Mrs. Wilson to undertake such a journey?''

"Do you think I would refuse?" Amanda cut in. "Mr. Chandler, I owe my life to you and your friends. Helping you to see your father is the least I can do.'' She regarded him closely. "However, I must admit that learning you have a Sioux father is quite a surprise. You don't look much like an Indian.''

"Doesn't *my* opinion matter?" Janice asserted forcefully. "I'm sorry that Mr. Chandler's father is ill, but I refuse to travel to his village!''

"Why don't we have a vote?" Amanda suggested. "All in favor of going on, raise their hands.'' Her own hand went up immediately; Sheila's followed quickly, then Luke's.

Amanda cast Janice a triumphant look. "Three against one. We go on to the village.''

Bart was deeply impressed with Amanda. She was quite a woman! That Sheila had so willingly agreed to the journey lifted his spirits considerably. Did that mean she had forgiven him?

"We'd better replenish our supplies and get back on the trail," Luke said, getting to his feet.

171

Bart rose beside him. "You ladies stay here and rest. I'll let you know when we're ready to leave."

The men were on their way outside when Yellow Bear halted abruptly and looked back at Janice. "Why do you not ask about your husband?"

"Ask what exactly?" She found the warrior's behavior rude.

"If he is still alive."

"Well, is he?"

"Your husband died before the medicine man could help him."

Janice didn't say a word.

Bart spoke softly. "We'll take his body with us and bury him in the meadow."

When the men left, Amanda turned to Janice. "How can you accept your husband's death so calmly?" she asked harshly.

"You have no right to preach to me! Your own husband has only been dead a day, and you certainly aren't mourning him!"

Her retort silenced Amanda. However, Janice was wrong, for Amanda was certainly grieving. Norman's death saddened her. She had cared, though she hadn't been in love with him.

On the other hand, Tom's death didn't sadden Janice in the least. In fact, she was glad he was gone. Their marriage had been a terrible mistake, and she was relieved to be free of him.

"Sheila," Amanda began. "Tell us about Mr. Chandler. If his father is Sioux, then why isn't he living with the Indians? It's apparent that he wasn't raised in a Sioux village. The man is schooled and very polished."

172

"He was raised by his grandfather, who owns a ranch in Texas."

Sheila preferred to avoid the discussion. If she said too much about Bart, the women might eventually pass the information on to her father. Then, he could very well put the pieces together and realize Bart was her Indian abductor.

"How did you meet Mr. Chandler?" Amanda asked. She wasn't prying, she was simply curious.

"We met quite by accident," Sheila replied evasively.

At that moment, Dream Dancer and Laughs-With-Birds returned. Sheila welcomed the interruption. Bart was a subject better left undiscussed.

The sun was on its westward course when the travelers left Red Owl's village. A few miles into their journey, they stopped in a grassy area interspersed with aspen and blue spruce. There, the men dug a grave for Tom Gilbert. Luke had a Bible in his bag, and he read from it over the man's final resting place. Amanda wept softly, for she had liked Tom very much. Janice's eyes, however, remained dry.

They moved on, and were soon on high ground that would take them into the mountains. The terrain grew more steep and gradually narrowed to a path bordered on both sides by wooded bluffs. They climbed for over an hour before reaching an area that was fairly flat. Bart decided it was a good place to set up camp. The sun was now sinking below the horizon, and traveling across the mountains after dark was too dangerous.

The women dismounted wearily. The Indians who had

173

captured Amanda and Janice had stolen the white men's saddles, as well as their horses. Fortunately for the ladies, Yellow Bear had convinced them to leave two saddled horses. Even though, Amanda and Janice weren't forced to ride bareback still, they were tired.

Bart built a fire under low branches, which would break up the smoke. They were now in hostile territory, and he couldn't chance a sudden attack.

Sheila and Amanda prepared a hot supper that was quite savory. Janice didn't offer to help. After all, she had been coerced into coming along, she shouldn't be expected to pitch in as though she were here of her own accord!

Bart, volunteering for the first watch, climbed to higher ground and took up a position where he could keep vigil over the campsite.

The women spread their pallets close together. The night air had brought a chill, and they used all their blankets to keep them warm.

"I have never been so miserable!" Janice complained. "Good Lord, I've worn this dress for days. I want a bath and a change of clothes." Her belongings had been left behind in the wagon. She had asked Bart to fetch them, or else send Luke or Yellow Bear, but he had refused, saying the wagon was now too far from the campside.

"I'd like a bath and clean clothes, too," Amanda replied. "But it's not possible, so there's no sense in complaining."

Janice was beginning to despise Amanda Wilson more with each passing day. The woman was insufferable. She didn't like Sheila, either! Someday she would find a way to get even with both of them. She'd make them sorry that they had treated her so unfairly.

Sheila threw off her blankets, and got to her feet.

"Where are you going?" Amanda asked.

"I'm not sleepy. I think I'll join Bart for a while."

She followed the path Bart had taken. The climb was somewhat precarious and she had to tread carefully.

Her unexpected visit pleased Bart, and he greeted her with a warm smile. He was sitting beneath a tree, and she sat beside him.

"Couldn't you sleep?" he asked.

"I didn't really try. I need to talk to you."

"Yes, I'm sure you do. You have a lot of questions to ask."

"You must know what they are."

"Why don't I tell you about my life. In doing so, I'll most likely answer your questions."

Sheila listened raptly as Bart gave a full account of his years with the Sioux. He told her about his father, sister, and Golden Dove. He spoke with warmth, and memories of his Sioux family tugged at his heartstrings. In his mind, he relived Charles Dwyer's massacre; his voice was thick with anger as he explained that tragic day to Sheila. She was shocked to learn that Donald's brother had done something so horrible.

Bart grew silent for a moment as he calmed his thoughts. He then recounted his meeting with Luke, the day he had met J.W., and his years at the Triangle-C.

"Your grandfather must be very worried. This isn't a good time to return to your Sioux family, for there is so much unrest and hate between the Indians and the whites.

And to make matters worse, your father has declared war against the Army.''

"I didn't know that when I left the ranch. I thought I'd find Iron Star on the reservation.''

Your father is half white. How can he be so warlike; since the soldiers are also his people.''

"Iron Star was raised as a Sioux, and that's what he is.''

"If Golden Dove hadn't insisted that you leave with Luke, you would also be Sioux.''

Bart smiled ruefully. "Yes, I suppose I would be.''

She placed a hand on Bart's arm. "I hope Iron Star gets well.''

"Thank you, Sheila.'' He gazed tenderly into her eyes. "You've forgiven me, haven't you?''

"Yes,'' she admitted. "But don't you dare lie to me again.''

"I won't,'' he said, grinning.

His smile was like a magnet pulling her closer. Almost without thought, she boldly wrapped her arms around his neck and kissed him on the lips.

Before Bart had a chance to respond fully, Sheila drew away and was on her feet. She could hardly believe she had been so brazen, and her cheeks reddened with embarrassment.

"Good . . . good night,'' she stammered, then turning around, she left as quickly as the steep incline would allow.

Chapter Eleven

Amanda was sleeping fitfully, for she was dreaming of her husband's death. An arrow had pierced his heart, killing him instantly. She had been crouched behind the wagon, reloading the men's rifles, when her husband fell. She had rushed to his side, hoping to find him alive, but the arrow had done its work too quickly.

Now, emerging suddenly from her dream, she sat up with a start. It took a moment to clear the nightmare from her mind, and she stared about the camp as though she didn't know where she was, or how she had gotten there.

Amanda's vivid dream had made her heart pound rapidly, and as it gradually slowed, she managed to calm her thoughts. Now she was wide awake, and falling back asleep was out of the question. She looked about. Janice, lying beside her, was deep in slumber. Sheila, on

Amanda's other side, was also asleep, and next to her, Dream Dancer slept deeply.

Amanda glanced toward the campfire. It had burned down to glowing embers. Yellow Bear and Bart were wrapped in their bedrolls, which were placed close to the dying fire. She peered up at the sky. The horizon was beginning to lighten. It would soon be dawn.

She threw off her blanket and got to her feet. She ran her fingers through her mussed hair. The golden-brown tresses weren't too tangled, for last night she had used Sheila's hair brush. She made a futile attempt to straighten her wrinkled dress, then moved away quietly. She knew exactly where she was going. She hadn't consciously told herself to go there; she was simply allowing her emotions to guide her. Luke was not in his bed, which obviously meant he was taking the last watch. She carefully followed the same path Sheila had taken earlier, and the short climb led her to where Luke's vigil overlooked the camp.

Luke had been sitting beneath a tree, but he was now standing, for he had seen Amanda's approach. Her visit came as no surprise, he surmised she would grasp an opportunity to talk alone with him. Although he wasn't surprised, he was nevertheless apprehensive, for he wasn't sure how to act. They had once been lovers, and treating her now as a casual acquaintance was difficult. Moreover, he had never fully recovered from the pain of losing her.

Now, as he watched her come closer, he couldn't help but admire her beauty. As a girl of eighteen she had been striking; she had matured into an exceptionally attractive woman.

Amanda paused in front of him, and he gazed down into her hazel eyes. Her thick mane of hair was tousled, and a wayward lock had fallen over her shoulder. Luke fought back the temptation to reach out and caress its silky softness.

Returning Luke's intense scrutiny, Amanda was finding him ever more attractive. A splattering of gray dappled his beard and hair, but it lent a distinguished touch that was very flattering. She decided she approved of his beard; it was well groomed and added to his good looks. His smoky-blue eyes hadn't lost the power to completely mesmerize her, but with great effort she tore her gaze from his and allowed her eyes to wander over his tall, heavily muscled frame. His dark trousers adhered smoothly to his long, muscular legs, and his cream-colored shirt, made of suede, stretched tightly across his burly chest and the wide width of his shoulders. Amanda's heart skipped a beat. He was indeed a fine figure of a man!

Luke, finding Amanda tempting, stepped back and put her out of arm's reach. He intended to keep his distance. He didn't feel he could erase the past twenty years, furthermore, he didn't even want to try. Also, though less important than his determination to remain uninvolved, her husband had been dead only a couple of days.

"What do you want?" he asked. The question was spoken flatly and without emotion.

What did she want? Amanda wasn't sure. Had she come here to ask for his forgiveness—to try to explain something she had done twenty years ago? After so much time, did it really matter? Yes, it mattered to her! She had a feeling, however, that it wasn't important to Luke.

She pushed the past to the far recesses of her mind, and answered softly, "I woke up and couldn't go back asleep. So I decided to come up here and talk to you."

It was on the tip of his tongue to say they had nothing to talk about. But he didn't say it. She had jilted him a long time ago; it was buried in the past, and he was determined to keep it there.

Glancing up at the sky, Luke murmured, in lieu of having anything else to say, "It'll soon be dawn."

"Yes," she replied quietly, as uncomfortable with the conversation as Luke.

A frown crossed Luke's face. "You know, I've been thinkin' 'bout goin' back and buryin' your husband and the others. But I'm kinda hesitant to leave Bart and the rest of you. If there's trouble, my gun will be needed. You all are alive; your husband and the other men are dead. I can't do nothin' for 'em but bury 'em, but I might be able to help keep you and the others from meetin' the same fate."

"I understand. And you're right. You must think of the living. All of us must."

"I'm sorry 'bout your husband, Amanda. I reckon I should've told you that before now."

"Thank you, Luke," she murmured so quietly that he barely heard.

"How come you and your husband decided to make this trip?" he asked suddenly. "I mean, I understand you all wantin' to find gold, but why were you so desperate? Didn't your husband realize goin' into the Black Hills is like committin' suicide? Hell, you all didn't even make it to the mountains! Didn't the Army advise you against tryin' something so crazy?"

"Yes, of course the Army did. But Norman wouldn't listen. He was obsessed with being rich again. He despised his poverty. He was born to riches and didn't know how to live any other way. As I told you, he invested the bulk of his money into the Confederacy and lost every penny of it. Afterward, he used what little he had left to try to build back his fortune. But again he made bad investments and soon lost all his inheritance. He went to work as an accountant for an old colleague of his father. Desperate, and driven by love of money, he started to embezzle. He was caught, his employer pressed charges, and Norman spent the next four years in prison."

Luke was astounded. For the past twenty years, he had always imagined Amanda living in luxury; instead, she had struggled to survive. "How did you manage to support yourself?"

"When my parents died, they left me their home. If you remember, it was very large. I turned it into a rooming house, and I took in enough money to live comfortably."

"Did you and Norman have any children?"

She hesitated, then murmured, "No, we didn't."

Luke failed to detect her hesitancy. "How did he get it in his head to prospect for gold?"

"He met a man in prison who claimed that his brother had found a fortune in the Black Hills. After that, prospecting for gold became an obsession. Janice and her husband were my boarders, and when Norman came home from prison, he and Tom Gilbert spent a lot of time together. Tom was young, and miserable because he couldn't earn enough money to please Janice. He was easy pickings for Norman, and in no time at all, he talked Tom into a partnership. Tom had a small but tidy inheritance. Norman needed that money and convinced Tom to turn it over to him. He assured Tom that prospecting for gold was a sure investment. My father had left his home to Norman and me, but the title was in Norman's name. He sold the house so that he could put up his half. Shortly after, we were on our way out here. Janice and I couldn't stay behind even if we had wanted to because our husbands had sunk all their money into making this trip."

"Norman was a very foolish man," Luke said, not meaning to sound unkind.

"Yes, I know. And his foolishness cost him and Tom their lives. It was a terrible price to pay."

He looked at her speculatively. "You didn't love him, did you?"

"No, but I cared. Norman was weak, impulsive, and not very smart, but in his own way, he could be charming and likable. He wasn't really a bad person, he was . . . he was . . ."

"Selfish?" Luke helped.

She appeared a little embarrassed. "Yes, I suppose 'selfish' describes Norman Wilson."

"I'm sorry your marriage wasn't all you had hoped for." He smiled kindly. "I mean that, Amanda."

"I know you do," she replied. She remembered Luke's character well enough to know he wouldn't say something like that if he didn't mean it. "What about you, Luke? Are you happily married?" She awaited his answer with bated breath.

"Never got married," he mumbled.

It was difficult for Amanda to hide her joy.

Luke grinned offhandedly. "I reckon I just ain't the marryin' kind."

"But that's not true!" she blurted out impulsively. *"We* were planning to get married!" A cold mask fell across his face, and she wished she hadn't spoken so rashly.

"That was a long time ago," he said unemotionally. "I was barely more than a youngster. Back then, I didn't realize I wasn't the marryin' kind. But I know better now. I ain't the kind of a man who can be tied down with a wife and kids. I relish my independence too much."

She nodded. "I understand. Time has a way of changing people. Neither of us are the same as we were twenty years ago."

Luke checked the sky. The sun was cresting. "Well, let's get back to camp and build up the fire. We'll be leavin' soon."

Amanda took the lead, and Luke walked closely behind her. He held her arm as they descended the steep hillside. His touch sent a tingly sensation racing through Amanda's entire being. She knew such a reaction could mean only one thing. She still loved Luke Thomas as passionately as ever!

The travelers stopped at noon to eat a cold lunch of pemmican, a food eaten often by the Sioux. The fare was made from dried strips of meat pounded into paste, mixed with fat and berries, then pressed into small cakes. It was as tasty as it was filling.

The sun, shining brightly in a cloudless sky, warmed the countryside, as well as the travelers. Bart, deciding to give everyone second cups of water, went to the mule to get a full canteen, then passed it around. Bart drained his cup quickly, then returned to the mule to replace the canteen.

Janice, wanting a moment alone with Bart, followed him. Flashing an alluring smile, she said sweetly, "I hope you don't think badly of me."

"I don't understand."

"I didn't mean to sound unfeeling when I objected to visiting your father's village. It's just that I'm terribly afraid. I was raised in the East, and I know nothing about Indians. It's only natural that I should fear them."

"You should fear them, and with good cause. The Sioux are tired of being pushed around and lied to. A large number of them, as well as other Indians, are going to rebel. When they do, no white person will be safe. However, as a guest in my father's village, no harm will come to you."

She studied him intently. "I can't believe you're part Indian. You don't resemble them at all."

"The resemblance is there. You just don't see it."

"Maybe I don't want to see it."

"Why do you say that?"

"I don't find Indians handsome. In fact, to me they are very threatening. The only contact I had with the Sioux wasn't very pleasant. They killed my husband and took me prisoner." She smiled again; as alluring a smile as the first. "However, I have a feeling meeting you will change my opinion of Indians, that I will learn to see them in a different light." Janice was lying through her teeth. Indians were savages, and nothing Bart could say or do would change her mind. In her opinion, Bart Chan-

184

dler wasn't a savage. His Indian blood was so slight that it wasn't important. Nonetheless, it was apparent to Janice that he was loyal to the Sioux, and in order to win his affections, she knew she must pretend a certain amount of compassion.

Bart had no trouble seeing through her facade. However, he thought her flirtation harmless and saw no reason to challenge her. He had met women like Janice before; they cared for no one but themselves. Also, like Janice, most of them were beautiful and believed their beauty could win over any man they desired.

He replaced the canteen, then escorted Janice back to the others. He noticed Sheila was watching them. He wondered if she was jealous. He couldn't help but hope that she was, for that would mean she was falling in love with him.

Bart's suspicion was right; Sheila was indeed experiencing a pang of jealousy. She didn't like the feeling, for she considered jealousy unbecoming; she willfully cast the emotion aside. Moreover, she had no right to be jealous. She and Bart had made no pledge of loyalty to each other. He was free to do as he pleased. But, she couldn't help but think he had more sense than to fall for Janice.

Sheila turned her eyes to Janice, who was standing nearby. The young woman's sensuality hit her full force and her spirits fell. Why wouldn't Bart, or any man for that matter, fall victim to Janice's enticing charms? Furthermore, Janice was as manipulative as she was beautiful. Sheila supposed it would be almost impossible for any man to reject her, Bart Chandler included!

Jealousy surged again, but Sheila managed to thwart

it. She had no right to feel such an emotion, especially since she was *engaged* to Donald. Her engagement, however, certainly wasn't going to last. She intended to end it as soon as she returned to the fort. She didn't love Donald, and she wasn't about to marry him. She now realized that she had agreed to marry him only to please her father. She had always felt that her father didn't really love her, and she had foolishly believed that if she could win his approval, she'd also win his love. Now, as she considered her own behavior, she could hardly believe that she had come so close to making such a huge mistake. Her father's favor wasn't worth the price of marrying a man she didn't love. Nothing was worth that sacrifice!

Again she wondered how her abduction was affecting her father. She didn't doubt that he was concerned and afraid for her life. She was certain that in his own way he loved her.

Colonel Langsford mounted his horse gingerly. His rheumatism was bothering him, and his joints ached terribly. He and his troops had stopped for a short rest, and it was now time to move on. Lieutenant Dwyer was already mounted and waiting for Langsford to give the order to move out.

The colonel was in considerable pain. He felt as though hundreds of sharp pins were puncturing his flesh. He rubbed a hand down each leg as though he could brush away the discomfort. A heavy sigh escaped his lips; he dreaded the remainder of the journey. He and the other soldiers were on their way to Flying Feather and Big

Buffalo's villages. Langsford was hoping to hear news of Sheila in one of these villages. During the thwarted exchange, Yellow Bear had been wounded, and Langsford was sure Sheila's abductor had sought care for Yellow Bear in one of these nearby villages.

It was a long ride to both Indian encampments, and Langsford decided to shorten the journey. He spoke to Dwyer. "Take half the men with you and ride to Flying Feather's village. I'll visit Big Buffalo's, with the rest, then meet you back at the fort."

"Yes, sir," Dwyer replied.

"You know what questions to ask, but do so with tact. Flying Feather is a peaceful chief, and has never caused the Army any trouble."

Dwyer passed the command to move out down to his corporal, who quickly organized an orderly departure. Within a few minutes, Dwyer was leading his men toward Flying Feather's village. In the meantime, Langsford, followed by his soldiers, was on his way to visit Big Buffalo.

It took three hours to reach Flying Feather's village. The people watching the soldiers ride into their encampment were apprehensive. Mothers gathered their children into the folds of their arms like mother ducks protecting their ducklings under widespread wings. The elders stood outside their tepees and stared at the bluecoats with a trace of fear; they somehow knew that the soldiers' visit was not a friendly one. The village's warriors weren't present; they had gone hunting.

Flying Feather, standing in front of his tepee, quietly awaited Dwyer's approach. He had dealt with the lieutenant before, and had sensed the man's deviousness. He was also familiar with his brother, Charles Dwyer. Among the Sioux, Major Dwyer was notorious. Outwardly, the old chief appeared calm, but anxiety knotted his stomach. If Captain Evans were leading the soldiers, or even Colonel Langsford, he wouldn't be quite so anxious, for both officers had shown signs of integrity. In Flying Feather's estimation, Evans was more compassionate than Langsford; still, the colonel usually dealt fairly with the Sioux. But the chief suspected that Lieutenant Dwyer, like his brother, was the despotic spawn of an evil spirit.

As the lieutenant drew closer to Flying Feather's tepee, the old men of the council gathered around their chief. They stood proudly as they waited for the soldiers to rein in.

Dwyer didn't bother to dismount; he simply eyed Flying Feather coldly, then motioned for his translator to come forward. A young soldier rode up to the lieutenant. He had been captured by the Sioux when he was six years old and had lived with them ten years before the soldiers gained his release. The young man eventually joined the Army; the cavalry was glad to get him because he spoke the Sioux language fluently.

Now, Dwyer told him to ask the chief if Yellow Bear was in his village.

Flying Feather responded by shaking his head.

"Has he been here?" the translator asked, again repeating the lieutenant's words.

Flying Feather hated to lie, but it was necessary now. "I have not seen Yellow Bear." Mouthing untrue words had caused him to speak a little haltingly.

The young man gave Dwyer the chief's answer.

Donald had heard the hesitation in Flying Feather's voice. He suspected the man was lying. "Tell the chief I know he's lying. Also tell him that he has one minute to tell the truth before I order my men to open fire on his people."

The translator hoped the lieutenant's threat meant nothing and that he was merely trying to scare Flying Feather into a confession. Reluctantly, he passed the threat on to the chief.

A jaw muscle twitched; otherwise, Flying Feather remained unmoved in appearance. He took Dwyer's threat seriously, for he was certain the man was capable of cold-blooded murder. As he spoke to the translator, he kept his eyes glued to Dwyer's. "Yes, Yellow Bear was here. He stayed a short time, then left." Flying Feather was perfectly aware that his confession might lead to his arrest, but, at the moment, his sole concern was to protect his people.

The words were quickly translated. Dwyer smiled smugly. Getting the old man to talk had been surprisingly easy. "Ask him about Miss Langsford and her abductor."

The questions were given to the chief, and he answered them truthfully.

"Miss Langsford was here," the interpreter said to Dwyer. "She left with Yellow Bear and his brother, who is called White Cloud. It was White Cloud who kidnapped Miss Langsford. The chief swears that the woman is unharmed and shows no hostility toward White Cloud."

Dwyer was seething. No hostility! Then his suspicions were right—she was bedding down with that savage and enjoying it! A merciless rage came over him as he remembered all the nights he had lain awake craving Sheila's body but denying himself the pleasure of taking her. Like a fool, he had decided to wait until their wedding night, and now she was giving that warrior what rightfully belonged to him.

His anger was so intense that he could barely control it. He turned to his corporal and ordered harshly, "Arrest Flying Feather! He knows it's against the treaty to harbor a fugitive!"

The soldier complied eagerly, for he hated Indians as much as the lieutenant.

Flying Feather accepted his arrest peacefully; he knew fighting it was futile. His wife, afraid she would never see him again, clung desperately to him. He reluctantly freed himself from her grasp, handed her over into his daughter's arms, then ordered his young grandson to bring him his favorite horse.

The wailing of women and children followed Flying Feather as he accompanied the soldiers out of the village. He didn't look back; he was afraid if he did, his composure might crumble. He could only hope that the white man's court would understand the circumstances and show him leniency.

They had traveled about five miles when Dwyer issued the command to halt. Sheila's betrayal was still raging through his mind. He felt he had to release some of his anger or he would explode like a keg of dynamite.

Flying Feather was mounted at his side. He looked at him and tersely told him to leave.

The chief knew a few of the white man's words, but

he didn't understand the meaning of "leave." He shook his head, indicating to Dwyer that he didn't comprehend.

"Go! Fast!" Donald ordered authoritatively.

This time, Flying Feather understood. The lieutenant was setting him free! Happiness washed over him. Apparently Lieutenant Dwyer was more merciful than he had thought. Flying Feather felt guilty that he had judged him so harshly. He gave Donald the Indians' sign for a friendly parting, then, turning his pony about, he sent it into a brisk canter.

Dwyer, grinning sadistically, drew his rifle from its scabbard. Peering through the weapon's rear sight, he aimed the barrel at Flying Feather's back. Before anyone had a chance to grasp what was happening, Donald pulled the trigger. He hit his target; the fired bullet slammed into the chief, sending him toppling from his pony and onto the ground.

Returning his rifle to its scabbard, Dwyer told his corporal to make sure the chief was dead. The violent act had released some of Donald's pent-up anger and he felt much better. Killing Indians always had a positive effect on him.

He glanced a little apprehensively at the soldiers under his command. He knew that not all the men were completely loyal; some troopers were visibly angry and shocked. Yet Dwyer wasn't really worried. What could they do? Try to bring charges against him? No enlisted man was that daring! An uncrossable line existed between officers and enlisted men, and neither group ever tried to cross it.

Returning, the corporal reported that Flying Feather was dead.

Dwyer then spoke to his troopers. "Flying Feather was shot while trying to escape."

They said nothing, but Dwyer, could see by their faces that they weren't about to refute his words. A wide, complacent grin spread across his face.

Lieutenant Dwyer had never looked more evil.

Chapter Twelve

He-Who-Stands-Tall drew up his pony, gesturing for the seventy odd warriors behind him to do the same. The Sioux band was an ominous sight, for they were fully armed and painted for war. He-Who-Stands-Tall was indisputably fierce; his face was painted black and red on opposite sides and red was also painted around his eyes, which he believed would help him detect an enemy from afar. In this case, it had worked. The warriors had crested a hill and on the other side, down in a fertile glade, they spotted Colonel Langsford and his soldiers. The column, riding in leisurely fashion, was on its way back to the fort from Big Buffalo's village.

The warrior's eyes were tight slits of animal cunning as he watched the soldiers. His heart, filled with anger, craved revenge. He and the others belonged to Flying

Feather's village. Their hunting excursion had been successful, and, laden with fresh meat, they had been on their way home when they came upon Flying Feather's body. They had taken their chief back to the village. There they learned what had happened.

Enraged, He-Who-Stands-Tall and the other warriors cried out to the council for retaliation. The old men of the council, their own blood running hotly, gave the warriors permission to seek revenge. He-Who-Stands-Tall and his warriors planned to find the bluecoats and attack without warning. In the meantime, the people would prepare to leave and move into the mountains where they would join up with the other Sioux who had refused to surrender.

As He-Who-Stands-Tall drew his rifle from its sheath, his mouth watered with the taste of revenge. It didn't occur to him that he was about to attack the wrong soldiers; he simply took it for granted that these were the ones who had murdered his chief.

Meanwhile, Colonel Langsford, tired and tortured with rheumatic pain, was looking forward to reaching the fort. He longed for a hot bath and a glass of brandy. With great effort, he pushed his discomfort to the back of his mind and thought about what he had learned at Big Buffalo's village. It was rumored that a white woman was traveling with Yellow Bear and his brother, who was called White Cloud. Langsford had never heard of White Cloud, and wondered why he hadn't. He had asked Big Buffalo about White Cloud, but the chief said he knew nothing about him. Langsford believed Big Buffalo knew more than he was willing to admit, but further questioning would have been pointless. The chief clearly had said all he was going to say.

A sudden war cry, vociferous and blood-chilling, took the colonel and his soldiers completely by surprise. Langsford was stunned by the sight confronting him. A large band of warriors, seeming to appear out of thin air, was racing toward him and his soldiers. His mouth went dry with fear, a shiver rippled up his spine, and his stomach roiled. But the colonel was a true soldier, and, controlling his fright, he took command. They were on open ground, but a green wall of trees stood in the distance; if he and his men could beat the warriors to the area, they could dismount and take shelter. The battle would then swing in their favor, for they could pick off the Indians as they charged.

Langsford gave the order to run for the trees, and the soldiers forced their tired horses into a desperate race toward nature's refuge. About halfway, the Indians hit with full force. Gunfire was exchanged, soldiers fell wounded or dead, but the Army's response was just as potent. And the soldiers were better marksmen than the Indians', their accurate shots sent several warriors to their deaths.

The troop had almost reached the trees where they planned to take up their position when He-Who-Stands-Tall got off a shot that hit Langsford in the back. The powerful blow nearly knocked him off his horse, but he somehow managed to stay in the saddle and reach the wooded area. There, he lost consciousness and fell to the ground.

He-Who-Stands-Tall and his warriors gathered their

fallen brethren and retreated. They knew charging the woods would be deadly. But they were nonetheless satisfied with the attack; they had killed many of the soldiers and had avenged their dead chief. Later, after they joined forces with the Sioux in the mountains, there would be more battles to fight. They didn't doubt that they would reign superior. The bluecoats would be taught a lesson they would never forget.

Dwyer and his men entered Fort Laramie wearily; it had been a long and exhausting day. The lieutenant went straight to Colonel Langsford's office to make his report. He was surprised to find that the colonel hadn't yet returned. Major Forster and Captain Evans were also waiting for Langsford, and the officers sat about the desk, each with a brandy in his hand.

Dwyer told his comrades that he had been forced to shoot Flying Feather as the man was escaping. Although both officers doubted his story, neither disputed it. Major Forster, thinking an Indian's life of little value, didn't care enough to question the lieutenant's report. Captain Evans, on the other hand, cared very much; he simply knew it would be useless to say anything.

The men were having a second glass of brandy when they were disturbed by a commotion from outside. Before they could get to the door to see what was happening, Sergeant Bosworth, who had ridden with the colonel, burst into the office.

With a rush of words he told the officers about the attack and that they had suffered several casualties, Colonel Langsford among them. He quickly let them know that the colonel was still alive and had been taken to the infirmary.

"Is Colonel Langsford conscious?" Evans asked.

"No, sir," the sergeant replied.

Evans looked at Forster. "That means you're now in command."

The major stood straight and squared his shoulders, as though his sudden position had made him taller. Eugene Forster had been in the Army for fifteen years; a dedicated soldier, he planned to stay in the service until he retired. "Do you have any idea which village these Indians came from?" he asked Bosworth.

"Yes, sir!" he answered crisply. "I recognized some of them. The one who appeared to be their leader was He-Who-Stands-Tall. He's from Flying Feather's village."

Immediately both officers looked at Dwyer. Evans's expression was condemning, Forster's disapproving.

Donald attempted to justify his actions. "I had no choice but to shoot Flying Feather. Don't you understand that I had to make an example of him? We must teach these Indians on the reservations to obey the rules. Otherwise, the savages will run all over us."

Forster could see Dwyer's logic, and, for the most part, agreed with him. However, he wished he had taken the chief alive. "Well, what's done is done," he said to the lieutenant. "You're a superb officer, and as far as I'm concerned, your conduct remains above reproach."

"Thank you, sir," Dwyer replied, gloating inwardly. He eyed the major shrewdly. "Sir, you aren't going to let He-Who-Stands-Tall get away with this, are you?"

"Of course not!" Forster blustered, angry that Dwyer should even think that might be the case. "I want you to get fresh horses, a full company, and find He-Who-Stands-Tall!''

''I'm sure he and his tribe have left the reservation and are on their way into the mountains. I'll have to head them off.''

''That shouldn't be a problem. Traveling with women and children will slow their progress.'' The major paused, planned a quick strategic move, and continued. ''I'll have a telegram sent to Fort Swafford. A detachment from there can head them off from the north. And since you'll be coming from the south, by this time tomorrow, your two columns should have the tribe caught in the middle.''

Dwyer grinned eagerly. ''He-Who-Stands-Tall will not get away. That, I promise you!'' He preferred not to leave it there. ''But Major, don't you want me to arrest all the warriors who attacked the colonel and his men?''

''Good God, no! There are too many! Do you expect us to hang every one of them? In any use, the tribe will perish without their young men. No, just bring back He-Who-Stands-Tall; I'm sure he was the instigator. After you arrest him, see that the rest of the people are escorted back to the reservation.''

''Yes, sir,'' Dwyer replied. He was disappointed, for he would have relished bringing in, or killing, every warrior who had participated in the attack. However, he was pleased that a detachment from Fort Swafford would be involved. He hoped his brother would be leading it.

The forested slopes of the Black Hills were steep and precarious, and as trouble was brewing back at Fort Laramie, Yellow Bear, whose wound was healing nicely, was leading his fellow travelers up a sharp incline. They made the climb without mishap. The land that now stretched out before them was a flowered valley interspersed with thick groves of trees. Rugged cliffs presented a stunning backdrop.

They traveled for another hour or so; then, as the sun was making its glowing descent, they stopped and set up camp. Again, Bart built the fire with dry kindling and under low branches to break up the smoke. They ate a hot supper, and as the men saw to the animals, the women washed and stowed the dishes. This time, Janice pitched in and helped; however, her assistance was given with an ulterior motive. She wanted to make a good impression on Bart.

Bedrolls were laid out, the women's on one side of the camp, the men's on the other. Bart, taking the first watch, left the site and found an ideal place to stand guard.

Dream Dancer and Yellow Bear were alone at the fire, for everyone else had gone to bed. They were sitting side by side, and their proximity was thrilling to Dream Dancer. Yellow Bear, obviously deep in thought, was staring straight ahead. Dream Dancer took advantage of his preoccupation to study him closely. His deerskin shirt, decorated with porcupine quills, was a perfect fit, and so were his fringed leggings. His black hair was cut to shoulder length, and he wore a leather headband adorned with an eagle feather. Such a feather was a symbol of prowess and attainment; an eagle feather could only be worn by men.

Yellow Bear, as though he could feel Dream Dancer's

eyes on him, turned his face to hers. His good looks made her heart pound so thunderously that she wondered if he could hear it.

Yellow Bear was finding her equally desirable. Dream Dancer had been in his thoughts frequently, and her beauty had totally entranced him. That the white trappers had molested her preyed heavily on his mind. He wanted his wife to be untouched. An Indian girl's innocence was protected, and after her ceremony of maidenhood, her virtue was closely guarded by her parents and relatives. Yellow Bear looked deeply into his heart, and asked himself if he could accept this beautiful young woman as his bride. Could he erase the trappers' assault from his mind? Yes, he thought he could. Besides, in way, Dream Dancer was still a virgin, for he was certain no man had ever taken her to passion's glorious peak. All at once, Yellow Bear knew that he wanted to be that man.

He smiled tenderly. "Dream Dancer, when we reach my father's village, I will ask his good friend, Brave Antelope, to let you live with him and his family. Then, with his permission and yours, I will pay you court."

She was flabbergasted, and, for a long moment, could say nothing. At last, she found her voice. "You want me for your wife?"

"Yes, I do," he assured her. "I want to marry you very much."

"But what about those white trappers, can you . . ."

He put a finger to her lips, silencing her. "We will never speak of them. From this moment on, they never existed. Do you understand?"

"Yes," she whispered. "I understand, Yellow Bear."

"Good," he murmured, his eyes regarding her with desire, as well as love. "Now, it is time for sleep."

She rose gracefully, gazed down at him with adoration, and said softly, "Tonight I will dream only happy dreams." She turned around quickly and moved to her bedroll as though she were gliding on air. She had never been happier. Her thoughts went to Black Elk. She was now glad he hadn't wanted to marry her. Yellow Bear would undoubtedly make a better husband; in addition, he was more handsome, and Dream Dancer didn't doubt that he was kinder and more understanding. She wished she could see her parents and tell them the wonderful news. As far as they knew, she had gone to the mountains to enter the spirit world. Once she and the others had reached Iron Star's village, she would ask Yellow Bear to get word to her parents that she was alive and about to get married. Her thoughts took a sudden swing as her gaze moved to Luke, who was in his bedroll. She owed her life, her future with Yellow Bear, and the children she would bear him, to Luke Thomas. If it were not for him, she would now be waiting for death instead of awaiting her marriage. As her gaze lingered on Luke, her heart filled with gratitude. She hoped someday she could help him as much as he had helped her.

The morning dawned sunny and warm. Spring had arrived and summer was near. Down the mountain, across the valleys, and miles away from Yellow Bear and the others, Flying Feather's people were moving toward the sanctuary afforded by their sacred land in the Black Hills.

They were covering the same ground that Yellow Bear and his party had crossed days before.

He-Who-Stands-Tall rode his pony proudly, for he was still savoring his assault on the bluecoats. It had made him feel good to watch the soldiers fall, but, most of all, he was overjoyed that he had shot the officer in charge. He hoped the Great Spirit had guided his bullet through the man's back and into his heart. He-Who-Stands-Tall believed that officer was responsible for Flying Feather's murder. However, if he had known that Langsford wasn't involved, he would still have wished him dead. The warrior hated all soldiers, and prayed earnestly for their extinction.

The sun was creeping toward its summit when three warriors, who had been scouting ahead, returned to He-Who-Stands-Tall and the others with disturbing news. Over the rise, they had spotted a large column of soldiers.

He-Who-Stands-Tall knew these soldiers weren't from Fort Laramie, for they were coming from the north. A stab of fear shot through his heart. Could they be from Fort Swafford? The notorious Major Charles Dwyer was the fort's commander, and He-Who-Stands-Tall, in fact all Sioux, regarded the man as extremely dangerous. As a child, his mother had kept him close to home by telling him Dwyer would steal him away if he wandered too far. Charles Dwyer was the Sioux's version of the bogeyman. As a child, He-Who-Stands-Tall had feared the man as though he were some kind of two-headed monster.

Now, He-Who-Stands-Tall forcefully pushed his childish fears aside. He and his warriors were fearless and strong. They would confront this man and his soldiers,

202

but before he killed Major Dwyer, he would prove that he was not afraid of his childhood monster. He-Who-Stands-Tall carried his coup stick on his horse; he slowly withdrew it, and held it up for all to see. Proudly, he proclaimed, "I will use this to touch the bluecoat called Dwyer before I slay him. I will do so in the face of flying arrows and bullets."

His listeners were duly impressed, for He-Who-Stands-Tall's act symbolized much courage.

Two Kiowa scouts, riding under Lieutenant Dwyer's command, had spotted He-Who-Stands-Tall and his people. They had also located the troopers from Fort Swafford. Donald's soldiers were advancing from the rear, but the company from Fort Swafford was approaching the Sioux head-on. The two military units now had the Indians trapped.

As He-Who-Stands-Tall was proclaiming his prowess, Lieutenant Dwyer's command rode into view. Simultaneously, the soldiers from Fort Swafford appeared over the distant rise. The Indian warrior's heart hammered against his chest, and heavy perspiration beaded his brow. He hadn't expected a flank attack, and was alarmed to find that he and his people were caught between two armies. For a fleeting moment he considered surrender, but quickly dismissed the notion. He suspected the bluecoats were here to arrest him and the other warriors who had taken part in yesterday's attack. Many soldiers had died, and the white man's court would undoubtedly sentence the participating Indians to death. He-Who-Stands-Tall was determined not to perish at the end of a rope. He would rather die making a run for it.

Some of the other warriors felt the same way. A mile or so to their left the landscape was thick with trees and shrubbery, and behind the verdant shelter, wooded slopes led up into a meandering path across the mountainous region. If they could reach the area ahead of the soldiers, they were certain they could then lose them.

The warriors planning to take flight gathered around He-Who-Stands-Tall; the ones who refused to leave stayed close to their families. These Indians, hoping the soldiers intended simply to return them to the reservation, decided to remain with the tribe.

He-Who-Stands-Tall, his adrenaline flowing, bid a proud farewell to his people by raising his rifle and giving a blood-chilling war cry. The warriors with him responded in kind. Their noisy parting was misconstrued; Lieutenant Dwyer, watching from a distance, found their behavior threatening. Certain they were about to charge him and his men, he gave the order to advance with caution.

The soldiers, led by their lieutenant, rode steadily toward the Indians, their rifles unsheathed and ready to fire.

A young warrior, believing they were about to be massacred fired the first shot; his panic set off a full attack. The Indians and the soldiers exchanged fire; meantime, the detachment from Fort Swafford raced speedily toward the battle.

The Indians were now greatly outnumbered, and the soldiers' victory was swift. Dozens of warriors fell dead or badly wounded. Women, children, and old men had been trapped in the cross fire; several of them received injuries, but none were fatal.

The battle's aftermath was filled with children's cries and the wailing of women. The wounded Indians were rounded up and attended by the doctor from Fort Swafford. There was little he could do but stand by and watch the more seriously injured die; He-Who-Stands-Tall, a gaping hole in his chest, bled to death. The Army men had received some minor casualties; the doctor riding with the Fort Laramie troops took care of them.

Lieutenant Dwyer's mood was buoyant. Not only was He-Who-Stands-Tall dead, but his brother had led the Fort Swafford detachment. The brothers hadn't seen each other in months, and their reunion was joyful. They embraced enthusiastically and slapped each other fondly on the back. The Dwyers' resemblance was uncanny. If Charles wasn't twelve years older, they could have passed for twins.

Moving away from the troops and the subdued Indians, the brothers talked in private. Donald told Charles about Sheila's abduction and that he suspected she was White Cloud's lover.

A frown of revulsion appeared on the major's face. "Good God, surely you're mistaken!"

"I wish I were," Donald answered miserably.

"You don't still intend to marry her, do you?"

"Of course not! But I do intend to see White Cloud hang from the end of a rope with his manhood severed from his body!"

Charles chuckled. "You'll never get Colonel Langsford or Major Forster to agree to that. They pamper these damned Indians! However, in a few more days you'll be

205

under my command. Then you can do what you please with White Cloud.''

Donald grinned with anticipation. ''All I have to do is find the swine!''

Charles placed an encouraging hand on his brother's shoulder. ''Don't worry, Donald. I know where Yellow Bear's people are camped. White Cloud will no doubt be there. Soon we'll capture him, and you'll have your revenge.''

Chapter Thirteen

Golden Dove, knowing she was about to see White Cloud, could barely contain her joy. The day the runners from Flying Feather's village arrived with the startling news of her grandson's return, she had reacted with mixed emotions. She wanted desperately to see White Cloud again, but he had chosen a dangerous time to return to the Sioux. Much animosity existed between the whites and the Indians. Even Iron Star had declared war against the soldiers. Golden Dove was afraid the majority of the Sioux would no longer see White Cloud as one of them; he had been living in the white man's world too long. She feared his return might cost him his life!

Despite her anxieties, the thought of seeing him again filled her with happiness. White Cloud had always been her favorite grandchild. She knew she shouldn't feel that way—she should love her grandchildren equally. And she did adore Yellow Bear and Spotted Wing, but White Cloud had always been very special. She supposed her deep feelings came from the fact she had practically raised him. Iron Star's marriage to Red Blanket hadn't really interfered, for her daughter-in-law had generously allowed her to continue caring for White Cloud.

The day Yellow Bear had left with Three Moons and the others to ride to Flying Feather's village, Golden Dove had watched them leave with conflicting emotions. A part of her prayed that Yellow Bear would return with White Cloud, yet her more practical side hoped White Cloud would refuse to come into the mountains. The Black Hills were no place for a white man; they were swarming with hostile Indians.

Yellow Bear had been gone only a short time when Iron Star fell ill. At first, his sickness had seemed mild, but within two days his fever had risen drastically and his condition became critical. Golden Dove knew her son was dying, and only his desire to see White Cloud was keeping him alive. She wasn't sure how she would go on living without Iron Star; she loved him as much as it was possible for a mother to love a child. Since her husband's death, she had lived almost solely for Iron Star and White Cloud. Now she would soon lose her son, and surely White Cloud would return to his white grandfather! She could feel herself shriveling up and dying inside. The thought of her own death didn't sadden her; her life had been her love for Iron Star and her memories of White Cloud. As much as she loved her grandson, she hoped his stay would be very short. After Iron Star died, he might not even be safe in this village. The warriors here were hot headed and despised all whites. They would undoubtedly view White Cloud as an enemy.

Now, as Golden Dove braided her long hair, which was streaked with silver, she thrust her worries aside. A few moments ago, three warriors who had been combing the surrounding area for enemies had ridden back to the village to announce Yellow Bear's return. They had come across his camp, and he had sent them ahead to let everyone know that he was coming home with White Cloud. The warriors had said that three white women, a white man, and an Indian girl were with Yellow Bear. Golden Dove was very curious, and wondered why her grandsons were traveling with these people. Also, she was shocked that they had brought them into the mountains.

When Golden Dove finished grooming her hair, she got off her pallet and moved across the tepee to her son's bed. Red Blanket and Spotted Wing were sitting beside him. The man was deeply asleep, and they hadn't been able to awaken him to let him know that White Cloud would soon arrive.

Golden Dove placed a gentle hand on Red Blanket's shoulder. "I will go outside and wait for my grandsons."

The woman lifted grief-filled eyes to her mother-in-law. "If Iron Star wakes up, I will tell him that White Cloud is on his way." She choked back a sob. She feared her husband would never awaken, at least not in this world.

Golden Dove managed a feeble smile that failed in its attempt to give Red Blanket encouragement. Then, looking at her granddaughter, she asked, "Do you want to come outside with me?"

"No," Spotted Wing mumbled sullenly.

"But why not?"

"I don't care that White Cloud has come back. He is not Sioux, he is a white man!"

"He is your brother!" Golden Dove insisted.

"No, he is no longer my brother!" she spat back hatefully.

Golden Dove preferred to avoid any unpleasantness with Spotted Wing, and she left the tepee. Standing outside, she peered in the direction her grandsons would arrive, but the riders were not yet in sight. She shifted her weight anxiously from one foot to the other. She tried to imagine White Cloud's appearance. Ten long years had passed since she last saw him; he was now a full-grown man. She knew he would be handsome, for he had been an exceptionally good-looking boy. She also knew he wouldn't look much like Iron Star, for he had taken after his mother's side of the family.

She couldn't help but wonder how she would look to White Cloud. The ten years that had separated them had aged her. She wasn't sure of her exact age, but she knew she was around fifty-nine. She had lived with the Sioux since she was sixteen, and it had been a hard, laborious life. She felt as though the years had taken their toll, and that she wasn't nearly as energetic as she should be. She owned a mirror, but hadn't looked in it for a very long time. She had stopped seeing any purpose to it.

In truth Golden Dove judged her looks much too harshly, for she was still attractive. The strenuous life she led kept her in good physical condition, and her slender frame was as supple as that of a woman much younger. Her complexion was smooth and barely wrinkled, and her eyes were bright and vivacious. She actually appeared younger than her years; it was her heart and soul that had given in to age. Inside, she had lost the will to face her remaining days. The many worries preying on her mind didn't help her outlook. Iron Star's impending death; White Cloud's dangerous return; the Sioux's war with the soldiers; the certainty that the white Army would prevail—and most of all, the secret that she had always carried deep in her heart. All the Sioux, including her son Iron Star, believed she was really one of them, but she wasn't. In her heart, she had never forgotten that she was white!

Bart could hardly wait to see his family, and as he rode toward the village, his heart beat with anticipation. From the depths of his memory he recalled each family member in vivid detail. Spotted Wing had been eight years old when he last saw her; now she was a young woman about to be married. That he had missed so much of her life saddened him. In the mirror of his mind, he could still see Golden Dove as she had been the day he had left. Standing outside the tepee, tears rolling down her cheeks, she had watched him ride away with Luke. Looking back, he had kept her in sight for as long as he could. It was hard for Bart to imagine Iron Star ill; he couldn't remember ever seeing his father sick—the man had always been robust and healthy.

Sheila, riding behind Bart, urged her horse alongside his. She smiled tenderly. "Are you excited?"

He grinned somewhat hesitantly. "Yes, I guess I am. I'm also a little nervous about seeing everyone. It's been such a long time."

She understood. "I was always nervous when I knew my father was coming to Kentucky to see me. He was always away so long that I never knew how to act around him when he returned."

"Why would he stay away so long?"

"I don't know. I used to think it was because he didn't care, but now I'm not so sure. I think he simply cared more about his work."

Her admission took Bart by surprise; he hadn't realized that she had grown up believing her father didn't love her. He chastised himself for not taking time to question Sheila about her life. He had been so wrapped up in his own life that he had sorely neglected hers.

"I'm sorry, Sheila," he murmured.

"Sorry?" she questioned. "About what?"

"That I haven't taken time to get to know you the way I should."

"You've had a lot on your mind."

"That's no excuse," he replied, still angry with himself.

"You're wrong, Bart. It *is* an excuse, and a very good one. Besides, there's not much to learn about my life. It hasn't been very interesting. . . ." She smiled pertly. "That is, until I met you. Thanks to you, my life is no longer boring."

"I hope you mean in a favorable way."

Her smile widened. "That depends."

"On what?"

"On how everything turns out."

Bart chuckled heartily. "You're as shrewd as you are beautiful."

Yellow Bear, riding on Bart's other side, got his attention and pointed toward the sky. Cooking smoke from Iron Star's village could be seen swirling upwards to disappear into billowing clouds. The camp was not yet in sight though, for it was situated beyond the grassy hill that lay ahead.

Urging their horses into fast canters, the travelers reached the hill and scaled it quickly. On the other side, a placid river flowed in front of the Indian encampment. The Sioux had made their home in a beautiful, fertile location, and as the riders descended the hill, Sheila admired the stunning scenery. On the horizon, the mountain range loomed magnificently, the towering peaks nearly touching the passing clouds. The land was overflowing with indigenous pines, aspen, and blue spruce. However, the village was situated in the open so that an enemy could never approach undetected.

Camp dogs barked loudly at the visitors as they crossed the narrow river and entered the camp. Several young boys ran over to them, silenced the dogs with sharp commands, then waved eagerly to Yellow Bear. They stared at Bart with puzzlement. They knew he had to be White Cloud, for the other man was too old. But they didn't understand why Iron Star's son looked like a white man. White Cloud's return had been the talk of the village, and the boys had envisioned him as a some kind of phantom warrior returning from a fate worse than death. They were terribly disillusioned. Iron Star's long-lost son was no god, he was a white man, which, in their opinion, made him lower than a snake.

Iron Star's tepee was located in the heart of the village, and the people stared openly at the visitors as they passed their lodges. Their expressions varied from friendliness to downright hostility. Many of the people accepted White Cloud's return with good wishes, but there were others who resented him; these feelings were especially felt by the younger warriors. They didn't consider White Cloud one of the People, but as the enemy.

As Bart neared his father's tepee, he saw Golden Dove waiting for him. The sight of her filled his heart with joy, and brought tears to his eyes. Dismounting, he hurried to her, swept her into his arms, and embraced her tightly.

She clung to him with all her strength, and as tears flowed copiously, she cried with happiness, "White Cloud, I can hardly believe you're here. I never thought I would see you again!"

As Sheila watched their reunion, her own eyes turned misty. She looked closely at Golden Dove, and was surprised to find that the woman didn't seem very old. For some reason, she had pictured Bart's grandmother as elderly. That Golden Dove was not an Indian was obvious, for her silver-streaked hair was the color of seasoned wheat and her eyes as blue as the sky.

Bart and his grandmother were speaking in the Sioux tongue, and when Bart all at once appeared troubled, Sheila wondered why. Had his father died? She didn't think so, for Yellow Bear had joined Bart and Golden Dove, and he didn't seem upset.

Bart was indeed troubled, for Golden Dove had just told him that Spotted Wing no longer considered him her brother.

"Where is she?" he now asked Golden Dove.

She waved a gesturing hand toward the tepee. "She is with Red Blanket and Iron Star."

Spotted Wing chose that moment to step outside and glare maliciously at Bart.

Her anger tore into his heart. He cursed his stupidity for thinking he could ride back into her life as though he had never been away. She had been a child when he left, and she probably could barely remember him. In her mind, he was nothing more than a hated white man. Stepping back, Bart looked her over from head to foot. She had grown into a lovely woman. Her slender frame was softly curved, hair, as black as ebony, cascaded to her waist; her facial features, accentuated by pronounced cheekbones, bore little resemblance to those of her white forefathers.

"Spotted Wing . . ." Bart began, his tone tinged with pleading.

She cut him off sharply. "Go back to your white grandfather! We do not want you here!" She spit on the ground, emphasizing her disgust. "You are a traitor, and I hate you!"

Yellow Bear intruded forcefully. "Spotted Wing, that is no way to talk to White Cloud! He is still our brother!"

"He is no longer *my* brother!" she retorted, then, wheeled about and stalked away.

"I am sorry," Yellow Bear said to Bart. "But Three Moons has much influence on our sister, and he has hardened her heart."

"I suppose she has every right to feel the way she does. But before I leave, maybe I can find a way to reach her."

"I would not count on it, my brother."

Bart spoke to Golden Dove. "May I see my father?"

"Yes, but I think he is asleep."

"Then I will sit with him until he awakens." He indicated Sheila and the others. "Where can my friends stay?"

"You and Luke can stay with me in my tepee," Yellow Bear answered. "I have decided that Dream Dancer will live with Brave Antelope and his family, but I will take the other women to Talking Deer's home. She is Brave Antelope's mother. She is a widow and lives alone, but her son provides for her. She does not live with Brave Antelope because she does not get along with her daughter-in-law." Remembering, Yellow Bear laughed softly. "Brave Antelope was married only a short time when he moved his mother into her own tepee. He said he could no longer bear the women's bickering."

Bart turned and looked at Sheila. "You and the others will be fine. After I talk to my father, I will come see you."

Golden Dove, watching her grandson, saw that his eyes were tender as he talked to the young woman. She suspected that he was in love with her.

"Grandmother," Bart said, "later I will introduce you to everyone, but now I'd like to see Iron Star."

Golden Dove was looking the group over. She recognized Luke, and nodded to him. He responded by tipping his hat.

She faced Bart and said for him to come with her. She pushed aside the tepee's leather flap, bent over, and went inside. Bart followed, closing the flap behind him.

It was dark inside; the only light came from above through the smoke opening. After a moment, Bart's eyes adjusted to the change, and he saw Red Blanket sitting at Iron Star's bedside. She got quickly to her feet and bid him a warm welcome.

He took her into his arms and hugged her tightly. He had only fond memories of his stepmother.

The women stood back as Bart moved to his father's bed and sat beside him. The man was still asleep, and Bart hoped he wasn't unconscious. He touched Iron Star's brow; he was burning up with fever. A water-filled bowl was within reach, in which a piece of cloth was soaking. Bart wrung it out and used it to wash his father's face, chest, and arms. As he carried out his ministrations, he examined Iron Star closely. He couldn't be sure, but he suspected he had lost a lot of weight; still, the man's tightly muscled physique was impressive. Bart gazed into his father's face. He could see a resemblance to Golden Dove, but Iron Star had taken mostly after his father, High Hawk. Despite his illness, he was still a handsome warrior, and Bart could easily understand why his mother had fallen in love with him.

Minutes dragged by, and Bart had been with his father for almost an hour when Yellow Bear came inside. He sat beside his brother, and said quietly, "The others are settled." He looked closely at Iron Star, and was saddened to see the spirit of death on his face. "Our father is dying," he mused aloud.

"Yes, I know," Bart replied somberly. "If only he would awaken so I could talk to him!"

"He will!" Golden Dove spoke up. She had been sitting at the cooking pit, but she now came forward and joined her grandsons. "Only his desire to see White Cloud has kept him alive. He will not die without seeing

217

his firstborn." She placed a consoling hand on Bart's shoulder. "White Cloud, your father loves you very much. He always has."

A stab of guilt, as sharp as a knife, jabbed mercilessly into Bart's heart. Dear God, had he been wrong to leave his Sioux family? He had believed his place was with J.W. Could he have been mistaken? *Mistaken, hell!* he thought angrily. *I stayed with J.W. because I preferred his way of life over my father's! Spotted Wing was right, I am a traitor! I betrayed Iron Star!*

As though Golden Dove could read his mind, she said strongly, "You must not feel guilty, White Cloud. Your father understood why you left—it was the Great Spirit's wish."

Bart appreciated his grandmother's kind encouragement, but it did little to ease his guilty heart.

Talking Deer saw to her guests, then left the tepee. She walked importantly through the village, for she knew she was the center of attention. After all, she had three white women in her home, and her neighbors would indeed be curious to hear all about them. And in no time at all, she was surrounded by inquisitive women, asking all sorts of questions at once.

Inside Talking Deer's tepee, her guests were experiencing varying emotions. Sheila's thoughts were centered on Bart. She wondered how he was. Seeing his father under such grave circumstances had to be very hard on him. Amanda's mood was as somber as Sheila's; however, her mind was completely on Luke. He was still treating her as though she were a mere acquaintance, and she desperately longed for a more personal relationship. Unlike her companions, Janice's disposition wasn't grim, but sour. She resented being in this village and wanted to leave as soon as possible. That she had been so rudely coerced into making this trip was infuriating to her.

"Lord, what I wouldn't give for a bath and clean clothes!" Janice complained. She had never felt so filthy.

Her companions were in complete accord, and their wishes coincided with hers.

"When I see Bart, I'll ask him what can be done," Sheila decided.

"I suppose we'll have to bathe in the river," Janice replied crankily. "I doubt these Indians even know what a bathtub is."

"The way I feel," Amanda began, "I wouldn't mind bathing in a horse's water trough if it was the only way to get clean."

Sheila voiced her agreement.

At that moment, Bart came inside. Golden Dove was with him, and he introduced her to everyone.

"How is your father?" Sheila asked him.

"The same. I'd have been here sooner, but I kept hoping he'd wake up and talk to me. I can't stay, because I want to be at his bedside when, or if, he comes to. I'm sure you ladies are longing for clean clothes and baths. Golden Dove will tend to everything." Bart's eyes captured Sheila's. "I'll be back as soon as possible."

Again, Golden Dove noticed the way her grandson looked at the young woman. She was now quite certain that he was in love with her.

Sheila watched as Bart left the tepee. Her heart ached for him, for she had seen the pain in his eyes.

Golden Dove, speaking English, said, "I will get soap, clean clothes, then take you downstream so you can bathe." Her gaze measured each woman.

Janice, finding her scrutiny rude, asked, "Why are you looking at us like that?"

"I need to find clothes that will fit all of you."

"What kind of clothes?" Janice asked, her eyebrows raised sharply.

"Indian apparel, of course." She met the young woman's skeptical stare. "Unless you prefer to put your dirty clothes back on. Or course, if you please, you can wear nothing at all."

Huffing, Janice retorted, "You don't have to be nasty!"

Golden Dove, not bothering with a reply, turned around to leave, but was detained by Sheila's sudden question. "Please, what was your white name?"

She found the question odd, but saw no reason not to answer, "Margaret Latham. Why do you ask?"

"My father has been in the Army for a long time, and he might know of your family."

"My family is here," Golden Dove said. Although she spoke softly, her tone was nonetheless firm. Promising to return soon, she left the tepee.

Sheila was quite taken with Bart's grandmother. She said to Amanda, "Golden Dove speaks English very well, doesn't she? You'd think after so many years, she would have forgotten most of it."

"I'd say she made sure she didn't forget. Apparently,

she has spoken English every day. Most likely, to herself.''

"That means she never really became a Sioux," Sheila
murmured thoughtfully. "Deep in her heart, she's still
Margaret Latham.''

Chapter Fourteen

Sheila bathed and washed her hair as quickly as possible. The river was warm and she was tempted to remain in the water for a while, but Golden Dove was at the bank washing their clothes and she was anxious to help.

Leaving Amanda and Janice still bathing, Sheila made her way to shallow water and onto dry land, where she dried herself with a blanket.

Golden Dove watched her with admiration. She thought the young woman quite beautiful, and could see why her grandson was obviously smitten with her. Golden Dove called to her, lifted a bundle of clothes, and handed them over. "I think these will fit," she said.

Sheila looked first at the dress, which was made of deerskin. She slipped the garment over her head; the soft leather was pleasant against her skin. The dress, fringed and ornamented with colorful beads, was really striking. Golden Dove had also brought her moccasins decorated with quills. Sheila put them on and was pleased that they fit. A sash came with the dress. She tied it around her waist, and this final touch completed the outfit.

"How do I look?" Sheila asked Golden Dove.

"You're very beautiful. No wonder my grandson loves you."

"Loves me?" Sheila questioned, thrilled. "Did he tell you that?"

Her delight was so apparent that Golden Dove had to smile. "No, he didn't tell me. But I can tell."

Sheila wanted to believe her, but she was afraid to allow her hopes to soar too high, for Bart might send them plunging back to earth. If he was in love with her, then why hadn't he told her?

She got her brush and ran it through her long tresses briskly but thoroughly. Golden Dove had returned to her laundry, and kneeling beside her, Sheila began to help.

"Golden Dove," she began, "your English amazes me. Considering how many years you've been with the Sioux, I should think you'd have forgotten most of it."

"Teaching English to others has kept it fresh in my mind."

"I'm sure it has," Sheila replied, watching her speculatively. "But I think it's more than that. English is the only link you have left to Margaret Latham. Is that why you won't let yourself forget?"

"You're a very extraordinary young lady. You've only known me a few hours, and already you have seen into my heart." She sighed heavily, turned to Sheila, and admitted somewhat wistfully, "Yes, I never wanted to forget who I really am."

"Did your husband know this?"

She shook her head. "He wanted me to be Sioux in every way. I loved him and longed to please him. He never knew. No one knows."

"But if you feel this way, why didn't you leave the Sioux along with Bart?"

"Let me explain. I didn't want to forget who I am, true, but that didn't mean I longed to return to my former life. Or maybe I should say, to living with whites again. Our people, Sheila, can be very cruel and unforgiving. Most of them would have scorned me, ridiculed me, and found me repulsive. Why should I leave the Sioux who love me and respect me, to return to my own people who would degrade me?"

Sheila started to disagree, but Golden Dove held up a silencing hand. "I know what you're about to say. But, trust me, not *all* our people would be so cruel, but most of them would. I see no reason to subject myself to their cruelty when I'm perfectly content with my husband's people. Furthermore, Yellow Bear and Spotted Wing need me. They're my grandchildren, and I love them very much. I would never leave them."

"But you wanted Bart to leave?"

"It was the Great Spirit's wish."

"It was also your wish, wasn't it?"

Golden Dove smiled faintly. "He was still a child, and I knew our people wouldn't scorn him. Why shouldn't I want a better life for him? If his mother had lived, she would have felt the same way. Bart belonged with J.W.

Chandler; this way of life was not for him. He's more white than Indian. The road the Great Spirit sent him on was the right one."

"Do you really believe in the Great Spirit?"

"Don't you?"

"I believe in God."

"Then you believe in the Great Spirit." Golden Dove smiled, touched her arm, and murmured, "They are one and the same."

Amanda and Janice came out of the river, dried themselves, then took the clothes Golden Dove handed them. Amanda, finding the Indian apparel quite lovely, was anxious to get dressed. Janice, however, turned up her nose as though the garments were offensive. But she didn't voice a complaint; she knew she had to wear the Indian clothes or keep a blanket wrapped about her nakedness. Certain every warrior in the village coveted her body, she wasn't about to have only a blanket between her and their lust.

With help from the others the laundry was done quickly and spread over bushes to dry. The women were about to return to the village when Dream Dancer found them.

The girl's eyes were shining brightly and a radiant smile was on her face. Her words tumbled forth. "Yellow Bear say I can now tell wonderful news. He and I will soon marry!"

"Dream Dancer, I'm so happy for you!" Sheila exclaimed.

Golden Dove and Amanda extended their good wishes.

Dream Dancer, appearing a little embarrassed, murmured, "Now I feel foolish that I wanted to die."

Sheila laughed. "Love can work miracles, Dream Dancer!"

"Yes," she replied. "But I owe my happiness to Luke. He save me from dying. He is a good man."

Amanda, listening, agreed wholeheartedly.

Bart, sitting at his father's bedside, stretched his cramped muscles. He was alone with Iron Star. Yellow Bear had been there earlier; he had left saying he would return soon. Bart was considering getting himself a cup of coffee when Iron Star stirred and moaned in his sleep. Hoping he was about to awaken, Bart moved closer to the bed and laid a hand on the man's shoulder.

"Father," he said softly. "Can you hear me?"

Iron Star moaned again, and his eyelids fluttered. He came to slowly, his mind struggling back to consciousness. He looked at Bart through a hazy blur, blinking his eyes in a futile effort to bring them into focus; but his son's face remained blurry.

"Father, do you know who I am?"

"I cannot see you very well, but yes, I know who you are. You are my firstborn. I do not have to see you to know you are here. I can see with my heart."

"Forgive me for waiting so long to come back."

"It is good that you stayed away. You do not belong here, White Cloud. You must leave."

"No, I cannot do that! I will not leave until you are well."

"I will not get well, White Cloud. But I am grateful that my heart has seen you one last time. You are the child my first wife bore me, and that makes you very special. Your mother was my greatest love. Soon I will see her again. She waits for me in a world much better than the one I leave behind.''

Bart's eyes filled with tears. ''Father, my heart tells me that I should not have left you.''

''What does your mind tell you?''

''Not to listen to my heart.''

The barest trace of a smile touched Iron Star's lips. ''Sometimes, my son, the mind is wiser than the heart. Do not torment yourself, White Cloud. You took the life the Great Spirit chose for you. It is wrong to question the Great Spirit's wisdom.''

Bart, ridden with guilt, wished it were that simple. But the ten years he had spent away from Iron Star tore into his conscience. This man was his father, and he felt as though he had deserted him.

''These past days,'' Iron Star began, his voice growing weaker, ''I stayed alive because I knew you needed me.''

''Needed you, Father?''

''Yes, to take away your guilt. After I fell ill, a vision came to me. I was riding my favorite horse through the woods when a half-grown white buffalo appeared before me. I reined in and stared at this young buffalo who so bravely blocked my path. He turned his head, gesturing for me to ride ahead and look at what lay beyond. I rode past him and to the edge of a cliff. A dead buffalo lay at the bottom. I asked the white buffalo, 'Why did you want me to see this?' He replied, 'That is my father. I am young and foolish. I was showing my prowess and running at full speed. I did not know that a cliff lay before me. My father, desperate to save my life, raced ahead of me to block my fall with his body. But I skidded into him, and sent him over the cliff. Now my father is dead, and my guilt is heavy.' The young buffalo said no more. He simply raced past me and leapt over the cliff. His dead body then lay beside his father's. When I awoke, I knew the spirits had spoken to me. I could feel that your guilt was as heavy as the white buffalo's. I am still alive, my son, to tell you that it is wrong to feel that way. The life you have led was not of your choosing, but I feel that it has been a good life.''

"It *has* been good, Father.''

"Your grandfather, is he a honorable man?''

"Very much so.''

"Have you been happy with him?''

"Yes, I have.''

"Then your heart should be grateful, not guilty.''

Bart smiled warmly. "I am very proud to be your son.''

"A father can ask for no more. I want to talk to Red Blanket, Golden Dove, and my other children. Please find them for me.''

Bart clasped his father's hand, squeezed it gently, then left the tepee to locate his family.

Dusk was covering the land when Bart went to Talking Deer's lodge and asked Sheila to walk with him. She was anxious to be with him, and agreed readily. Taking her hand, he led her down to the river's bank and away from the village.

Coming upon a well-concealed area where they could be alone, Bart stopped, turned to her, looked at her with admiration. "You look very beautiful." He looked over her Indian apparel, noticing the way the pliable garment adhered smoothly to her ample breasts and rounded hips.

She read desire in his eyes, and her heart reacted at once. Never had she felt such an amorous response to any man. With Bart, she was totally vulnerable. If he were to draw her into his arms, she knew she would be his for the taking.

He smiled tenderly, reached out and traced her face with his fingertips. "You're so lovely," he murmured, his deep voice tinted with passion.

"Thank you," she whispered. A blush rose to her cheeks, causing her to be a little angry at herself. He probably thought she was impossibly naive.

Bart, however, found her wonderfully refreshing. A lot of women as beautiful as Sheila flaunted their good looks, used them to manipulate, and were completely wrapped up in themselves.

"How . . . how is your father?" Sheila asked, his masculine closeness causing her to stammer.

Bart stepped back. "He's dying."

"I'm sorry," she murmured. "Have you talked to him?"

"Yes, for a few minutes."

"Seeing you again must have been very wonderful for him."

A scowl crossed his face. "I shouldn't have waited so long to come back. If I had returned sooner, I could have seen my father healthy. But no, I had to stay at the Triangle-C and think only of myself!"

"Bart, I don't believe that! You aren't capable of thinking only of yourself. Furthermore, how could you foresee your father's illness? He's still quite a young man. There was no reason for you to feel that you had to rush into the mountains to see him.''

''Rush?'' he questioned harshly. ''Good God, I waited ten years!''

''You mustn't punish yourself like this. I'm sure Iron Star doesn't think you deserted him.''

''No, he doesn't,'' Bart replied. He recounted his conversation with Iron Star. He even told her about Iron Star's vision.

''Your father sounds very impressive. You have good cause to be proud of him.'' She paused, then spoke somewhat hesitantly. ''Bart, I'm ashamed to admit this, but before all this happened, I never really thought about the Sioux's plight. I never even thought of them as individuals. I simply saw them as a whole. I didn't hate them as a lot of people do, but I didn't try to understand them either. I suppose I just found it easier to close my mind and look the other way.''

''That's understandable, since you never had much contact with them. And considering you're engaged to Dwyer, I'm amazed he didn't convince you to despise Indians as much as he does.''

Sheila lifted her chin defiantly. ''I'm not easily swayed. I have a mind of my own!''

''So I have noticed.'' A grin lit up his face.

His smile was charming, and it sent a wave of warmth flowing through her. Again, she became physically aware of him, and the surging power of his presence was spellbinding.

Sheila's response was reflected in her eyes, and Bart read the invitation in their dark depths. His heart raced

231

with passion as he suddenly drew her into his arms. He felt as though he had waited a lifetime for this moment. He held her so tightly that her body was molded to his; he could feel her womanly curves pressed against him. Bending his head, he kissed her demandingly, urgently, his lips overpowering hers with compelling persuasion.

Passion, suddenly born but nonetheless forceful, sent tremors through Sheila as she returned Bart's kiss. Never had she imagined that a man's kiss could arouse such a response; ecstatic, rapacious, and all-consuming love burned within her like wildfire.

Bart released her with reluctance; he wanted to make love to her and possess her completely. But he was too much a gentleman to take advantage of her.

Sheila, wanting him desperately, asked tremulously, "Bart, is something wrong?" Had she somehow disappointed him?

He smiled a little shakily. "Sheila, I wonder if you have any idea how much I want you."

"Yes, I think I do," she replied. "And I want you, Bart. I want you with all my heart."

"It wouldn't be right," he said. "I won't take advantage of you."

His chivalry didn't surprise her; his kindness was one of the reasons she loved him. A twinkle, as bright as it was seductive, shone in her eyes. "Bart Chandler, if you won't take advantage of me, then I shall take advantage of you." She slid her arms about his neck and pressed her body to his.

"Heed my warning; if I make love to you, I'll consider you mine for now and always." He spoke gently, yet there was a serious undertone that left no doubt in Sheila's mind that he meant what he said.

"I love you, Bart," she confessed. "And heed *my* warning; you will belong to me as much as I belong to you."

"That's the kind of warning I like to hear," he murmured thickly, before claiming her lips in a captive caress.

Bart, his rekindled passion blazing hotly, removed his shirt, placed it on the grass, then guided Sheila down upon it. He lay beside her, brought her close, and kissed her again.

Her hands feathered over his bare shoulders. She admired his lean, muscular strength. Explosive sensations ruled her heart and mind, sending reality soaring into space. Forgotten was her father, her fiancé, and the perilous situation surrounding her. She was conscious of nothing except Bart's lips on hers, his body agonizingly close, and the unanswered ache that was now spreading between her thighs.

Bart carefully untied her sash, then drew her dress up and over her head. She wore no undergarments and a warm breeze touched her bare flesh. Dusk had given away to night, but the moon's luminous glow fell across her body, illuminating her loveliness. Bart feasted upon her ravenously with his eyes, and he found her more desirable than any woman he had ever seen. His gaze hungrily raked her full breasts, the dark triangle between her thighs, and her long, shapely legs. Such perfect beauty almost drove him beyond the realm of rational thought. The male animal in him was tempted to take her aggressively, for he had never been so sexually aroused. But he controlled the powerful need, and kissed her gently and with exquisite tenderness. Then, slowly, his fingers etched a path over her warm flesh, exploring her thoroughly.

Responding freely, she writhed and moaned beneath his experienced touch, trembling with breathtaking ecstasy.

Bart's lips now traveled the path his hands had mapped, and as waves of new and compelling rapture washed over her, Sheila cried out, her passion soaring to even greater heights. She watched through love-glazed eyes as Bart raised himself up to undo his trousers. She made no protest as he moved to kneel between her legs. She wanted to consummate their union with all her heart and soul. Every fiber of her being was crying out for him. He freed his erect manhood, and she daringly wrapped her fingers about him. With a fevered groan, he placed his hand over hers, showing her how to give him pleasure. Sheila, ecstatic that her touch could affect him so profoundly, had never felt more like a woman.

Sheila's intimate caress nearly drove Bart over the brink, and he quickly moved her hand away. Suddenly, his mouth took hers in a savage assault that was totally consuming, intensifying the ache centered between her thighs. She wanted him. How desperately she wanted him.

"I love you, Sheila," he whispered tenderly, his hardness gently seeking entrance.

Sheila's aunt had prepared her for this moment, and she knew what to expect. Clinging tightly to Bart, she braced herself for a moment of pain.

His arm encircled her waist, lifting her thighs closer to his. Slowly, he sank into her warm depths; as he encountered the proof of her virginity, he paused only long enough to say again that he loved her. Then, not wanting to prolong her pain, he sheathed himself deeply inside her.

Sheila's soft outcry was smothered by his ardent kiss. He began gentle, steady strokes, and her pain was soon supplanted by a feeling of euphoria. She instinctively met his erotic rhythm, and, clinging to him, she whispered his name with deep longing.

Their bodies blended in love's union, each thrust carrying them higher and higher into ecstasy. Their desire became exquisite agony, causing their hips to pound more rapidly, driving them almost to passion's edge.

Bart's lips sought hers and captured them with punishing sweetness. Now his need was more than he could bear, and he dove into her deeply, time and time again, ultimately taking her with him to a wondrous fulfillment.

Sheila's ragged breathing matched Bart's, and his whispered endearment was breathless as he moved to lay at her side. He drew her possessively close, holding her as though he never intended to relinquish her.

She snuggled contentedly. Their lovemaking had been all she had dreamed it would be—even more so! "I love you so much," she told Bart softly.

He kissed her brow. "Will you marry me, Sheila?"

"You better believe I will!" she replied.

He chuckled. "As soon as we get back to civilization, I'll make an honest woman of you."

"Just for that male-focused remark, I might refuse to marry you." She smiled saucily.

"You'll marry me, all right, if I have to abduct you a second time!"

She was about to respond when Golden Dove's voice reached them. She was at a distance, but they could still hear her clearly. She was calling for Bart.

Bart quickly helped Sheila back on with her dress, then, as he was straightening his own clothes, she hastily ran her fingers through her mussed hair.

He took her hand, led her out of the foliage and into the open. Standing at the river's bank, he called to Golden Dove, "We're over here!"

Golden Dove appeared within a few moments. Her face was pale and haggard. "Come—you must hurry!" she said to Bart. "It's your father! We're losing him!"

Bart squeezed Sheila's hand, and his eyes stared sadly into hers.

"Go on," she encouraged him.

He was gone quickly, leaving Sheila and his grandmother behind.

Sheila went to Golden Dove and murmured sympathetically, "I'm sorry about your son."

She nodded numbly. Losing her only child was a hard cross to bear.

Chapter Fifteen

Iron Star's people knew their chief had been dying, so his death came as no surprise. However, their grief was none the less for having known they would lose him. Iron Star had been a popular chief, among the old as well as the young.

Golden Dove felt the loss of her son as acutely as the others, but Iron Star was gone and there was nothing more she could do for him. She knew she would have the rest of her life to mourn and that for now she must set her grief aside and think of White Cloud. As long as Iron Star had lived, he was safe here, but she felt that he and his friends were now in great danger. She would insist that they leave without delay. She sent word to White Cloud that she wanted to see him at once.

She was alone in her home when Bart arrived. His

sorrow was apparent, and her heart went out to him. She was sitting at the lodge fire, and motioned for him to join her.

He sat beside her, then took her hand and held it tightly. "Are you all right?" he asked.

"Yes," she murmured. "I sent for you because I want you to leave right away. Don't even wait for your father's burial ceremony."

"Why must we rush?"

"You and your friends are not safe here. The young warriors do not see you as Sioux; they think of you as a white man. Three Moons will be back soon, and he will incite the others. If you won't leave to protect yourself, then leave for the safety of your friends. You brought them here and are responsible for them." Her hand, enclosed in his, tightened. "I do not speak rashly, White Cloud. You and the others are in grave danger!"

He didn't dispute it. He had seen hostility on the faces of several warriors. "I will leave, Grandmother," he said softly. "But I want you to come with me."

She shook her head. "I don't want to leave. My place is here with Yellow Bear and Spotted Wing." Her tone was suddenly imploring. "White Cloud, please try to understand. Do not make this any harder for me! Losing you again is breaking my heart, but the pain will be easier if you do not press me."

"I understand," he acquiesced. A rueful smile touched his lips. "I really do understand, Grandmother."

She smiled through tears. "I wish you much happiness, White Cloud. Marry Sheila. She is a good woman and will make you happy. Now, you must go to the others and tell them to prepare to leave."

238

"All right. We will leave first thing in the morning."
He kissed her cheek, then got up and was stepping outside
when Spotted Wing appeared.

She started to brush past him and step inside the tepee,
but he caught her arm. "We must talk," he told her.

She flung off his hand. "I have nothing to say to you!"

"I'm leaving in the morning. If we don't talk now, we
never will."

"Good!" she spat out.

"Spotted Wing, why do you hate me so much?"

"I hate all white men."

"But I am your brother!"

"Are you?" she questioned furiously. Her eyes swept
over him with disdain. "You look like a white man to
me. You dress like one, act like one, and in your heart
you *are* one. I have only one brother, and he is Sioux!
Yellow Bear is my brother, you are not!"

"The clothes I wear don't change my blood. We share
the same forefathers."

"Yes, but you have forsaken yours!" She lifted her
chin angrily. "I am proud to be Sioux! I will soon marry
Three Moons, and he will proclaim a great war against
the white man. We will run you and your kind off our
lands."

With that, she pushed aside the tepee's flap and went
inside to see Golden Dove. Bart, knowing further talk
was pointless, didn't try to stop her.

He stopped at Yellow Bear's lodge to speak to Luke,
then went to Talking Deer's tepee to tell the others that
they were leaving.

* * *

239

Back at Fort Laramie, Lieutenant Dwyer and Major Forster were at the officers' club drinking brandy when the fort's doctor, Major Reed, found them. Pulling up a chair, he sat at their table.

"Colonel Langsford is out of danger."

"That's good news," Forster replied, meaning it sincerely.

"However," the doctor continued, "I told him he must apply for a medical retirement. After several threats to put in the paperwork myself, he finally agreed to do it."

"Is his injury permanent?" Forster asked.

"No, he'll mend. But the colonel has advanced rheumatism. In my opinion, he isn't physically able to continue his duties. He plans to move to Kentucky and buy a home close to his brother and his wife. Of course, he doesn't intend to leave until his daughter has been found, however."

"Speaking of Miss Langsford," Dwyer said to Forster, "she is the reason I asked you here for a drink. I want to lead an all-out search for her. That might take weeks, and I don't have that much time left at Fort Laramie. Sir, if you'll grant me an early transfer to Fort Swafford, I can organize a search party from there. Major Dwyer has already given his permission."

"I see no reason to deny your request, Lieutenant. I'll have your transfer papers in order by tomorrow."

"Thank you, sir."

Forster's expression turned grim. "I certainly hope you find the colonel's daughter. But I shudder to think what atrocities she has suffered."

Atrocities? Dwyer thought bitterly. He was certain

Sheila didn't consider White Cloud's sexual assaults atrocious. Quite the contrary, the lustful trollop was no doubt enjoying herself! He was filled with rage and could hardly wait to reach Fort Swafford, organize a detail, and begin his search. But he wasn't really looking for Sheila—he no longer gave a damn about her. He wanted to find White Cloud. He'd make the savage sorry that he had stolen what was supposed to be his.

As Lieutenant Dwyer was plotting revenge, Bart was telling Sheila and the others that they were leaving in the morning. The news was met by unanimous approval. They had all sensed the simmering hostility in the village and were anxious to be on their way.

Bart spoke to Amanda and Janice. "We'll take you ladies to Fort Laramie. From there you can make traveling arrangements to return to St. Louis." He regarded them with concern. "Do you ladies have any money?"

Janice answered harshly. "Of course not! Our husbands spent every dime we had to hunt for gold!"

"We aren't completely without funds," Amanda told her. "I sewed a few dollars in the hem of my skirt. Before Golden Dove washed my clothes, I told her about the money. She said she would remove it and put it in a safe place."

"Well, that money will get us back home, but then what?" Janice complained.

"You have relatives in St. Louis. I'm sure they will help you."

Janice pouted. She had relatives, all right. But she didn't like any of them.

241

"What about you?" Bart asked Amanda.

"I have an uncle who lives close to St. Louis. His home is in St. Charles. I'm sure I can stay with him."

"Well," Luke spoke up. "It seems everybody has some place to go. Now, all we gotta do is get out of these mountains with our scalps still intact."

Janice gasped. "Are you saying we might not make it to Fort Laramie?"

"Comin' here, we had Yellow Bear along for protection. Goin' back, we ain't got no one but ourselves. Yellow Bear can't come—he's a wanted man."

Sheila's eyes darted to Bart's. "Are we really in danger?"

"I won't lie to any of you. Yes, there is some danger. But the odds of making it out of these mountains alive are in our favor."

The group talked a few minutes longer, then Bart and Luke, reminding the women they planned to leave at dawn, left for Yellow Bear's tepee.

Sheila, following, called to Bart. He sent Luke on to the tepee, and walked back to Sheila.

"I must talk to you," she said.

He took her arm and guided her to the river. They walked a short way downstream before stopping. Sheila hadn't seen him alone since Iron Star died, she put her arms about him. Holding him close, she murmured, "I'm so sorry about your father."

He clung to her tightly for a moment, then kissed her softly before releasing her.

"Bart," she began. "I need to talk to you about Janice and Amanda. When we get back to the fort, my father

242

will ask a lot of questions. They are bound to tell him
who you really are.''

"Yes, I know," he replied. "I guess I'll have to face
the consequences."

"Maybe not," Sheila said. "If you have no objections,
I'll ask Janice and Amanda to keep your identity a secret.
I've given this considerable thought, and I think we
should tell my father that White Cloud stayed behind with
Yellow Bear."

"And where does Bart Chandler fit in?"

"There's no reason to mention you. I think you should
forget Fort Laramie and go directly to Texas. We will
tell my father that White Cloud set us free, and Luke got
us back to the fort."

"And what about us?" he asked. "You said you would
marry me."

"I will," she assured him. "I'll come to Texas with
Luke."

"And what excuse do you intend to give your father
for going to Texas?"

She sighed impatiently. "What difference does it
make? I'll think of something. Bart, right now, my only
concern is protecting you."

"I appreciate your concern, Sheila. But if I confess to
abducting you, there's not too much the Army can do
about it."

"They'll have you arrested."

"But I might get off with a sharp reprimand."

"But you might get a prison sentence!"

"I'm sorry, Sheila," he said stubbornly. "I don't think
can hide behind a woman's skirts!"

"What does that mean?"

"Exactly what it implies. I won't have you lying for me."

"That's not the way you felt before!"

He frowned. "I should never have abducted you in the first place. But, damn it, now I can't run from the consequences. Don't you understand? I have too much pride!"

She did understand. Bart was a man of principles, and she knew he would stand behind them firmly. She fought back tears. "But what if you go to prison?"

"I'll manage if you promise to wait for me."

"I'll wait," she cried, flinging herself into his arms. "I'll wait a lifetime!"

"Well, let's hope it won't be that long," he said, trying to lighten the atmosphere.

"Oh, Bart!" she sobbed. "I love you so much!"

He kissed her. "I love you, too."

He drew her as close as possible. He was pleased that she was willing to lie for him, for that meant she cared with all her heart. But Bart had decided to face the consequences of his actions, whatever they might be. Even if he received a prison term, it was worth it, for Yellow Bear's life had been spared.

He moved Sheila away from him so that he could gaze down into her face. "In the beginning, my plan to take you back to the fort as Bart Chandler was simple. But things are now much more complicated. I think we must abide by the adage that honesty is the best policy. Our love will see us through."

"You make it sound so easy," she murmured.

"I know it won't be easy. But considering who we are and how we feel, it's the only course we have. I won't live a lie, and I don't think you want to live one either."

She didn't, not really. She went back into his arms, and clung to him with all her strength. She was overcome with admiration for him. No wonder she loved him so much!

Janice was standing outside the tepee when Sheila and Chandler returned. "I need to talk to you," she blurted out to Bart.

He waited until Sheila had gone inside before taking Janice's arm and leading her down to the river. They stood on the bank; the myriad of stars reflected in the water glittered as brightly as diamonds.

Janice moved closer to Bart, and slipped her arm in his. "Do you mind?" she asked, feigning a timid smile.

"What do you want to talk to me about?" he asked, sounding impatient. He had a feeling Janice was about to try to use her flirtatious charms on him.

Bart's feeling was right. However, Janice wasn't certain how to go about it. She had never encountered this particular problem before. Enticing a man had always been easy; she never had to put forth much effort— her beauty alone was enough. But to her dismay, Bart Chandler didn't seem to be smitten with her looks. She gazed up at him, batted her long lashes, and said sweetly, "Bart, I hope you don't find me too forward, but I want to let you know . . ." She purposefully paused, appeared somewhat embarrassed, then continued. "I want you to know that I'd like for us to become better acquainted. I mean, we've been traveling together a long time, yet we barely know each other.''

Bart repressed an amused smile. The lady wasn't very subtle. His eyes swept admiringly over her voluptuous body. She was indeed an attractive woman. Her borrowed Indian apparel clung seductively to her curves, and her auburn tresses were the color of a red sunset. Looking deeply into her eyes, he read the sensual invitation smoldering in their depths.

He removed her hand from his arm, stepped back, and said evenly, "I don't think there's any reason for us to become better acquainted. There would be no purpose to it.''

"But why not?'' she asked.

"Earlier tonight I asked Sheila to marry me.''

"Well, it would seem that I waited too long to let you know how I feel.''

"It wouldn't have made a difference. I think I fell in love with Sheila at first sight.''

"You surprise me, Bart. I would never have thought you had such romantic notions.''

"I didn't, not until I met Sheila.''

Sheila! Sheila! Sheila! Janice thought heatedly. The man was apparently stuck on the name. Didn't he know how to talk about anyone else? Seeing no reason to fight a losing battle, however, she decided to dismiss Bart as unattainable. She was bitterly disappointed though, for she was terribly attracted to him and would have relished conquering him. Also, she suspected that he was a virile, exciting lover, and, in her experienced opinion, such men were few and far between.

She smiled flirtatiously, ''Well, if you should change your mind . . .''

''I won't,'' he was quick to say. He took her arm. ''I'll walk you back to the tepee. You need to get some sleep, as we'll be leaving at dawn.''

He took her to the lodge, bid her a terse good night, then left.

As Janice stepped inside, Sheila merely glanced at her, then looked away. She assumed Janice had wanted to be alone with Bart so she could flirt with him. Her presumption didn't spark any jealousy. She had confidence in Bart's love, and trusted him completely.

The next morning, everyone was ready to leave before the sun had fully risen. Most of the villagers stayed inside their homes, for they saw no reason to bid farewell to their visitors. Too many of them resented their presence and were glad that they were leaving.

As Luke and Yellow Bear saw to the horses and mule, Golden Dove invited the others inside her tepee, where she gave them packages of food that she had prepared for their journey.

Tears kept threatening, but Golden Dove fought them back. She felt that she would never see White Cloud again. She loved him dearly, had loved him since the day he was born, and now for the second time she would have to watch him ride out of her life. It was almost more than she could bear. But she believed his leaving was the right thing for him to do.

Yellow Bear, pushing aside the tepee's flap, stuck his head inside and told Bart that the horses were out front.

Janice, anxious to leave, mumbled a quick goodbye to Golden Dove and hurried outside, where Yellow Bear helped her up onto her horse. Amanda's farewell was much warmer. She embraced Golden Dove and thanked her for her kindness. Then she, too, left the tepee.

Spotted Wing, sitting in a corner, hadn't uttered a word since Golden Dove had brought her guests inside. Now, Sheila glanced over at the girl, and was taken aback by the look of hate on her face. For a moment their eyes met, and Sheila could tell that Spotted Wing wished she was dead. She was certain it wasn't personal. The girl simply despised anyone who was white.

Going to Golden Dove, Sheila hugged her fondly. "I wish you would come with us."

"My place is here." Golden Dove smiled warmly. "White Cloud told me that you are marrying him. I am very happy for both of you."

"Thank you," Sheila said. She hugged her again, then left quickly so Bart could be alone with his grandmother and sister. Bart, determined to make one last attempt to reach Spotted Wing, went to her and sat down. She moved back, recoiling, as though he were repulsive.

"Spotted Wing, I may never see you again. Can't we part with warmth, if not with love?"

"Go away, white man. I hate you!" She glowered at him.

Bart pressed on. "Spotted Wing, think back. When you were a child, don't you remember how you used to follow me around like a little puppy? I was never impatient with you. In fact, I often let you accompany me on my pony. I sat you behind me, and as we raced across the plains, you'd pretend that I was a warrior who saved

248

you from a terrifying death. And remember all those walks we took in the woods, and how we would discuss our futures . . ."

"Stop it!" she demanded. "Yes, I remember those days. They are gone forever! The brother I loved then is dead!"

"No, I'm *not* dead. I'm still the same brother!"

She bounded to her feet and glared down at him. "You are my enemy, and the enemy of every Sioux! Go back to your own people! I pray to the Great Spirit that my eyes never see you again!"

Bart, torn, watched as she stalked outside. With a heavy sigh, he got up and walked to Golden Dove.

"I am sorry," she said. "But Spotted Wing thinks like Three Moons. Her thoughts are no longer her own."

"Now that my father is gone, will the council appoint Yellow Bear as chief?" Bart didn't speak the name of Iron Star, for it was the Sioux custom not to speak the name of a deceased person.

"He is your father's son. I am sure he will now be chief." She touched Bart's arm in an encouraging gesture. "You must leave. The sun is climbing quickly. It is best that you be gone before the people begin their day."

Bart took her into his arms and held her close. "I love you, Grandmother."

She embraced him tightly, then stepped back. "Go, White Cloud. My love goes with you." She handed him the packages of food.

Bart had to force himself to turn away from his grandmother and walk outside. Leaving her ripped into his heart. He attached the fare onto the mule, then went to

Yellow Bear, who was waiting for him. Dream Dancer, having already said her goodbyes, was standing beside Yellow Bear.

"Goodbye, my brother," Yellow Bear said to Bart, sadness in his voice.

They embraced for a long moment, then Bart swung up onto his horse. Golden Dove had come outside to see him off. Yellow Bear went to her and put an arm around her shoulders. Bart's gaze settled intently on the pair; he wanted to implant their images forever in his mind. With effort, then, he tore his gaze away, kneed his horse, and started out of camp.

The others followed closely, and they soon reached the nearby hill and rode to the top. Reining in, Bart looked back at the village. He could barely make out Golden Dove and Yellow Bear, who were still standing outside the tepee. He lifted his hand and waved to them.

They returned his parting gesture, then watched as he turned his horse around and disappeared over the rise.

Chapter Sixteen

Amanda awoke with a start. She was trembling and her heart was pounding. She had been dreaming again about her husband's death, and the nightmare had been horribly real. She flung off her blanket and sat up. Her eyes swept over the quiet campsite. Sheila and Janice were asleep, Bart was taking the first watch, and Luke was sitting by the fire.

Amanda was surprised that Luke was still awake; he would take the second watch and needed his sleep. They had been on the trail now for days, and their journey was almost over.

She got up, moved to the fire and sat beside him. The coffee pot was still warm, and she poured herself a cup.

"Couldn't you sleep?" Luke asked.

"I *was* asleep, but I had a bad dream."

" 'Bout your husband's death?" he guessed.

"Yes," she replied heavily. "I keep reliving it in my dreams."

Luke turned his face to her, and looked at her closely. The gash on her forehead was healing well and wouldn't leave a scar. "Maybe you cared for Norman more than you realized," he speculated.

"No, I know exactly how I felt. I cared, I cared very much, but I was never in love with Norman. He wasn't a good husband or provider. Norman was too wrapped up in himself to be aware of someone else's feelings. But he wasn't all bad. At times, he could be very likable and charming. He was also quite handsome, and had a way with women. He had several romantic liaisons."

"If he was cheatin' on you, why didn't you leave him?"

She spoke wistfully, and so softly that Luke barely heard. "I didn't leave him because I was just as guilty. In my heart, I was unfaithful to him every day of our marriage."

Luke guarded his emotions. "If you're about to tell me that you never stopped lovin' me, then do us both a favor and don't say it. You can't come back into my life after twenty years and act as though what happened between us took place a short time ago. Too much has transpired. I'm sorry your marriage wasn't as happy as you thought it would be. But you've got no one to blame but yourself. You didn't have to marry Norman Wilson. You knew I was comin' back for you!"

"Luke, why were you gone so long?"

"When I left St. Louis, I told you I had to trap all winter to make enough money for us to get married. I also told you I might not make it back by spring, but that it could be as late as early summer. Well, I got back in June, only to learn that you had married someone else.''

"Yes, my father told me that you came to the house.''

"Yep, I sure did!,'' he said. "I came to tell the woman I loved that I was back!'' He chuckled bitterly. "Your father seamed to enjoy tellin' me that you married Wilson, and no longer lived there. He sure as hell didn't want you to marry me. He never thought I was good enough for you.'' Luke shrugged as though it wasn't really important. "I reckon he was right. Why would he want his educated, high-society daughter to marry a man like me? Hell, I ain't got much learnin', and what little I got my ma taught me, and I don't think *she* knew all that much.''

"Your lack of schooling never mattered to me.''

"Hell, Amanda, I can't even read or write more than a few words.''

"It's never too late to learn.''

"I'm forty-four years old. It's too late for *me*.''

"That's nonsense. You may not be schooled, but you're still a very intelligent man. Learning to read and write would not be a problem.''

"Who's gonna teach me?''

"I will,'' she was quick to offer.

"Haven't you forgotten somethin'?''

"What's that?''

"You're goin' back to St. Louis.'' It sounded more like an order than an observation.

"Yes, I'm going back,'' she agreed. "For a moment I forgot. But Sheila and Bart are getting married. I'm sure if you asked her, Sheila would tutor you.''

"I'll think about it," he mumbled.

A cold reserve had come over Luke. Amanda could sense it—almost feel it. She knew he wanted her to go away, go back to bed and leave him alone. She finished her coffee quickly, muttered good night, and returned to her pallet.

Luke remained at the fire, staring thoughtfully into the darting flames. He could still feel Amanda's presence: her image was clear in his mind. Her mussed hair, falling past her shoulders, had created a sensual vision, and the flickering flames reflected in her hazel eyes had been entrancing. Why, after twenty years, did he still have to find her so damned desirable?

Thrusting her from his thoughts, Luke went to his bedroll and lay down. However, despite his efforts to erase Amanda from his mind, a long time passed before he finally fell asleep.

Much later that night, he relieved Bart and took the last watch, which would last until morning.

Dawn was breaking when Bart was awakened by Luke's hand on his shoulder. "There's a group of soldiers camped in the valley," Luke said. "We didn't spot 'em last night 'cause they didn't have a fire. You reckon we oughta contact 'em?"

Bart, sitting up, answered, "Yes, I think we should. They might be a detachment from Fort Laramie. Also, we must consider the women. They'll be a lot safer if we travel with the Army."

Luke agreed. "Let's wake them, have something to eat, then ride down to the soldiers."

Luke started to move away, but Bart stopped him. "Luke, wait a minute. When are you going to tell me about you and Amanda Wilson?"

"What do you mean?"

"Don't hedge with me, Luke. Sheila told me that you and Amanda know each other."

"I met her in St. Louis years ago. I fell in love with her, but she jilted me and married someone else. That's all there is to it."

Bart eyed him knowingly. "It's not that cut and dried, Luke. But if you don't want to talk about it, then I won't press you."

"Well, now that we got that settled, I'll wake up the ladies."

Bart watched his friend as he sauntered over to the women. He had always suspected that Luke had been hurt by love. Luke had never said anything directly, it was just a feeling Bart had. He wondered if Luke was still in love with Amanda. If he had to bet on it, he would say that he was.

The women were glad to hear that soldiers were nearby, but Janice was by far the most elated. Since leaving Iron Star's village, she had lived each day in fear of an Indian attack. Thank God, the Army was now here to protect her!

They ate their morning meal, repacked the supplies onto the mule, then headed for the soldiers' camp.

The unit was getting ready to leave when the group rode into view. The troopers looked them over curiously as they entered their camp.

Captain Harrison, the officer in charge, came forward to greet them.

"Bart wished them a good morning then introduced himself and the others.

The captain stared incredulously at Sheila. "Are you Colonel Langsford's daughter?"

"Yes, I am," she replied.

"Ma'am, I'm stationed at Fort Swafford, but we were notified of your abduction." His gaze went over her. "Apparently you're all right." He turned back to Bart. "Mr. Chandler, I insist that you and the others accompany me back to Fort Swafford."

"We're going to Fort Laramie," Bart replied.

"No, sir! You're coming with me! I intend to see to it that no harm comes to Colonel Langsford's daughter. At the fort, a wire can be sent to her father. If he wants her to come to Fort Laramie, then she will be given a military escort."

Bart didn't argue, for he knew the captain was adamant. He did, however, dread going to Fort Swafford. He knew Charles Dwyer was the post's commandant, and he didn't want to come face-to-face with him. He hadn't seen him since he led the massacre on Iron Star's village and he had hoped he would never have to see him again.

Harrison spoke to Janice and Amanda. "Ladies, a few days ago a patrol from Fort Swafford came upon four men who had been killed by Indians. Do you know anything about this?"

Amanda told the captain what had happened. She finished by asking where her husband was buried.

"The soldiers buried the men where they found them." He didn't tell her that wild animals had found the bodies first and there hadn't been much left to bury. The captain continued. "I'm very glad that you found our camp.

256

When the patrol returned to the fort and reported the deaths, Major Dwyer sent us to look for survivors. It would seem our mission is a success. Incidentally, we passed an abandoned wagon a few miles back. I suppose it's yours."

"Yes, it is," Janice told him. She favored the officer with an alluring smile. "Please Captain, may we go to our wagon? All my belongings are in it." A worried frown suddenly wrinkled her brow. "The wagon wasn't ransacked, was it?"

"No, ma'am, not that I could tell. It appeared as though it was searched, though—probably by the Indians who attacked you. However, we found three chests inside containing ladies' clothes."

Janice beamed. Thank goodness, she still owned a wardrobe!

The soldiers were ready to leave, and the captain told his sergeant to break camp. The troopers mounted, and Harrison gave the command to pull out. The column rode in a formation of twos, but they left a center space for the civilians. That way, they could better protect them.

Sheila rode between Bart and Luke. She had an uneasy feeling about going to Fort Swafford. Not only was she hesitant about meeting Donald's brother, but she was afraid for Bart to see him. The massacre had taken place ten years ago, but she knew it was still very real in Bart's mind.

Luke's thoughts were the same as Sheila's. "When you see Charles Dwyer, you gotta keep calm," he said to Bart. "You can't do nothin' 'bout what happened ten years ago."

"I know that," he replied. "I don't intend to start

257

anything. However, he's going to realize that Bart Chandler and White Cloud are the same person. After all, he was there when you informed me that I was J.W. Chandler's grandson.''

Luke was worried. "You might be in a heap of trouble.''

"Sheila's abduction has nothing to do with Fort Swafford. If I'm arrested, I'll be taken to Fort Laramie.''

Sheila didn't say anything, but she had made up her mind that Bart's arrest would never take place. She was ready to swear that she had not been abducted but had left with Bart of her own free will. She hadn't told Bart about her decision because she knew he would be opposed to it. He had made it quite clear that he didn't want her to lie in order to save him. Her thoughts suddenly shifted to Donald. She wasn't sure how long she had been away from Fort Laramie; the days had seemed to run together. But she was fairly sure that Donald's transfer hadn't yet been activated. She was thankful for that. She preferred to confront him at Fort Laramie on her father's turf. She had a feeling he would react angrily to what she had to tell him.

The wagon was located, and its contents were removed and crammed into the Army supply wagon. Farther down the road, the column came upon the area where Amanda's husband and the others were buried. The captain respectfully ordered his troops to halt, and he gave Amanda a moment alone at the graves. There was no way of knowing which one was Norman's.

That her husband would spend eternity in a shallow,

unmarked grave saddened Amanda. She didn't want to grieve in front of strangers, but she couldn't hold back the tears as she returned to her horse. To her amazement, Luke dismounted, went to her, and held her close for a moment. He then helped her back on her horse, and offered a tender smile before moving away.

Harrison was anxious to reach the fort, and didn't stop to make camp until after nightfall. Bart, knowing the truth would come out at Fort Swafford, drew Janice and Amanda aside, and with Sheila and Luke looking on, he told them what he thought they should know about Sheila's abduction. At break of dawn, they continued onward. The captain, setting an arduous pace, insisted they ride steadily through the day and into the night. The land had been shrouded in darkness for hours before the weary travelers finally approached Fort Swafford. The sentries on duty quickly opened the heavy gates and admitted the troops.

The captain motioned for the civilians to follow; they came to a halt in front of Dwyer's office. Two young soldiers promptly took their horses and led them to the stables.

Sheila took a quick glance about the fort. Compared to Fort Laramie, it was sorely lacking. It was much smaller, and several of the log-constructed buildings leaned obliquely, giving the impression that they were about to fall. She had heard that the post had been built hurriedly and without much planning. Now, after seeing it, she knew the rumor was true. She had also heard that the Army was considering closing it down.

The sentry standing at the major's door saluted Harrison, then stepped inside and announced the captain.

Harrison, followed by the others, walked into the office. Major Dwyer was sitting at his desk, but got quickly to his feet. The captain, indicating Sheila, immediately informed his commanding officer that he had found Miss Langsford.

Charles's resemblance to Donald gave Sheila quite a start. Their likeness was uncanny. She was aware that another soldier was present, but she hadn't really looked at him. Now, as she turned her gaze to the other man, she gasped out loud and exclaimed, "Donald! What are you doing here?"

Bart moved closer to Sheila. The lieutenant's presence made him uneasy. If the bastard dared to lay a hand on her, he would kill him!

Donald was as shocked as Sheila, and it took a moment for him to find his voice. "What am *I* doing here? What in hell are *you* doing here?"

"My friends and I were on our way to Fort Laramie, but Captain Harrison insisted that we come here instead."

He didn't consider her answer much of an explanation. Later, he would get the whole truth. "I received an early transfer," he told her. "I had planned to organize a search party to look for you, but that is no longer necessary, is it?" His eyes, staring into hers, were accusing.

She wasn't intimidated. "No, that isn't necessary," she replied calmly. She faced Charles Dwyer. "Major, I insist that you allow my friends and me to leave in the morning for Fort Laramie."

"Insist?" he repeated, a brow raised sharply. "I think not, Miss Langsford. All of you will stay here until your father can be notified." He looked her over. She was very beautiful; he could see why his brother had wanted

260

to marry her. Turning from Sheila, he studied the two women with her. He found them exceptionally attractive, and he was especially drawn to Janice. He could see a strong resemblance between her and his dead wife.

Captain Harrison quickly told the major what he knew about Amanda and Janice.

Charles's gaze then moved on to Bart and Luke. He immediately recognized Thomas. He was surprised to see the mountaineer after so many years.

"Luke Thomas," he said thoughtfully. "I figured you were dead, scalped by Indians or chewed up by a grizzly bear."

"You ain't seen me, 'cause I left these parts."

The major spoke to Bart. "What's your name?"

"Bart Chandler," he replied.

"Chandler?" Charles mused aloud. Enlightenment suddenly shone in his eyes. "Of course. Chandler! Well, I'll be damned! You must be J.W.'s half-breed grandson! The last time we met, you were a scrawny kid."

"And you had just led a raid on my father's village," Bart added, his tone as hard as steel. "A raid that killed women and children!"

The major laughed coldly, for he had just put the pieces together. "I also remember your Indian name," he said to Bart, a sly grin curling his lips. "I heard it recently, but it didn't ring a bell. But now it's clear. Your Indian name is White Cloud!"

"What?!" Donald burst out. "You mean, this man is Yellow Bear's brother?"

"In the flesh," Charles said. His grin was now like that of the proverbial cat who swallowed the canary. Then, suddenly, his expression changed, and he shot

261

Captain Harrison an official look. "Place Mr. Chandler under arrest."

The captain started to obey, but was stopped by Sheila's sudden outcry. "Wait! You have no reason to arrest Bart!"

"No reason?" Charles said forcefully. "He abducted you and aided in Yellow Bear's escape!"

"If you arrest him, then you'll have to arrest me, too. You see, he didn't abduct me. I conspired with him to save Yellow Bear."

"She's lying!" Bart intruded. "She wasn't involved."

"I'm sure she wasn't," Charles concurred. "Miss Langsford, your attempt to help Mr. Chandler is very admirable, but totally unacceptable." He again told the captain to arrest Bart.

Sheila watched, helpless, as Harrison slipped Bart's pistol from its holster, then led him outside at gunpoint. With her anger barely under control, she said to the major, "I want a wire sent to my father at once, telling him to come here immediately."

"That will be taken care of in the morning. Now, it's quite late, and I'm sure all of you would like a hot meal before retiring. Our accommodations are lacking, but I do have a fairly comfortable home and a cook. You will all be my guests for dinner. Afterward, I'll arrange suitable sleeping arrangements." He moved out from behind his desk. "Please follow me. I'll take you to my home."

"Charles," Donald said. "Take the others, but leave Sheila here. We need to talk. I'll bring her to your quarters later."

"Of course." The major was quick to comply. He

opened the door, and gestured for the others to leave with him.

Luke hesitated. He didn't like leaving Sheila alone with Lieutenant Dwyer. But she understood his hesitancy, and assured him that she would be all right.

The moment the others were gone, Donald tore into her furiously. "You cheap little harlot! You've given yourself to that half-breed, haven't you?"

She lifted her chin defiantly. "What if I have?"

He drew back his arm and slapped her across the face. "You whore!"

The vicious whack brought tears to her eyes, but she held them in check and responded by slapping him back. "You bastard!" she uttered fiercely.

"I should break your neck!" Donald raved.

"And just how would you explain that to my father?" she countered. Her eyes shot daggers at him.

It wasn't easy for Dwyer to bridle his temper, but he somehow managed. When the time was right, he would get even with her, but this was neither the time nor the place. First, he had to plot his revenge.

He turned away, moved to the liquor cabinet, and poured himself a brandy. He swallowed a liberal amount before facing Sheila again, trying to collect himself. "I suppose you're in love with White Cloud."

"His name is Bart Chandler."

"Excuse me," he said mockingly. "Bart Chandler."

"Yes, I'm very much in love with Bart. We're getting married. I realize I owe you an explanation. I didn't plan on falling in love with another man; it just happened. But I had decided to call off our engagement even before I fell in love with Bart. Our marriage would never have worked. I wasn't in love with you. I agreed to marry you because you and my father pressed me."

"Don't you have any decency?" he asked, his tone tinged with revulsion. "How could you give yourself to an Indian? You're worse than any barroom whore!"

"In the first place, Bart is not exactly an Indian! He's three-quarters white and is also an educated gentleman. And in the second place, even if he were a Sioux in every sense of the word, I would still have fallen in love with him!"

Donald laughed derisively. "I can't visualize you living in a wigwam and raising papooses!"

"No, I suppose you can't! Now, if you don't mind, I'd like to join my friends."

He gulped down the remainder of his brandy and put away the glass. "Very well, madam. But don't think this completes our business. I have more to say to you, but it will have to wait."

"Don't waste your breath, Donald. I'm not interested in hearing anything you have to say."

Regarding her intently, he cursed himself for still desiring her. Her riding apparel was frayed and stained in places, her hair was wind-blown, and she was covered with trail dust, yet she stood before him as regally as a queen, her beauty breathtaking!

Donald didn't want to marry a woman who had been with another man, especially one with Indian blood. He did, however, long to take Sheila to his bed. Imagining her unclothed and at his mercy, was sexually arousing. His manhood, growing erect, strained against his confining trousers. He routed the lustful picture from his mind as he went to Sheila, grabbed her arm, and ushered her outside.

As he led her toward the major's quarters, he silently vowed to have Sheila at his beck and call. He would find a way to force her to do his bidding! A nasty grin spread across his face. He would break her rebellious spirit— one way or another!

Chapter Seventeen

Major Dwyor's home had two bedrooms. The larger one was his, but the second bedroom was a spare, containing a double bed and a bureau. He decided two of the ladies could sleep there. He'd spend the night on the sofa and let the last of the women use his room. Luke could stay in the barracks. Tomorrow, he would have a cot moved into the second bedroom. Sheila and Amanda offered to bunk together, which pleased Janice. Having a bed to herself sounded heavenly.

Following dinner, Luke left for the barracks, and Sheila and Amanda retired to their room. Janice, however, joined Charlcs in the parlor for a nightcap. He poured a brandy for himself and a sherry for his guest.

The parlor's furniture was threadbare and badly worn, and except for two woven rugs, the floor was uncovered.

Drab-colored curtains framed the windows, and cheap paintings hung on the walls.

Charles noticed that Janice was eyeing the decor critically. "I'm sorry," he said, "that my home is so shabby, but this fort is old and has never been renovated. The Army is considering closing it down, because it would cost too much to remodel it. I really don't care what they decide, for I hope to transfer soon. My brother and I hope to join General Custer's 7th Cavalry." Reverence shone in his eyes. "There's no one I admire more than George Custer!"

Janice couldn't have cared less if he received his transfer or not. She had no real interest in Charles Dwyer. Not only did she consider him too old for her, but she wasn't about to marry a soldier. The next time she married, it would be for money.

Janice sat on the sofa, and Charles promptly joined her there. He took a sip of his brandy and turned to her. "You remind me of my wife," he said. "She died ten years ago. She had hair the color of yours."

This remark annoyed Janice. She didn't like reminding him of another woman. She wanted all men to find her beautifully unique. She changed the subject. "What will happen to Mr. Chandler?"

"I'm not sure," he replied. "Considering his grandfather is J.W. Chandler, he'll most likely get off scot-free."

"Is J.W. an important man?"

For a moment he was astonished that she hadn't heard of J.W., but then, remembering she was from St. Louis, he explained, "J.W.'s name is well known in the West.

He's a cattle baron and one of the richest men west of the Mississippi River.''

"He's rich?" she repeated, giving Charles her undivided attention.

"Not only is he wealthy, but he's close with generals and politicians. The man has a lot of influence. That's why Chandler will probably go free.''

Janice was impressed. Bart's grandfather was rich, which meant someday Bart would inherit a fortune. Oh, if only he wasn't infatuated with Sheila! What she wouldn't give to marry Bart and share in his riches! In addition, he was irresistibly handsome. Such a husband would certainly sweeten the kitty! A wave of despair washed over her, though. Bart was not available—thanks to Sheila Langsford!

The front door suddenly opened, and Donald barged into the room, cutting into Janice's thoughts.

"Excuse me," he said, his apology sounding perfunctory. He looked at Charles. "I must talk to you.''

Janice finished her sherry and placed the glass on the coffee table. As she got up, so did Charles.

"I'm sorry about my brother's intrusion," he told her.

"That's all right. It's late and I'm very tired. Good night, Major, and thank you for your hospitality.''

"You're more than welcome, and please call me Charles.''

She smiled sweetly, said good night to Donald, and left.

Charles turned angrily to his brother. "Your interruption is inexcusable! I was trying to get better acquainted with the young lady!''

"I'm sorry," Donald replied. "But I really must talk to you."

The major's anger waned, and he poured himself another brandy, and one for Donald. He returned to the sofa and watched as the younger man, drink in hand, paced the room anxiously.

"Charles," he began, sounding desperate. "When I was courting Sheila, I behaved as a perfect gentleman. I wanted very much to take her to bed." He rubbed a hand over his brow. "God, how badly I wanted her! But I held myself in check. I was determined to wait until our wedding night. Well, as we both know, now that night will never come. But, damn it, I still want her. I don't care if it's only one time, but I've got to have her!"

"I sympathize with you, Donald. But I don't know how I can help you."

"Think, Charles! Surely, there's some way I can get to her!"

"If you want my help, then sit down and stop pacing like a male dog caged from a bitch in heat. I can't think otherwise. Your pacing is too distracting."

Donald perched on the edge of a chair. As he sipped his brandy, he watched his brother expectantly. He was certain Charles would think of something.

Time passed, and Donald was drinking his second glass of brandy when Charles finally came up with an idea. "You say you don't care if you have her only one time?"

"Once will suffice."

"In that case, I have a plan that might work."

Donald's spirits rose. "What is it?"

"It's obvious that Sheila is in love with Chandler. You can get to her through him."

"How?" he asked, excitement bubbling.

"To start with, Chandler will never see a day in prison. His grandfather has too much influence. So we might as well set him free."

"What?" Donald exclaimed. "I want that bastard dead!"

"Don't worry, Chandler won't live past tomorrow. In the morning, I'll release him. After he leaves the fort, he'll be ambushed. We can trust Sergeant Kent to take care of that for us. He'll make it look as though Chandler was killed by Indians."

"But what about Sheila?"

Charles grinned. "Listen closely, and I'll tell you exactly what to do . . ."

The next morning, Sheila awoke early. Amanda was sleeping soundly, and Sheila dressed quietly so she wouldn't disturb her. Last night, Amanda had looked through her cedar chest and found a dress and a pair of shoes that fit Sheila. She slipped into the gown quickly, put on the shoes, then moved to the bureau and brushed her hair.

Leaving the bedroom, she closed the door soundlessly behind her. She went to the dining room, where she found Major Dwyer at the table, eating breakfast.

He pushed back his chair and stood up. "Good morning, Miss Langsford," he said politely. His eyes traveled over her. She was a picture of loveliness. Her borrowed gown was white percale with dark-blue polka dots, and the same royal-blue shade bordered the hem and low neckline. Sheila's rich brown tresses, brushed back from

271

her face, fell past her shoulders and halfway down her back. Her delicate nose and lips were exquisitely feminine, but her most remarkable feature were her coffee-brown eyes that were perfectly framed by dark, arched eyebrows. Charles Dwyer found her incredibly beautiful, and he could understand Donald's obsession with her.

He drew out a chair, helped her be seated, then sitting next to her, he poured her a cup of coffee.

Dwyer's cook, a middle-aged Kiowa woman, asked Sheila what she would like for breakfast.

"Nothing, thank you," she replied. She was much too worried about Bart to eat.

The woman went back to the kitchen, and Charles remarked that Sheila should eat something. "Skipping meals is unhealthy, Miss Langsford," he added.

"I'm not hungry," she said tersely. She came straight to the point. "Major, I want to see Bart."

"The stockade is no place for a lady."

"I don't care! I insist that you let me see him!"

"I'll think about it," he replied evasively.

Her temper rose. "I also want to send a wire to my father."

"I'll see to that myself."

"Major Dwyer," she began angrily. "I am not your prisoner. How dare you refuse to allow me to wire my father!"

"Miss Langsford," he said, sounding very tolerant, "I have to send a wire to the colonel anyhow, and sending two is totally unnecessary."

"But I don't want him simply notified that I've been found, I want him to come here!" Surely, she could convince her father to help Bart!

"I don't think it's possible for the colonel to travel."

"Why ever not?" she demanded.

"He was seriously wounded."

"Wounded?" she cried. "But how. . . . When?"

"He and his troops were attacked by a band of warriors from Flying Feather's village. Your father was shot in the back. However, I'm glad to report that he will make a complete recovery."

"Thank God for that!" Sheila said. She looked questioningly at Dwyer. "But I don't understand why Flying Feather's warriors would attack soldiers. Flying Feather's people are at peace with the Army."

"They were, and they are again. The warriors who led the attack are either dead or back on the reservation." He explained in more detail, "Donald went to Flying Feather's village to ask about you and Yellow Bear. The chief deliberately lied and was arrested. He was shot while trying to escape."

"Shot? Was he killed?"

"Yes, he was. And that's why his warriors attacked your father. Apparently, they thought the colonel's troops were responsible for their chief's death."

A hardness came to Sheila's eyes. "Who killed Flying Feather? Was it Donald?"

"Yes."

"Your brother is a cold-hearted murderer! Flying Feather was an old man; he couldn't possibly have escaped. Donald killed him for no reason at all."

"Miss Langsford, I find your remarks concerning my brother quite offensive. He is a soldier and was merely carrying out his duty. Obviously, you have allowed Bart Chandler to prejudice your views. You are a white

273

woman, and Colonel Langsford's daughter. You should be more loyal to your own people.''

''Loyal to a murderer like Donald? Never! Also, I heard about your raid on Iron Star's village! Apparently, you and Donald are two of a kind!''

Dwyer didn't say anything, he merely stared at Sheila with a blank expression. In a way, he admired her frankness. Nevertheless, in his opinion, she needed to be taught a lesson. If Donald wasn't so obsessed with humbling her, Charles would have enjoyed doing it himself.

Charles glanced at his pocket watch. It was time for his brother to arrive. The two had plotted carefully last night, and this morning Donald would put their plan in motion.

Donald suddenly entered the house and joined his brother and Sheila in the dining room. He exchanged a conspiratorial glance with Charles, then looked at Sheila. ''I must talk to you alone.''

She didn't trust him. ''What about?''

''About Chandler.''

''He's all right, isn't he?''

''For now.''

''What do you mean by that?''

''You'll know exactly what I mean after we talk.'' His arm made a sweeping gesture toward the parlor. ''Shall we?''

She pushed back her chair and got to her feet. She walked to the parlor with outward composure; inside, though, her stomach was tied in knots and her heart was pounding. She somehow knew that Donald's visit carried a terrible import.

Folding her arms tightly, Sheila stood in front of the

sofa and stared unflinchingly into Donald's eyes. "All right, we're alone now. Tell me what you have to say."

He found her impertinent and could hardly wait to have her at his mercy. He chuckled to himself. Mercy? He planned to show no mercy!

"I intend to give you a chance to save Chandler's life," he said calmly.

Her body went rigid. "What do you mean?"

"Unless you agree to cooperate fully, Chandler will be shot while trying to escape."

"Is that the only way you know how to kill?" she blazed furiously.

"I don't understand." He was truly confused.

"I'm referring to Flying Feather's death."

Donald smiled. "Ah, yes! And Chandler will be just as dead as Flying Feather if you don't agree to my terms."

"Are you mad? You can't kill Bart! The Army didn't care that you murdered Flying Feather, but it will care very much if you kill Bart. He's a white man."

Donald was relieved that she didn't mention J.W. She evidently wasn't aware that Bart's grandfather was a very influential man. He had counted on her not knowing.

"Chandler might be a white man in most people's opinion, but he posed as a Sioux warrior, abducted you, and helped Yellow Bear escape. He committed a crime, and it is my brother's duty to place him under arrest. If Chandler should attempt an escape, and my sergeant is forced to shoot him to protect himself, then it's clearly a case of self-defense."

"Bart won't try to escape."

Dwyer raised an eyebrow. "Sheila, you're smarter than that. Must I draw you a picture?"

"No!" she spat fiercely. "You sorry bastard! Bart will be shot in his cell, won't he? Then his body will be carried outside to make it look as though he was trying to escape."

He grinned. "That wasn't too difficult to figure out, was it?"

"You'll never get away with it!"

"Why not? Do you plan to run to my brother?"

"Of course not! He's probably in on it. But there are other officers on this fort."

He went to her, grabbed her wrist, and held it in a viselike grip. His eyes, staring into hers, were deadly serious. "If you dare speak to any officer, I promise you Chandler won't live to see another sunrise! There's a deserter locked in the same cell with him. If you talk to any officer on this fort, he's agreed to kill Chandler. In return, he'll be allowed to escape." This was a lie; Donald hadn't approached the deserter. It was merely a well-calculated ploy to keep Sheila from going to one of the fort's other officers. He could see by the fear in her eyes that she believed him. Pleased, he continued in a icy tone. "If necessary, one of the guards will slip a knife to the deserter and he will plunge it into Chandler's heart. Make no mistake, madam. If you don't live up to your part of the agreement, Chandler will cease to exist!"

"Agreement?" she lashed out, breaking his hold on her wrist. "What kind of agreement?"

He shrugged as though it wasn't of any real importance. "It's very simple, Sheila. Tonight you will come to my quarters, get undressed and into my bed. I will join you there, and you will let me do whatever I please. You will not fight, and you will not refuse anything I ask of you. In return, you will be compensated, for tomorrow morning Chandler will be set free. On that, you have my word and my brother's.''

She stared at him as though she couldn't believe what she had just heard. ''You must be mad!''

''Mad? I think not. I merely want what is mine!''

''You are mad!'' she came back furiously. ''I'd rather die than succumb to you!''

''But it isn't *your* life that's threatened, is it? It's Chandler's. The question isn't if you're willing to save yourself, but if you're willing to save your lover.''

She loved Bart and would do anything to keep him alive. There was no reason to think over Donald's threat; there could be only one answer. A sickening sensation settled in the pit of her stomach. ''All right, I'll agree to your terms,'' she murmured.

He smiled with satisfaction. ''I thought you would see it my way.''

Anger, vivid in its intensity, flared in her eyes. ''I swear to God, Donald, if you don't honor your part of the agreement, I'll kill you!''

She sounded like she meant it, and, for a moment, Donald's confidence was shaken. But he quickly regained his poise. The arrogant bitch would pay dearly for making such a threat. When Bart left in the morning, he'd personally see to it that she left with him. During the ambush, she would die along with her lover. He laughed inwardly—the Army would think the Sioux had killed them. His sergeant and the men who would ride with him intended to use unshod Indian ponies. After they killed their victims, they would take their scalps. The sergeant was as cold-blooded as the Dwyer brothers, and he had agreed readily to the ambush, for he enjoyed the privileges that came his way when he cooperated with officers. The three men who would accompany him, however, were not quite so eager. But the Dwyers had obtained their alliance through bribing them, which hadn't been very difficult. They were an unsavory threesome who would kill anyone for the right price.

Donald stared into Sheila's fiery eyes. "Threats are unnecessary," he said calmly. "I will honor my part of the bargain."

"Surely you must realize that I'll tell my father everything."

"Tell him if you wish. By then, it will all be over and he can do nothing. It will be your word against mine. Furthermore, your father is retiring. He will have no authority over me or my brother. In fact, by now his retirement papers have probably come through." Donald hid a complacent grin. Sheila would never say anything to the colonel, or anyone else, for by this time tomorrow she would be dead!

Sheila felt completely defeated. Donald had her blocked at every turn. There was nothing she could do but cooperate. Imagining the degradation that lay ahead sent a shiver of revulsion up her spine.

She forcefully thrust the night ahead of her to the back of her mind. "When can I see Bart?" she asked.

"In the morning. In fact, if you wish, you can leave the fort with him."

"I will. You can count on it!"

"And if Bart learns about this," she continued, "he'll kill you!"

"Who's going to tell him? You? I don't think so. Why

would you go to such lengths to save his life, only to put it in jeopardy again? If he were to kill me, he would certainly be arrested and tried. Also, my dear, I'm sure you'd rather he never knew about tonight.''

She was filled with a furious hate. The cold-hearted cad had her totally beaten!

''If you'll excuse me,'' he said, his tone mocking, ''I must be about my duties. I have a lot of work to keep me busy. There's a bedroom off my office. Be there tonight at ten o'clock, naked, and in my bed.'' Self-confidence and lust shone in his eyes. ''You know what, my darling? You might find tonight pleasantly surprising.''

With that, he turned on his heel and left the room.

Sheila, emotionally drained, dropped down on the sofa, tucking one foot under her. She was utterly defeated, for Donald had shrewdly covered every angle.

She was suddenly aware of another's presence, and, looking up, she saw Major Dwyer poised in the doorway. A knowing smile was on his face.

''Miss Langsford, you seem distraught. Perhaps a cup of hot tea might make you feel better.''

Bounding to her feet, she responded with cold fury. ''Go straight to hell, Major Dwyer. And take your brother with you.''

He laughed. ''We Dwyers do not take kindly to betrayal, as you well know. Miss Langsford, you were unfaithful to Donald, and you must now pay the price. We Dwyers don't get angry, nor do we get even; instead, we triumph.''

He laughed again, then turned about and left the house.

Chapter Eighteen

Captain Harrison's wife invited Sheila, Amanda, and Janice to her home for lunch. Amanda and Janice accepted the invitation; Sheila, however, didn't feel like socializing and pleaded a headache.

Following a pleasant visit with the captain's wife, Janice and Amanda, on their way back to Charles's home, passed by his office. He had seen the ladies from the window, and he quickly stepped outside to intercept them.

"Good afternoon," he said. Smiling, he gave Amanda a cursory glance before his eyes settled on Janice. Her resemblance to his wife was striking. Charles had never loved any woman other than his wife; they had been childhood sweethearts and had always known that someday they would marry. His wife's death had been devastating to him; now, after ten years, he still wasn't fully recovered.

"Where have you two been?" he questioned, still looking at Janice.

"Mrs. Harrison invited us to lunch," she answered.

"Didn't Miss Langsford attend?" he asked, trying to hide an amused smile.

"No, she has a headache," Amanda answered.

"That's a shame," Charles said, still amused. Tonight, his brother surely would take care of her headache.

"If you'll excuse me," Amanda said, "I need to check on Sheila." Amanda knew there was more wrong with Sheila than a headache, but she thought Sheila was simply distraught over Bart.

"If her headache doesn't improve," Charles remarked, "Doctor Owens can give her something for the pain."

"I'll tell her what you said," Amanda said; then she looked at Janice. "Are you coming?"

Charles spoke up before Janice could answer. "Mrs. Gilbert, I have some sherry in my office. Won't you join me for a drink?"

Janice still didn't like Sheila and Amanda, and she didn't relish returning to the major's home and spending the remainder of the day with them. So she accepted Charles's invitation.

Pleased, he quickly ushered her into his office, where he poured two glasses of sherry. He sat behind his desk, and Janice took the chair across from him. As he nursed his drink, he studied her across the span of his desktop. She was wearing a colorful calico gown with short, puffed sleeves and a low neckline. Her auburn curls were drawn back away from her face and held in place by a green ribbon the same shade of emerald as her teardrop earrings.

Janice was aware of his admiration. It was obvious that he found her beautiful. She wished Bart would look at her in the same way.

She took time to look the major over closely. He was indeed a handsome man. She supposed he was in his late thirties. Janice had married at nineteen and was now twenty. If the major was wealthy, the difference in their ages wouldn't matter, for he wasn't past his prime. But she saw no reason to have a dalliance with Charles; it'd merely be a waste of time. Nevertheless, his good looks were tempting, and making love to him certainly wouldn't be unpleasant. Charles's flaxen hair was still full, his mustache was impeccably groomed, and his winter-blue eyes had the power to weaken a woman's resolve. Janice was tempted, for she craved sexual fulfillment.

She lowered her eyes and took a sip of sherry. There was no reason to make a hasty decision; she would give having an affair with him more thought. After all, she would probably be stuck at Fort Swafford for quite some time. With Bart locked in the stockade, Luke and Sheila certainly wouldn't leave; therefore, she would have to remain here until Colonel Langsford sent a detachment to escort her and the others to the fort.

"Charles," she began, her thoughts focused on remaining at the fort. "Don't forget to have a cot delivered to the house. I wouldn't want to put you out of your bedroom again."

That Sheila would be absent for the evening couldn't

very well be kept a secret from Janice and Amanda. Thus, Charles saw no reason to hedge. "A cot won't be necessary," he said. "Miss Langsford has decided to spend the night with my brother."

"What?" Janice exclaimed, totally shocked. "I . . . I don't know what to say!"

"Miss Langsford and Donald used to be engaged. Maybe they have decided to rekindle their love."

"Sheila was engaged to your brother?" Janice remarked. "I didn't know that!"

"Yes, but that was before Mr. Chandler came between them."

Janice couldn't imagine why Sheila had decided to go back to Donald. Why in heaven's name would she choose the lieutenant over Bart? The woman must be mad! Hope suddenly sprang into her heart. That Sheila had chosen Donald now made her very happy! Bart had become free game, and she intended to snare him for herself. But a dark cloud fell across her newfound happiness. She couldn't very well entrap Bart as long as he was in jail.

"When do you suppose troops from Fort Laramie will arrive to take Mr. Chandler back?" she asked, sounding much calmer than she felt.

"He won't be taken back. I don't intend to keep him locked up; there's no real purpose to it. His release is inevitable. I've decided to set him free in the morning."

Janice felt mixed emotions. She was glad that he'd be released so soon, but that meant Sheila would snare him right back. After all, her dalliance with Donald might be nothing more to her than an avenue of sexual release. Sheila was not a fool; why would she marry a soldier when she could marry Bart, who would someday inherit a fortune. She probably figured Bart would never learn that she had given herself to Donald. But she had thought wrong! Janice quickly decided to tell Bart exactly what was going on.

She favored Charles with one of her sweetest smiles. "I wonder if it's possible for me to visit Mr. Chandler."

Dwyer was suspicious. Did Janice have feelings for Bart? "Why do you want to see him?"

She knew what was going through Charles's head; she also knew that she had to play her cards wisely. If he believed she was romantically interested in Bart, he'd refuse to let her visit him.

She spoke casually. "Mr. Chandler helped rescue me from the Sioux. I feel as though I'm in his debt. Now he's in jail and I think it's my Christian duty to visit him." She shrugged insouciantly. "Of course, if you'd rather I didn't, I'll understand. Actually, I must confess that his connection to the Sioux unnerves me somewhat. I think his savage upbringing lurks just below the surface. Nevertheless, I was raised to be kind to others, and whether I like it or not, I am beholden to him. My conscience tells me that the least I can do is pay him a visit." Her eyes looked pleadingly into his. "You do understand, don't you?"

He was caught in her web. "Yes, of course I understand. When would you like to see him?"

"Now, if I may," she answered unhesitant.

"Very well, Mrs. Gilbert."

"Please call me Janice," she said, her voice laced with sugar.

He was flattered. "When we finish our drinks, I'll take you to the stockade."

"That will be fine, Charles."

Janice no long considered Charles a possible lover, and as he escorted her to the stockade, his arm in hers, she felt no attraction for him. The chance that she might win Bart had completely wiped any romantic notions concerning Dwyer from her mind.

Dwyer, afraid Bart might try to escape, had placed several sentries at the stockade. Now, one of them promptly unlocked the door, admitting the major and his lady companion.

Another soldier was seated at a desk, but as the major entered, he got immediately to his feet.

Janice looked around the small room with distaste. It was stuffy and didn't smell too clean.

"Do you want to see Chandler alone, or would you rather I came with you?" Dwyer asked her.

She pretended to think it over. "No, I suppose I'll see him alone."

Charles told the guard to remove the prisoner sharing Bart's cell. The young man unlocked an adjoining door, went inside another room, then returned a couple of minutes later with a bedraggled soldier.

The door was standing open. Dwyer gestured toward it. "You may go in," he said to Janice.

She walked as though she wasn't in a hurry, but she really wanted to race to Bart's cell. She was indeed anxious to tell him about Sheila and Donald.

As she moved into the next room, an offensive odor

struck her, and she took a perfumed handkerchief from her pocket and held it under her nose. There were no windows to admit fresh air, and the room was stifling. A barred cell occupied most of it; Bart, standing behind the bars, was watching her.

She wrinkled her nose. "It smells in here."

"There's no ventilation, and prisoners aren't allowed to bathe very often. In fact, I think my cellmate hasn't bathed in over a year."

She pretended deepest sympathy. "Oh, Bart, I'm just mortified to find you in a dreadful place like this!"

"I'll survive it," he replied lightly, his eyes darting behind her as though searching for something or someone. "Didn't Sheila come with you?"

She answered with obvious hesitancy. "Sheila? No . . . no, she isn't with me." She then feigned elation. "Bart, I have wonderful news for you! Major Dwyer plans to set you free!"

He was astounded. "When?"

"Tomorrow morning."

"I don't understand. It doesn't make sense."

"I could be wrong, but I think it's because of your grandfather. He knows you're certain to be released anyway. He figures keeping you locked up is pointless."

"Does Sheila know I'm being released?"

Again, she acted as though she wished to avoid discussing Sheila. "I . . . I don't know." She saw a worried frown cross his brow, and she was pleased. "Bart," she began, sounding anxious. "Do you plan to leave Fort Swafford?"

"Yes, as soon as I get out of here."

"Will you go to Fort Laramie?"

He nodded. "Sheila will want to stop and see her father. Also, it's the closest place to buy supplies."

"May I go with you? I don't want to stay here, and at Fort Laramie, I can make traveling arrangements to St. Louis." She had no intention of going to St. Louis. Between here and Fort Laramie, she planned to entrap Bart, get him to propose marriage, then journey with him to J.W.'s ranch. She didn't foresee failing, for Sheila wouldn't be around to interfere. Once Bart learned about Sheila's being with Donald, he would certainly refuse to take her with him.

"You're more than welcome to travel with us," Bart told her. "I imagine Amanda will want to come along, too. Tell Sheila and the others that I want to leave as soon as I'm released."

Janice lowered her eyes, giving the impression that she hadn't the heart to look into his face.

"Is something wrong?" he asked.

She waited a long moment before raising her eyes back to his. "Bart, I don't know how to tell you this!" She sounded terribly concerned.

"Tell me what?" he demanded impatiently.

"Well, I don't think Sheila will be leaving with us. You see, she and Lieutenant Dwyer, they are . . . they are back together." She stamped her foot in anger. "Sheila should be ashamed of herself for not coming here and telling you this herself! I don't like being the bearer of bad news!"

"What do you mean, Sheila and Dwyer are back together?"

Pretending to be hesitant, she dropped her gaze and

288

studied him through half-lowered lids. His swarthy good looks made her heart pound with expectation. She could hardly wait to be in his arms, for she found him irresistible. His black hair, dark complexion, and steel-gray eyes were so appealing. Bart's tall frame was perfectly proportioned, with wide shoulders, strong chest, narrow waist, and muscular hips. Janice couldn't help but notice the way his tan trousers fit like a second skin. Imagining what waited for her beneath those trousers caused an ache to spread between her thighs.

Bart, having no idea where her thoughts were, demanded again that she tell him about Sheila and Donald."

"I found out about them quite by accident. Major Dwyer planned to have a cot delivered to his house for me to sleep on tonight. Last night, I used the major's room. He slept on the sofa, and Sheila and Amanda slept together in his spare bedroom. Well, by chance, I reminded Major Dwyer not to forget the cot. He told me that it wouldn't be needed because Amanda and I would be sharing the same bedroom. Naturally, I wondered where that would leave Sheila. Before I could even ask him, he told me that Sheila planned to spend the night with Lieutenant Dwyer. He said that they were getting back together. The major believes that seeing each other again rekindled their love."

Bart's initial reaction was one of disbelief. "That's absurd! Major Dwyer intentionally lied to you, then sent you in here because he knew you would have to tell me. It's nothing but a trick on his part to punish me!"

"I don't think so. The major didn't send me to you. In fact, he had misgivings about letting me come here. I'm sorry, Bart, but I think he's telling the truth."

"It doesn't make sense! Sheila doesn't care anything about the lieutenant."

"Well, she must have cared at one time. She was engaged to him, wasn't she?"

Bart didn't answer, but Janice's innuendo got him to thinking. His disbelief faded into confusion. Did Sheila care more for Donald than she had admitted? Was the major right; did seeing Donald again renew her feelings? No! That wasn't possible. She loved him, had even agreed to marry him. But then she had agreed to marry Donald, too, his judgment intruded. What was she thinking? Couldn't she make up her mind?

His confusion disappeared, and picturing her in the lieutenant's bed filled him with rage. He grasped the bars tightly, and fury blazed in his eyes. "Tell Sheila I want to see her right away!"

"I'll tell her," she said, knowing full well that she wouldn't. Now, Janice felt there was nothing to gain by remaining. She would leave Bart alone with his troubling thoughts. "I'll see you in the morning. And thank you, Bart, for allowing me to ride with you to Fort Laramie."

She turned gracefully and walked to the open door with a satisfied smile on her face.

Amanda, sitting on the sofa, watched Sheila closely as she stood at the parlor window, staring vacantly outside. Amanda was very worried about her friend. She could tell that Sheila was deeply troubled. When Amanda returned from her lunch with Mrs. Harrison and Janice, she had found Sheila lying on the couch. She had asked about her headache, and Sheila said that it hadn't gone away.

Amanda remembered Major Dwyer's advice and suggested that Sheila visit Owens. She replied that she would think about it.

After that, Amanda tried to draw her friend into a conversation, with hopes that she might tell her what was making her so ill. She knew there was more wrong with Sheila than a headache. But her attempts to get Sheila to confess failed, and she finally gave up.

She went into the kitchen, prepared a pot of hot tea, then returned to the parlor. Sheila had left the sofa and was now standing at the window.

Amanda tried to coax her into having a cup of tea, but Sheila firmly declined. Now, the tea had grown cold, and Sheila was still poised at the window.

Sheila's head was indeed pounding, but the pain was bearable. It was the ache inside her heart that she couldn't bear. She felt as though she would rather die than be unfaithful to Bart. A bitter expression fleeted across her face; if she killed herself, Donald's fury would surely drive him to murder Bart! The devil had her completely under his control.

She leaned her head against the windowpane as tears welled in her eyes. She wanted desperately to cry, but was afraid if she gave in, she might cry herself into madness.

An innate force in Sheila struggled to the surface, giving her sudden strength. She swallowed back her tears, and stood ramrod straight. She was determined she wouldn't let Donald destroy her. Somehow, she would survive the ordeal that lay ahead!

Earlier, Sheila had put her depression behind her and had actually gone to the stockade. Her plan was to look the jail over and find a way to plot Bart's escape. But her hopes had been quickly dashed, for Major Dwyer had more than doubled the guards. Getting Bart out of jail would be impossible.

Her spirits crushed, she had come back to the house. Despondent, she had lain down on the couch and had still been there when Amanda returned.

"Sheila," Amanda suddenly said, "I know you're worried about Bart, but, honey, you can't worry yourself sick. You'll be no help to Bart if you become bedridden."

She turned away from the window, went to the sofa, and sat beside Amanda. "I'll be all right," Sheila murmured, putting forth a brave front.

Amanda was about to say that she didn't believe her, but was stopped by Janice's coming into the house. The young woman stepped lively into the parlor. She was somewhat puzzled to find Sheila looking so forlorn. As she apparently preferred Donald over Bart, and was even planning to renew their love—or at least, to have an affair—Janice had expected to find Sheila glowing.

She sat in a chair, and stared thoughtfully at Sheila as she wondered why she was so obviously upset. She could think of no reason why, and quickly decided she didn't care anyhow. Nevertheless, she couldn't let a chance like this go by, and turned with a catty smile. "My dear, are congratulations in order?" she said to her.

"What do you mean?" she asked, perplexed.

"Major Dwyer told me that you and Donald are back together."

Sheila leapt angrily to her feet. "How dare he tell you that!"

"Well, isn't it true?"

292

She was about to deny it heatedly, but was stopped by her own common sense. She must tread cautiously, for Bart's life was on the line! She feigned a calm composure. "Why does Major Dwyer think that?" She wondered just how much Janice knew.

The young woman raised a brow. "Charles knows everything."

"What does *that* mean?"

Janice glanced at Amanda, then looked questioningly at Sheila. "Do you really want me to say this in front of Amanda?"

Sheila's temper was dangerously close to exploding. "Tell me what?"

"That you are planning to spend the night with Donald."

"What?" Amanda exclaimed, jumping to her feet and clutching Sheila's arm. She forced the younger woman to look at her. "That isn't true, is it?"

Sheila desperately wanted to confess the truth, but she knew she couldn't. If Donald or Charles were to learn that she had broken her part of the agreement, they would have Bart killed. Although she wanted to confide in Amanda, she couldn't take that chance with Bart's life. There was no guarantee that Amanda might not tell someone. And if she did, the Dwyers would certainly find out.

"Answer me!" Amanda insisted. "Is Janice telling the truth?"

Sheila drew a long, calming breath, then answered tersely. "Yes, it's true."

"But why?" Amanda demanded.

Sheila forced anger into her voice. "It's really none of your business, Amanda!"

Her friend was taken aback. "Sheila, this isn't like you."

"What do you mean, this isn't like me? You act as though you've known me for years. Actually, you don't really know me at all. And you certainly know nothing about Donald and me!"

"I thought you were in love with Bart."

Sheila whirled about brusquely and headed for the guest bedroom. "Please mind your own business!" she said sharply over her shoulder. "That goes for both of you!"

She darted into the bedroom, slammed the door closed, hurried to the bed, and fell across it. Doubling her hands into fists, she pounded them into the pillow. Damn Donald and his brother! The devious pair were not only forcing her to betray the man she loved, but had now forced her to turn against her dearest friend! She hated them. God, how she hated them.

Janice remained in the parlor, letting Amanda know that Bart would be released in the morning. She also told her that he planned to leave for Fort Laramie as soon as he was free. If she wanted to come along, then she should be ready first thing in the morning. Janice was concerned about her wardrobe; she knew Bart would want to travel horseback. She didn't stay concerned too long, though, for she realized she could send for her things. Detachments were always journeying back and forth from Fort Swafford to Fort Laramie.

Deciding to take a rest, Janice left the parlor and went

to Charles's bedroom. Amanda was getting ready to carry the teapot and cups back to the kitchen but was detained by a knock on the door.

It was Luke; she let him in gladly. She hoped he had come to see her, but as she waved him into the parlor, his first words sent her hopes fleeing.

"Is Sheila here? I'd like to see her."

"Yes, she's here. But I don't think this is a good time. She has a bad headache."

"She has probably worried herself sick over Bart."

Amanda was no longer so sure. Something was bothering Sheila, that was obvious, but she wasn't sure if it had anything to do with Bart. She wondered if she should tell Luke about Sheila and the lieutenant. She thought it over for a moment, then decided not to say anything. He would probably tell Bart, and she didn't want to stir up trouble.

"Luke," she began. "Did you know that Bart is being released in the morning?"

His surprise was evident. "No, I didn't. I tried to see him, but Major Dwyer ordered the guards not to let me in."

"Why do you suppose the major is letting him go?"

"He probably thinks no charges will be brought against him. Bart's grandfather is too important, and he's got too many political connections. I reckon Dwyer locked him up just to teach him a lesson."

"Such a lesson doesn't make sense."

"Well, I've known Charles Dwyer for years, and I ain't ever known him to be sensible."

"For some reason, the major gave Janice permission

to see Bart. She said that Bart wants to leave in the morning for Fort Laramie. Janice and I will be leaving with him."

"You make it sound like Sheila and I ain't goin'."

"I didn't mean it the way it sounded. Of course, you're coming with us."

Bemused he asked, "Ain't Sheila goin'?"

"I . . . I'm not sure," she stammered.

"I thought she and Bart had an understandin'."

"So did I, but maybe I was wrong."

"Is somethin' goin' on I should know about?"

Amanda didn't answer right away; then, with an angry expression, she replied. "Luke, a few minutes ago, Sheila informed me that her life is none of my business. Therefore, I intend to stay out of it."

"It's Lieutenant Dwyer, ain't it? Is Sheila considerin' goin' back to him?"

Amanda offered no comment, but the truth was written on her face.

A cold hardness came to Luke's eyes. "Women!" he said disgustedly. "Why can't you women stick to one man? Why do you have to be so damned fickle?"

Amanda knew he was speaking of their past relationship, and she retorted defensively. "Why do you men have to be so hard-headed?"

"Am I supposed to take that personally?"

"If the shoe fits . . . !"

Without a word, he wheeled about abruptly, opened the door, and stomped outside.

Amanda took a step to stop him, but then decided to let him go. She shouldn't have lost her temper, but Luke Thomas was so . . . so exasperating!

Chapter Nineteen

Donald was gloating as he walked to the stockade. His expression was exultant. It was late, and the soldiers guarding the jail were surprised by his visit. One of the sentries quickly let him in, and Donald told the guard at the desk that he wanted to see Chandler alone. The young man, as he had done earlier, went into the adjoining room and returned with the soldier who shared Bart's cell.

Donald stepped briskly through the open doorway. A cold smile curled his lips as he saw Bart standing in the barred cell. He was looking back at him with murder in his eyes. Charles had told Donald about Janice's visit to Bart and that she might have mentioned his liaison with Sheila. Now, the glare in Chandler's eyes assured Donald that she had indeed. He was glad that Chandler knew. It served the bastard right!

"What the hell do you want?" Bart asked, fuming.

"I just wanted to let you know how lucky you are."
A sarcastic grin was on his face.

"Lucky? What do you mean by that?"

"When I thought Sheila had been abducted by a warrior, I planned to catch you, then castrate you before killing you. It's lucky for you that you aren't really an Indian. Now, I can't very well do something like that to J.W. Chandler's grandson, can I?" A hateful sneer distorted his mouth. "You rich, arrogant sonofabitch! Just because your grandfather is J.W. Chandler, you figure you can get away with anything! Well, why the hell not? You did get away with breaking the law, didn't you? My brother is setting you free because there's no reason to keep you locked up; your release is inevitable." Donald suppressed a smile; Chandler would be released all right, released straight into an ambush! That he had been denied the pleasure of personally killing him was infuriating, but knowing that Bart would still die assuaged his anger. Moreover, everyone would believe that he had died at the hands of the Sioux, and that lifted Donald's spirits considerably. He was almost jubilant!

"Now that you've said what you came here to say, why don't you leave?" Bart's hands gripped the bars so tightly that his knuckles turned white.

"Yes, I suppose I might as well leave. It is getting late, and following dinner, I have an important engagement." His expression was smug. "I certainly wouldn't want to be late. The lady doesn't like to be kept waiting."

Bart, his jaw clenched, said quietly but with an undertone of rage, "Don't play games with me, Dwyer! I already heard about you and Sheila, and I don't believe it!"

He shrugged indifferently. "Then you're a fool." With that, he turned around and strutted into the other room.

Bart released his grip on the bars. He had been clutching them so tightly that his fingers were stiff. He flexed his knuckles, then moved to his cot and sat down. The air was stifling, and he rubbed a hand across his perspiring brow. He was too tense to sit for very long, and, getting up, he paced back and forth.

He wanted to trust Sheila and to believe in their love, but his confidence was shaken. Why hadn't she come to see him? He had told Janice to tell her that he wanted to see her. Maybe she hadn't visited him because the Dwyers wouldn't give their permission. Or maybe, he thought angrily, she hadn't visited because she did plan to reconcile with Donald.

Furious, he suddenly made a fist and slapped it viciously into his other hand. Donald was probably right—he was a fool! He had trusted Sheila completely and had believed she loved him! Now, she had thrown him over for the lieutenant!

But Bart was too sensible to let his anger totally rule his judgment, and as he considered the situation more rationally, he decided to give Sheila the benefit of the doubt. He'd not find her guilty on hearsay alone, especially considering that the informants were Janice and Dwyer. In his opinion, neither of them were to be believed.

Dr. Owens' office was located in the infirmary, which was constructed of logs. It was the fort's largest structure, but like the rest of the buildings, it was in dire need of repair. As Sheila walked slowly toward the medical facility, she noted that the dreary-looking fort matched her mood. The post was a disgrace, and should be abandoned. The officers' quarters were grim and primitive, the enlisted men's barracks even worse. The high wall surrounding the fort was built of logs. It was unsteady and rotten in places. Sheila didn't think Fort Swafford could hold off a full attack.

Reaching the infirmary, she went inside. Cots were lined against the walls, but only a couple of the beds were occupied. She hoped the doctor was still here, but considering the late hour, he was most likely gone. His office was to her right, and she went over and knocked on the door.

"Come in" was the reply.

Thank goodness he hadn't left. She took a long breath before entering. She wanted to appear controlled. It wouldn't do for the doctor to get suspicious. She knew she couldn't get through the night without something to calm her nerves, and she planned to ask Owens for a sedative.

Sheila entered the office quietly. The doctor was at his desk, his head bent over a stack of papers. It was a moment before he looked up. "Miss Langsford," he said, surprised to see her. He got to his feet, and gestured toward the chair facing his desk. "Please sit down."

Sheila perched on the edge of the chair, and, folding her hands in her lap, she clutched them together nervously.

"What can I do for you?" Owens asked. "Are you ill?"

The doctor was fatherly looking middle-aged, with a kind, trusting face. Sheila restrained her sudden impulse to tell him how the Dwyers were manipulating her. She sensed that he would believe her and would protect her from their evil shenanigans. But could he protect Bart as well? She was afraid he couldn't, and she wasn't about to gamble with Bart's life.

"Doctor Owens," she said calmly, "I have trouble sleeping. Could you give me a sedative, or perhaps a sleeping powder?"

"Yes, of course I can. My dear, you've been under a lot of pressure, and insomnia is certainly understandable. However, you don't want to rely on medicines to help you sleep."

"I'm sure my inability to sleep is only temporary."

"Yes, I'm sure it is, too. I'll give you a sedative, and I want you to take it right before you go to bed. But don't mix it with a nightcap, or you'll become too heavily sedated."

She decided immediately to have several nightcaps. The more sedated she was, the better!

Leaving the infirmary, Sheila went to Donald's office. No sentries were posted out front, and the door was unlocked. She walked inside, and, looking about, she saw a corner cabinet where Donald kept his liquor. She went over to it and grabbed a bottle at random. She didn't care what she drank as long as it contained alcohol.

Carrying the bottle, she moved to the door that led into Donald's bedroom. She stepped inside, where a lantern was lit and the bedcovers pulled back. A bottle of champagne, ensconced in a silver-coated bucket, and two long-stemmed glasses, had been placed on the nightstand.

She hurried past the bed and went to a table that held a water pitcher and washbowl. A water glass was there, too. She picked it up and dropped in the powder Dr. Owens had given her. She then poured water into the glass, and drank down the contents in gulping swigs.

She moved to the bed, sat on the edge, and opened the bottle, taking a whiff. It was whiskey, and the strong odor caused her nose to wrinkle in distaste. Bracing herself, she drew a long breath, put the bottle to her lips, and took a big drink. The liquor burned her throat, and the taste of it almost gagged her. A violent shiver ran through her and bile rose in her throat. She swallowed strongly, put the bottle back to her mouth, and took another drink. This time, the whiskey went down a lot easier, and she quickly took two more swallows.

She glanced at the clock on the wall, and was alarmed to find that it was almost ten o'clock. Donald would be here soon. That thought drove her to take three more generous swallows of whiskey.

She placed the bottle on the nightstand, and stood up to remove her clothes. Her balance was off and the floor seemed to sway beneath her feet. She knew the powder mixed with the liquor was beginning to take effect.

She undressed awkwardly, for her hands were trembling and her head was swimming. Finally, she managed to shed all her clothes, letting them fall haphazardly at her feet. She got into bed, drew up the covers, and leaned back against the headboard. Grabbing the whiskey bottle, she quaffed down a generous mouthful. She intended to drink herself into oblivion. Her thoughts were now hazy, but somewhere in her mind she wondered if all this whiskey combined with the sleeping powder could be fatal. Afraid that could be the case, she took one last swallow, then set the bottle aside.

By now, perspiration was beading heavily on her brow, and the room was spinning. Sheila snuggled down into the covers and closed her eyes. The darkness didn't take away her dizziness though. She now felt as though her whole body was whirling around in space. She didn't like the feeling; it was scary, and she tried to open her eyes. But they wouldn't open, for her lids seemed as heavy as lead. Despite her efforts to regain consciousness, she remained floating aimlessly in an infinite darkness.

Donald was whistling a lively tune as he approached his office, opened the door, and stepped inside. He had waited a long time for this night, and could hardly wait to enjoy Sheila to the fullest. As he stopped whistling, a cold, anticipating smile curled his lips. He planned to humble her, degrade her, then arouse the cheap bitch's passion until she begged him to take her. Donald laughed aloud. He would take her all right! He planned to ram his hardness so far inside her that she would writher in ecstasy! Oh, yes, the little tramp would certainly ride him with wild abandon! Afterward, he would slap her around just for the fun of it, then take her again!

Anxious to get started, he hurried to his bedroom door and swung it open. His manhood was erect and throbbing, and cold-hearted lust was in his eyes.

Sheila was in bed; though the covers were drawn up

past her breasts, her shoulders were bare, and Donald knew she was naked. She had kept her part of the bargain.

"Your lover is here," he said thickly. He waited for her to open her eyes and look at him. She didn't move. What in hell? he thought. He spoke again, louder this time. "I'm here, goddamn it! Open your eyes and act like you're happy to see me!"

There was no response.

He sat on the edge of the bed, grasped her shoulders, and shook her roughly. Her head rocked back and forth like a rag doll's. "What in hell's wrong with you?" Donald demanded angrily.

He released his grip, and she fell back limply. Suddenly, he caught a glimpse of the whiskey bottle. The damned bitch was drunk! Drawing back his hand, he slapped her soundly across the cheek. "Wake up, you slut!"

The stinging whack brought Sheila to for a moment, and her eyes fluttered open. She saw Donald's face through a cloudy haze. She struggled vainly to grasp a semblance of reality, but the powder and whiskey combination was too sedating, and she dropped back into a fathomless darkness.

Donald was livid. His anger quickly burst out of control. He slapped her a second time, but still she remained unresponsive. "I'll wake you up, by God!" he cursed, flinging the covers aside. The lantern's saffron glow fell across Sheila's nakedness, and Donald's gaze traveled over her hungrily. He found her beautiful beyond compare. His hands sought her out roughly, greedily, his fingers digging into her soft flesh.

Donald's mauling brought Sheila back from the darkness, and she was dimly aware that he was defiling her with his hands. Deep in her mind she tried to bring life back into her body so she could push him away. She knew she was supposed to succumb to him, but letting him touch her was more than she could bear. Before she could find the strength to fling his hands aside, she again slipped into oblivion.

Sheila's lifeless response was infuriating to Donald. He couldn't very well humble, degrade, and conquer an unconscious woman! He could get on top of her and take her, but, by God, there would be no triumph in that.

The hardness inside his pants shriveled, and his passion died. His anger, however, remained alive. He grabbed the champagne bottle, uncorked it, and filled one of the glasses. He gulped the drink as though it was water and he was dying of thirst. As he reached for the bottle to take another drink, he accidentally dropped the glass. It fell to the floor unbroken and rolled to a stop at his feet. He picked it up, and placed it on the nightstand. Taking the unused glass, he filled it with champagne, and guzzled it as greedily as the first.

He made a face; champagne wasn't what he really wanted. He needed something much stronger. He took the whiskey bottle, got up, and walked to the door. He turned back and glared at the sleeping woman. "I'll give you a couple of hours to sleep off your drunk," he said. "Then I'll be back! Goddamn it, you bitch! You're going to pay for this!"

Taking the whiskey bottle with him, he stalked outside. He needed to be alone, have a few drinks, then sleep for a couple of hours before returning to Sheila. As he wondered where to go, his gaze fell across the stables.

He crossed the quiet courtyard, and walked inside the stables. He found an empty stall filled with hay. He made himself comfortable, opened the bottle, and took a liberal swallow. The liquor soothed his anger and appeased his disappointment; he continued swigging. The more he drank, the better he felt. He was certain that Sheila would soon come around and he would still have plenty of time to play out his fantasy. He checked his watch; he'd give her two hours, but not one minute longer. If she was still unresponsive, he'd wake her up one way or another!

He continued to drink until the bottle was completely drained. Then, feeling warm and drowsy, he snuggled down into the surrounding hay. His eyelids grew heavy and he closed his eyes. Now he'd sleep. A calculating smile crossed his face. Considering what he had in mind for Sheila, he would need his rest!

A few minutes later, Donald, sound asleep, was snoring softly.

It was five o'clock in the morning when a guard unlocked Bart's cell and told him he was free to leave.

Bart, lying on his cot, was awake. His arms were folded under his head, and he was staring up at the ceiling. His thoughts had been on Sheila and Donald when the guard arrived.

He got up and bid his cellmate, who had been awakened by the guard, a terse goodbye. The barred door was immediately locked behind Bart, and the guard motioned for him to follow.

They went into the other room, where Bart's pistol

and gunbelt were returned to him. He strapped them on, walked outside, and asked a sentry where he could find Lieutenant Dwyer's quarters. The soldier gave him directions.

There was a purposeful intent in Bart's steps as he headed away from the stockade. The morning sun picked up a vicious glint in his gray eyes, and his lips were drawn into a thin line.

Reaching Donald's office, he stopped, drew a long breath, then tried the door. He was pleased to find it unlocked. If Dwyer and Sheila had spent the night together, they certainly would have locked the door.

Still, he went inside. He had to know for sure, to see for himself that Sheila wasn't there. The outer office was unoccupied, but the door leading into the bedroom was standing open. Moving quietly, Bart stepped through the portal, and the sight that awaited slammed into him with a terrible force.

There, on the bed, lay Sheila. Asleep, she was on her stomach, uncovered, her long brown hair draped across the side of her face. Bart quickly drew the covers up over her naked body. He stood riveted, glaring down at Sheila with tremendous anger. He was tempted to awaken her and release some of his anger by telling her exactly what he thought of her. He made a move to do just that when he happened to glance at the nightstand. He stared furiously at the half-filled champagne bottle and the two used glasses. Apparently, Sheila and Dwyer had had quite a romantic evening! He wondered where Dwyer was. Maybe he had an early-morning appointment! He'd probably be back soon and crawling into bed with his two-timing girlfriend!

307

"To hell with you!" he muttered to Sheila, his tone one of utter disgust.

Whirling around abruptly, Bart left the room, crossed the office, and went outside. He was enraged, but he was also hurting. He had never known such heartache. It cut into him without mercy.

He headed toward the barracks to get Luke. He wanted to leave this fort and Sheila behind and never see either of them again.

Donald, unconscious from too much whiskey, was flat on his back; his mouth was open, and he was snoring loudly. The air had dried his throat, and as he swallowed, the dryness caused him to gag. He came awake coughing, and, at first, he was too groggy to think clearly. Slowly, though, everything came back to him, and the morning light filtering into the stables sent him leaping to his feet. Good God, it was morning! He had planned to sleep only a few hours—how could he have stayed out so long? Intense anger raced through him, and his features twisted into a deranged scowl. He looked quickly at his watch; it was past five o'clock. Damn it to hell; now he didn't have time for Sheila. He and Charles were supposed to leave within the hour, travel to Yellow Bear's village, and destroy it. No more powwows would take place there to invoke hostility against the Army. He and Charles intended to make sure of that! By the time they finished, the village would be too weak to declare war.

Looking forward to obliterating Yellow Bear and his warriors eased Donald's disappointment. He had lost his chance to conquer Sheila, but an even greater victory lay ahead. After all, Sheila was only a woman, and a used one at that. He wouldn't let losing her depress him. She wasn't worth it; no woman was!

His mood much improved, he left the stables and went to his office. Sheila was still asleep. He studied her lustfully for a moment, and even considered making hurried love to her, but he dismissed the notion. Rushed passion was too unfulfilling.

He went to his wardrobe and removed a clean uniform. He quickly stripped off all his clothes. He was about to put on his undershorts when he heard Sheila moan softly. He turned toward the bed and looked at her.

As her eyes fluttered open, she became aware first of a harrowing headache pounding at her temples. Her mouth felt as dry as cotton, and she desperately wanted a drink of water. She swallowed dryly, then, as her drugged mind slowly cleared, she realized she was still in Donald's bed. She glanced at the nightstand and was puzzled to find the champagne bottle half empty. Had she and Donald drunk champagne? Then, all at once, sensing another's presence, her glance darted across the room. She was taken aback to find Donald there, naked, looking at her.

He smiled, but it was more like a sneer.

Sheila turned her eyes away, drew up her legs, and sitting up, leaned her head on her knees. She was sick all the way to her soul. She tried to recall last night, but everything was so vague. She did remember Donald talking to her, remembered he had slapped her—maybe even more than once. She also remembered his hands on her, and that memory sent a repulsive shiver up her spine. After that, however, she remembered nothing.

309

She sank back down onto the bed and buried her face in the pillow. She wondered why she couldn't remember more about last night, but then, it didn't really matter. She didn't need to recall everything in vivid detail to know what happened. In fact, it was more merciful that she didn't remember. Suddenly, she grasped on to a fleeting moment of hope. Maybe the assault never took place! Was that why she couldn't remember? But her hopes dissolved quickly. Of course it had happened! Otherwise, why would Donald be standing in the room naked?

She strove futilely to recall the night with some kind of clarity, but her mind remained blank. Such total amnesia was frightening.

"Get up, and get dressed!" Donald told her sharply.

She was more than ready to leave. She wanted to get as far away from Donald as was possible. Sitting, she swung her legs over the side of the bed, holding the covers over her nakedness.

Donald looked away from her, and began to put on his clothes. He was tempted to ogle her, but didn't want to become aroused.

Sheila was surprised he had turned away, but then why should he want to watch her? Last night, he had no doubt had his fill of her.

She gathered up her discarded clothes and dressed hastily. Her head was still pounding, and her mouth was terribly dry. She ran her fingers through her tangled hair, but the tresses remained in disarray. She knew she must look a sight.

She staggered to the mirror and studied her reflection. Her eyes were puffed and swollen, and her face was as pale as a ghost. It also appeared somewhat bloated. She stared at herself in shock. It was hard to believe that the face looking back was hers.

Donald, finished dressing, went to her, grabbed her arm, and forced her out of the room, through the office and outside.

The bright sunlight hurt her eyes, and she blinked against the harsh rays. Donald tightened his hold on her arm, but she flung his hand aside. She couldn't stand having him touch her! During the short walk to Charles's home, he didn't utter a word, and neither did Sheila.

Donald opened the front door, stepped inside, grabbed Sheila's arm in a hold she couldn't break, and pulled her in behind him as though she were excess baggage.

Bart was in the parlor, along with Luke. Amanda and Janice were also present, and so was Charles. The group looked on in silent wonder as Donald entered, practically dragging an unkempt Sheila at his heels.

Donald stared coldly at Bart, who was standing in the middle of the room. His fingers clutched Sheila's arm in a viselike grip, then he slung her toward Chandler so roughly that she lost her balance and went tumbling into his arms.

"You can have your whore back!" Donald sneered.

Chapter Twenty

Silence followed Donald's remark, but the tension in the parlor was so thick that it was almost tangible.

Sheila moved awkwardly out of Bart's arms. Her head was still hammering and her body ached. Hesitantly, she lifted her gaze to Bart's, and the frigid expression in his eyes chilled her to the bones.

"You don't look well, Miss Langsford," he said calmly. "Do you have a hangover?"

She didn't know what to say. She hadn't expected to see Bart under these circumstances. The hope that he would never learn about her and Donald had been the strength that sustained her. Now, she felt totally drained.

"I . . . I can explain," she said, her voice terribly weak.

Bart arched a brow sharply. "I'm sure you can, but I'd rather not hear it." He turned to Luke. "Let's go to the stables and saddle the horses. The sooner we're out of here, the better.''

Janice spoke up. ''Bart, you're coming back for Amanda and me, aren't you?''

''I told you I'd take you to Fort Laramie and I will.'' He and Luke started to leave, but Amanda stopped them.

''Wait!'' she said. She looked at Sheila. ''Are you staying here, or coming with us?''

''I'm not staying,'' she replied firmly. ''I plan to leave for Fort Laramie if I have to travel alone.''

Amanda decided to speak to Luke instead of Bart. ''Sheila will be leaving with us. Please saddle a horse for her.''

Luke agreed to do so, then he followed Bart, who was already on his way outside.

Amanda went to Sheila and draped an arm around her shoulders. She couldn't understand why she had cast Bart aside for Donald. She was gravely disappointed in Sheila. Nevertheless, the young woman was obviously miserable, and she looked dreadful. Amanda's heart went out to her, and she said soothingly, ''Come with me. You need to wash up and change into riding clothes. Bart and Luke will be back soon.''

As Amanda was taking Sheila into the bedroom, Charles was motioning for Donald to follow him outside. The moment they were on the porch, he turned to his younger brother. ''Sergeant Kent hasn't left yet,'' he said strongly. ''Find him and tell him the ambush is off!''

''Off?'' Donald whined. ''But why?''

''Are you out of your mind?'' he snapped. ''By God, it's obvious why! Chandler's got three women traveling

314

with him! I don't give a damn about Chandler or Thomas, but I do give a damn about the women!''

"Then why did you set up the ambush?"

"I didn't know Janice and the others would decide to leave with Chandler. I figured Thomas and Chandler would be alone. This morning, when they arrived to tell the ladies that they wanted to leave right away, I was totally shocked. I had no idea that Janice and Mrs. Wilson planned to go with them. I hope to talk Janice into staying, but that still leaves Mrs. Wilson and Sheila.''

"Why should you care if Sheila dies? You didn't care about her last night.''

"Taking her to bed isn't quite the same thing as killing her. I don't murder white women! Now, get the hell out of here and stop Sergeant Kent!''

Donald left reluctantly, and Charles hurried back into the house and to the parlor, where he was pleased to find Janice. She was sitting on the sofa, dressed in riding apparel. The morning sun, shining through the window, slanted across her hair, accentuating the reddish highlights in the long tresses. She was a picture of beauty, and Charles knew losing her would be a big disappointment. He had hoped to win her heart.

"Janice," he said, "I wish you would reconsider leaving with Chandler and the others.''

She wasn't about to reconsider. that Sheila would be traveling with them hadn't changed her mind. She was still determined to snare Bart. She didn't see Sheila's presence as a deterrent; Bart was obviously through with her.

She smiled amiably, then lied with ease. "Charles,

315

you're very sweet, and I do appreciate your kindness. However, I'm very anxious to reach Fort Laramie so I can make arrangements to go home.''

He moved quickly to the sofa, sat beside her, and took her hand into his. ''My dear, you don't understand. I want you to stay here because I'm falling in love with you. I hope soon to ask you to marry me.''

Janice almost laughed. The man was such a silly fool! Marry him, indeed! She intended to marry Bart Chandler. Feigning a subdued expression, she continued to lie. ''Charles, I'm very flattered, but my husband has been dead only a short time. I couldn't possibly consider marrying so soon. Surely you understand. But, if you like, we can correspond. As soon as I'm back home, I'll write you a letter. Then, when the time is right . . . ? Maybe you can take a furlough and come to St. Louis.'' There! she thought. That should pacify him.

Charles could sympathize with her grief; he still hadn't fully recovered from losing his wife. ''I understand completely. I will certainly be looking forward to receiving your first letter.''

Janice smiled sweetly.

Sheila filled the washbasin with water, stripped away her apparel, and washed herself so vigorously that the cloth chafed her skin. She rubbed her flesh over and over again as though she could wash away Donald's defilement of her.

Amanda laid Sheila's riding clothes on the bed, then, turning to her, she said firmly, ''I want you to tell me why you spent the night with Donald! I can tell by the way you're scrubbing your body that you hated what he did to you."

Sheila dropped the cloth into the basin. She was as clean as she was going to get. She went to the bed and began putting on her clothes.

"Well?" Amanda insisted, her arms folded across her chest. "Are you going to tell me or not?"

"If I tell you, will you promise that you won't say anything to anyone until I've had a chance to talk to Bart?"

"Yes, I can make that promise."

As Sheila continued to dress, she told Amanda exactly how the Dwyers had manipulated her. She explained her visit to Dr. Owens, and that the sedative mixed with the whiskey had clouded her mind. She had no clear memory of last night, but she did remember Donald talking to her and slapping her and fondling her. After that, her mind was totally blank. But this morning, she awoke to find Donald in the room, naked. Also, though the champagne bottle was half empty, she couldn't remember drinking with him. But she must have, for both glasses had been used.

Amanda listened to the incredible story with shock and anger. She could hardly believe the Dwyers were so devious, but she didn't doubt that Sheila was telling the truth.

"Those sorry bastards!" she fumed. "They should be court-martialed and sent to prison!"

"They wouldn't be found guilty; it would only be my word against theirs. I can't prove that I was coerced."

"If Bart finds out what they did to you, he'll . . . he'll . . ."

317

"He'll *what*? Try to kill them? Don't you realize I've considered that? The Dwyers are very important military officers, and if Bart kills them, or even injures them, he might very well go to prison."

"Maybe not. I understand his grandfather is very influential."

"Not even J.W. could save him from a murder charge." Sheila wiped a hand nervously across her brow. "I may never be able to tell Bart the truth. The consequences could be too severe."

"But if you don't tell him, he'll think the worst."

"Yes, I know," she replied dejectedly. "Either way, I lose."

Amanda placed a firm hand on Sheila's arm. "You can't keep the truth from Bart! You must be honest with him!"

"But I'm afraid the truth will lead to his own destruction. I know Bart. He won't let the Dwyers get by with what they did to me!"

"Nevertheless, you owe him the truth."

"I'll think about it," Sheila replied.

"Well, while you're thinking, I'll go to the kitchen and get you a cup of coffee."

Amanda left the room and walked through the parlor, where Janice was now sitting alone on the sofa. The dining room was between her and the kitchen. The door was closed, but as she started to open it, the voices on the other side gave her reason to pause.

"I don't think we should take Yellow Bear back to Fort Laramie to hang." Donald was speaking. "I say, we kill him and all his warriors!"

"I agree," Charles replied. "We'll leave as soon as

318

Chandler and the others are gone. It wouldn't do for Chandler to get drift of this. He'd beat us to Yellow Bear and warn him.''

The Dwyers' decision to attack Yellow Bear and his people had been made the night before. They had always planned to carry out the mission eventually, but had postponed it until Sheila could be found. Now, there was no reason to delay. Furthermore, preparations were already made; they would simply use the supplies that had been packed for Donald's thwarted search for Sheila. The troops were ready to leave, the supply wagon was loaded, and there was nothing to keep them here.

''I think we should wreak such havoc on the village that it will put fear in every Sioux's heart,'' Donald remarked. ''The murdering savages will be only too glad to leave the mountains and return to the reservation.''

Amanda, still eavesdropping, was stunned. She thought about Golden Dove and Dream Dancer—would they die during the soldiers' onslaught? She knew the Dwyers well enough to know they would show no mercy, not even to women and children!

The front door suddenly opened, and Amanda jumped back as though she had been caught. She moved away from the dining room, and went to the parlor to find that Bart and Luke had returned.

''Are you ladies ready?'' Luke asked her.

''Yes, we are. I'll get Sheila.'' She moved to do so, but was stopped by Sheila's entering the parlor.

At the same moment, the Dwyers appeared. Charles promptly took Janice's arm and led her outside; the others followed behind them.

The horses and the pack mule were tied out front. As

Charles helped Janice mount, Luke assisted Amanda. Bart made no move to give Sheila a hand, so Luke aided her as well.

Sheila kept her eyes averted from Donald and Bart. She couldn't stand looking at Donald, and it pained her too much to look at Bart.

Only Janice said goodbye to the Dwyers, then the group turned their horses around and headed toward the fort's open gates.

Bart took the lead. Sheila rode in the rear alongside Luke. She didn't say anything to Luke; their eyes had met briefly, but the resentment in his gaze dissuaded her from starting a conversation. She didn't blame him for feeling such bitterness; after all, he loved Bart like a brother.

They hadn't ridden very far before Amanda caught up to Bart. "There's something I think you should know," she told him.

"If it's about Sheila, I don't want to hear it." He sounded determined.

"It's not about Sheila. I overheard a discussion between Major Dwyer and the lieutenant. They are planning to attack your brother's village. They intend to leave right away. From what they said, I don't think they mean to leave too many survivors."

Startled, Bart reined in sharply, causing the others to do likewise. Luke quickly rode up to see what was wrong.

"May God damn the Dwyers to eternal hell!" Bart muttered viciously.

"What's goin' on?" Luke asked.

Amanda repeated what she had told Bart. She spoke clearly; so, Janice and Sheila heard every word.

"I must warn Yellow Bear," Bart vowed. "Luke, you can take the women to Fort Laramie."

Janice, listening, was strongly opposed to returning to Yellow Bear's village; however, she was more opposed to being separated from Bart. She couldn't very well win his affections if they weren't together. "Bart," she said, forcing concern into her voice, "I don't think you should go alone. What if you should meet with an accident? There would be no one to warn Yellow Bear. I think we should all go with you." She cast Sheila a snide expression. "Of course, if you're opposed to going to Yellow Bear's village, you can go back to Fort Swafford."

"No, she can't!" Bart said irritably. "If she goes back, the Dwyers will know that I plan to warn Yellow Bear."

Sheila was instantly piqued. "Are you implying that I would tell them?" Fire danced in her eyes.

"Let me put it this way, Miss Langsford. I don't trust you any farther than I can see you!"

Janice hid a smile behind her hand. Their bickering delighted her!

"Once before," Amanda began, "when we were undecided, we took it to a vote. I see no reason not to do so again. All in favor of going to Yellow Bear's village, raise their hands."

Every hand, including Sheila's, went up immediately.

Bart, grateful for their concern, let his eyes rest briefly on Luke, Amanda, and Janice; he intentionally ignored Sheila. "I'm fortunate to have such good friends." Janice's unselfish offer had totally astounded Bart. Maybe he had judged her unfairly. She was evidently a much nicer person than he had originally thought.

"I know a shortcut through the mountains," Luke said.

"I used to travel it back in my trappin' days. It's steep in places and ain't no easy climb. But if we take it, we can reach the village a day or two ahead of the Dwyers."

They decided to take Luke's shortcut.

They stopped at noon and ate a cold lunch, but wanting to make good time, they didn't linger. Traveling steadily, they covered a lot of ground before nightfall. At twilight, they came upon an area well surrounded by thick foliage. They dismounted, and made camp there.

Luke built a fire, and the women prepared a hot meal. Although the food was tasty, no one ate very much. Everyone's appetite was poor.

Bart offered to take the first watch. He moved away from the campsite and found a good place to keep vigil.

Sheila, sitting at the fire, watched him leave. Amanda was next to her, and she gently nudged Sheila with her elbow. Too softly for the others to hear, she said, "Now's your chance to talk to Bart. Follow him."

Sheila sighed miserably. "I'm not sure what to tell him."

"Tell him the truth."

"You make it sound so simple."

Amanda, keeping her voice hushed, replied, "Sheila, if you don't tell Bart the truth, then the Dwyers will have won. Don't let those monsters destroy your happiness and Bart's."

"You're right, of course." Dreading what she must do, she got up slowly. She wondered how Bart would react to what she had to tell him.

Following the path Bart had taken, Sheila found him sitting beneath a full-branched tree. He was leaning against the trunk, his rifle propped at his side.

His gray eyes squinted with anger as he watched her approach. He hadn't expected her to follow him. She certainly had a lot of gall. What in hell did she want? Now that Dwyer had thrown her over, did she expect him to take her back? It'd be a cold day in hell!

Sheila stood before him. "Bart, I must talk to you." Her heart was pounding, and nervous perspiration had accumulated on her palms. She distractedly rubbed her hands together.

The sky was cloudless and a three-quarter moon shone down on Sheila, bathing her in a golden hue. Her dark-brown tresses flowed past her shoulders in shimmering waves, and her beautiful coffee-brown eyes were staring unwaveringly into Bart's.

Bart didn't say anything, but responded with a long, silent scrutiny. His gaze swept over her slender figure. She was wearing the riding apparel she had worn the day he had abducted her. The garment had been mended and was spotted with stains that would not wash out. He noticed that she stood proudly, her head high and her shoulders squared. But the nervous rubbing together of her hands told Bart that she wasn't nearly as calm as she appeared to be.

Sheila waited a long time for him to speak to her, then, giving up, she said again, "I must talk to you."

Bart sprang gracefully to his feet. His expression was stern and his voice as hard as granite. "I don't think we have anything to talk about."

323

"I want to tell you about Donald."

"You can't tell me anything I don't already know!" he said sharply.

"What do you mean by that?"

"I knew you were going to spend the night with Dwyer before it happened. Do you think I didn't find out until he threw you in my arms?"

"How did you know?"

Bart decided to leave Janice out of it. "Dwyer came to see me at the stockade."

"And he . . . he told you—"

Bart cut in furiously. "What the hell do you want from me, Sheila? Surely to God, you don't expect me to take you back after you spent the night with that bastard!"

Sheila stared at him incredulously. Donald had gone to the stockade? Exactly what did he say to Bart? "Did Donald tell you *why* I was spending the night with him?"

"He told me everything!" Bart snapped, his anger causing him to spit out the words before he could stop them. He started to retract what he said, to answer more honestly, but was put off by Sheila's sudden outburst.

"I don't see how I could have thought I was in love with you!" She was on fire with anger. Bart knew she had given herself to Donald to save his life. How dare he treat her so abhorrently! He should despise Donald, not her.

"Well, at least we have that in common," he responded. "I don't see how I could've loved you, either!"

Furious, she drew back a hand and swung out to slap him, but he caught her wrist in midflight.

His fingers tightened painfully. "If I were you, I

wouldn't resort to physical violence. You'll come out the loser!''

"You're hurting me!'' she cried with a grimace, trying vainly to break his firm hold.

He released her abruptly. "Go back to camp, Sheila. And, hereafter, stay the hell away from me!''

"With pleasure!'' she spat. She whirled about sharply and hurried back to camp. Amanda had placed Sheila's bedroll next to her own, and Sheila went to it and lay down.

"Well?'' Amanda questioned. She had been almost asleep, but Sheila's return brought her wide-awake. She sat up and looked expectantly at her friend. "Did you tell Bart?''

"I didn't have to,'' Sheila mumbled angrily. "He already knew. Donald told him!''

Amanda was astounded. "Bart knew? Then why did he treat you so horribly?''

"Because he's a contemptible, heartless . . . jackass! He doesn't care why I spent the night with Donald; he only cares that another man trespassed on his property. Bart's a selfish, callow cad, and I hope after this trip is over, I never have to see him again. In fact, I don't know if I can stand being around him that long. I'd leave him now if I could.'' That last thought struck her suddenly. Reckless anger took control over her better judgment, and she started contemplating leaving. She knew the way to Fort Laramie from here. Although Bart probably wouldn't care if she left, she knew Luke and Amanda would stop her. Therefore, it would be necessary for her to slip away. She wasn't sure how she could manage it, but she'd find a way. She knew she had to make her move soon. Once they reached the mountains and Luke's shortcut, she might get lost trying to find her way to the fort.

"I certainly misjudged Bart Chandler," Amanda said, breaking into Sheila's thoughts. "I thought he was compassionate and very warm-hearted."

"Well, he's not!" Sheila snapped. "He's a cold-blooded, despicable skunk! I wish . . . I wish . . ."

"You wish what?"

Sheila's voice dropped to a whisper that sounded terribly forlorn, "I wish I had never met him." She drew up the top blanket, then rolled to her side. Tears glazed her eyes. She tried to hold them back, but the effort was futile. She was too heartsick not to cry. Not wanting anyone to know, she kept her sobs muffled.

But Amanda could see that she was crying, for her shoulders shook with each racking sob.

Janice was still sitting at the fire. She was alone, for Luke had retired. She had a pleased smile on her face, having seen Sheila's angry expression when she came back from talking to Bart. She had passed the campfire quickly, but Janice still caught her expression. Apparently, Sheila had failed to inveigle Bart back into her good graces.

Janice was tempted to leave camp and go talk to Bart herself, but she resisted the urge. She suspected Bart was the kind of man who liked to make the first move. She wouldn't rush him. After all, she had plenty of time.

Chapter Twenty-One

The forest-covered slopes of the Black Hills still lay ahead, but the travelers had reached high ground. They stopped at noon, ate a cold lunch, and were about to move on when Luke, looking down in the valley below, spotted smoke coming from a distant campfire. He drew it to Bart's attention. The smoke was swirling upward over pines and aspen to disappear into a cerulean sky.

"We'd better check it out," Bart decided.

"You reckon it's Indians?"

He shrugged. "I don't know, but I hope not. They might not be friendly."

"More than likely, it's trappers."

"That's my guess, too. All the same, we'd better make sure." Bart turned to the women. "You ladies stay here. That campfire's probably two, three miles away. We'll be gone a while, but you should be safe here." He went to the pack mule and removed two extra Winchesters and ammunition. He looked at Janice and asked if she knew how to use a rifle.

"No, I don't," she answered. She had never shot a gun in her life. "But, Bart, surely you aren't serious about leaving us here alone!"

"Whoever built that fire is too damned close for comfort. We have to make sure they aren't hostile."

"Can't Luke go without you?" she pleaded.

"This is a job for both of us," he answered firmly. He turned to Amanda. "Do *you* know how to use a rifle?"

"Yes, I do. However, I'm not that good a shot."

He handed her a Winchester and a box of cartridges, then cast a steely gaze in Sheila's direction. "I already know *you're* a good shot, Miss Langsford. One day I had the pleasure of watching you shoot. You hit every target your fiancé pointed out." He quickly gave her a rifle and ammunition, turned to Luke, and said, "Let's go."

Sheila, torn between tears and anger, watched as Bart and Luke rode away. Bart's cold reserve hurt her deeply, yet, it also provoked her anger—how dare he be so cold-hearted and cruel!

"I can't believe they left us here alone!" Janice exclaimed irritably. Her eyes darted back and forth from Amanda to Sheila as she waited for them to agree.

"As Bart said, we're safe here," Amanda replied calmly.

"Oh?" Janice asserted. "Then why did he leave us rifles?"

"I'm sure it's simply a precaution." Amanda went to her horse, removed a rolled blanket from behind her saddle, then spread it on the grass. "I don't know about you two, but I'm going to use this time to get some rest. We have a lot of hard traveling ahead."

Janice decided to lie down also, but she was certain she wouldn't get much rest. After all, at any moment they could be accosted by Indians, or even attacked by a wild animal! She arranged her blanket beside Amanda's. Not that she craved Amanda's closeness, but she wanted to be close to the woman's rifle. That way, if danger approached, Amanda could protect her.

A breeze, drifting warmly, and the melodious chirping of birds, had a lulling effect, and Amanda was soon sleeping soundly. Janice, despite her fear, fell asleep shortly thereafter.

Sheila stepped quietly to the women, and their deep, steady breathing assured her that they were both sleeping soundly. She had hoped for this; she didn't think she'd find a better time to leave.

Her gaze rested a long moment on Amanda. She was a true friend and Sheila liked her immensely. She prayed that Amanda and the others would reach Yellow Bear's village safely. She also uttered a prayer for their safe journey from the village to Fort Laramie. She hesitated for just a fraction—maybe she should stay with her friend—but as Bart's heartless treatment of her crossed her mind, she knew she couldn't remain. Bart's cruel rejection was more than she could bear!

Sheila moved furtively to her horse. Bart had reclaimed his stallion, and Luke had borrowed an army gelding for her to ride. She slipped the rifle into the scabbard, then put the cartridges in the saddlebags' pouch. Hurrying to the pack mule, she found a package of dried jerky, two cans of beans, and matches. These she put in the saddle-bags' other pouch. Her canteen was full, but water wouldn't be a problem; she'd soon reach the Platte River.

She swung up onto the army-issue saddle, kneed the gelding gently, and rode away quietly.

A couple of hours after Sheila left, Bart and Luke returned. They galloped into camp, and as Luke got down from his horse, he said, "It was only trappers; nothin' to worry about."

Bart, dismounting, noticed Sheila's gelding was missing. At the same instant Amanda exclaimed, "Sheila's gone!"

"Damn it!" Bart raged.

"Janice and I took a nap, and when we woke up Sheila wasn't here." Amanda was terribly worried. "I can't believe she did something so foolish!"

"*I* can believe it!" Bart snapped. "Hell, she took off once before. That's how she met up with you and Janice!"

"Yes, and she was also taken captive," Amanda replied. "You'd think that would have taught her not to be so reckless."

"Not that stubborn, deceitful woman!" he uttered fiercely.

"She might be stubborn," Amanda retorted reproachfully, "but she isn't deceitful!"

"The hell she isn't!" Bart was steaming. "But I don't have time to argue with you." He spoke to Luke. "You all go on, but leave a trail I can follow. I'll find Sheila,

330

then we'll catch up to you if we have to ride through the night."

"Where do you think she's headed?" Luke asked.

"Fort Swafford!" Bart said bitterly.

"No!" Amanda disputed. "She wouldn't go there. Bart, if you head in that direction, you'll never find her. She's going to Fort Laramie. You must believe me. I know what I'm saying." Amanda, imagining the danger that could befall Sheila, shuddered visibly. "You must find her, Bart. But you won't accomplish that backtracking toward Fort Swafford!"

She sounded as though she knew what she was talking about. "All right," Bart replied. "I'll head toward Fort Laramie. But, for Sheila's sake, I hope you aren't wrong."

"I'm not," she said firmly.

Bart grabbed a few supplies, then mounted his stallion and took off at a fast canter.

"I ain't never known a woman to be as much trouble as Sheila Langsford!" Luke mumbled.

Amanda turned on him with sudden fury. "Don't you dare say anything bad about Sheila! It breaks my heart to think what that girl has gone through!"

"What *she's* gone through?" he countered. "What about Bart?"

Amanda suppressed her anger. Luke might not know that the Dwyers had manipulated Sheila; maybe Bart didn't tell him. She considered telling him herself, but preferring not to talk about it in front of Janice, she changed her mind. She wasn't sure if Sheila wanted Janice to know.

"Shouldn't we be leaving?" Amanda asked Luke.

That she had dropped the discussion so abruptly surprised him. Women! he thought crankily. There was no figurin' 'em!

At dusk, Sheila stopped to spend the night beside the Platte River. Worried that Bart or Luke might be looking for her, she decided not to build a fire. She ate dried jerky. It wasn't very tasty, but it satisfied her hunger.

Night descended, but the moon's golden rays illuminated the landscape. In the distance, Sheila could hear a wolf's lonesome howl. She wondered if the animal was a female crying for its mate; if so, then she knew exactly why it sounded so forlorn.

The wolf finally stopped wailing. Then, except for the river's gentle lapping, silence reigned supreme. The quiet was unnerving, and she wished for the sounds of nocturnal creatures. Anything was better than total silence.

Sheila lay back on her blanket, and drew her rifle close to her side. She didn't think she would be able to fall asleep. The vast wilderness was frightening, especially after dark. For a moment her courage weakened, and she wished she had stayed with the others. But as Bart's cold manner came to mind, she decided she'd rather take her chances out here alone then subject herself to his contempt.

Sheila's fatigue eventually took its toll, and she drifted into sleep. But slumber brought her no peace, for she dreamt of Bart.

She had been sleeping about an hour when her horse, picking up a scent, whinnied softly. But the animal's warning was too quiet to awaken Sheila.

Chandler rode stealthily to the river's bank, dismounted, and tied his stallion next to Sheila's horse. Bart was a superb tracker, and finding Sheila had been easy. Moving soundlessly, he went to Sheila and knelt beside her. She was moaning softly in her sleep, and her face seemed tormented. She was obviously having a bad dream. He wondered if her conscience was bothering her!

Bart placed a firm hand on her shoulder. "Wake up, Sheila."

Her eyes flew open instantly, and she sat up with a bolt. "Bart!" she exclaimed. She wasn't surprised that he had followed her, but she was very alarmed to find him leaning over her. If he had been a predator, she would have been totally vulnerable to him. How could she have slept so soundly?

A reproachful scowl was on his face. "Damn it, Sheila! Didn't the last time you ran away teach you anything?" He was furious. She was as hard-headed as she was beautiful!

"Why did you come after me?" she asked angrily. "Why should you care what happens to me?"

"Whether I like it or not, you're still my responsibility!"

"Well, I hereby relieve you of that obligation. I'll take responsibility for myself."

"That's very funny!" he retorted.

She wanted to defend herself, but how could she? He was right, damn him! He had walked right up to her while she slept like a baby.

"I hate you!" she declared fiercely, in lieu of anything better to say.

Fury lurked beneath his sudden smile. "I really don't

333

care if you hate me or not, Miss Langsford. You're coming with me in any case. You'll remain my responsibility until I hand you over into your father's care. Unless you'd rather I hand you back to Lieutenant Dwyer.''

She sprang angrily to her feet. "You detestable, cold-hearted cad!"

He stood up slowly, with the litheness of a panther. He spoke evenly, but there was a fierce glint in his eyes. "You'll behave civilly, or find yourself tied and gagged.''

"You'd do it, too, wouldn't you? You damned bully!"

"I would, without a doubt.'' Their gazes locked in silent warfare, then with uncanny calmness, he said, "Get undressed.''

"What?'' she cried sharply.

"You heard me. Get undressed. I've decided to take a bath.'' He hadn't bathed since leaving the stockade, and the river was tempting. "I don't intend to leave you on the bank so you can run away,'' he continued. "That leaves me only two choices. We bathe together or I tie you up so you can't leave.'' He arched a brow. "Which one shall it be?''

She certainly didn't want to be tied up, but she didn't want to bathe with him, either. "How dare you give me such an ultimatum!'' she spat, hands on hips, and her foot tapping angrily.

He was through bickering, for he was anxious to get his bath over with. They had a long night of traveling ahead. "Apparently, you don't want to cooperate, so I'll get the rope and tie you.'' He reached down and picked up her rifle. He wouldn't put it past the woman to use it to her advantage.

"Wait! I'll go in the water with you," Sheila decided. "But you better keep your distance!"

He responded with a cold grin. "That goes both ways."

"Don't flatter yourself! I'd rather wallow with a pig!"

"You already did!" The image of Lieutenant Dwyer flashed in his mind.

Bart whirled about and went to his horse; he delved into his saddlebags and removed a bar of soap. He walked downstream, but not very far from Sheila, then propped her rifle against a tree and began taking off his clothes.

Sheila, turning away, undressed as quickly as possible and waded into the water. The river was shallow, and the bottom was flat. She had to sit down in order for the water to cover her breasts. Fuming over Bart's rudeness, she remained seated with her back facing him. She could hear the gentle slapping of water as he bathed. Then, he suddenly appeared behind her. She looked over her shoulder and was astounded to find him standing over her, his outstretched hand offering her the soap.

She took it in a shaky grasp, for she was fully aware of his naked maleness. Against her will, an intense desire surged through her, and her love for Bart sprang to life, taking control of her heart and mind. Despite his unfair treatment of her, she still wanted him. How furiously she wanted him!

Bart read the invitation in her enchanting brown eyes, and it sent his resolve fleeing to the far corner of his mind. Caught up in the magic moment, he sat beside her, then moved her so that she rested between his legs, her back resting against his chest. He took the soap from her hand and began to rub the bar gently over her bare flesh.

He sudsed her arms, shoulders, taking tender care to wash her full breasts with a stimulating motion. Slowly, he moved the soap down to her stomach. She raised her knees so that he could brush the bar over her legs. He intentionally saved the best for last, and the soap stroked across her thigh, then down to her womanly softness.

Sheila moaned with longing, and her head moved back and forth against his shoulder. She was devoid of all rational thought, was conscious only of Bart's tender yet fiery ministrations.

He dropped the bar so that his hand could cup her firmly. As his finger entered her warm depths, his lips trailed a path along the side of her cheek, then down to her neck. Forcefully, he turned her in his arms, bent his head over hers, and kissed her roughly.

Standing, he swept her up, carried her to the bank, and placed her on the spread blanket. He gently eased his body on top of hers, and as his hardness rested against her moist crevice, his lips seized hers in a demanding caress. "I want you . . . I want you," he murmured with desire, his mind filled only with longing. Suddenly, his lips claimed hers again.

Sheila, a prisoner of rapture, returned his kiss with equal passion. "Bart! Bart!" she cried throatily, her body aching for him to possess her fully.

His lips traveled thoroughly over her breasts before they dipped down past her stomach to relish her completely.

Tremors of ecstasy rocked through her as she surrendered breathlessly and with unbridled abandon, her passion now flaring uncontrollably.

His lips once again moved over her stomach, then

etched a blazing path across her breasts before capturing her mouth in a kiss so exciting that explosive sensations wafted through her entire being.

Bart's need was demanding release, and he urged her legs about his waist. She instinctively locked her ankles, and waited expectantly for his exciting entry.

With one deep thrust, he was fully inside her, causing Sheila to cry out with desire. He began moving against her with masterful strokes, and she responded eagerly to his rhythmic thrusting. He kissed her passionately, his tongue tasting, exploring the sweetness of her mouth.

Bart cupped her buttocks firmly, and drew her thighs as close to his as possible. As his strokes grew faster, deeper, she clung to him, his aggressive rhythm driving her toward love's glorious peak.

Bart's passion soon reached total fulfillment, and his body trembled with ecstasy as he spilled his seed deep inside her. Sheila also achieved a shattering climax, and sighed with rapture.

He moved to lie at her side, but she didn't snuggle against him. Now that her passion was sated, the trouble between them loomed back into focus. She despised herself for letting desire weaken her resolve. What was wrong with her? Didn't she have any self-restraint, any pride? She sighed defeatedly. She apparently had no defense against Bart Chandler!

Bart's thoughts were very similar to Sheila's. He was also disappointed in his behavior. It had taken only one seductive look from Sheila, and he had been putty in her hands. Hereafter, he swore resolutely, he would have to be more firm. How did he expect to get over Sheila if he kept making love to her? Reminding himself that she was

337

deceitful and totally untrustworthy, he got quickly to his feet, cast her a steely glance, and muttered gruffly, "Get dressed. It's time to leave."

His curt manner came as no surprise. She hadn't expected him to act otherwise. The cold-hearted devil was determined to treat her like a trollop!

"Why are we leaving now?" she asked. "Why not wait until morning?"

"I told Luke we'd catch up to him if we had to ride all night. Just because you were self-centered enough to run away doesn't mean I'm going to lose a day's travel. It's imperative that we reach Yellow Bear before the Dywers do."

Sheila agreed in part; they *did* need to reach Yellow Bear without delay. However, she didn't consider herself self-centered. That her flight could cost a day's travel to Yellow Bear's village hadn't crossed her thoughts. Leaving Bart had been the only thing on her mind.

Bart walked downstream to where he had left his clothes, and Sheila began putting on her riding apparel. She had finished dressing when Bart returned carrying her rifle.

"What happened tonight doesn't change anything between us," he said. His tone was icy cold.

She threw him a defiant look. "Oh, yes, it changes one thing, Bart Chandler! It changes my opinion of you. I thought you were callous and cold-hearted. But now I know you're much worse than that—you're a low-down, unfeeling varmint!" With that, she knelt beside the blanket, rolled it, then moved to her horse and attached the blanket behind her saddle. Returning, she grabbed her rifle from Bart's hands, went back to her horse, mounted, then slapped the reins against the gelding's neck and was gone in a flash.

Bart mounted his stallion, and quickly caught up to her.

Luke was drowsy, and he poured himself a cup of coffee. He was sitting alone at the campfire; the women were asleep. He considered dozing off for a little while, but instantly discarded the notion. They were in dangerous territory, and falling asleep was too risky. He took a large drink of coffee. For his sake and the women's, he needed to stay alert.

Detecting movement, he glanced over his shoulder and was surprised to see Amanda leaving her bedroll. Carrying her rifle, she came to the fire and sat beside him. "I'll take the second watch," she said.

"You don't have to do that," he replied, even though he was grateful for her offer.

"I know I don't have to," she said impatiently. "But you need your sleep."

"Are you sure you can stay awake until mornin'?"

She sighed testily. "Honestly, Luke! Just because I'm a woman doesn't mean I'm not dependable!"

"I'm sorry. Sometimes I can act like a real heel."

She wasn't about to argue with that.

"I shouldn't be so cranky," he continued, "but considerin' what Sheila did to Bart—"

Amanda cut in irritably. "Sheila didn't do anything to Bart!"

He looked at her as though she were daft. "The hell she didn't! She told him she'd marry him, then the first chance she got, she crawled into bed with Dwyer."

"Not willingly, she didn't."

"What do you mean by that?"

"Didn't Bart tell you that she was manipulated by the Dwyers?"

Luke shook his head.

"I should be surprised, but I'm not. Evidently, he doesn't want you to know what a jackass he really is!" She poured herself a cup of coffee, and as she drank it, she told Luke everything.

"Those lousy bastards!" he seethed. "I oughta break their damned necks!"

"Well, you can start with Bart! The way he treated Sheila was inexcusable! She gave herself to Donald to save his life, and in return, Bart treated her like . . . like dirt!"

Luke was baffled. "Bart's behavior doesn't make sense. I know him better than anybody else, and he's not capable of this kind of cruelty. He obviously doesn't know why Sheila went with Dwyer."

"How can you be so sure?"

"If Bart knew the truth, Dwyer's face would be a bloody pulp."

"But Sheila said that Donald told Bart what was going on."

"I have a feelin' that somehow Sheila and Bart didn't make themselves understood to each other. They probably let their tempers get in the way." Amanda wondered if Luke was right.

Stretching, Luke stifled a yawn. "Well, Bart will catch up to us tomorrow; I'll have a long talk with him then."

She watched as he got to his feet and moved away. Luke placed his blanket a short distance from the fire, then, using his saddle for a pillow, he lay down and rolled to his side.

Amanda noticed that he had left his rifle behind. She picked it up and went over to him. Kneeling, she placed the gun beside him. "Here; you forgot this."

His back was toward her, and he turned over.

"I'm not a very good shot," she explained. "I think you should keep your rifle within reach."

Their gazes locked, and Luke was acutely aware of her incredible loveliness. She still looked very much like the young girl he had once loved. Her looks hadn't changed; she had simply matured with grace and elegance.

Amanda could sense his thoughts, and her heart began to pound expectantly. She was desperate for him to take her into his arms and kiss her.

Luke, desiring her, came very close to throwing caution to the wind, but was stopped suddenly by cold logic, which doused the flame Amanda had rekindled. He was still bent on leaving the past behind, and, turning his back to her, he mumbled, "Wake me up at dawn."

Amanda returned to the fire and stared unblinkingly into the darting flames. Wistfulness, like a recurring pain, washed over her. Luke was beyond her grasp, so why did she keep reaching out for him? She had lost him twenty years ago—a sob lodged in her throat—and she had also lost their baby. Memories cut painfully into her heart as she remembered the son she had borne, only to lose him two hours later. He had lived such a tragically short time, barely long enough for his mother to hold him, love him, and have the minister christen him Luke, after his father.

Tears welled in Amanda's eyes, overflowed, then rolled steadily down her cheeks. She wept quietly, but from the depth of her heart.

Chapter Twenty-Two

Afternoon shadows were blanketing the landscape when Bart and Sheila caught up to Luke and the women. Thomas had left a discernible trail for Bart to follow.

Amanda was greatly relieved to see that Sheila was all right. Janice, on the other hand, had hoped Bart wouldn't find Sheila, and she resented her return. Trapping Bart would be much easier without Sheila around.

Anxious to keep moving, they didn't stop to converse. The passage ahead was steep and perilous, and Luke wanted to complete the dangerous climb before nightfall.

The inclined path was narrow, and the travelers had to ride in single file; Luke led the way and Bart brought up the rear. The horses were held to a slow, steady climb and finally reached the top without a misstep.

The precarious trek had taken a long time, and the sun was now setting. Luke and Bart decided to make camp;

another steep climb loomed ahead, and they didn't want to attempt it until morning.

They were now in Sioux territory, and Bart informed the women there would be no more campfires. From here on, they would eat cold meals and do without coffee.

As the others nibbled on dried jerky, Bart tended to the horses and the pack mule. Luke waited until Bart had watered and tethered the animals before approaching him.

"Bart, let's take a walk," he said.

"A walk?" Bart questioned.

"I wanna talk to you, but what I got to say is private." He gestured toward the women. "I don't want them hearin' us."

A testy frown creased Bart's brow. "Luke, are you about to stick your nose where it doesn't belong?" He wasn't angry, but he sensed Luke wanted to discuss Sheila, and he didn't want to talk about her.

"It's my nose, and I'll do what I please with it!" Luke muttered gruffly. His hand swept toward the distant foliage. "Let's go. What I got to say won't take long."

Bart, complying, followed him into the dense vegetation.

Meanwhile, Amanda, sitting on her bedroll, which was placed beside Sheila's, watched the men move away. She knew why Luke wanted to be alone with Bart, and she prayed that Luke's speculation was right. Maybe Bart *didn't* know that the Dwyers had forced Sheila into submitting! Sheila was on her blanket, sitting Indian-style with her elbows propped on her knees and her chin cupped in her hands. Amanda gave her a sidelong glance. She looked crestfallen. A hopeful smile touched

Amanda's lips. If Luke was right about Bart, then Sheila's heartache would soon disappear.

Amanda longed to talk to Sheila about Bart, but Janice's bed was beside Sheila's, and Janice was awake. If she tried to draw Sheila into a conversation, Janice would hear every word. And in Amanda's opinion, Bart's and Sheila's relationship was none of Janice's business.

Bart, impatient, crossed his arms over his chest, eyed Luke sternly, and said, "Okay, we're alone now. Say your piece."

"It's got to do with Sheila."

"I figured that."

"Do you know why she gave herself to Dwyer?"

"I suppose she was hoping to resume their relationship."

Luke shook his head with wonder. "Bart, you thick-skulled jackass! Didn't you ask her why she was with him?"

"Why should I?"

" 'Cause if you had, you'd know she did it to save your life!"

Bart was taken aback. "What are you saying?"

Slowly, and in detail, Luke explained how the Dwyers had manipulated Sheila, leaving her no choice but to submit to Donald's demands to save Bart's life.

"How did you learn about this?" Bart asked.

"Amanda told me. She didn't even know about it until it was all over. She persuaded Sheila to confide in her."

Bart was sick . . . sick all the way to his soul! My God, he had treated Sheila horribly! No wonder she was

345

so angry! Remorse cut into him without mercy, causing him to groan audibly. Could he ever make it up to her?

"She might never forgive me," Bart murmured, speaking his thoughts aloud.

"She'll forgive you," Luke said. "Considerin' she loves you enough to give herself to Dwyer, she loves you enough to forgive you."

"Dwyer!" Bart muttered murderously. "I'm going to kill that sonofabitch!"

"Don't do nothin' rash," Luke advised. "Killin' him ain't gonna get you nowhere except in a lot of trouble. If you wanna beat the hell out of him, then that's fine. I'll even hold the bastard for you!"

Bart pushed his anger to the far recesses of his mind. At the moment there was nothing he could do about Dwyer. Now, only Sheila's feelings were important. He despised himself for the way he had treated her. "God!" he moaned. "Sheila might forgive me, but I don't think I'll ever forgive myself!"

"Don't be so hard on yourself, Bart. You didn't know." Luke placed an encouraging hand on his arm. "Stay here; I'll send Sheila to you." Luke hurried back toward camp.

Sheila dominated Bart's thoughts, dulling his instincts and his ability to sense danger. He was thus not attuned to his surroundings, which made it easy for Three Moons, who was hidden in the shrubbery, to sneak in closer. Three Moons and the warriors with him had come upon the campsite by accident. They had completed a successful raid on an isolated ranch, and were now on their way back to their village. Three Moons had indeed been surprised to come upon White Cloud, but he wasn't sure if he wanted to attack him and his companions. Not that he wouldn't relish killing Bart, but the man was Yellow Bear and Spotted Wing's brother—killing him might arouse the Great Spirit's anger!

Three Moons remained hidden in the foliage. He'd wait for White Cloud to return to camp, then he would slip back to where his warriors were waiting. Fear of the Great Spirit's wrath had persuaded him to let White Cloud live.

Luke emerged from the thick shrubbery, and went straight to Sheila. With a wide grin on his face, he told her that Bart wanted to see her.

"Well, I don't want to see him!" she mumbled peevishly.

Luke, impatient, reached down, grasped her arm and drew her to her feet. "He's waitin' for you. Just walk into the bushes and keep goin' straight ahead. You can't miss him."

She flung off his hand. "I said, I don't want to see him!"

"My goodness!" Janice interrupted. "Luke, you have no right to insist that she see Bart!"

"Stay out of this!" Amanda told her. She had seen the smile on Luke's face. Bart apparently hadn't known about the Dwyers' evil trickery!

"Ma'am," Luke said to Sheila, "what Bart's got to say to you is mighty important." When she didn't respond, he encouraged, "I think you oughta hear him out."

"All right!" she gave in. "I'll talk to him!" She

moved away quickly, and her long, determined strides concealed her hesitancy from the others. She didn't want to be alone with Bart; she saw no purpose to it. They had been alone last night and until this afternoon, and the hours had been spent in almost total silence. Why did Bart want to see her, now? Hadn't he hurt her enough? Did he want to bury the knife a little deeper?

She made her way into the bushes, and pushed aside the bristly branches that kept trying to grab at her skirt. Dusk was falling rapidly, for the sun had made its entire descent. It would soon be fully dark.

Sheila found Bart, and stood stiffly before him. "What do you want?" she snapped.

"Sheila . . ." he began, but that was as far as he got, for at that moment Three Moons sprang from the shrubbery. He had a rock in his hand, and as he lunged forward, Bart caught a quick glimpse of him before he slammed the rock against Bart's head. The hard blow knocked him unconscious, and he fell heavily to the ground.

Sheila started to scream for Luke, but Three Moons was suddenly upon her, his hand clamped tightly over her mouth. She struggled wildly, but was helpless against his superior strength.

Three Moons's hand moved up until it also covered her nose. Unable to breathe, her struggles grew weaker until, finally, she passed out.

The warrior slung her across his shoulder, then trudged his way through the thicket and to the place where his men awaited. He draped his captive across his pony, mounted, then motioned that it was time to leave.

The Indians rode away stealthily and headed toward

the narrow path that led farther into the mountains. The passage was steep, but the warriors had traveled it often and were not afraid to make the climb at night.

Three Moons's decision to capture Sheila had been made in a moment; there hadn't been time for him to think it over. But, now, as he considered what he had done, he was pleased with himself. He remembered Sheila very well; she was Lieutenant Dwyer's woman. That was why White Cloud had abducted her. The exchange between the woman and Yellow Bear had failed, and White Cloud had been forced to keep the woman with him. Three Moons wondered why they were still together; he pondered the question for a moment, then dismissed it. It made no difference; the woman was still linked to the lieutenant, and he intended to use her to his advantage. Flying Feather's son, Slow Coyote, would pay many horses to own the lieutenant's woman. That Dwyer had killed Flying Feather was now widely known among the Sioux. Three Moons was certain that Slow Coyote craved revenge for his father's murder. Killing the woman would give Slow Coyote much satisfaction.

Three Moons knew that Slow Coyote was riding with Crazy Horse, and through their many raids, Slow Coyote had stolen many horses. Three Moons was determined to have some of those horses for himself! He wasn't sure, however, of Slow Coyote's whereabouts, but the old medicine man, Lame Crow, would know. He had recently visited Crazy Horse, and, upon his return, had mentioned seeing Slow Coyote. He had also elaborated on Slow Coyote's valuable possessions and his herd of horses.

Three Moons was hesitant about taking his captive

349

back to his village, but he knew that was where he would find Lame Crow. Yellow Bear would undoubtedly try to convince him to set his captive free. A harsh frown crossed the warrior's brow—Yellow Bear could argue until he ran out of breath, but it would do him no good. This woman was his prisoner, which made her his property to do with as he pleased.

Sheila, regaining consciousness, moaned weakly. Her eyes fluttered open. At first, everything was a hazy blur, and she blinked several times to clear her vision. The night was bathed in moonlight, and she could make out a pony's hooves slowly covering a well-beaten path. She knew she was on that pony, flung facedown like a slaughtered deer. The position was uncomfortable; her back ached and the blood running into her head made her temples throb.

Three Moons's attack flashed across her mind. It had happened so quickly. He had sprung out of the thicket without warning. She remembered him hitting Bart over the head, but she wasn't sure what he had used—a rock maybe? Then he had put his hand over her mouth and nose until she passed out.

She wondered why Three Moons had taken her captive. What did he want with her? Did he plan to kill her? But why? Why would he want her to die? She was suddenly afraid, terribly afraid, but, at the moment, her discomfort was more pressing than her fear. Riding facedown across Three Moons's horse was awkward and painful. Her chest was flat against the pony's back, and Three Moons's arms, pressed against her spine, had her pinned so tightly, she could barely breathe. Her arms and legs were dangling over each side of the horse, and she was powerless to lift her head, which was hanging as limply as a rag doll's. She tried to sit up, but Three Moons's arms dug into her, pressing her chest more firmly against the horse.

"Please let me up," she managed to plead.

Three Moons didn't speak English, but it wasn't necessary to understand her words to know that she wished to sit upright. A malicious smile curled his lips. He intended to leave her slung over his pony for a long time. She was his captive, and Three Moons didn't treat captives kindly.

Sheila didn't ask a second time. She figured it wouldn't do any good, and she wasn't about to beg. She tried to relax, hoping it might make the ride a little less jarring and uncomfortable. But it didn't help much. Her thoughts went to Bart. Three Moons had struck a severe blow across Bart's head. Dear God, what if he was dead? That fear tore into her ruthlessly. Bart had aroused her anger, true, and had disappointed her terribly; nevertheless, she still loved him. That he might be dead was too heartbreaking even to consider, and she forcefully thrust the possibility from her mind.

Janice was sleeping soundly, her bedroll next to Amanda's. Not wanting to awaken her, Amanda moved away quietly and went over to Luke, who was lying on his blanket. His arms were folded under his head, and he was gazing up at the many stars lighting the vast heavens.

"Luke," she said, sitting beside him, "I'm a little worried about Sheila. She and Bart have been out there a long time."

He wasn't concerned. "I reckon they're makin' up. Sometimes, that takes a while . . ." He arched a brow. "If you know what I mean."

She knew what he meant, and she supposed he was right. "I'm glad everything worked out between them."

"Yeah, I'm glad, too." Then, sounding somewhat bitter, Luke added, "But not all love stories end happily ever after, do they?"

Amanda stiffened. "You're a nice man, Luke Thomas, but you have a very serious flaw."

He chuckled amusedly. "Only one? You gotta be kiddin'."

"One *serious* flaw," she emphasized.

He sat up and looked at her. Anger lurked in his azure eyes. "Go ahead, tell me what it is. You're probably dyin' to say it. What's my serious flaw?"

"You aren't forgiving."

"You want me to forgive you for jiltin' me twenty years ago?" He waved his hands impatiently. "All right, I forgive you. Now, are you satisfied?"

"No! Are you?"

"Me? What do you mean by that?"

"Don't you want to know why I married Norman? How can you be satisfied without answers?"

"You already said you didn't love him, so I reckon you married him for his money."

Her eyes flashed petulantly. "Yes, I did marry him for his money!"

He regarded her quizzically. "So? Do you want a pat on the back from me? Congratulations?"

"I want you to listen to me."

He sighed. "Amanda, for God's sake, let it be. After twenty years, what difference does it make?"

"It might not make any difference to you, but it does to me."

"All right," he gave in, but his expression told her that he wasn't really interested. "Tell me what you gotta say, but make it fast."

He was exasperating, and she was tempted to leave and never talk to him again. But she forced herself to remain. She was determined to explain why she had married Norman Wilson. She could no longer stand Luke thinking the worst of her. Her pride, as well as her heart, demanded that she tell him the truth.

She drew a long breath, sorted her thoughts, then began softly. "Two months after you left St. Louis, I realized I was pregnant."

Luke tensed, but he didn't say anything.

"It didn't take long," she continued, "until my mother caught on. I was terribly sick in the mornings. I tried to keep it from her, but she found out nonetheless. She confronted me, and I had to tell the truth. She went to my father . . ." Amanda's voice grew raspy. "God, how hard it was for me to face him! I was only eighteen, and I was scared to death. I was alone with him in his study, and I can still remember the rage on his face. It was frightening! He was so angry that I thought he was going to explode. He began ranting and raving, but somewhere along the way, I suddenly realized he was no longer shouting about my pregnancy, but about his own problems. He was deeply in debt, and the bank was threatening to take away not only our home but also my father's business. This was all a shock to me. I had no inkling that he was on the brink of financial ruin.''

Amanda paused, and Luke saw that she had tears in her eyes.

''My father felt he couldn't live with destitution and a daughter pregnant out of wedlock. That was too much for him. He preferred death over living with such shame. I didn't know that he was planning to kill himself the day I barged into his study unannounced. I caught him at his desk with a pistol aimed at his head. Somehow, my pleading got through to him, and he put the gun away. That night, Norman came to the house to see me. Norman was my beau before I met you. I don't know if he loved me, but it was clear he desired me and wanted me. Norman always wanted what he couldn't have, and although I allowed his courtship, I consistently said no to his marriage proposals.''

Again, Amanda paused. She waited a long moment before continuing. ''I was in the garden that night, and my mother sent Norman to me. He could see that I was terribly upset. I must give Norman credit where credit is due. He was very concerned and troubled to find me so disturbed, which was unlike Norman; usually he was too wrapped up in himself to be so considerate. I responded to his kindness and told him everything. I cried and he consoled me. We were in the garden a long time. I alternated between talking and crying. He would listen as I talked, and hold me as I cried. Through it all, Norman seemed to be battling with his own inner conflict. Did he want me badly enough to marry me even though I was carrying another man's child? His need to have me obviously won the battle, and he asked me to marry him. I

354

was stunned. He assured me that my pregnancy didn't matter and that he would raise the child as his own. I was touched by his kindness, but nevertheless I refused to marry him. I didn't love him, and I also knew he wasn't usually so considerate of my feelings. But then he offered me something I couldn't refuse. Norman had inherited his father's fortune; he was very wealthy. He said if I would marry him, he would pay off my father's debts and invest in his business.''

"So you married him to save your father," Luke said flatly.

"Yes," she replied. "But I'm not a martyr, Luke. I admit I was aware that marriage to Norman would protect me and my baby; and that fact influenced my decision.''

"But I would have married you," he said firmly.

"But you weren't there. Norman was. Oh Luke, can't you understand how I felt? We had only known each other a few weeks. Our romance was a whirlwind. The night before you left, I let you make love to me. If you'll remember, you were the first! The next morning, you rode out of my life telling me you'd be back someday. My God, I didn't know you, not really. How could I be sure you would come back?''

"I told you I would!" he said angrily.

"And I was supposed to build my future and my child's future on that? A promise from a man I didn't know? Furthermore, you were a trapper. How could I be sure that you wouldn't die out there in the mountains? It happens all the time. Trappers have accidents and bleed to death or perish in the snow. I couldn't turn my back on my father, nor could I bring my child into this world out of wedlock on the slim chance that you might come back to me. I had to make a choice, and I made the one I thought was best for everyone concerned."

"What about the child?" Luke asked so quietly that Amanda barely heard. He somehow knew the answer would tear into his heart.

"We had a son," she said, a sob in her throat. "He was born two months too early. He only lived a couple of hours. I named him Luke Thomas Wilson."

Luke responded with silence.

Amanda looked at him intently, trying desperately to see into his mind, but his expression was unreadable. Luke's thoughts were his own.

The silence between them dragged into minutes. Amanda, her nerves stretched to their limit, was about to insist that Luke tell her his thoughts when, suddenly, she caught sight of Bart staggering out of the shrubbery. He was holding his hand to his head, but she could still see the blood oozing through his fingers. Bounding to her feet, she cried, "Bart, my God, what happened?"

"Sheila!" he groaned. "She's gone! Three Moons took her!"

Chapter Twenty-Three

Amanda cleaned Bart's wound where the rock had struck his temple, leaving a gash that, despite the profuse amount of blood coming from it, wasn't very deep. The laceration was discolored and swollen, but it looked worse than it really was.

"I'm going after her," Bart said the moment Amanda finished.

"It won't do you any good," Luke commented. "You can't track Three Moons in the dark. Furthermore, that warrior knows these mountains like the back of his hand. He can lead you in circles, get you lost, then sneak up on you and shoot you in the back."

"What am I supposed to do then?" Bart questioned sharply. "Let him have Sheila?"

"He's most likely headed for his village, and that's

where we're goin'. When we get there, we'll get Sheila back.''

"What if he isn't going to the village?" Bart eyed Luke intensely.

"Then we'll get Yellow Bear to help us find him.''

"No," Bart mumbled. "I'm going after her now." As he got to his feet, he tottered precariously.

"You ain't in no condition to go anywhere alone," Luke told him. "You probably have a slight concussion. You were knocked out for more than an hour.''

"Three Moons and Sheila aren't that far ahead of us," Amanda said. "If we leave now, we can reach the village shortly after they do.''

"We got a steep climb awaitin'," Luke replied. "Goin' up that narrow path is dangerous in daylight, and I got bad misgivings 'bout you and Janice tryin' to make it at night.''

"The sky is cloudless and the moon is almost full," Amanda said. "It isn't that dark.''

Janice, standing nearby, was listening closely. Bart's reaction to Sheila's capture had upset her. Was he still in love with her? Good Lord, the woman had been in another man's bed. How could he still care about her? Janice's confidence was shaken. Had she made this trip for nothing? Despite everything that had happened, was she going to lose Bart to Sheila after all? She found herself wishing Three Moons would eliminate her once and for all.

Janice, immersed in thought, wasn't aware that Luke was speaking to her until he raised his voice and repeated his question. "Do you think you can make the climb at night?''

Attempting such a steep trek in the dark terrified her.

However, she wanted to remain in Bart's good graces. She might be wrong about his feelings; maybe he was only concerned about Sheila's abduction because he felt responsible for her. She decided to be agreeable. "If everyone wants to leave now, I have no objections. The climb is no doubt dangerous, but I'm sure I can do it."

Amanda studied Janice suspiciously. She knew the young woman very well, and this kind of consideration was not Janice's usual behavior. Amanda wondered if she had an ulterior motive for cooperating.

"Then it's settled," Luke remarked as he turned to Bart. "We're goin' with you. Let's pack up and move out."

Time passed agonizingly slowly for Sheila. Three Moons left her draped across his horse, and the unnatural position caused her arms and legs to turn numb. For a long time she had felt a tingling in her dangling limbs, but the tingle of life had finally given way to complete numbness. Her head, which rested between her hanging arms, throbbed with each beat of her heart. If Three Moons didn't relent and let her up soon, she felt as though she would not last.

But Sheila had more grit than she realized, and as this force surfaced, her eyes flamed with anger and a look as hard as granite came to her face. Damn it, she wasn't going to ride facedown across this horse one moment longer! She was suddenly determined to sit upright . . . regardless!

They were now on flat ground, and Sheila knew a struggle between her and the warrior wouldn't cause the pony to lose its footing and fall over a cliff. Forcing her arms and legs to move was no easy feat, for they felt lifeless. Through sheer willpower, she managed to wiggle her limbs, which helped the blood circulate, then, as feeling returned, she began to squirm.

Three Moons pressed his arm firmly against her back, trying to hold her in place. But Sheila was struggling too forcefully, and he couldn't control her. He jerked roughly on the reins, bringing the pony to an abrupt halt.

Sheila braced her hands against the horse's side, and gave one huge push, which sent her sliding off the animal's back. As her feet touched the ground, her legs toppled beneath her and she fell helplessly. She lay sprawled for a moment, catching her breath, then, with effort, she managed to stand up. She stared unwaveringly into Three Moons's eyes. His expression was stern; he looked furious. Sheila was scared, but she wasn't about to back down. Without a word, she reached up, grasped his arm for support, then swung herself up behind him.

Three Moons was shocked, but he was also impressed. The white woman was very spirited. He admired her strong will, and decided to let her remain astride.

As the warrior coaxed his pony into a steady canter, Sheila sighed with relief. She had apparently earned her place behind him. Now that she had achieved a more comfortable position, she considered escape. That flicker of hope was quickly doused, however. Escaping from Three Moons and his warriors was impossible. She wondered where he was taking her. She hoped he was going to his village, for Yellow Bear and Golden Dove would certainly help her. Her thoughts moved to Bart. She prayed that he was all right, but Three Moons had struck him severely. Her heart lurched—Bart could be dead! No! she quickly told herself. He's alive!

Tears misted her eyes, but she brushed them away with the back of her hand. She was determined not to cry.

Bart and the others scaled the steep path successfully, and had ridden several miles before stopping to give the horses a short rest. Dawn was only minutes away, and a pink hue, dappled with purple streaks, marked the eastern horizon. They had stopped in a fertile area dotted with towering trees, green shrubbery, and colorful wild flowers.

Bart, leaving the others, walked a short distance away. He paused and gazed northward as though he could somehow spot Sheila through the thick forest. That she was Three Moons's captive, and totally at his mercy, had Bart's nerves at full stretch. If Three Moons harmed her, he would kill him. So help him God!

He had failed to protect Sheila, and blamed himself for her capture. If he had been on his guard, Three Moons couldn't have slipped up on him. Twice now, he had failed Sheila miserably. First, he had believed the worst about her and Donald Dwyer, and now he had let Three Moons whisk her away. He considered himself totally at fault.

Detecting footsteps, Bart glanced over his shoulder.

Janice was coming toward him. She was tired of waiting for Bart to make the first move; also, she was beginning to fear that he never would. She decided it was time to make her feelings clear. Offering a tender smile, she paused at his side and gazed sweetly into his eyes. "Bart, I must talk to you," she murmured.

He wasn't in the mood for Janice, but considering that she had been helpful and cooperative, he figured he owed her the courtesy of listening. "What's on your mind?"

"You are," she replied.

He looked at her inquiringly. "Me?"

Her hand rested on his arm. "Don't you know what I'm trying to say?"

"No," he answered.

"Bart, you aren't making this very easy for me." She summoned her most alluring smile. "I'm very attracted to you. I have been from the first moment I saw you. But you already know that, don't you? I mentioned it to you once before. However, at the time, you were involved with Sheila—"

"I still am," he interrupted. He didn't want to be unkind, however, and he continued gently. "Janice, you're a very lovely young lady. That you find me attractive is very flattering, but I'm in love with Sheila."

"How can you still love her?" she spat shrilly, anger bringing out her true personality. "Good Lord, she gave herself to Donald Dwyer! Have you no pride?"

"She was forced into submitting to him. She did so to save my life."

Janice was astounded. "Is that what she told you?"

"No, she didn't tell me. I found out through Amanda and Luke."

"I don't believe she was forced."

"It's the truth," he replied calmly. Moving past her, he asked her tersely to excuse him.

Steaming, Janice watched as he walked over to Luke and Amanda. Oh, she had been such a fool to come on this trip! Bart was blindly infatuated with Sheila, and nothing she could say or do would change his mind. One shred of hope, however, still remained. Three Moons might kill Sheila; then Bart would certainly be hers for the taking. He would be grief-stricken; a sly smile curled her lips—she would console him tenderly and passionately. Her confidence returned, and with victory on her mind, she went back to the others.

The horses had rested long enough. The group mounted and started toward Yellow Bear's village. Luke estimated they would arrive early the next morning.

Three Moons and his warriors brought their horses to a stop. They intended to eat pemmican and relieve themselves. They had made good time, for Three Moons hadn't bothered with covering their tracks. He saw no purpose to it; White Cloud knew the way to their village. He was sure White Cloud would show up there, demanding his woman be returned. A hard mask fell across Three Moons's face. White Cloud could demand all he wanted, but it would be to no avail. This woman was his captive, and he intended to keep her. White Cloud would undoubtedly offer to fight for her. Three Moons had no objections to that—he would enjoy killing White Cloud in a fight. The Great Spirit couldn't find fault with him for protecting himself. His wrath thus would not be aroused.

Three Moons slid off his pony's back, then reached up and assisted Sheila. He pointed toward the warriors who were relieving themselves. They hadn't bothered to seek the privacy of surrounding shrubbery. Sheila quickly averted her eyes from the Indians and looked back at Three Moons. He was now pointing at her, letting her know she could do the same.

She made a half turn to go into the bushes, but Three Moons's hand clutched her arm and held her in place. He gestured at the spot where she stood.

Understanding his meaning, Sheila's face turned red, but not with embarrassment. Anger flamed in her so fiercely that her cheeks flushed scarlet. She was about to explode. In a flash, the Dwyers and Bart crossed her mind. She was sick and tired of men taking advantage of her! The Dwyers had forced her to swallow her self-respect and do their evil bidding to save Bart's life. In return, Bart had treated her cruelly and selfishly. Now, Three Moons wanted her to submit to his every whim. Well, she was fed up. She could take no more. She'd rather die than allow another man to control her.

With a strength driven by anger, she flung Three Moons's hand from her arm. Eyeing him dauntlessly, she pointed toward the bordering bushes, then whirled about brusquely and headed toward them. She expected him to come after her, but he didn't.

She moved into the thick shrubbery and fought back angry tears. She didn't try to run away; she knew it would be futile.

When she returned, Three Moons handed her a pemmican cake. She was hungry and accepted it without hesitation. As she ate, Three Moons watched her intently. That a white woman could elicit his admiration surprised him. He had thought all white women were of little worth.

Despite Sheila's bravery, Three Moons remained determined to sell her to Slow Coyote. He admired her, true, but not enough to forfeit trading her for several horses. In his opinion, horses were more valuable than women.

Although Sheila kept her eyes turned away from his, she could feel his long, silent scrutiny. She wondered what he was thinking about. Was he trying to decide what to do with her—sell her, make her into a slave, or kill her? All three possibilities sent a chill rippling up her spine.

She intentionally cleared her head of such thoughts, and concentrated on their destination. She hoped, prayed, they were going to Three Moons's village. Surely, Yellow Bear and Golden Dove would save her.

Golden Dove pushed aside the flap on her tepee and stepped inside. She wasn't surprised to find Spotted Wing lying on her bed, staring dejectedly into space. The girl had been terribly depressed since Three Moons left. The warrior had returned the same day White Cloud and the others had departed. He had stayed one day, then was off on another raid. Spotted Wing had wanted him to stay home and plan their wedding. But Three Moons was young and restless, and raids seemed to mean more to him than Spotted Wing.

"Get up and put on your clothes," Golden Dove told the despondent girl. "Today is your brother's wedding day. The ceremony will start soon."

Spotted Wing rose reluctantly. "Oh, Grandmother!"

she moaned. "I envy Dream Dancer! Yellow Bear is so anxious to marry her! I wish Three Moons was as anxious to marry me!"

"Three Moons and Yellow Bear are very different. Your brother feels much compassion for women. Three Moons considers them only a convenience."

"That's not true!" Spotted Wing argued. "He loves me very much, and he will make a wonderful husband!"

Golden Dove sighed impatiently. They had been through this discussion before. Many times she had tried to make Spotted Wing see that Three Moons would not be a tender, loving husband, but her granddaughter was blindly in love and refused to open her eyes. Golden Dove decided to let the subject drop; she was too tired to argue. The last few mornings she had awakened feeling so fatigued that she had barely made it through the day. Now, she felt almost too weak to stand, and she moved slowly to the cooking pit and sat down. She brushed a hand across her brow. It was layered with perspiration. Her skin was warm and clammy, and she knew she was running a fever. She was tempted to go to her bed, lie down, and give in to her illness. But she didn't want to miss Yellow Bear's wedding ceremony. Also, if he knew she was sick, she thought he might postpone his marriage. She was much too happy over his wedding to let it be delayed. She thought highly of Dream Dancer and was thankful that Yellow Bear had found her. She would be a loving wife for her grandson. Her musings shifted to White Cloud, and a pleased smile touched her lips. He had also found a wonderful woman with whom to share his life. It was apparent to Golden Dove that Sheila loved White Cloud with all her heart. She was also kind and compassionate. Yes, her grandsons had done well! If only . . . if only Spotted Wing had chosen as wisely as her brothers!

Night shrouded the village like a dark cowl, but a large fire located in the heart of the encampment illuminated the dancers who were actively enjoying the festivities.

Yellow Bear's wedding was a reason to celebrate, and the people were feasting on wild game, fruits, and several different kinds of nuts. The meat was skewered on spits and was still roasting before the fire; it was the task of many matronly women to make sure the spits were turned to assure that the meat was cooked evenly.

Yellow Bear, standing a short way from the gaiety, watched the activities a little impatiently. He was waiting for Golden Dove to leave his tepee, come to him and tell him that his bride was ready to receive him. The passing minutes seemed long, for his loins were on fire for Dream Dancer. He loved and desired her intensely.

Finally, he caught sight of his grandmother coming toward him. Impatient, he met her halfway.

She smiled at his eagerness. "You may go to your bride."

He hugged Golden Dove briefly, then made a beeline to his tepee. Hurrying inside, he found Dream Dancer in bed, the covers drawn up past her breasts. He knew that underneath the blanket, she lay totally naked.

Dream Dancer's gaze swept appreciatively over her husband. He was strikingly handsome. His shoulder-length hair was freshly washed, and light from the fire smoldering in the cooking pit made the black locks shine

367

with shimmers of blue. His fringed shirt and leggings adhered smoothly to his masculine body, and as Dream Dancer boldly lowered her gaze, she was pleased to see his manhood straining against his tight-fitting pants. Evidently, he desired her as powerfully as she desired him.

He saw where her gaze had wandered. He smiled wryly and a twinkle sparkled in his dark eyes. Hastily, he stripped away his apparel until he wore only his breechcloth.

Dream Dancer, watching with adoration, held out beckoning arms to him. He quickly doffed his final garment, and joined his bride beneath the blanket.

Sweet endearments were exchanged, and they both pledged their undying love, meaning it sincerely. Consummating their marriage, their bodies came together in perfect balance, each erotic stroke a testament to their marriage vows. They moved together rhythmically, and were soon lost in rapturous paradise.

Yellow Bear and Dream Dancer were snuggled together, and were discussing their future when Spotted Wing called to her brother from outside the tepee.

Yellow Bear slipped into his breechcloth, opened the leather flap, and waved his sister inside. He knew something had to be terribly wrong for her to disturb him on his wedding night.

"Golden Dove is very sick," Spotted Wing said, worry etched deeply on her face.

"Sick?" he repeated, as though he needed to hear the word again to actually believe it. He couldn't recall his grandmother ever being ill.

"You must come," Spotted Wing coaxed.

Dream Dancer hurried from her bed and began putting on her clothes. In the short time she had known Golden Dove, she had learned to love her as though she were of her own blood.

Dressed, she went to her husband, placed a gentle hand on his arm, and said softly, "Golden Dove is strong. Maybe she will not die."

A sob lodged in Yellow Bear's throat, making it impossible for him to answer. He took Dream Dancer's hand into his, and with Spotted Wing leading the way, they rushed to Golden Dove's tepee.

Chapter Twenty-Four

Dawn was breaking when Three Moons rode into the village. The people, tired from last night's festivities, were still inside their homes, most of them sound asleep.

Three Moons wasn't sure where to put his captive, and was considering it when Yellow Bear stepped out of Golden Dove's tepee. Yellow Bear wasn't surprised to see that Three Moons had returned, he was about to turn away and head for Lame Crow's lodge when he suddenly caught sight of Sheila. Shocked to find her with Three Moons, he stood as though fastened to the ground, his mouth agape and his eyes staring incredulously. He recovered quickly, and waved the warrior, to a stop.

Reining in his pony, Three Moons faced Yellow Bear. "The woman belongs to me," he said, his eyes daring the man to disagree.

Yellow Bear moved so that he could see Sheila better. "You all right?" he asked her.

"Yes," she answered feebly. She was so fatigued that she could barely stay on the horse.

Yellow Bear, speaking to Three Moons, lapsed back into his own language. "Why do you have this woman?"

"She is my captive."

"You had no right to capture her!"

Before Three Moons could reply, he was distracted by Spotted Wing. She had been with Golden Dove, but the sounds of voices had brought her outside. She hurried to the man who was to be her husband and exclaimed breathlessly, "Three Moons, you are back!" The words had barely passed her lips when she noticed his captive. Her countenance turned angry. "Why do you have this woman with you?" she spat.

"We will talk later!" he replied firmly. His gaze turned to Yellow Bear. "Now, I take my captive to my father's tepee. Tomorrow morning, I will leave and she will leave with me." With that, he coaxed his pony into a slow gallop and headed farther into the village.

Yellow Bear was visibly upset. "I must call a meeting of the council. The woman belongs to White Cloud. It was wrong for Three Moons to take her."

Spotted Wing was just as upset as her brother but not for the same reasons. That Three Moons had treated her so coldly was infuriating. Also, he was planning to leave again in the morning! If he truly loved her, he would not go away so much! A pang of jealousy coursed through her. The white woman was very beautiful, and she wondered if that was why Three Moons had taken her.

"Go back to our grandmother," Yellow Bear told his

sister. "I will ask Lame Crow to mix some medicinal herbs for Golden Dove." Lame Crow was a distinguished healer among the Sioux. "Then I will arrange a meeting of the council."

Spotted Wing, her emotions turbulent, returned to her grandmother.

Meanwhile, Three Moons had reached his parents' lodge. Dismounting, he reached up and drew Sheila to the ground. Taking her inside the tepee, he found his father and mother sitting at the cooking pit eating their morning meal. The sight of the white woman sent them bounding to their feet.

Three Moons let them know that he wanted to leave his captive with them.

Remembering Sheila as White Cloud's woman, his father refused to keep her. He had been good friends with Iron Star, and he was very fond of Yellow Bear; thus, he was determined not to become involved. He was angry at his son for taking the woman, and spoke his mind without hesitation.

Sheila wished she could understand what they were saying. She could see that the older man was very upset with Three Moons. She wondered if these people were Three Moons's parents.

Fuming, Three Moons grabbed Sheila by the arm and practically dragged her outside. Taking a rope from his pony, he drew Sheila across the compound and over to a pole used for hanging fresh meat. Shoving her to the ground, he bound her to the stake and left her there.

His parents, standing in front of their tepee, watched as their son tied his captive. They made no move to stop him; to own a captive was Three Moons's right. Only the council had the power to interfere, and no one else would dare take it upon himself to set her free.

Riding at a steady pace, Bart and the others crossed the narrow river and rode into the Sioux encampment. Camp dogs greeted them with a succession of rapid barks as the villagers looked on with mixed emotions.

Bart, leading the way, headed straight for Yellow Bear's tepee. His brother, aware of their arrival, was waiting outside. Dismounting, Bart asked him anxiously if Sheila was there.

"Yes. Three Moons brought her here earlier this morning. He tied her to a stake."

Fury flashed in Bart's eyes.

"Try to stay calm, my brother. Soon the council will meet to decide if Three Moons has the right to keep Sheila. It is good that you are here; now you can speak to them on your own behalf."

"First, I intend to see Sheila."

"White Cloud, have you been away so long that you cannot remember our customs? For now, Sheila belongs to Three Moons. You cannot talk to her without his permission."

"His permission, hell!" Bart raved. "If he tries to stop me, I'll kill him!"

The brothers were conversing in English, which made it much easier for Luke to understand them, for he could speak the Sioux tongue, though not fluently. He got down from his horse, stepped to Bart, and said firmly, "Yellow Bear's right. If you expect to get Sheila back, you've got to cooperate. You get the council angry at you, and they'll refuse to help you."

"Luke speaks wisely," Yellow Bear concurred.

Bart gave in, albeit reluctantly. "All right, I'll cooperate. When is the meeting?"

"Very soon," Yellow Bear replied. He swallowed deeply, drew a long breath, then said, "Our grandmother is very ill."

Bart staggered as though the words had struck him physically.

Yellow Bear touched his brother's arm. "Come; I will take you to her." He told Luke and the women to make themselves at home in his tepee.

Sheila's capture, coupled with the revelation of Golden Dove's illness, had forced the Dwyers' imminent attack to the far recesses of Bart's mind. But now, as he walked beside Yellow Bear, he suddenly remembered. "We were coming here to warn you of an attack. Major Dwyer and his brother are planning to destroy this village."

Yellow Bear stopped dead in his tracks. "How do you know this?"

"We were at Fort Swafford, and Mrs. Wilson overheard the Dwyers talking about it."

"I do not understand how they can attack us when they do not know where this village is located."

"Well, they apparently do know. Major Dwyer is always sending out scouts. One or more of them probably found this village."

Yellow Bear was deeply distressed. "Are they coming here because of me?"

"I'm sure you have something to do with it."

"Then I will surrender to them and spare my people."

"One man's blood won't be enough to appease those two leeches! You have to convince the people to pack up and move out as soon as possible. The Dwyers will be here in another day or two."

"I will tell the council what you have said. It must be their decision to leave or stay."

"I'll talk to them with you."

"Good," Yellow Bear replied.

They entered Golden Dove's lodge. Dream Dancer and Spotted Wing were at her bedside. The pair wasn't surprised to see Bart; they had assumed he would come for Sheila.

Spotted Wing cast Bart a cold, cursory glance, then hurriedly left as though she couldn't stand being in the same place with him.

His sister's rejection still had the power to wound, and Bart watched her leave with pained look in his eyes. He then moved to Golden Dove's bed and sat down. The woman was asleep, and Bart studied her face closely. Her features were drawn and her complexion was very pale. He took her limp hand into his and held it gently.

Spotted Wing, looking for Three Moons, found him coming out of his parents' tepee. She rushed over to speak to him. "White Cloud is here," she said anxiously.

The warrior was undisturbed. "The woman is mine. If he tries to take her, I will kill him."

Watching him suspiciously, she asked, "Why does the woman mean so much to you? Do you find her beautiful?"

"Yes, she is very beautiful, but her beauty is not important to me. I plan to sell her to Slow Coyote. She is Lieutenant Dwyer's woman, and Slow Coyote will give me many horses for her."

"She is White Cloud's woman," Spotted Wing argued.

He shrugged. "It makes no difference. She once belonged to the lieutenant."

Spotted Wing was disappointed in Three Moons. She had always thought he was the bravest and most fearless warrior in the village, but it didn't take much courage to capture a woman.

"What pride is there in selling a woman for horses?" she asked, her eyes flashing. "A warrior who gains his horses through raids can hold his head high. But to trade a woman is weak and cowardly."

Three Moons was livid, but he was also astounded. Spotted Wing had never before spoken to him in such a way. She had always treated him with respect and had believed him above reproach.

He clutched her shoulders firmly, his fingers digging into her flesh. "I will not marry a woman with a sharp tongue!"

"If you want me as your wife, then you must earn my respect! Give the woman back to White Cloud!"

"Never!" he uttered angrily. He turned her loose, whirled about, and walked away.

Spotted Wing, fighting back tears, watched him for a moment; then she turned and looked over at Sheila, who was tied to a stake, the sun beating down upon her.

Spotted Wing asked permission to enter the tepee belonging to Three Moons's parents, and his mother invited her inside. She asked for a cup of water. The woman gave it to her, and, going back outside, Spotted Wing carried the water to Sheila.

Kneeling, she held the cup to Sheila's lips, and Sheila drank from it thirstily.

Spotted Wing's compassion surprised Sheila. When she was here previously, she had gotten the distinct impression that Spotted Wing didn't like her.

"Do you speak English?" she asked.

"Yes. Golden Dove taught me your words." Her English was impressive.

"Why are you helping me?"

"Three Moons should not have taken you."

"Why don't Yellow Bear and Golden Dove make Three Moons set me free?"

"They must obey our customs. You belong to Three Moons. Only the council can set you free."

"Will they?" She waited breathlessly for Spotted Wing's reply.

"I do not know. But White Cloud is here. He will talk to the council."

"Bart is here?" she exclaimed. Thank God he was alive! "But why hasn't he come to see me? How can he just leave me tied like this?"

"White Cloud must also obey our customs."

To hell with their customs! Sheila thought angrily. If Bart still had feelings for her, he wouldn't stay away! That she might be judging him unfairly flashed across her mind, but she was too upset and miserable to care.

"I must go," Spotted Wing said. "Golden Dove is very ill, and I want to be with her." Following that somber announcement, she moved away quickly.

378

Golden Dove's condition weighed heavily on Sheila's mind. She liked the woman very much and was sad to hear that she was sick. Bart loved his grandmother dearly; she could well imagine how worried he must be. She suddenly strained against the ropes binding her, wishing she could go to Bart, hold him close, and give him comfort. The urge passed quickly, however. Bart obviously didn't want her comfort, he didn't want anything from her—except wanting her out of his life! That thought fueled her anger. As far as she was concerned, she couldn't do that fast enough.

If Three Moons has his way, she told herself, *I'll be out of Bart's life very soon—and forever!* The possibility was frightening, and she found herself praying that the council would vote to set her free.

Bart, with Yellow Bear at his side, entered the council's lodge. Eight men sat on thick buffalo rugs that were placed around a bed of hot coals smoldering in an open pit. The old medicine man, Lame Crow, pointed to two unoccupied rugs and told Yellow Bear and Bart to be seated.

They sat down, and crossed their legs Indian-style. Bart was tense, and his nerves were strained. He wanted to jump to his feet and demand that they set Sheila free. But he kept his patience; if he angered the council, they might decide in Three Moons's favor.

Lame Crow was the spokesman. "Does the white woman belong to you?" he asked Bart.

Did she? Yes, if he could persuade her to forgive him! He could only pray that she loved him enough to

379

understand. "Yes, she belongs to me," he answered. "I plan to marry her."

"White Cloud, you are no longer one of the People. You have chosen to be a white man. But your father was a great Sioux warrior and a great leader. His spirit has spoken to me, and he wants what is best for you. He asked me to let you have your woman. The other members of the council and I have decided that Three Moons was wrong to take her from you. We want you to take your woman, and the ones who came here with you, and leave at once."

Relief flooded over Bart. Thank God, Sheila would go free! But he didn't want to leave now. Not with Golden Dove seriously ill. "I am grateful for your kindness, but how can I leave when my grandmother is very ill?"

Lame Crow spoke firmly. "I am sorry, but you must leave!"

At that moment, Three Moons barged inside. He stalked to a rug and sat down. "I did not mean to be late," he said. "But I just now got word of this meeting. I am here to claim my captive."

"We have already decided that the woman rightfully belongs to White Cloud," Lame Crow told him. "You were wrong to take her."

Three Moons was enraged, but he didn't say anything. He respected the Sioux customs and would abide by the council's decision, regardless of how much it angered him. Nevertheless he couldn't help but feel as though Lame Crow and the others had betrayed him.

Yellow Bear spoke up clearly. "White Cloud has something very important to say."

"What do you wish to say, White Cloud?" asked Lame Crow.

"Major Dwyer and his brother are planning to attack this village," he began. "Somehow, they learned where you are camped. They are bringing many soldiers with them, more soldiers than you have warriors."

"How do you know about this?" Three Moons questioned, eyeing Bart distrustfully.

"My friend, Amanda Wilson, overheard the Dwyers discussing the attack." He turned to Lame Crow. "They will be here in another day, two at the most. That gives you time to tell the people to pack up and leave."

"Leave? But where do you think we should go?"

"Back to the reservation. It's the only place where you'll be safe."

"Reservation?" Three Moons thundered.

Lame Crow, glowering at Three Moons, held up a silencing hand. He gave the angry brave a warning look, then turned back to Bart. "Go on, White Cloud. What more do you have to say?"

"I think you should take my advice and return to the reservation. Except for Yellow Bear, of course. He is wanted by the Army, and if they find him, they will hang him. I want Yellow Bear to hide out. My grandfather has many friends in the Army. They are distinguished chiefs. I will ask my grandfather to talk to them in Yellow Bear's behalf. A new trial can be arranged, and this one will be fair. I'm sure Yellow Bear will be found innocent."

Yellow Bear regarded his brother with surprise. Bart hadn't said anything about this to him. But he wasn't opposed to the plan, and was willing to cooperate.

"May I speak?" Three Moons asked the medicine man.

"You may speak."

"I do not believe White Cloud tells the truth. It is only a trick to get us to surrender to the bluecoats. I say there will be no battle! The soldiers are too afraid to fight us!"

"If you believe that," Bart uttered, "then that belief is going to cost you your life. Don't underestimate the Army. They aren't afraid to fight."

Lame Crow looked at Yellow Bear. "What does our young chief have to say?"

"I believe my brother."

Lame Crow smiled tolerantly. "Yes, White Cloud is your brother, and that is why the others and I decided you should not sit in council. Love for family can be stronger than wisdom." He moved his eyes to Bart. "Leave and go to your woman. Take her to Golden Dove's tepee, and wait there. Yellow Bear and Three Moons will stay here. We have much to settle."

Bart got up. As he left, he could feel Three Moons's heated gaze searing into his back. He did not intend to take the warrior's hate lightly; he knew he was a dangerous enemy.

Earlier, Yellow Bear had told Bart where he could find Sheila, and, hurrying away from the council's lodge, he went straight to the spot where she was tied.

Sheila saw him coming, and a smile lit up her face. But as his recent treatment of her swept fiercely across her mind, her smile faded abruptly.

The sight of Sheila bound to the stake pained Bart. His heart went out to her. Taking a knife that was sheathed about his waist, he knelt beside her and cut the ropes. He gently helped her to her feet.

"Thank God you're all right," he said thickly.

She drew free of his grasp. "Does this mean the council decided in my favor?" She eyed him frigidly.

He understood her coldness, and he didn't blame her. "Yes, you're free."

"Is Golden Dove feeling any better?" she asked.

"No, she's still very sick. But how did you know she was ill?"

"Spotted Wing told me. When she brought me a drink of water."

"My sister gave you water?" he questioned, amazed.

"Yes, she did. I don't think she is too pleased with Three Moons."

"Good. Maybe she'll decide not to marry him." Bart placed his hands on her shoulders. She tried to pull away, but he held her firm. "Sheila, there is something I must tell you." He was about to admit that he had misjudged her, and to ask for her forgiveness, but, at that same moment, Dream Dancer called his name. Glancing over his shoulder, he saw her rushing toward him.

"White Cloud!" she cried, her expression anxious. "You must hurry! Golden Dove is awake and is asking for you!"

Chapter Twenty-Five

Lieutenant Dwyer paced the army tent restlessly. His brother, sitting on the edge of a cot, watched as Donald covered the small space again and again. Charles was just as upset as Donald, and the periodic wringing of his hands revealed his anxiety.

The brothers and their soldiers had been camped for hours. The unit had been making good time; the Dwyers had been pleased with their progress and were sure they would reach Yellow Bear's village on schedule. Then, early in the day, a trooper fell ill. Two more soldiers came down sick shortly thereafter. Now, over a dozen men were afflicted.

Donald stopped his pacing to speak to his brother. "Why don't we just leave the sick behind and go on? We can pick them up on our way back. There's only a dozen or so ill; we can manage without them."

"That's true," Charles replied. "And if no more of our men get sick, we'll leave in the morning. However, if this sickness continues to spread, we'll have to stay here until the men are well. We can't attack Yellow Bear's village if we're shorthanded."

Donald was about to agree when the medic, Corporal Parker, suddenly stepped inside the tent. His face was lined with worry. "Six more are sick," he reported. "And I'm sure there will be more."

"Damn!" Charles cursed, rising angrily from his cot. "What the hell is wrong with them?"

"They are acutely nauseated, I think they have food poisoning. However, I'm fairly sure it's not too serious. In another day or two, they should be fine."

Contaminated food was not that uncommon on maneuvers, for the soldiers' diet consisted of canned rations. Charles wasn't concerned for himself or Donald, for they hadn't eaten the same food as the others. Officers' rations were separated from the enlisted men's.

"It seems we have no choice but to stay here," Charles decided. "We'll still carry out our mission; we'll just be a couple of days late."

The corporal left to see about his patients, and Donald opened a bottle of brandy for himself and the major. He filled two glasses, handed one to his brother, and mumbled, "Damn the bad luck."

"We have to look on the brighter side, Donald. At least the men aren't seriously ill. I've heard of food poisoning wiping out practically a whole detachment. But just in case there's more tainted food, we'll get rid of the canned rations. I'll have Sergeant Kent take a few men with him to hunt wild game. This area should be filled with sources of fresh meat.''

The brighter side, however, did little to ease the lieutenant's disappointment.

Charles placed a hand on his brother's shoulder. ''I understand how you feel, Donald. You're young and you're impatient to see action. But you'll see plenty of battles before the Indians are permanently placed on reservations or else exterminated.'' A wide smile crossed the major's face. ''Once our transfers are approved and we're riding with General Custer, we'll be part of a great crusade. Mark my word, George Custer will go down in history, and we'll go down with him!''

''Yes,'' Donald agreed. ''But, first, I intend to get rid of Yellow Bear. I just wish to hell I could eliminate his half-breed brother at the same time.''

''You might as well forget Bart Chandler.''

Donald considered that much easier said than done. The man had abducted the woman he planned to marry, then he had defiled her. For that, Donald craved vengeance!

Bart entered Golden Dove's tepee behind Dream Dancer and Sheila. As the women stood back, he moved to his grandmother's bed and sat down. He was pleased to see that she had lost some of her pallor. Her eyes, which were gazing into his, were lucid. He was sure she was getting better.

''White Cloud,'' she murmured, ''why did you come back?'' He didn't want to upset her, and revealing the

Dwyers' planned attack to her would certainly do just that. "Later, when you're feeling stronger, I'll tell you why I'm here. But now, I think you should rest."

"Yes," she sighed. "I am very tired."

He took her slim hand into his. "You're going to get well."

A weak smile brushed her lips. "You say that like it's an order."

"It is," he replied with a grin.

Sheila, looking on, was relieved to see that Golden Dove seemed to be recovering. Dream Dancer was standing at her side. She touched Sheila's arm to get her attention.

"You very tired," Dream Dancer said. "Come; I take you to my tepee. You can sleep."

Sheila complied readily. She was exhausted and sleep sounded heavenly.

Bart had heard Dream Dancer's invitation, and he watched as the women left. He wanted Sheila with him; he was anxious to make amends. But Golden Dove was still awake, and he didn't want to leave her. Also, Sheila needed rest. He would talk to her later.

Dream Dancer showed Sheila which tepee was hers, then she hurried back to be with Golden Dove.

As Sheila entered the lodge she was immediately embraced by Amanda, who was overjoyed to see that she was all right. Luke gave her a warm hug as well. Janice, however, remained seated on her buffalo rug, her expression childishly sullen.

Venison stew was simmering at the cooking pit, and Amanda dished up a full bowl and gave it to Sheila. Famished, she ate heartily, then went to a bed of furs

388

and practically collapsed. Within minutes, she was sound asleep.

Yellow Bear left the council meeting ahead of Three Moons, and moved quickly to his grandmother's lodge. Stepping inside, he found Bart still seated beside Golden Dove, who was now sleeping restfully.

Dream Dancer hurried to her husband. "Golden Dove is better," she told him.

"The Great Spirit is kind."

Bart moved to sit at the cooking pit, where Yellow Bear joined him. Dream Dancer poured cups of coffee for the brothers, then took her place beside her husband.

"What did the council decide?" Bart asked anxiously.

"That this is their home, and they will not order the people to pack up and move. They are against running farther into the mountains, and are strongly opposed to returning to the reservation. They have decided to stand and fight."

"But that's insane! The Dwyers are probably coming here with a full battalion. What few guns you have and your arrows will be useless against cannons."

"I know that, my brother. But Lame Crow and the others are not sure if they believe you. Three Moons almost convinced them that you were sent here by the Army to trick them into returning to the reservation. Three Moons does not believe the soldiers plan to attack. You say that the Army is one or two days behind you, so the council voted to prepare the village for war. But if there is no attack, then they will believe Three Moons was right about you."

389

"There will be an attack, all right," Bart said with certainty. "And some of your people will be killed."

"Yes, I believe you. But I could not make Lame Crow and the others believe. They do not completely trust you."

Bart's muscles tensed. Damn Three Moons for swaying the council! These people would be massacred, and there was nothing he could do about it.

"There is more," Yellow Bear said softly.

Bart looked at him questioningly.

"The council decided that you must stay here for two more days. If the soldiers do not come, then they will believe that Three Moons was right and that you are working for the Army."

"And what happens then?" Bart asked the question calmly, despite the knot of sudden apprehension in his stomach.

"Sheila will be given back to Three Moons, and you and your friends will be killed."

"Good God!" Bart exclaimed. "Is that the thanks we get for coming here to warn you?"

"It was not my decision."

"I know that. But, damn it, Lame Crow and the council were good friends with our father. They knew me when I was a boy. How can they be so quick to sentence me and the others to death?"

"If the soldiers do not come, they will see you as an enemy and a traitor. The price is death."

Bart rubbed a nervous hand across his brow. "I can't believe it's come to this—but I hope the Dwyers aren't detained. If they're late getting here . . . !" He fell silent.

No one said anything for a long moment, then Yellow Bear remarked heavily, ''The Dwyers will be on time, for they enjoy killing too much. Their arrival will prove you are not a traitor, but the price will be paid in the blood of my people,''

''Yellow Bear, you don't understand. There is no guarantee that the Dwyers will arrive in another day or two, as you say. They might be detained, or maybe Amanda misunderstood when they were leaving.''

His brother's eyes were somber. ''I do understand, White Cloud. You and your friends are in grave danger.''

Sudden anger, directed at himself, fused hotly through Bart. He should never have allowed Sheila and the others to accompany him here. But, God, he had never imagined it would turn out like this!

Yellow Bear wished he could ease his brother's mind, but there didn't seem to be any way to do so.

Later, as Bart joined his friends, he did so with a heavy heart. He intended to be completely honest with them. They had a right to know that they were in critical danger.

He wasn't surprised to find Sheila asleep; he could well imagine how tired she must be. He hated to disturb her, but knowing it was necessary, he asked Amanda to awaken her.

She did so at once, and without question, for Bart's grave expression told her something was terribly wrong.

It took a moment for Sheila to fight off her drowsiness, then she and Amanda joined Luke and Janice, who were standing with Bart, waiting to hear what he had to say.

As calmly as possible, Bart told them what the council had decided. His news was met by shocked expressions and stark silence.

The silence, however, was quickly broken by Janice's outcry. "My God, what kind of savages are these people? We came here to save their lives, and they show their gratitude by executing us!"

"I don't think it will come to that," Bart said. "I am fairly certain the Dwyers will arrive on schedule."

"A lot of good that will do us!" Janice complained harshly. "We'll die in this village along with the rest of them."

"You won't die," Bart replied. "We'll see the soldiers before they attack. If you, Amanda, and Sheila make a run for them, no one will stop you." Bart turned to Luke. "You should make a run for it with the women."

"Me?" he asked. "Ain't you leavin' with us?"

"I can't leave Golden Dove; she's too ill."

"Then I ain't leavin' either," Luke said. He sounded adamant.

Meanwhile, Bart's confidence hadn't soothed Janice's fear, and she said in a strident voice, "I can't believe you all can take this so calmly! Good Lord, none of us will come out of this alive! These savages won't let any of us flee to the Army. We'll be shot down in cold blood!"

"Your screeching isn't helping the situation!" Amanda declared angrily. She was just as frightened as Janice, but losing control wasn't the answer.

Janice's fear was now mingled with rage, and, glowering at Amanda, she said in a voice so high-pitched that it was nerve-shattering, "I don't need your advice. That's all I've heard since we left St. Louis. Well, I'm sick of it, and I'm sick of you!"

"Janice!" Sheila interrupted. "Why don't you do us all a favor, and be quiet!" Her nerves were tightly strung, too, but Janice's shrieking only seemed to make everything worse.

The distraught woman turned on Sheila with a fury. "Don't you dare tell me to be quiet! Who do you think you are to talk to me like that? Everyone here knows what you are, so you can stop pretending to be so perfect. You're nothing but a slut, and that's probably why Three Moons wants you back! You not only went with Donald, but you wallowed with Three Moons, too, didn't you?"

Fiery anger burst in Sheila. She wanted to slap Janice across the face, but she wasn't about to stoop to brawling. Nevertheless, she knew she was on the brink of doing just that!

Bart quickly took control, and placed himself between Sheila and Janice. "There'll be no more bickering!" he said testily. "And damn it, Janice, what you said was totally uncalled for!"

Janice glared up into Bart's face. Apparently, the man was hopelessly infatuated with Sheila. She had been completely wrong to think that she might win his affections. Her anger intensified as she realized that she had put her life in jeopardy for nothing. Absolutely nothing! She had never stood a chance with Bart. And now, because she had made such a terrible mistake, she was probably going to die! The possibility of her death was more than she could cope with, and she brushed past Bart, went to Dream Dancer's bed, and dropped down onto the thick rugs. She cried loudly, desperately, not caring that the others heard.

No one hurried over to console her. Instead, they sat around the cooking pit, drank coffee, and discussed their situation calmly. At last, to everyone's relief, Janice's sobs subsided and she drifted into sleep.

Yellow Bear arrived and was glad to report that Golden Dove was awake and well enough to eat. Amanda was very fond of Golden Dove. She wanted to pay her a visit, and she asked for Yellow Bear's permission, which he readily granted.

Luke, wanting to pay his own respects, offered to accompany Amanda. Together, they left the tepee and walked the short distance to Golden Dove's lodge.

They had a pleasant visit, but didn't stay long, for they knew Golden Dove needed her rest. As they stepped outside, the sun was sinking westward and the horizon was streaked with a golden hue. The camp was active; several children were playing games, the women were finishing their afternoon chores, and the men of fighting age were cleaning and sharpening their weapons.

"Looks like the warriors got word to prepare for battle," Luke concluded.

Amanda shivered in spite of the warm weather. "It's a little frightening," she replied.

"A little?" he questioned. "Hell, it's enough to send a chill up your spine!" He paused, took her arm, and brought her steps to a halt. Gazing down into her face, he said gently, "Amanda, it's all right to be frightened, you know. It don't make you a coward; it just means you got common sense."

"Then I have a lot of common sense," she replied with a timorous smile.

"You got that, all right," he said, meaning it sincerely.

"Do you have a special reason for making such a statement?"

"Yep, I sure do. I've been givin' what happened between us a lot of thought, and you were right to marry Wilson. Hell, it's true you had no guarantee that I'd come back. 'Sides that, I wasn't plannin' to come back until spring or early summer—you'd had to gone through your pregnancy out of wedlock. That's a lot of disgrace for an eighteen-year-old girl to face. Furthermore, marryin' Wilson saved your father. Considerin' everything, you made the right decision."

She stared at him in pleased surprise. "Does this mean you have finally forgiven me?"

"Forgiven you?" he questioned. "*I'm* the one who should be askin' for forgiveness. I haven't treated you very nice."

She gazed lovingly into his smoky-blue eyes, and her heart pounded with expectations. "Luke, do you think . . . ?" She couldn't bring herself to go on, for she was too afraid his response would cast her hopes aside.

"Do I think what?" he prodded.

"Never mind," she replied, evading the issue.

His hands gripped her shoulders gently. "Do I think *what?*" he persisted. "Tell me, Amanda."

She swallowed heavily and mustered her courage. "Do you think there's any hope for us?"

A warm twinkle sparked in his eyes. "I still love you, Amanda.

I reckon if you still love me, then that's all the hope we need."

She smiled radiantly. "Oh, Luke, after twenty years you still love me? It's almost more than I can believe!"

"Why do you find it so surprising? You never stopped lovin' me, did you?"

"Never!" she exclaimed.

He brought her into his embrace, bent his head, and kissed her with deep longing. His lips on hers made her pulse race with desire as well as with happiness. She had waited so long for this glorious moment!

Holding her as close as possible, Luke murmured thickly, "Amanda, I ain't never loved any woman but you. God, I never got over you!"

"I know, my darling. It was the same with me."

He held her at arm's length so that he could look into her face. "You're still beautiful."

"Thank you. And, darling, you're so handsome that just looking at you makes my heart beat wildly."

He rubbed a hand across his face. "If you want me to shave off my beard, I will."

She laughed lightly. "Don't you dare! I love your beard!"

He drew her back into his arms. Now that he had found her again, he never wanted to let her go. "Amanda, my darlin', will you marry me?"

"Oh, yes!" she cried happily.

Luke sealed their pledge with a long, breathtaking kiss. Then, releasing her somewhat reluctantly, he said, "J.W.'s been wantin' to sell me some land for a long time. Reckon now I'll buy it, build us a house, get up a good-sized herd of cattle, and become a rancher. You got any objections to livin' on a ranch?''

"None whatsoever," she was quick to reply. She'd live on an open prairie if that was the only way she could be with Luke.

"It won't be a mammoth spread like J.W.'s," he explained.

"I don't care. Besides, I'm the richest woman on the face of the earth, for I have the man I love!''

"We're gonna be happy, Amanda. I promise you.''

"I'm already happier than I've ever been in my life!'' she exclaimed, flinging herself into his arms.

He embraced her tightly. "Darlin', I just want you to know that I'm sorry 'bout the baby. I wish I had been with you.''

"Oh, Luke!" she cried somberly. "Losing our baby was heartbreaking!''

He kissed her tenderly.

Gazing up at him through eyes that shone with love, she said a little hesitantly, "Luke, I can still . . . I mean, we can have . . .''

"Are you tryin' to tell me we can have another baby?'' He was grinning.

A blush rose to her cheeks. "Yes, that's what I was trying to say.''

"Havin' a baby would certainly be a blessing, but if we don't have one, I'll still be happier than any man's got a right to be.''

"You have every right to be happy, my darling! You're a wonderful man!''

At that moment three warriors, carrying their weapons,

passed by. Their presence put a sudden damper on the couple's joy. A foreboding cloud, like a thick cloak, fell over Luke and Amanda, covering them with dread.

"Oh, Luke!" Amanda moaned. "For a while I was so happy that I forgot where we are!" Tears misted her eyes. "We may never get married, build a ranch, or have a baby. We might die right here in this village!"

Luke struggled for encouraging words, but he could think of none. Their situation was indeed perilous. He drew her back into his arms and held her close.

Chapter Twenty-Six

Sheila had gone to bed and the others were having dinner when Amanda and Luke returned to Yellow Bear's tepee. Janice, now awake, was toying with a bowl of venison stew. She was too upset to have much of an appetite.

When Yellow Bear and Bart finished eating, they left to check on their grandmother. Sheila awakened a few minutes later and decided that she also wanted to see Golden Dove.

As Sheila was leaving, Luke went to the cooking pit and poured himself a cup of coffee. Janice, seated next to him, put aside her half-eaten dinner.

"You don't like venison stew?" Luke asked her.

She shrugged. "It's all right, I guess. I'm just not hungry." Janice was surprised when Amanda sat on Luke's other side and took his hand in hers. The couple's eyes met and glowed with love. Janice steamed with envy. Not that she was interested in Luke, he certainly wasn't her type. But she was interested in *love*, and it seemed everyone had someone except her! It had now become apparent to Janice that Sheila had her hooks buried so deeply into Bart that he would never be free. She had decided to give up on Bart, he was a hopeless cause. It was, however, a tremendous disappointment—she had been looking forward to marrying a man as handsome and as rich as Bart. She thrust the loss from her mind, dwelling on it was too depressing. Her thoughts moved on to Charles. She now wished she had remained at Fort Swafford. At least there she would be safe, and Charles would certainly appease her sexual frustrations. She needed a man desperately. As her musings lingered on the major, she turned to Luke and asked, "How well do you know Charles Dwyer?"

"I don't know him all that well, but I know his kind." He wondered why she had asked.

"His kind? What do you mean by that?"

"He's got high ambitions, and he don't give a damn how many people he has to destroy to reach his goal."

"Goal? Does he want to become a general?"

"He's aimin' for higher than that. He once told me he plans to make a reputation for himself in the Army, then move on to politics. Well, he's made a name for himself, so I reckon as soon as the Indian situation is taken care of, he'll retire from the Army and run for Congress or the Senate."

Janice's interest was aroused. Becoming a politician's wife appealed to her. She could live in Washington,

D.C., and mingle with the elite. She suddenly grew terribly angry at herself. She had been such a fool to set her cap for Bart when she could have had Charles!

Luke continued. "Hell, knowin' Dwyer, he probably won't be satisfied until he runs for President."

"President!" Janice gasped.

Amanda, eyeing Janice knowingly, asked, "Are you planning on becoming the First Lady?"

She cast Amanda a furious scowl. "You say that like you think it's impossible. Well, that's how much you know! It just so happens that Charles is quite smitten with me."

"Then why did you leave Fort Swafford?"

"That's none of your business!"

Amanda smiled. "Were you hoping to snare Bart?"

Her response was a harsh frown.

"Cheer up, Janice," Amanda continued. "The Dwyers will be here soon, and I'm sure you can cajole your way back into Charles's good graces."

"There's little chance of that!" she snapped. "I'll probably be shot down trying to reach him!"

"No, I don't think so," Luke told her. "If the Army shows up, Lame Crow and the others will know Bart was tellin' the truth. They ain't gonna care if you leave." He turned to Amanda. "And that goes for you, too. When the soldiers get here, I want you to leave with Janice and Sheila."

She shook her head adamantly. "No, I won't leave you!"

"I ain't gonna argue with you 'bout this, darlin'. I want you with the soldiers where you'll be safe."

401

"I won't leave unless you come with me."

"You know I can't do that. How can I leave Bart? I gotta stay here in case he needs my help."

"Then I'll stay, too," she said stubbornly.

Luke decided to let it drop for now. But he was determined that she leave. If she stayed here, she would very likely die. He had witnessed massacred villages before. Women and children were invariably killed during the onslaught.

Janice, listening, thought Amanda a complete fool. Such loyalty was beyond her comprehension.

Bart, finding his grandmother asleep, decided to leave and return in the morning. Dream Dancer and Yellow Bear planned to spend the night in Golden Dove's tepee. As Bart stepped outside, he almost collided with Spotted Wing, who was about to enter. She swept past him. However, he noticed that this time her stare was less hostile. It gave him reason to hope.

He was heading back when he caught sight of Sheila coming toward him. He stopped and waited.

She paused in front of him. "Is it all right if I visit Golden Dove?"

"She's asleep. Why don't you wait until morning?"

Sheila agreed, turned around quickly to leave, but was halted by Bart's hand on her arm. "I must talk to you," he said.

She flung off his hand and eyed him coldly. "Go ahead; talk! I'm listening!"

"Let's walk down to the river."

She complied, but when he tried to take her hand, she

drew away. "Don't touch me!" she ordered. "I'll talk to you, but that's all!"

He understood her hostility, and he certainly didn't blame her. They reached the river's bank, and, keeping her eyes turned away from Bart's, Sheila gazed blankly at the moon reflected in the water. The sounds of the village floated about them, and in the distance an owl's hoot echoed off and on.

"Bart," Sheila began, facing him. "Before you say whatever it is you're determined to say, may I ask you something?"

"Of course."

"Why aren't you planning a way for us all to escape?"

He pointed behind them, and her eyes followed his finger. Four warriors stood nearby, watching their every move.

"We're being watched all the time," Bart told her. "Also, our horses and supplies are guarded."

She sighed heavily. "Then there's no way to escape."

"I didn't say that. Maybe, with Yellow Bear's help, we can find a way."

"But the odds certainly aren't in our favor, are they?"

"No," he answered honestly.

Her voice came out strained. "If the Dwyers don't show up, you and the others will be . . . killed! God, the thought alone is more than I can stand!"

"Sheila," he said gently. "What about you? Why are you only afraid for the rest of us?"

"I am afraid for myself," she admitted softly.

"But more so for me and the others?" It was a question that didn't require an answer. It was obvious her greatest concern didn't lie with herself.

"Bart, if I'm given back to Three Moons, do you know what he plans to do with me?"

"Yes, I do. Yellow Bear said he intends to sell you to Slow Coyote."

"Who is Slow Coyote?"

"Flying Feather's son. Three Moons figures he will want to kill you to avenge his father."

"But why? I had nothing to do with Flying Feather's murder!"

"Three Moons will tell Slow Coyote that you are Lieutenant Dwyer's woman."

"So that's why I was abducted!" she asserted. "Damn Donald! He doesn't even have to be with me to destroy my life."

"Sheila, what I have to say to you concerns Dwyer."

Rage burst in her. "I won't discuss Donald with you, nor will I subject myself to more of your insults!"

"You don't understand. I want to apologize. I was wrong, so damned wrong!"

"Wrong about what?"

"I didn't know that the Dwyers manipulated you. I thought you spent the night with Donald because that was what you wanted."

She stared at him with astonishment. "But you said that Donald told you everything!"

"He didn't. When I told you that, I spoke rashly and out of anger."

She turned away from him, and gazed across the river. "I went with Donald to save your life and for no other reason."

"I believe you."

"Do you?" she said somewhat bitterly. She wondered

why Bart's understanding didn't take away all the hurt inside.

"Can you forgive me?" he asked intently.

She turned her face to his. Forgive him? There was no question about it, she loved him too much not to forgive him. He was more important than her pride—or anything else! "Yes, I can forgive you," she murmured.

Relieved, he reached for her, but she stepped back. "What's wrong?" he asked.

The degradation she had suffered suddenly overwhelmed her, and she cried out, "How can you want me in your arms after I was with Donald? I never wanted you to find out! I had hoped to keep my shame to myself! God, I never wanted you to know!"

He brought her into his embrace, and held her tenaciously. "Sheila, I love you! We can't let what Dwyer did come between us! Don't you understand? I still love you and desire you as much as ever!" He brushed his lips across her brow, whispering, "Darling, I love you so much. You're my whole life. Without you I'm nothing."

Her hands pushed against his chest, and he let her go hesitantly.

"Bart, I know I can't let Donald ruin my life, and I hope in time I can put what happened behind me." She rubbed a hand across her forehead, as though she could bring forth the memory of that night. "If only I could remember! I think it's the blankness that bothers me the most. I was defiled in the worst way, and I can't even remember going through it."

Bart was confused. "Why can't you remember?"

She told him about getting a sedative from the doctor, then mixing it with whiskey. "The combination put me out like a snuffed candle. I can vaguely recall Donald being in the room. He yelled at me, and even slapped me a couple of times.'' A harsh grimace crossed her features. ''I can even remember his hands touching me. But, after that, I draw a complete blank.''

''Maybe nothing happened.''

''God, how I wish that was true! But when I woke up the next morning, he was standing in the room without his clothes. If he didn't force me, then why was he naked?''

''I don't know.'' A cold, murderous glare came to Bart's eyes. ''But if we come out of this situation alive, I promise you'll find out exactly what happened that night. I can also promise you that bastard will pay for what he did.''

''Bart, no!'' she cried. ''If you kill him, then what I did to save your life will be for nothing! Nothing! You'll hang, or else spend the rest of your life in prison!''

''I don't intend to kill him,'' Bart replied, his voice coldly calm.

''Then what do you intend to do?'' She regarded him intensely.

''Well, let me put it this way—when I finish with that sonofabitch, he'll be missing some teeth, and will have to breathe through his mouth because his damned nose will be broken! His bones won't be in such good shape, either!''

Visualizing Donald's face battered and bloody put a smile on Sheila's lips. A beating was more merciful than he deserved.

Bart arched a brow questioningly. ''Why are you smiling?''

"I was just picturing Donald in my mind, imagining how he will look when you get through with him."

Bart reached for her, and this time she went into his arms very willingly. He held her close. "What happened with Dwyer makes no difference to our love. In fact, I love you all the more for what you did. You saved my life."

She clung to him tightly. All her hurt was now dissolved. "Oh, Bart, when I thought you had turned against me, I was so heartbroken!"

"If I remember correctly, you were also quite angry."

"Yes, that's true," she replied with a smile. "But I was more heartbroken than angry. I love you fiercely!"

He kissed her deeply and with passionate longing. She returned his ardor with all her heart, wishing this moment in time could last forever.

He broke their kiss to gaze down into her beautiful brown eyes. The saffron moonlight slanted across her face, and he took time to admire her delicate features. He found her more lovely than words could describe.

Sheila was returning his admiration in kind. His gray eyes framed by long, dark lashes were so handsome, and his coal-black hair, coupled with his swarthy good looks, made him irresistible. As her gaze fell across his full lips, the need to kiss him became overwhelming. Standing on tiptoe, she pressed her mouth to his in a wild, hungry caress.

Drawing her body close to his, Bart responded passionately as his tongue entwined with hers, turning their kiss into a rapturous exchange that left them starving for more.

With searing reluctance, Bart released her. He wanted

her desperately and his body was aching for fulfillment, but there was nothing he could do about it for now. The four warriors were still nearby, and Bart knew they wouldn't let him and Sheila out of their sight.

Sheila wanted Bart as much as he wanted her, but she also knew they couldn't be alone. "Maybe we should go back and join the others," she said, forcing a timorous smile.

"I think you're right," Bart agreed. "But you owe me a night of blazing passion."

"Promise?" she questioned with a smile.

"You can count on it."

"Don't think I'm not."

"Wanton little vixen, aren't you?" he teased.

"It's your fault. You shouldn't be so irresistible."

"Look who's talking." He slipped his hand into hers, and they began walking back to the tepee. They kept up their teasing exchange, for it was the only shield they had against their present peril. They were both acutely aware that their promised night of passion might never be more than a dream.

Yellow Bear checked on his grandmother and was pleased to find that she was sleeping restfully. He then went over to Spotted Wing, who was lying in bed. She was in her nightdress and under the covers, but was still awake. He sat beside her. "We must talk," he said.

"About what?" she asked guardedly.

"About Three Moons and our brother."

"He is your brother, not mine!"

"Stop acting like a child! You are trying my patience!

408

You behave as though you no longer have a mind of your own. You have let Three Moons think for you! You know White Cloud is not a traitor."

"Yes, I know that. He loves you and Golden Dove, and he would never betray either of you."

"Or you," he completed. "He loves you."

"That is too bad, for I do not love him." Her voice, however, wasn't too convincing.

"Hasn't White Cloud's return triggered your memories of him? Don't you remember how much he cared about you?"

"I was very young when he left. It is hard for me to remember."

"You do not speak the truth."

Her dark eyes snapped petulantly. "Very well. I do remember. And I also remember how I adored him!"

Yellow Bear spoke kindly. "You are angry at White Cloud because he went away. You were only a child, and you thought he betrayed you. Am I right, Spotted Wing?"

"I suppose," she mumbled.

"And you still have not forgiven him for leaving you. That anger you carried in your heart made it very easy for Three Moons to control your thoughts. Spotted Wing, you do not hate White Cloud because he lived in the white man's world, you hate him because he left you. But it is very wrong to hate him for something that was not of his doing. He was forced to leave."

"Why didn't he run away from his white grandfather's home and come back?"

"It became his way of life. Our brother is more white than Sioux, so why is it so hard for you to understand why he chose to stay with his grandfather?"

"I do understand! He loved him more than us!" She spoke bitterly.

"*Us?*" he questioned. "You think only of yourself, Spotted Wing. You are angry because he did not come back to *you.*"

She didn't deny it. Deep in her heart she knew Yellow Bear was right.

"It is time to set aside these feelings and act like a woman. You must help me plot White Cloud's escape. If the soldiers are late coming here, he and his friends will die. They came here to warn us, and it is not right that any of them should die. I also want you, Golden Dove, and Dream Dancer to escape with them."

"No!" Dream Dancer spoke up. She was sitting on her bed, but had heard every word exchanged between her husband and sister-in-law. Bounding to her feet, she hurried to Yellow Bear and knelt beside him. Her expression was one of determination. "I will not leave you! You are my husband and my place is with you!"

"She is right," Spotted Wing asserted. "My place is here, too! This is my home and these are my people! I will not leave!"

Yellow Bear understood. "You two may stay. But we must send Golden Dove with White Cloud. She is old and sickly. When the cannons fire and the bullets fall, she can not run for cover."

The women agreed with him.

"But she will not want to leave," Spotted Wing said to Yellow Bear.

"Somehow, I will make sure she goes." He looked deeply into his sister's eyes. "Can I depend on your help in plotting an escape for White Cloud and his friends?"

410

"Yes, I will help you."

"Even at the risk of losing Three Moons's love?"

She was no longer so sure she had ever had his love. "I said I will help you, and I will."

"Good," Yellow Bear replied, smiling. "Now, it is time to go to bed. Tomorrow, we will try to plan an escape."

"It might be impossible," Dream Dancer murmured gravely.

"Nevertheless, we will try."

Yellow Bear and Dream Dancer went to their bed, and Spotted Wing was left alone with her thoughts. She considered everything her brother had said to her. She wondered if he could be right. Did her hate for White Cloud stem from childhood? Was that hate merely an excuse to cover the hurt she had suffered when White Cloud left her to live with his grandfather?

Sudden tears glazed her eyes. Oh, yes, it had hurt her terribly to lose White Cloud. She had loved him so much. Turning to her side, she buried her face in the buffalo rug to muffle her sobs. She still loved White Cloud! He was her brother; they shared the same blood, and it was a bond that still held them together! Her years of resentment and Three Moons's influence had failed to completely break the bond with White Cloud. It had always been there, but she had refused to admit it. Now, however, she could no longer deny it!

411

Chapter Twenty-Seven

The next morning, Bart and Sheila visited Golden Dove, and were pleased to find that she was feeling much better. Dressed, she was sitting up in bed, and Dream Dancer had brushed and braided the woman's long, silver-streaked hair. She was still weak, though. It would be days before her full strength returned.

As Bart and Sheila sat down, Golden Dove asked, "White Cloud, now will you tell me why you came back? I know something is wrong. I can see it in your eyes, and everybody else's."

Bart stole a questioning glance at Yellow Bear and Dream Dancer. They both nodded slightly, letting him know it was all right to tell Golden Dove the truth. Spotted Wing wasn't present; she had left before breakfast and hadn't returned. No one knew why she had left or where she had gone.

As gently as he could, Bart told his grandmother about the Dwyers' planned attack, and the council's reaction.

Golden Dove was afraid for Bart, his friends, and her people, but she was also angry at Lame Crow and the others for their suspicions. If the soldiers didn't arrive on time . . . ? A shudder ran up her spine.

She clasped her grandson's hand as tightly as her weakened condition allowed. "White Cloud, you and the others must escape! If the soldiers are detained, the people will believe Three Moons is right about you!"

"I will help them escape," Yellow Bear said. "And so will Dream Dancer and Spotted Wing."

"Spotted Wing?" Bart questioned, surprised.

Yellow Bear smiled. "Our sister loves you. She always has."

"What makes you so sure?" Bart asked.

"Last night, we had a long talk. She does not want you to die."

The news cheered Bart, for he loved his sister very much.

"Be cautious, my grandsons," Golden Dove warned. "Three Moons has much influence on Spotted Wing. Her heart is surely torn between White Cloud and the man she wants to marry."

"Our grandmother speaks wisely," Bart told his brother. "Maybe we shouldn't be so quick to trust Spotted Wing."

Yellow Bear disagreed. "She can be trusted. She told me she would help you escape. She would not lie to me."

Golden Dove tended to believe him. "Spotted Wing has tried my patience many times, and I was disappointed when she chose to marry Three Moons. However, the girl has never lied to me or to Yellow Bear. Sometimes, she is truthful to a fault."

"All right," Bart replied. "Then it's settled. We'll trust her." He hoped they weren't making a serious mistake.

"How do you plan to help White Cloud and the others escape?" Golden Dove asked Yellow Bear.

He sighed with regret. "I have not thought of a way as yet. But I will keep trying."

"We will all try," Golden Dove said.

"Bart," Sheila began. "Let's go back and tell the others. Maybe Luke or Amanda can come up with a plan." She intentionally omitted Janice; that she might think of something wasn't likely. The woman could do nothing but whine and complain!

Bart got up, but as he reached down to assist Sheila, Yellow Bear spoke. "Wait. Before you leave, I have something to say."

"What is it?" Bart asked.

Yellow Bear looked away from Bart and eyed his grandmother firmly. "If we find a way for White Cloud to escape, you will go with him."

"No! I will stay here!"

"You will leave!" he insisted. "Listen to me, Grandmother! When the soldiers attack, you will still be too weak to run for shelter. Do you expect Dream Dancer and Spotted Wing to help you? You will only slow them down and they will die with you." Yellow Bear didn't mean to sound so harsh, but he knew it was the only way to convince Golden Dove to leave.

415

"I will not need their help," she said.

"Are you saying that you can run as fast as Dream Dancer and Spotted Wing?"

"Of course I can't. But I will insist that they leave me behind."

"Tell me, my grandmother; if they were ill, would you leave them behind to save yourself?"

"No, you know I wouldn't."

"Then why do you expect less from them?"

Golden Dove sighed heavily. "Yellow Bear, you are very shrewd. You are also wise." She gazed lovingly into his eyes. "You are very much like your grandfather."

Yellow Bear, flattered, stood a little taller. That Golden Dove compared him to High Hawk was a great compliment. His grandfather's superb leadership and prowess were well known among the Sioux.

"Grandmother, does this mean you will do as I say?" he asked.

"What other choice have you left me?" Tears touched her eyes.

Bart knelt beside her and took her hand into his. "Don't look so sad, Grandmother. You will have a good life with me, and with Sheila."

"He's right," Sheila pleaded. "We love you, Golden Dove."

"You two make my heart happy, but there will be many others who will break it. I will be ridiculed and scorned."

"It won't be as bad as you think," Bart said. "And the ones who do scorn you can go straight to hell. Why should you care what they think?"

"I do not want to ostracize you from your neighbors."

"Don't let that worry you," Bart said with a grin. "I can assure you that my neighbors will accept you. They're good people."

"What about your grandfather? He might resent me."

"There's no chance of that," he replied without hesitation. "J.W. is kind and generous."

"But my son stole his daughter; how can he help but resent me?"

"You aren't to blame for my father's actions." Honoring the Sioux's customs, he didn't speak Iron Star's name. "Besides, J.W. lost his bitterness a long time ago."

Golden Dove didn't say anything, but she wasn't totally convinced. White Cloud could be wrong about J.W.; the man might very well take exception to her presence. She didn't want to come between White Cloud and his grandfather—she would rather die! She lay back on her bed, for she was suddenly very tired.

Bart and Sheila left, but as they stepped outside, they caught sight of Spotted Wing. She was coming toward them. Bart wondered where she had been.

"White Cloud," she said. "I must talk to you."

Bart sent Sheila on to Yellow Bear's tepee, then he walked downstream with Spotted Wing. Four armed warriors followed at a distance.

They stopped on the grassy bank. Spotted Wing wrung her hands nervously. "Last night, Yellow Bear talked to me, and his words made me look deep into my heart. I am sorry that I was so mean to you. White Cloud, all these years, I thought I hated you."

"Thought?" he questioned.

"I did not really hate you. I was angry and hurt. I never forgave you for leaving me."

She turned her back to him and stared across the placid water. "I used to dream of your return. In my dream you'd come charging into camp whooping and waving your lance like a warrior returning from battle. But as the months passed, the dream appeared less and less frequently. Finally, I knew you were never coming back. You had gone to the white man's world to stay. I felt betrayed, and I began to see you as a traitor. You turned your back on me and your Sioux family. After a while, my pain turned into anger and then into hate."

She whirled around and faced him. "Our father told me the Great Spirit had chosen your way of life, and you had no choice but to obey. But that was not what I wanted to hear, and I turned a deaf ear. I did not care about your vision, I only cared that you were gone. I loved you so much that the only way I could bear losing you was to turn that love into hate."

A look of abject remorse covered Bart's face. "I shouldn't have stayed away this long. But the years passed so quickly, and I had so much to learn. Also, my grandfather needed me, and I had grown to love him very much."

"I think I understand now," she replied.

Bart studied her face intently. Her eyes, no longer hostile, met his and did not waver. She looked a lot like her mother, Red Blanket, who had left after Iron Star's death to live in another village with her brother.

"Spotted Wing, believe me, the soldiers will attack this village, and many will die. I don't want you to be

418

one of them. If the others and I escape, will you come with us?"

"No. My place is here. I will not leave my people and my family."

Her expression told him it would be useless to try to change her mind. "What about Three Moons? Do you still want to marry him?"

"I am not sure, but, in any case, Three Moons is not as bad as you think. He hates the white man, true, but he has good reason to hate them."

Bart couldn't argue with that. All Sioux had cause to loathe the whites. He knew the whites also had reason to hate. It was a vicious circle with no end.

He placed a tentative hand on Spotted Wing's arm. "Have you finally forgiven me for leaving you?"

"Hating you for going away was childish, and I am now a woman. The Great Spirit chose different roads for us to travel. I do not understand why, but it is not my place to question his wisdom."

"That's true, but he brought us back together and took the hate from your heart. We are, and always will be, brother and sister. Distance cannot break the bond that holds us together."

"Yes, I know that now."

He beckoned her into his arms, and she went quickly into his embrace. Holding her close, Bart murmured, "I love you, Spotted Wing. I always have."

Later, Bart and the others sat about the cooking pit trying to plan an escape. Now that Golden Dove had agreed to leave, Bart was free to go also, for his grandmother would be with him. Suddenly, they were interrupted by Yellow Bear. He came inside the tepee wearing a worried expression.

Bart, knowing something was amiss, asked him anxiously, what was wrong.

"Three Moons convinced the council that you and the others are planning to escape. The council has decided to separate you. They believe if you are divided into two groups, you cannot plot a way to leave. A tepee is being prepared for you and Sheila; the others will stay here. Also, they have forbidden your family to come into contact with you or the others."

"Then how did you get in here?" Bart asked.

"Lame Crow gave his permission. But once you are moved, I can no longer talk to you."

"Damn!" Bart cursed. "How the hell are we going to find a way to escape if we can't even talk to each other?"

Yellow Bear sighed gravely. "We cannot, my brother. Three Moons is smarter than we thought. He knows you will try to escape, and that I will help you."

"Yes!" Janice exclaimed angrily. "And we all know how Three Moons found out, don't we? Spotted Wing told him!" She glared at Bart furiously. "Your own sister betrayed you!"

"We don't know that!" Bart replied. "Three Moons could have figured it out on his own! He's not stupid!"

"No, but you are if you believe Spotted Wing didn't go running straight to him!" Janice retorted.

Bart looked at Yellow Bear. "Where did Spotted Wing go this morning?"

"She said she took a long walk because she wanted to be alone with her thoughts."

"Do you think she went to Three Moons?"

"I do not want to think that."

"Neither do I," Bart sighed.

"Well," Luke spoke up, "it don't make any difference one way or the other. What's done is done. I reckon we're stuck here until the end."

"Come; I will take you to your tepee," Yellow Bear said to Bart and Sheila.

Amanda went to Sheila and hugged her. "I'll miss you," she whispered.

"Me, too," she replied softly, then added in a voice too low for the others to hear, "I'm sorry you and Luke are stuck with Janice."

Amanda laughed quietly. "By the time this ordeal is over, she'll have my nerves shuttered. Luke's, too."

Last night, Amanda had told her that she and Luke were getting married, and that they planned to live close to Bart's ranch.

"I'll see you in another day or two," Sheila said, her voice shaky with uncertainty.

"Of course you will," Amanda replied. But like Sheila, she feared they would never see each other again; or if they did, it would be under much graver circumstances.

Sheila's emotions were mixed. She hated leaving Amanda and Luke, for their company meant a lot to her, but she couldn't help but savor being alone with Bart. Their perilous future made their time together very precious. At least they would now have the privacy they both needed so desperately. She remembered Bart's promised

421

night of blazing passion; she had every intention of holding him to it.

Bart and Sheila, alone in their temporary quarters, were starting a fire in the circular cooking pit when Lame Crow announced his presence from outside, then pushed aside the leather flap and entered.

The medicine man, dressed in a beaded robe, fringed leggings, and a headband adorned with colorful feathers, was very impressive. Sheila stared at him with awe; his overwhelming aura of authority was undimmed by age. His long gray hair hung in two neat braids, and his face was heavily lined. His eyes, however, were alert and penetrating—and Sheila also saw intelligence and wisdom in those dark, piercing eyes.

Lame Crow, speaking his own language, said to Bart, "Scouts have been sent to spot the enemy before he arrives. We will be warned in time to send you and your friends away. White Cloud, if you have told the truth, and the soldiers are on their way to attack us, then it is not right that you, too, should have to face danger. The council agrees with me. When the soldiers are spotted, you and the others will be released. I give you my word."

"You and the council are very fair, Lame Crow. But how many days will your scouts await the soldiers?"

"Today and tomorrow. Did you not say the soldiers can be no more than two days behind you?"

"Yes. But there is no guarantee. They could always be detained."

"I think not, White Cloud. An army on the warpath does not stop to idly pass the time. Warriors, as well as the bluecoats, rush to battle." He turned around abruptly, went to the flap, and pushed it open. "I have spoken," he said on his way out. "We wait two days, no longer."

"What did he say?" Sheila asked the moment Lame Crow was gone.

Bart quickly told her.

She smiled with hope. "If the Army shows up on time, we'll be set free!"

"If," Bart mumbled. "That's a mighty big word."

"God, I hope Amanda heard the Dwyers correctly and they planned to leave right after we did!"

"So do I," Bart replied. "Our lives may very well depend on it."

With Bart's help, Sheila received permission to go to the river and bathe. Three older women went along to guard her. Dream Dancer had sent her a set of clothes. After having worn her traveling gown for so long, it was wonderful to put on clean apparel. The Indian garment, made of soft doeskin, hugged her ripe curves flawlessly, and the high-topped moccasins were a perfect fit. She also washed her hair, but had forgotten to bring a brush. When she returned to the tepee, Bart insisted that she allow him to brush her damp tresses until the thick locks cascaded down her back in dark, lustrous waves.

"You're so lovely," he murmured in her ear; his breath sent delightful chills up her spine.

She turned and went into his arms, clasping her hands around his neck. "I love you, Bart Chandler," she declared throatily before kissing him with unbridled desire.

Bart gently eased her down upon the plush softness of

the thick buffalo rug they sat upon. "I love you," he whispered; then his lips seized hers passionately.

"Oh, Bart," she murmured in a seductive tone. "I want you so desperately. Make love to me."

"Yes . . . yes," he groaned, his loins burning. His mouth returned to hers as his hand slipped beneath her Indian dress. She wore no undergarments, and his fingers caressed her bare flesh.

Sheila, finding his touch pure heaven, writhed and moaned with pleasure as he fondled her intimately.

Wanting her totally naked, Bart drew her dress up and over her head and flung the garment carelessly aside. He then removed her moccasins. Dusk had fallen, but an oil lamp was burning, and its soft glow illuminated Sheila's full breasts, her small waist, and the dark mound between her silky thighs.

Bart's hands, mouth, and tongue explored her delectable body; and, Sheila, savoring every minute, soared upward onto a cloud of weightless splendor.

Impatient to possess her fully, Bart rose and removed his clothes with haste. Sheila admired his strong, masculine frame, and her eyes took in every inch of him. His hard, throbbing arousal added fuel to her passion, and she trembled in fiery anticipation.

He lay beside her, and her hands skimmed lightly over his shoulders, across his chest, and down to his erect member.

"Sheila! . . . Sheila!" he moaned thickly, her touch arousing him to even greater heights.

Giving him pleasure fascinated her, and she continued to caress him with rhythmic motion that nearly drove Bart over the brink of rapture.

Rising up, he moved between her legs, placed his hands beneath her thighs, and sank into her velvety depths with one quick thrust. His hardness inside her made her cry out with fathomless desire.

Bart made love to her with a demanding force that she met with equal fervor. Their present peril was blocked from their minds; their hearts were in complete control. Their passions climbed to a wondrous rapture that lifted them to love's ultimate climax, causing their bodies to quake with total fulfillment. They lay still for a moment, savoring their perfect union, then Bart kissed her tenderly and moved to lie at her side.

Sheila snuggled into his arms, resting her head on his shoulder. Now that her desire was temporarily sated, cold reality set in, and it chilled her all the way to her very soul. She shivered.

Bart drew her close. "Are you cold?" he asked

"No, not really. I'm just a little chilled."

"But it's warm in here."

"The temperature didn't chill me."

"I don't understand."

"The Dwyers!" she clarified harshly. "They are the evil force that surrounds us! Bart, what if they don't show up in time? You and the others will die, and I . . . I will be given back to Three Moons!"

Bart held her tightly. "Try not to think about it. Besides, I'm sure the Dwyers will arrive on schedule."

She moved out of his arms, sat up, and looked him directly in the eyes. "But what if they don't?"

The question didn't call for a reply.

Bart suddenly drew her back into his arms as though she were about to disappear and only his embrace could prevent it. "Sheila, you must stop thinking the worst. Damn it, we're going to come out of this alive! I promise you I'll get you out of this village unharmed! So help me God!"

She didn't say anything more, for she knew there were no definite answers.

Bart, still holding her close, was tormented. Why had he made such a promise? Just how in hell did he intend to keep it? Well, by God, he would keep it or die trying! He still held himself responsible for getting Sheila into such a dangerous situation, yet not once had she blamed him. He wondered what he had done to deserve such a wonderful woman.

He turned to her; his lips sought hers in a loving exchange, which quickly triggered their unquenchable desire.

"Speaking of promises," he said with an askew grin, determined to lighten the mood. "If I remember correctly, I promised you a night of blazing passion."

"You certainly did," she replied. She thrust their troubles to the far recesses of her mind. Tonight, she wanted to lose herself in ecstasy. "Do you intend to fulfill your promise?" she asked, her brown eyes twinkling saucily.

"That is for certain," he remarked.

"Then, my darling, why don't you get started?"

"Can you keep up with me?" he teased.

"Of course I can. In fact, I'm willing to go above and beyond the call of duty."

He arched a brow. "I suppose you're ready to prove that?"

"Put me to the test," she dared.

"I will," he came back. Then his lips captured hers urgently.

Again, their bodies came together with love, and the rapture they achieved was absolute perfection.

Throughout the night, and into the wee hours of the morning, they alternated between dozing and making love with a passion that was utterly complete and wonderfully consuming.

Chapter Twenty-Eight

The next day went by slowly for Sheila and Bart, and as the passing hours failed to bring the soldiers, their precarious situation began to look even worse. They were now very worried that Amanda had mistaken the Dwyers' time of departure.

The sun set, and darkness fell over the village. Despite the horrors tomorrow could bring, Sheila and Bart spent the night making love and snuggled in each other's arms. They clung tenaciously, desperately, for they knew they might never be together like this again.

The new day emerged with the musical chirping of birds, and the sun shining brightly. Soon thereafter, children were yelling playfully as they romped through the village, and camp dogs, barking rapidly, followed at their heels. Women left their tepees to work outside, and men sat about in groups, discussing the soldiers; they now believed the attack, would never happen. Apparently Three Moons was right about White Cloud; the bluecoats had sent him here to trick them into returning to the reservation. The more they leaned toward believing Three Moons, the more resentment they harbored toward Bart. Iron Star's son was a traitor. They were glad Iron Star hadn't lived to see this day. White Cloud's disloyalty would have broken his heart.

As the men in the village began to think Bart guilty of treason, Yellow Bear and Spotted Wing, standing outside their grandmother's tepee, watched the gathered groups with apprehension.

"The men think Three Moons was right about White Cloud." Yellow Bear sounded worried. "The soldiers should have been here yesterday. If they do not show up soon, the council will decide that White Cloud lied to them."

Spotted Wing's heart was heavy. "Do you think Lame Crow will give me permission to talk to White Cloud?"

"I do not know."

"I must see him!"

"Why are you so desperate to see our brother?"

"Yellow Bear, you believed me when I told you I didn't betray White Cloud. Now, I must convince White Cloud of that! He probably thinks I told Three Moons that he was planning to escape." Spotted Wing spoke the truth; she hadn't said anything.

Yellow Bear was about to reply when he suddenly spotted warriors cresting the distant hill. He watched as they sped down the grassy slope, across the meadow and to the river. The scouts the council had posted were among the band; the other warriors belonged to another village. As they drew closer, Yellow Bear recognized Running Bull and the braves who always rode with him.

As the people gathered around to greet them, Yellow Bear hurried over. Spotted Wing was close behind. The old men of the council arrived, along with Three Moons. He stayed clear of Yellow Bear's sister, however, for he no longer knew her opinion of him.

The scouts' return was expected, for two days had passed; it was Running Bull's arrival that had piqued the villagers' curiosity.

Smiling proudly, Running Bull leapt from his pony. He was quick to boast. "Yesterday my men and I came across the white eyes. They had three wagons filled with supplies the white use to prospect for yellow nuggets. The fools are now dead for trespassing on our sacred land." He lifted his lance, showing off the fresh scalps he had taken; then, with a wide smile, he continued. "The wagons were also filled with whiskey!"

This announcement brought cheers from most of the warriors in the village. In their opinion, the only good thing the white man brought to their land was his firewater.

There were others in the village, however, who profoundly disagreed. Whiskey made men act like fools. Yellow Bear and Lame Crow both felt this way, and they watched with consternation as Running Bull's braves handed out bottles of whiskey. Three Moons craved the liquor and gladly took a bottle for himself.

Lame Crow made a futile effort to stop the warriors from accepting the white man's drink, but his pleas fell on deaf ears. Yellow Bear, hoping they would listen to him, was about to voice his disapproval but was distracted by Spotted Wing's hand tugging at his arm.

She pulled him to the side. "Yellow Bear, let the warriors drink the whiskey. They will soon be drunk and many of them will pass out. It will then be easy for us to help White Cloud and the others to escape."

Yellow Bear was impressed. Why hadn't he thought of that? He smiled at his sister. "Spotted Wing, you are very shrewd."

She glanced over at the warriors. Several of them had already uncapped their bottles and were swigging down the contents. Her eyes searched for Three Moons. She found him in the middle of the group. He had a bottle tilted to his lips and was guzzling from it. She looked away, for the sight sickened her. Why did he and the others make such fools of themselves over the white man's firewater? Although she hated to see the warriors act so foolhardy, she was nonetheless thankful for this opportunity to save her brother.

Spotted Wing and Yellow Bear remained in Golden Dove's tepee, waiting for the whiskey to have its full effect on the warriors. When the sun had reached its zenith, they stepped outside and were followed by Dream Dancer. The sight that confronted them was pathetic. Warriors, and quite a few of the older men, were sprawled about the camp. Several of them were passed out, and the others were so inebriated that they could barely hold up their heads. No one was mingling about, for the women and children were in their homes, and the men who refused to partake of the whiskey were with their families.

Yellow Bear spoke quietly. "Dream Dancer, go to Luke and tell him to take the women to the river's bank. Then return for Golden Dove. Spotted Wing, you go to our brother. I will get their horses, weapons, and supplies."

The threesome went their separate ways. When Spotted Wing reached Bart's tepee, she wasn't surprised to find there were no guards. They had obviously left their post to take part in the drunken revelry.

She hurried inside, where she found Bart and Sheila tied up. Before leaving their posts, the guards had restrained their prisoners with ropes about their arms and legs. Finding a knife, Spotted Wing quickly cut them loose.

Bart and Sheila had heard the drunken carousing from outside, and Bart asked his sister where warriors had gotten the whiskey.

She told him about Running Bull's raid on the white prospectors. "I despise this drink called whiskey," she continued. "But it is good that Running Bull brought it to our village, for it gives you a chance to escape."

"Are all the warriors drunk?" Bart asked.

"The ones who are not are inside their homes."

"Where is Lame Crow?"

She shrugged. "I do not know." She placed a firm hand on his arm. "White Cloud, I did not betray you. I hope you will believe me."

He saw only sincerity in her eyes. "I believe you, Spotted Wing." He then hugged her warmly, and she returned his embrace.

"Come," she said. "You must hurry."

Moving cautiously by darting between tepees and keeping clear of the drunken warriors, they eventually made their way to the river's bank. Luke and the others were already there. A few minutes later, Yellow Bear arrived with their horses, mule, and supplies. His arrival was shortly followed by that of Dream Dancer and Golden Dove.

"We must make our goodbyes quick," Yellow Bear said.

Sheila noticed that Golden Dove carried a small bag, and as she attached it to the pony Yellow Bear had brought her, Sheila couldn't help but feel a little sad. The woman had only a small bag to represent over forty years of her life. Somehow it just didn't seem right.

It tore into Golden Dove's heart to say farewell to Yellow Bear, Spotted Wing, and Dream Dancer, but she forced herself to do so with dry eyes. Bart was also sorry to say goodbye, but he knew it had to be done quickly and with as few words as possible.

Hoping that someday he would see his brother and sister again, Bart mounted his horse to leave. Suddenly, spotting a distant figure, he tensed and his hand went to his pistol. He didn't draw it, however, for the figure had drawn closer; he saw that it was Lame Crow.

The old medicine man paused, then lifted a hand in farewell.

"Why isn't he trying to stop us from leaving?" Bart asked Yellow Bear.

"He loved our father very much, and I think he is doing it for him."

"Well, whatever his reasons are, I'm thankful he's not alerting the village. Will you tell him that for me?"

Yellow Bear assured him that he would, then he encouraged his brother to leave quickly.

The group slapped their reins against their horses, galloped across the narrow river, and headed toward the grassy hill that loomed ahead.

Amanda, riding beside Luke, thanked God for granting her a second chance with the man she loved. She could hardly believe they were actually free! Sheila was just as happy as Amanda. Now that their ordeal was over, she and Bart could get married and go to Texas. Neither woman, however, was more elated than Janice. She had been terrified of dying, but now that she was no longer plagued by that fear, her mind was free to concentrate on Charles Dwyer. She envisioned herself married to him and living in Washington, D.C., where she would consort with the upper crust of society. As far as she was concerned, Sheila was more than welcome to Bart and his dull ranch. She had much higher expectations for herself!

Bart, worried about Golden Dove, decided to stop and make camp before nightfall. Considering her weakened condition, he knew this trip would be very hard on her.

Bart and Luke were against starting a fire. It would be necessary to eat cold meals and do without coffee until they were safely out of the mountains.

The sun hadn't fully set. Still, the group gathered their bedrolls and were getting ready to lay them out when they heard the sounds of horses in the distance. They were holed-up on top of a steep hill, which was an ideal location, for it gave them a clear view in every direction. Bart and Luke hurried to the edge to look down in the valley below. Except for Golden Dove, who was resting, the women followed. No one was surprised to see the Dwyers leading a full company of soldiers. The long column came to a stop, and the troopers were ordered to dismount. Evidently, they were planning to camp there for the night.

"What should we do?" Luke asked Bart.

"Nothing. We can't let them know we're here. I want you to take the women, detour around the soldiers, and camp behind them. In the morning, start for Fort Laramie."

"What are you gonna do?" Luke asked.

"Go back and warn Yellow Bear."

Sheila clutched Bart's arm. "I want to go with you!"

He admired her courage, but he wasn't about to put her in danger again. He knew, though, that she would balk at that excuse. He decided to use a reason she couldn't argue with. "Sheila, I can travel much faster alone, and time is of the essence."

She understood, but she was afraid for his life. "Bart, please be careful!"

That Janice had slipped away went unnoticed, and they were all taken by surprise when she suddenly sped past them on horseback. She raced down the hillside and toward the soldiers without looking back.

"Damn it!" Bart cursed, enraged. "I should have known she'd pull something like this!"

"Go on, Bart!" Sheila encouraged. "We'll be all right. The Dwyers won't do anything to us."

"She's right," Luke confirmed. "If you're gonna warn Yellow Bear, you better get goin'!"

He gave Sheila a quick but affectionate kiss, then ran to his horse, mounted, and rapidly disappeared over the far side of the hill.

As Janice raced toward the soldiers, she was smiling with joy. Bart and the others had been such fools not to watch her. Did they really think she would stay with them when she could be with Charles and his army? Furthermore, she was glad that Charles intended to attack Yellow Bear's village. She hoped they would shoot down all the Indians! After all, the savages had planned to kill her, and she wanted to savor the sweet taste of revenge. That Yellow Bear, his sister, and his wife had helped them escape didn't matter to Janice. She was certain they participated only to save Bart and wouldn't have cared if she had died. She considered turnabout as fair play—she didn't give a damn if they died either!

She rode into the midst of the soldiers and was greeted with shocked expressions. The last thing they had expected to see was a lone white woman racing into their camp.

The Dwyers, elbowing their way through the crowd of soldiers, made their way to the front. The sight of Janice sent Charles's senses reeling. Good God, what was she doing here?

A trooper helped her dismount, and, rushing to

437

Charles, she exclaimed, "Bart has left to warn Yellow Bear. You must stop him!"

Charles's shock at seeing her was still too great for him to respond.

But Donald had his wits about him. He turned around sharply, spotted Sergeant Kent, and ordered briskly, "Take ten men with you and find Chandler! And don't come back without him!" Donald then spoke to Janice. "Where are the others?"

She pointed back at the hill. "Up there."

Taking a dozen soldiers with him, he left to go after them.

Janice gazed into Charles's shocked face with feigned longing. "I was only hours away from Fort Swafford when I knew I should never have left you! Oh, Charles, even though I've been a widow a short time, I cannot deny that my feelings for you are very ". . . very strong."

Somewhat recovered, he placed an arm about her shoulders and led her away from the soldiers. They went to a full-branched tree, stepped behind it, and were hidden from view by the wide trunk. Charles quickly brought her into his arms and held her soft body close to his. Her parted lips welcomed the major's amorous assault. His rough, fiery kiss easily aroused her passion, and she wished they were alone so he could satisfy her aching needs.

"Janice . . . Janice!" he moaned hoarsely, his heart beating with desire, as well as with love. "Now that I have found you again, I'll never let you go!"

"I want to marry you, my darling!" She pretended sudden embarrassment. "Forgive me! I shouldn't be so bold!"

438

He smiled with happiness. "Where our love is concerned, you can be as bold as you want." Then, eyeing her closely, he asked, "You do love me, don't you?"

"Oh, yes!" she cried.

"As soon as we get back to the fort, we'll be married." He urged her to sit down on the grass, and he quickly joined her there. "Now, darling, I want you to tell me what's happening. I thought you and the others were going to Fort Laramie. What are you doing here?"

Janice, complying readily, gave him a detailed account. She didn't, however, admit that she had traveled willingly to Yellow Bear's village, but made it sound as though she had been forced.

Sheila and the others had their bedrolls packed and back on their horses before the soldiers arrived. Standing at the edge of the hill, they watched as Dwyer led his men up the steep incline.

Reining in, Donald dismounted and stood before Sheila. She was wearing the Indian dress that Dream Dancer had given her, and Donald's eyes raked over her attire with distaste. An ugly sneer curled his mustached lips. "I see you have finally sunk to the lowest form of life—acting the part of an Indian squaw!"

"Go to hell!" she spat.

"To hell?" he questioned, his lips now curling into a chilling grin. "Tell me, Sheila, if I were to rub my body with buffalo oil, put on a breechcloth, and comb bear grease into my hair, would you still tell me to go to hell?"

"You better believe it!" she snapped.

He laughed bitterly. "Well, my dear, I have no intention of going to hell anytime soon. But I can't say the same for your half-breed lover!''

"What do you mean by that?"

"When I capture him, and I will, he will die along with his Sioux kin. Since his alliance lies with the Indians, he can die with them! And not even J.W. Chandler can do anything about it!'' With that, he wheeled about, went to his horse and swung into the saddle. "Mount up!'' he said gruffly to Sheila and the others.

They moved to their horses; then Sheila rode over to Donald. "What are you planning to do with us?''

"You're all under arrest for suspicion of treason. And since we can't lose the manpower to leave you behind under guard, we'll have to take you with us.'' He grinned evilly. "You can watch as we destroy Yellow Bear's village.''

"You lowlife!'' she seethed. "So help me God, if you murder those people, I'll see you court-martialed!''

His expression was coldly confident. "You have no real understanding of the military, my dear; otherwise, you wouldn't make such a ridiculous threat.'' He slapped the reins against his horse and started down the hillside. Sheila, riding between two soldiers, followed in his tracks. Amanda and Luke were next in line, Golden Dove was directly behind them, and the rest of the soldiers brought up the rear.

Amanda and Luke had heard the exchange between Sheila and the lieutenant. As they made their way down the slope, Amanda asked Luke, "Was Dwyer right about Sheila's threat? If he and Donald massacre the village, will the Army look the other way and ignore the slaughter?''

Luke shrugged. "Probably. The Army frowns on court-martialing their officers. 'Sides, they figure the more Indians the Dwyers kill, the less there are to fight."

"That's a horrible way to look at it."

"Yep, but that's the way it is, and there's nothin' we can do about it." He paused for a moment, then said with regret, "You know, darlin', I think we just jumped from one fryin' pan right into another. I'm beginnin' to wonder if we're ever gonna make it to Texas."

"We'll get there, all right!" she said, as though she could somehow control their destiny. "I didn't wait twenty years to lose you to Indians . . . or the army!"

Chapter Twenty-Nine

Charles gave the women the use of his tent; they needed privacy for they were surrounded by soldiers. Janice wasn't pleased about the arrangement; she knew the other women resented her. However, realizing she had no choice but to face them, she told herself she didn't care what they thought.

She entered the tent with her head held high. The others were already inside. She stared directly at each woman, and her flashing eyes dared them to say anything derisive; if they did, she would tell them exactly how she felt, then demand that Charles have them removed.

But to Janice's bewilderment, they barely looked her way. They seemed content simply to ignore her. That she had run to Charles hadn't really surprised them. The ladies were angry, but more with themselves than with

Janice. They had been such fools not to watch her more closely.

Janice moved to a far corner and sat down on Charles's cot. She watched the others, who were seated on blankets that would serve as their beds. That Janice would sleep on the major's cot went without saying; none of the others wished to use it.

Janice soon resented the women's silence, and said haughtily, "I am not the traitor, you know. The Sioux are our enemies, and it was my patriotic duty to warn the soldiers."

"We aren't stupid, Janice!" Sheila asserted sharply. "Patriotic, indeed! You don't give a damn about the soldiers. You only give a damn about yourself."

"You shouldn't curse, Sheila. It's not very flattering."

"If you don't keep your mouth shut, I'll do more than curse!"

"Are you threatening me?"

Amanda placed a calming hand on Sheila's shoulder. "Don't let her nettle you." She cast Janice a glance that revealed the repulsion she felt, then added, "She's not worth it."

Agreeing, Sheila cooled her temper. She turned to Golden Dove, who was staring into space. Knowing how worried she must be about her family, Sheila said encouragingly, "I'm sure Bart will reach the village and warn Yellow Bear. When he tells them the Dwyers have a full company of soldiers along with cannons, Yellow Bear and the others will agree to surrender. No one will be killed."

Golden Dove nodded. "I pray you are right."

Donald's sudden appearance caught them off guard.

444

Sheila and her companions got to their feet and stared at him with a touch of apprehension, wary of the gleeful grin on his face.

"Come with me," he said to Sheila, his hand grasping her arm.

She tried to pull away, but he held her too firmly. "I'm not going anywhere with you!" she snapped.

"My dear, we're only stepping outside. I don't intend to take you anywhere. There's something I want you to see."

She regarded him suspiciously, wishing she knew what was on his evil mind. "Take your hand off me!" she demanded. "I can walk outside without your help!"

He released her suddenly, laughed under his breath, then gestured for her to go ahead of him.

She moved outside and waited for Donald. He paused beside her, then pointed in the distance. Her eyes followed the direction of his finger, and the sight confronting her made her heart lurch. Sergeant Kent and his soldiers were riding into camp, and they had Bart with them. He was riding double with a trooper. Another soldier was leading Bart's stallion; it was limping badly.

"Oh, no!" Sheila moaned. "His horse is lame!"

Donald chuckled. "Chandler will be arrested, taken back to Fort Swafford, and tried for treason." His icy-blue eyes bore into hers. "And you, my dear, will be tried along with him." His lips curved into a smile, and he reminded her of a snake about to strike. "However, if you agree to become my mistress, I'll see that you are never put on trial."

"I would rather be tried, found guilty, and face a firing squad!"

"You say that now, but, in time, your courage will falter."

"Courage?" she lashed out. "It has nothing to do with courage. I loathe you more than I fear death!" She made a quick move to flee to Bart, but Donald's arm snaked about her waist.

"Go back inside, my dear. And you are forbidden to have contact with your half-breed lover."

She glared at him, then ducked back into the small tent.

A deep frown furrowed Donald's brow. His offer to help Sheila if she became his mistress had been spoken with no deliberation, and he was now aggravated with himself. He had thought he was completely over her, but apparently he wasn't. Damn it, just thinking about her aroused him. That he had drunk himself asleep that night in the stables still had the power to spark his anger. My God, Sheila had been in his bed naked, his to do with as he pleased, and he had fallen into a drunken stupor! Surely, if he could have her just once, his desire for her would not be so powerful.

A calculating grin spread across his face. Before they returned to Fort Swafford, he would enjoy her—if he had to tie her down to get what he wanted!

Luke, tied securely, watched as two soldiers brought Bart over, bound his hands, then shoved him to the ground. They wrapped a strand of rope about his ankles, then moved away.

Four guards remained nearby. They sat about a campfire and talked in low tones while keeping a close watch on the prisoners.

"Where are the women?" Bart asked Luke.

"In the major's tent." He sighed heavily. "I wasn't expectin' to see you."

"My horse tripped and pulled up lame. After that, it didn't take Sergeant Kent long to catch me."

Luke shook his head regretfully. "Well, Bart, you tried. We all tried, but maybe the Dwyers' attack is destined. You can't stop destiny."

Bart didn't agree, but he saw no purpose in discussing the matter. "When the Army arrives, I hope Yellow Bear and the others will realize that surrender is their only recourse. If they try to fight, they'll be destroyed. The village is too small to battle a full unit, especially one with cannons." Bart's eyes swept over the troops. "I don't want any of them to die, either. Hell, they're just soldiers obeying orders."

"Bart, you gotta stop carryin' all this on your own shoulders. Damn it, you did all you could do. Now it's out of your hands."

"Yes, I know," he replied somberly. "But warning Yellow Bear was vital."

"When the Indians see the soldiers outnumber them, they'll surrender."

"They won't know they're outnumbered."

"What do you mean?"

"I think I have the Dwyers' strategy figured out. They'll leave more than half of their men and their artillery out of sight, then ride into view of the village. Three Moons and the other warriors will believe they can win the battle. The Dwyers will wait for Three Moons or one of the others to fire the first shot, then they'll have the provocation they need to order a full attack. The rest of the Army will arrive, and the village will be destroyed."

"Which means no court-martial," Luke added. "The Dwyers were fired on first. The Indians started it."

"That's correct!" Bart replied harshly.

"Yep, you probably got it figured just like it's gonna happen. Too bad you didn't get to warn Yellow Bear how many soldiers there are."

"If only there was a way . . ."

"Well, there ain't," Luke remarked flatly.

Janice joined the Dwyers for supper at their campfire. Sheila and the other women stayed inside the tent. Their meals were brought to them, but none of them ate very much, for their appetites were poor. Golden Dove ate less than anyone. Sheila was worried about her. She was still weak and needed nourishment to keep up her strength. She tried to encourage the woman to take more food, but Golden Dove's stomach was too knotted with anxiety to accept food.

Now, with a deep sigh, Golden Dove said sadly, "If only White Cloud had gotten through to Yellow Bear."

Amanda attempted to ease her mind. "When Yellow Bear and the others see how many soldiers there are, they'll surrender without a fight."

Sheila, like Bart, understood the Dwyers. "The Indians won't know how big the Army is," she said. "Donald and his brother don't want them to surrender; they want an excuse to attack. I bet they'll leave most of the soldiers

448

out of sight, then provoke the warriors into firing the first shot.''

''Lord!'' Amanda groaned. ''I didn't even consider that.''

''That's because you don't know how evil the Dwyers really are. They think like devils!''

Tears welled up in Golden Dove's eyes. ''I'm so afraid for my people, especially for my grandchildren and Dream Dancer!''

''We must find a way to warn Yellow Bear,'' Sheila asserted.

''But how?'' Amanda asked.

''Bart and Luke are tied up. They are also under guard. Finding a way to set them free is impossible. However, *we* aren't tied up, nor are we being watched very closely. I intend to think of a way to escape so I can warn Yellow Bear.''

''But, Sheila, how can you possibly escape?'' Golden Dove cried.

''I don't know. I have to think about it. Why don't we all give it a lot of thought?''

The woman sat quietly as they tried to formulate an escape plan. Minutes went by before Sheila suddenly exclaimed, ''I have an idea that might work!''

''What is it?'' they asked in unison.

Sheila moved quickly to the oil lamp, picked up the matches beside it, returned, and handed them to Amanda. ''Here; keep these close.'' She leaned closer to her friends, and said it a low voice, ''This is my plan: Later tonight when Janice and most of the camp are asleep, I'll cut my way out the back of the tent. There's a knife in my carpetbag. As soon as I've cut my way through, I

449

want one of you to use those matches to start a fire. But don't awaken Janice until it's blazing, and you have only enough time to get out. Knowing Janice, she'll panic, scream, and carry on so hysterically that I won't be missed immediately. While all that is going on, I'll sneak to the horses, pick out a fast one, and ride away quickly——.''

"No," Golden Dove cut in. "Don't worry about the horse's speed. You'll be traveling in the dark and over treacherous terrain. You won't need a horse that is fast, but rather one that is sure-footed and familiar with the trail between here and the village. Take the pony I was riding; it was one of Yellow Bear's favorites. It has traveled this land many times, and it knows its way in the dark. Give it free rein, and it will get you safely to the village."

"But the Dwyers are certain to see her ride away, and they'll have her pursued," Amanda said. "That's why she needs a fast horse."

"No," Golden Dove insisted. "The soldiers will not catch her. It will be dark and the terrain steep; they will have to guide their mounts carefully. They will soon realize Sheila is far ahead, and they will turn around and come back."

"She's right," Sheila told Amanda. "I'll take the pony."

"For heaven's sake, Sheila, be careful!" Amanda said anxiously.

She smiled faintly. "I certainly don't plan to be careless." She patted her friend's arm. "I'll be fine, Amanda. Try not to worry."

It was well after midnight before Sheila decided it was time to leave. Janice had gone to bed over an hour ago. She was on Charles's cot, and her deep, steady breathing assured the others that she was sound asleep. The tent was shadowy, but they didn't dare light the oil lamp.

Sheila crept to the rear of the tent, knelt, and stuck the knife's blade into the canvas. Carefully, she sliced through the durable material until there was an opening big enough to crawl through.

Amanda and Golden Dove were crouched behind her. She turned and hugged them briefly.

"God be with you," Golden Dove whispered.

"Good luck," Amanda added.

"Start the fire," Sheila told them quietly.

Amanda said that they would, then Sheila ducked through the small opening and slipped outside.

Moving furtively so she wouldn't awaken Janice, Amanda picked up a carpetbag belonging to Charles. He had left most of his things inside the tent. A smile was on her face as she examined the bag and withdrew a change of clothes. "These will burn nicely," she whispered to Golden Dove. She stacked the clean uniform and underwear in a corner. Resentment sparked in her eyes as she gazed at the blue uniform. In her opinion, Charles didn't deserve to wear it. He wasn't a soldier, he was a butcher!

She started to strike a match, but Golden Dove placed a hand on her arm. "Wait," she said softly. Getting the lamp, she poured coal oil over the clothes.

451

"Now, they will blaze." Like Amanda, she was looking forward to watching the major's uniform burst into flames.

Amanda struck the match, then cupped the glow with her hand. She didn't want Janice to awaken, not just yet! She carefully dropped the lit match onto the clothing; darting flames took hold immediately.

The women stepped back out of harm's way. They watched, enthralled, as the fire spread rapidly, igniting nearby blankets, a stack of maps, and the canvas walls.

"It's time to get out of here," Amanda decided. She hurried to Janice, shook her shoulder, and cried excitedly, "Wake up! The tent is on fire!"

Janice's eyes popped open at once, and, sitting up with a bolt, she was terrified to see raging flames devouring part of the tent. She sprang from the cot, and, screaming hysterically, ran outside.

Amanda and Golden Dove were right behind her.

Janice's screams awoke the entire camp, and by the time the soldiers could get out of their beds, the entire tent was engulfed in flames. It burned as fiercely as a huge bonfire, and red-hot tongues of fire darted upward toward the night sky.

As though the conflagration had somehow put the soldiers and their officers into a daze, they stood by numbly and watched as the tent burned to the ground. Sheila's absence went unnoticed.

Sheila had hidden in the shadows behind the tent, where she had waited anxiously for the fire to begin.

She heard Janice's bloodcurdling scream, then almost immediately after the tent went up in flames.

She raced for the horses. They were tethered in three different groups; fortunately, the Indian pony was in the first group. There were no guards around, for they had left to watch the fire. For an instant, she debated slipping over to Bart and Luke and setting them free. The men guarding them were probably watching the fire along with everyone else. But she quickly dismissed the idea. Sneaking to Bart and Luke was too dangerous. She might be seen. Also, it would take too much time, and she must hurry!

The pony was wearing its bridle and blanket, Sheila started to swing up onto its back when she suddenly noticed a saddled roan. Finding it saddled didn't surprise her; the soldiers always kept a few horses ready to ride. But to her amazement, a rifle was still ensconced in the saddle's scabbard. She mounted her pony, edged it over to the roan, drew the rifle, and placed it across her lap. Then, turning the pinto around, she guided it past the other horses and into the open. She kneed the pony suddenly and slapped the reins against its neck. Startled, it took off with a bolt and raced away from the campsite.

Sheila's escape didn't go undetected; Bart and Luke, hearing the pony's pounding hooves, caught sight of her as she sped into the black of night. Fear, as sharp as a razor's edge, cut into Bart's heart. He knew the mission she had undertaken was filled with risks. The terrain between here and Yellow Bear's village was perilous; it

453

was also populated with hostile Indians. However, despite his fear, Sheila's courage filled him with pride.

The Dwyers had also heard Sheila flee, and Donald quickly took some men with him and left to bring her back. Donald wasn't concerned, for he was certain that she couldn't elude him and his soldiers. After all, she was only a woman: she couldn't very well get away. In fact, once she found herself alone in this treacherous land—in the dark no less!—she would undoubtedly hole up and wait to be rescued.

The fire was now only smoldering ashes, and as Charles eyed the ruins, rage rose inside him. Many of his personal belongings had been destroyed, in addition to maps and important papers. He turned angrily to Amanda and Golden Dove. "If you two were men, I would have you lashed for starting that fire. You will find that your act of arson was for nothing! Sheila will be caught and brought back! Since it is quite obvious neither of you can be trusted, you have forced me to keep you restrained." He spoke to a couple of his soldiers. "I want these women tied securely!"

"Where do you want us to put them?" one of the troopers asked.

"Keep them with the other prisoners."

As they led the women away, Charles moved to Janice and draped an arm about her shoulders. "My poor darling, are you all right?"

"Yes, I think so," she murmured. The fire had frightened her badly, and she was still shaken.

"I'm sorry, my dear, but you will now have to sleep outdoors. I'll have a bedroll prepared close to mine so I can protect you."

454

She gazed up at him with feigned adoration. "Charles, you're so kind and chivalrous. What would I do without you?"

He was flattered—as she knew he would be.

"Sheila will be all right," Golden Dove told Bart confidently. She was sitting beside him. The soldiers had tied her hands and Amanda's, then had taken them to where the men were being held. They were under a large tree, and could lean back against its wide trunk. Golden Dove had told Bart that the Indian pony would safely deliver Sheila to the village, and that it would also leave the soldiers far behind. He had found her words comforting, but they didn't stop him from worrying.

"God!" Bart groaned. "If anything happens to her . . . !"

"Nothing will!" Golden Dove remarked strongly. "I just know she's going to be fine. I feel it deep in my heart."

"I wish I did," Bart mumbled.

Time passed slowly as they waited for the soldiers' return. Bart and Luke weren't as confident as the women and were worried that Sheila would be brought back. But an hour or so before dawn, Lieutenant Dwyer and his men rode into camp. Sheila wasn't with them.

A pleased smile crossed Golden Dove's face. "See! I told you they couldn't catch the pony!"

Donald was steaming with anger as he dismounted and handed his horse over to a trooper. That Sheila had eluded him was a terrible blow to his pride. Damn her to hell, she was always getting the better of him! Someday, by

God, her luck would run out, and then he'd teach her a lesson she'd never forget!

Charles had been asleep, but the soldiers' return had awakened him. He was surprised to find that Donald had failed to apprehend Sheila.

"What happened?" hc asked his brother irritably. "I can't believe you let a woman get away!"

"I swear to God, Charles! She disappeared like an apparition!"

"Apparition?" the major ridiculed. "You expect me to believe the Great Spirit intervened and whisked her away?"

"Believe what you want!" Donald said angrily. "But I tell you, I couldn't find her!" He brushed past his brother and went to a campfire, where he poured himself a cup of coffee. That Sheila had disappeared like a puff of smoke was puzzling, but her escape aroused his anger more than his curiosity. The desire to get even with her filled his whole being. It had become an obsession.

Chapter Thirty

Donald, standing in the distance, looked on as the prisoners were untied and led to their horses. The stallion was still limping, so Bart was given an Army gelding to ride. Two soldiers assisted the women onto their mounts. Golden Dove was also issued another horse. More than forty years had gone by since she had used a saddle; it felt strange and a little awkward.

Bart was about to swing up onto the gelding when Donald came forward. Bart froze, and rage surged through him. Fury shone in his gray eyes, and his mouth twisted into a murderous sneer. His strong hands doubled into fists. God, how he wanted to send them slamming into the man's face! With effort, he controlled his temper; he would bide his time and wait for the right opportunity to beat the living hell out of him. He would make him pay for what he did to Sheila!

Bart's obvious rage caused a wide smile to appear on Donald's face. He was no doubt contemplating revenge. The man was a complete idiot. Did he really think that day would ever come? Earlier, as Donald had been drinking his coffee and sulking over Sheila's escape, his thoughts had turned to Chandler. Taking the man back to the fort for trial was too risky; he might be found innocent. Undoubtedly, like a raging bull, he would then avenge Sheila's honor. Donald had no intention of allowing that to happen. He didn't want to tangle with Chandler; he was too afraid that he'd come out the loser. So he had decided to get rid of Bart—permanently! When they reached Yellow Bear's village, he planned to release Bart, who would without question race into the Indian camp to find Sheila. Donald had already passed the word to Sergeant Kent and a few selected troopers to find Chandler and kill him during the attack. Not even J.W. could press charges; Bart's presence in the village would prove that he was fighting against the Army.

Bart looked away from Donald and mounted his horse. His hands shook with rage; his body was taut, and every muscle was tensed.

Luke, watching Bart closely, knew exactly how he felt. He edged his horse alongside Chandler's. "You gotta stay calm," he warned quietly. "Attackin' the sonofabitch now ain't gonna do you any good. You'd be lucky to get in one solid punch before bein' pulled away. Be patient—the time will come."

Bart nodded stiffly. "I know, but staying calm isn't easy."

"Right now, that's the only choice you got."

Donald, leaving, cast Bart a smug smile, then turned on his heel and strutted over to Charles and Janice.

Watching, Bart mumbled, "Apparently, my first impression of Janice was right. She's completely selfish and manipulative. She almost had one fooled. When she was so cooperative about returning to the village, I thought I had misjudged her."

Amanda heard what he said. "Bart, she was never cooperative. I figured out her motives very easily. She had hoped to inveigle you."

"Me? But why?"

"Your grandfather is rich, that's why. When she realized she couldn't get anywhere with you, she decided to go after the major."

"Why him? Officers aren't rich."

"That is true. But Charles plans to go into politics. Politicians live very comfortably, and are quite prestigious. Janice has high expectations. She hopes to become the First Lady of the country."

Bart laughed; he couldn't help it. "Dwyer President, and Janice the First Lady? God forbid!"

"You can say that again!" Amanda declared.

The Indians spotted Sheila the moment she crested the hill overlooking their village. Her pony was exhausted, and it was sweating profusely as she forced it to gallop down the grassy slope and toward the narrow river. Sheila loved animals, and it hurt her to subject the pinto to such an arduous pace. The beast was about to drop in its tracks, but innocent lives were depending on her and the pony.

Despite the lather that was now beading up on the pinto, she kept it at a steady trot.

Golden Dove had been right about the horse; it had indeed carried her safely across the perilous terrain, scaling the steep slopes as sure-footedly as a mountain goat. Guiding it had been unnecessary, for the pinto knew its way home. But staying on the unsaddled pony hadn't been easy when it was climbing sharp inclines, and several times she had come close to falling.

Through the long, treacherous night, Sheila had trusted the horse to deliver her safely to the village, and it hadn't disappointed her. She knew she would never forget the courageous pinto.

She had now reached the river, and the pony slipped as it sped across the water. The mishap made Sheila's heart lurch, but she was afraid for the pinto, not for herself. Fortunately it regained its footing and safely carried its rider into the village.

Yellow Bear, Dream Dancer, and several others were waiting for her. She still had the Army rifle, and, holding it securely, she slid off the horse's back. As a young Indian boy came up to take the pinto's reins, she said to Yellow Bear, "Tell him to walk the pony before giving it water."

"Do not worry," Yellow Bear replied. "Wolf Cub is good with horses." He moved closer to Sheila and asked, "Why did you come back? What has happened?"

She quickly told him about the Dwyers' army and that Bart and Luke were prisoners.

"How did you get away?"

She explained.

Yellow Bear grinned with admiration, but as the Dwyers' imminent attack filled his thoughts, the smile quickly disappeared. He turned to Dream Dancer. "Take Sheila to our tepee. The council and I have much to settle."

As Sheila followed Dream Dancer, she caught sight of Three Moons. He was standing in the crowd watching her with an expression she couldn't discern. Spotted Wing was at his side. She wondered if they were once more happily attached.

The women entered the tepee. Sheila laid her rifle aside, then Dream Dancer served her a cup of coffee and a bowl of food. Famished, Sheila did justice to her meal. "I noticed Spotted Wing with Three Moons," she finally asked. "Are they still engaged?"

"Yes. She love him, she want to marry him."

"She deserves better."

"A woman's heart not always wise."

Sheila's exhaustion was apparent, and Dream Dancer made her a bed. Needing rest, Sheila lay down, and within minutes she drifted into a restful sleep.

About an hour later, Sheila was awakened by Yellow Bear's voice. She sat up to find him standing over her. His face was grave, and she knew at once that he was troubled. Getting to her feet, she asked anxiously what the council had decided.

"Three Moons convinced them to stand and fight."

"What?" she exclaimed. "But didn't you tell them that the Dwyers have a full company of soldiers? They also have heavy artillery!"

"Yes, I told them. But Three Moons made them believe you are lying and that it is only another trick to get them to surrender."

"Tell them to send out scouts, and they'll see for themselves that I'm not lying!"

"Three Moons just left with others to find the soldiers." He summoned an encouraging smile. "They will soon return and say your words are true. Then, the council will have no choice but to agree with me. We must not confront the soldiers in battle."

Sheila sighed with relief. "Don't worry, Yellow Bear. When Three Moons sees the Dwyers' force, he'll know he can't fight them."

The soldiers had been traveling at a steady pace and making good time when Charles suddenly brought the troops to a halt. He motioned to the sergeant, who quickly rode up to talk to his commanding officer.

Bart wondered what was going on. He didn't like the looks of it. He watched intently as Sergeant Kent rode to the center of the column, and ordered it divided. Bart's heart slammed against his chest when he saw that the column leaving the formation took the cannons with them. He guessed the Dwyers' new strategy, and it not only scared him, but angered him to the core.

"What is going on?" Amanda asked.

"The Dwyers still plan to keep half the troops and the cannons out of sight. They figure Sheila warned the village, and that scouts will be sent out to see how many soldiers are on the march. That's why Dwyer is cutting the formation early. The scouts will find us all right, but they'll only see half of us. The others will trail a safe distance behind.''

''Maybe the scouts will take that into consideration and wait to see if there are more soldiers,'' Amanda said hopefully.

''Maybe,'' Bart mumbled. ''But I wouldn't bet on it.''

''When we spot the scouts, you can call out to them and warn them.''

''No.'' Golden Dove spoke up. ''White Cloud cannot warn the scouts, for we will not see them. They will be out there, but we will not know when or where.''

Luke, speaking to Amanda, explained, ''Indians have a innate gift for stealth that goes beyond reason. If an Indian don't want to be seen, believe me, he ain't gonna be seen.''

''Then Sheila's escape was for nothing!'' Amanda cried.

''We don't know that,'' Bart replied. ''I'm sure Yellow Bear took her at her word, and he has a lot of influence with the council.'' Bart wished he could totally believe what he said, but Three Moons's influence also carried a lot of weight. Despite Sheila's warning, the Dwyers' tactics might still succeed!

The bright sun, reaching its meridian, shone down on the quiet village. Birds of varying sizes and colors chirped different tunes; camp dogs barked sporadically; corralled horses whinnied and snorted; a baby's cry sounded now and then; and a northward breeze stirred the river, causing gentle waves to slap against the banks. Otherwise, the village was starkly silent. Families were gathered inside their lodges, mothers keeping their children close to them as fathers and sons prepared to defend their homes. A confrontation with the bluecoats was a distinct possibility, and every man in the village was readying himself for war.

Suddenly, the pounding of hooves carried into the hushed camp, sending the people rushing outdoors. They watched intently as Three Moons and the warriors with him cantered across the river and into the village.

They were met by Yellow Bear, Lame Crow, and the council. Sheila, standing between Dream Dancer and Spotted Wing, looked on anxiously. Three Moons's words carried loudly, and as he spoke, Spotted Wing translated his message for Sheila.

"Three Moons says he spotted the bluecoats, and there are less soldiers than we have warriors. They bring no cannons, only rifles."

"No!" Sheila cried. "I tell you, they have cannons!"

Spotted Wing raised a silencing hand so she could hear what the men were discussing. Angry words were thrown back and forth between Yellow Bear and Three Moons. Finally, Lame Crow quieted the heated exchange. Other warriors joined in, voicing their own opinions, and the conference continued for several more minutes before the group dispersed.

Taking Sheila's arm, Spotted Wing led her back inside the tepee. Dream Dancer followed behind them.

"It is best that you stay out of sight," Spotted Wing told Sheila. "The people believe you and White Cloud are working for the bluecoats. Three Moons did not see this huge army that you and White Cloud say are coming.

The warriors have decided to defend their homes against the soldiers."

"Dear God!" Sheila moaned. "I risked my life to come here, and it was for nothing!" She detected the faraway cry of an infant—and a chill of foreboding raced up her spine. "So many of you will die, including babies!"

"You are also in danger," Spotted Wing said.

"From Three Moons?"

"He is not your biggest danger; the soldiers are! When the battle starts, you will be here with us. If what you say is true, and the soldiers have cannons, they will use them on the village."

"*If* what I say is true! Spotted Wing, surely you believe me!"

She lowered her gaze from Sheila's. "I want to believe you."

"*If*, you don't completely trust *me*, you must certainly trust White Cloud! He wouldn't lie to you and the others!"

"You are right," she admitted a little sheepishly. "My brother would not betray his family."

Yellow Bear entered suddenly; their attention focused on him. He spoke authoritatively, and in English. "Dream Dancer, pack supplies for yourself, Spotted Wing, and Sheila. I want you women to leave the village, ride far into the mountains, and stay there until it is safe to return."

"No, my husband," she replied firmly in her own language. "I will not leave you!"

"I order you to go!"

"I will not obey! I love you, Yellow Bear! I would rather die at your side then live without you."

He could see that she was determined, and nothing he could do or say would change her mind. He turned to his sister, and continued in English so Sheila would understand. "Dream Dancer refuses to leave. You two will go alone."

She shook her head. "I also refuse to leave. I must stay here so I can help with the children."

Yellow Bear's eyes moved to Sheila. "You must go alone."

"I'm not running away, either," she replied. "Spotted Wing is right; mothers will need help with their children. I will not flee to save my own life, and leave innocent children behind to die."

Yellow Bear was impressed. "No wonder White Cloud loves you so much." He smiled. "I used to wonder if you were as beautiful inside as outside. Now I know that you are."

He turned away and went over to check his weapons. Sheila moved to the cooking pit, where a pot of coffee was still warm. She distractedly poured herself a cup, and drank it without really tasting it. She was tense and her stomach was roiling. She had never been in the midst of battle, had never even imagined that someday she would. Fear jabbed into her heart as fiercely as a lance, and her hands began to tremble.

Spotted Wing joined Sheila. Her own hands were shaking, and she reached over and entwined her fingers within Sheila's. The women held tightly, and their eyes met with mutual dread. In their minds, they could already hear the cannons firing.

Yellow Bear, watching, was deeply touched. He knew the pair were frightened, which was to be expected; however, their courage was much stronger than their fear. He was very proud of both of them!

Three warriors, who had been sent to await the soldiers, came charging into camp, whooping loudly and waving their lances. Their faces were painted for war, and their adrenaline was flowing.

As the older men stayed behind to oversee the women and children, the men of fighting age mounted their ponies. They were fully armed and anxious to prove their prowess.

As though moving in slow motion, the soldiers crested the distant hill, drew up their horses, and looked down at the village below.

The Dwyers weren't surprised to find the warriors armed and ready for battle. Evidently, Sheila had made it to the village.

"We'll draw them into a small skirmish, which will give the others time to get here," Charles said. He ordered his corporal to take a dozen soldiers and ride southward, which would make it look as though they planned to surround the village.

The corporal didn't like the order; it sounded dangerous. But he wasn't about to disobey. He and twelve chosen troopers carried out the major's command. They hadn't gotten very far before Three Moons decided to stop them. Leading over thirty warriors, he galloped away from the village and quickly intercepted the soldiers.

Outnumbered, the troopers were compelled to dismount, force their horses to the ground, take shelter behind them, and open fire.

Charles and Donald watched from a safe distance. The major's face was grim; he knew the troopers were doomed. When he sent the corporal on the mission, he knew it would be a lethal one. But sometimes it was necessary to sacrifice a few soldiers to win a battle.

"When we get back to the fort," Charles said to Donald, "remind me to write a letter to the families of those soldiers. I'll send them my deepest condolences, and tell them that their loved ones died heroically. Someday, when I run for President, they'll remember that I wrote them personally, and their votes will be mine."

Donald pointed at the Indians still in the village. "Why don't they charge us?"

"The ground between us and them is too open. They know we could easily pick them off. They'll wait until the skirmish is over and see if we'll charge first."

"And if we don't?"

"They'll risk the open ground and charge anyhow."

"Damn!" Donald groaned. He was getting frightened. "I hope the others hurry and get here. Those goddamned Indians have us outnumbered."

The major agreed. He returned to watching the small battle. Most of the soldiers were dead or badly wounded. If the troops didn't arrive soon, he might be forced to sacrifice more soldiers.

Bart and the others, still on horseback, were at the bottom of the hill. They couldn't see what was taking place but could hear the gunshots exchanged between the

Indians and the soldiers. Bart had glimpsed the corporal and his men riding southward, and had figured out the major's motive.

Now, as the shots slowly dwindled, he muttered angrily, "Damn Major Dwyer! He's a cold-hearted bastard!"

Amanda and Golden Dove looked at him quizzically.

"The major sacrificed those men intentionally," Bart explained.

The women didn't really understand, but Luke knew exactly what Bart meant. "If there's any justice in this world," Luke mumbled, "someday Major Dwyer will find himself surrounded by Indians on the warpath."

Janice's horse was close to Luke's, and she heard his every word. "There's no chance of that happening," she asserted petulantly. "Charles is sure he'll receive a transfer to General Custer's Seventh Cavalry. The general is a superb leader, and his troops will never be surrounded by Indians."

The gunshots ceased. An eerie silence prevailed, but was suddenly broken by the sounds of advancing horses. The rest of the troops could be seen in the distance; they were traveling swiftly. The caissons holding the deadly cannons bounced precariously across the terrain, and several times it appeared as though the two-wheel vehicles were about to topple over, sending their cargo spilling onto the ground.

But the soldiers arrived quickly, the cannons in place and unharmed. Major Dwyer rode down the hillside and began shouting orders.

Bart looked away from the troops and turned to his grandmother. Her eyes, staring widely at the cannons, were filled with tears. Bart urged his horse alongside hers. He touched her arm gently. "I'm sorry, Grandmother. God knows I did everything within my power to stop this from happening."

"I know," she replied somberly.

Bart knew the cannonballs would fly into the village, killing everyone within their range. Women . . . children . . . and Sheila! His heart pounded rapidly, and his stomach knotted with fear. God, if only he could reach the village and be with her.

Then, as though his prayer was answered, Donald rode over to him. "Chandler, since you love these Indians so much, you can join them."

Chapter Thirty-One

It was obvious to Bart why Donald was setting him free—to die in the village. That way, it would look as though he were fighting on the side of the Indians. However, his reasons didn't matter to Bart. He wanted to be with Sheila, regardless!

Donald spoke to Luke. "You can go with him," he said. He wanted Thomas dead, too.

"I will," Luke replied. Like Bart, he had figured out the lieutenant's motives. But he was willing to put his life on the line to help save Sheila and the others—especially the children!

"I want to leave with them," Golden Dove told Donald.

He shrugged, telling her he didn't care.

"No!" Bart insisted forcefully. "I mean what I say, Grandmother!" His eyes pleaded with hers. "Please

471

don't defy me! I have enough lives to worry about without worrying about yours too!''

Amanda agreed with Bart. That he and Luke would ride into the village terrified her, but she understood their reasons. Like Golden Dove, she longed to go with them, but why burden them with two more lives to guard? "Golden Dove," she said, "Bart's right; you must stay behind. We both must! We can be no help to them, only an added burden."

"Yes, you are right," Golden Dove relented. She looked at Bart. "I will stay behind."

Luke edged his horse closer to Amanda's, leaned over, and kissed her urgently. "I love you," he whispered.

She feared for his life. "Luke, please come back to me!"

He favored her with a twinkling wink. "I will, darlin'. We have a lot of years to catch up on."

Donald ordered the men to leave. They slapped their reins against their horses, took off with a bolt, and scaled the steep hillside.

Down below, the warriors watched them with misgivings. They recognized White Cloud and his companion, and wondered why they were returning. Was it some kind of trick? They didn't trust White Cloud, for they believed he had lied about the huge army with cannons.

Three Moons harbored much rage against White Cloud. He viewed him as a traitor and a liar. Slowly, he hefted his rifle to his shoulder and aimed the barrel at Bart. He had him in his sights and was about to pull the trigger when Yellow Bear grabbed the rifle.

"Do not shoot!" he ordered.

"Why not?" Three Moons argued fiercely. "Your brother is our enemy! He lied about the size of the Army! There are less bluecoats than we have warriors! And where are these cannons White Cloud warned us about?"

Yellow Bear pointed up at the soldiers.

Three Moons lifted his gaze to the hilltop and was astounded to see four cannons being rolled into place. His eyes bulged and his heart hammered.

"White Cloud did not lie," Yellow Bear asserted. Cold perspiration layered his brow, and he nervously rubbed a hand across his forehead.

Bart and Luke rode through the throng of warriors and reined in beside Yellow Bear. "Where is Sheila?" Bart asked at once.

"In the tepee with Dream Dancer and Spotted Wing." Yellow Bear sighed. "White Cloud, return to the soldiers and tell them we will surrender."

"The Dwyers won't accept your surrender. The skirmish you had with the soldiers gave them the provocation they needed to order a full attack."

Yellow Bear's expression was grave. "Then my people are doomed."

"We must save as many as we can," Bart said. "The woods are their best chance." A thick forest lay behind the village, but a long stretch of open land stood between it and the Indian camp. But, it was the only route available. If they moved quickly, they might be able to start the women, children, and old men on their way to the woods before the soldiers attacked. When the cannonballs started falling on the village, the people would be safer in the open than inside their homes.

"My warriors and I will stay and hold off the soldiers. You and Luke round up the people and tell them to head for the forest," Yellow Bear said.

Bart and Luke agreed. Their only purpose for returning was to try to save lives; neither man wanted to take up arms against the soldiers.

Lame Crow and his three great-grandsons, who were too young to fight, were standing nearby and heard the exchange between White Cloud and Yellow Bear. The old medicine man walked over. "My great-grandsons and I will help White Cloud and his friend gather the people," he said.

The group quickly split up. Lame Crow sent the youngsters in three different directions as he chose another. Luke and Bart headed toward Yellow Bear's tepee; their priority was to reach Sheila, Dream Dancer, and Spotted Wing. They hadn't gotten very far before the first cannonball exploded. It landed in the center of the village, blowing apart a tepee as though a stack of dynamite had gone off inside. Bart couldn't bear to think how many had died in the explosion. Another burst rocked the ground, and a second tepee was destroyed.

People now stampeded from their lodges. They were panic-stricken and disoriented. Most of them were women and children. Screaming mothers clutched their babies to their bosoms while trying desperately to keep the older children close to them.

Bart fought back his desire to reach Sheila, and pulled up to assist the others who were in need of help. It wasn't an easy decision, for he was worried to death about Sheila, but he couldn't race pass these people as though their lives didn't matter. He shouted to them to run for

474

the forest: a few heard and obeyed. There were many others, however, who were too paralyzed with fear to heed his advice. Bart dismounted, went to them and managed to calm them. Then he was able to persuade them to head for the woods. Through it all, more cannonballs fell. Some hit their targets, others veered out of harm's way.

Bart was surprised to find that his horse hadn't bolted. He ran to it and mounted swiftly. He looked about for Luke and spotted him assisting a group of women and children. As a sudden explosion reverberated dangerously close, Bart kneed the gelding into a fast gallop and raced farther into the village. He prayed he would find Sheila alive.

When the first cannon blast sounded, Sheila, Dream Dancer, and Spotted Wing wasted no time. Bolting from the tepee, they found as many women and children as possible and told them to flee the village. The carnage around them seemed like a nightmare.

But it was reality, and Sheila faced her own mortality as she remained in the village, searching for those who needed her help. She had lost sight of Spotted Wing in the chaos, but Dream Dancer was still close by.

Hysterical women, crying children, and elderly persons brushed past Sheila as they made their way to the village's outskirts, hoping desperately to reach the sanctuary of the forest.

Suddenly, Dream Dancer hurried to Sheila, grasped her arm, and said anxiously, "We can do no more! All the people now run to woods. We, too, must go!"

Sheila knew she was right. They were no longer needed and must think of their own lives. "Where is Spotted Wing?"

"I not know! Maybe she go to woods!"

Sheila quickly scanned her surroundings. Spotted Wing was nowhere in sight.

"Come!" Dream Dancer coaxed.

Clutching hands, the women began to run. The last stragglers were up ahead: they had almost caught them when Sheila detected an infant's demanding cry. She and Dream Dancer paused and listened closely. They tried to determine the baby's location, which was almost impossible, for three cannonballs struck one right after the other, as though they were playing follow the leader. The multiple explosions were ear-shattering, and completely drowned out the child's wailing. The booms faded like claps of thunder rumbling across the sky, and Sheila listened intently, hoping the baby would cry again.

Silence! God, she cried to herself, it must be dead! She wondered angrily which of the three cannonballs had killed the baby. She and Dream Dancer exchanged hopeless looks, then started to leave when the infant's weeping returned. The crying was now so pitiful that it sounded more like a mewing kitten.

The women, their ears cocked, retraced their steps. The child had to be somewhere close by. But where? Where?

Splitting up, they searched tepees and moved aside piles of rubble, but they failed to find the infant. It was no longer crying. Sheila prayed it wasn't dead. Frantically, she and Dream Dancer continued their pursuit.

Unbeknownst to Sheila and Dream Dancer, the last of

the cannons had been fired and the soldiers were now charging the village. Several warriors had been killed by the heavy artillery, and the soldiers encountered weak resistance.

Sheila was on the brink of giving up when she finally came upon the baby. It was lying beside a burning tepee, still wrapped in the arms of its dead mother.

"Over here!" she called to Dream Dancer. Sheila knelt and gently lifted the baby. It hiccupped and doubled its little hands into fists. Holding the child close, Sheila looked down at its mother through a teary blur. A deep gash was on her forehead. When the tepee exploded, something heavy must have struck against the woman's head. It probably killed her instantly. Sheila noticed a cast iron pot stained with blood.

Kneeling beside her, Dream Dancer gasped sadly. "The woman Brave Antelope's wife. The baby born two days ago."

They heard the pounding of horses' hooves, and bounded instantly to their feet. Sheila was uncertain whether to run or stay, but before she could decide, the riders came into view.

Elation swept through her when she recognized them as Bart and Luke, and with the baby still in her arms, she rushed to Bart, who leapt from his horse to draw her and her fragile bundle into his strong embrace.

"Thank God you're all right!" he groaned.

"Bart, is the battle over?" she cried, moving out of his arms to gaze into his face.

"I don't know," he replied. "But I doubt it. The soldiers are probably sweeping through the village. We must get out of here. The Dwyers want me dead."

477

Sheila readily agreed, but as she turned to tell Dream Dancer, a movement caught her eye. An old woman was stumbling toward her and the others. Her arm, which dangled lifelessly at her side, was bleeding copiously. "Bart, look!" Sheila cried.

As he left to help the wounded woman, Luke got down from his horse. He went to Sheila, and helped her onto Bart's gelding. She cradled the baby in one arm, and held the reins in the other. Luke then moved to Dream Dancer. "We'll have to put the woman on my horse, but you better ride with her," he said. He took Dream Dancer's arm and led her over to help her mount.

At that instant, Sergeant Kent came charging around the corner. He was looking for Bart, but failed to see him because he was tending to the old woman. But his search wasn't in vain, for he knew the lieutenant also wanted Thomas dead. He reined in abruptly, and pointed his pistol at Luke.

Within the blink of an eye, Luke's kindness flashed across Dream Dancer's mind. He had saved her life, and if it hadn't been for Luke, she would never have known Yellow Bear's love. Driven by heartfelt gratitude, she threw herself in front of Luke.

Before Luke could shove her aside, Kent pulled the trigger. The bullet meant for Luke plowed into Dream Dancer's back. She fell against Luke; he couldn't get to his gun.

The sergeant was about to fire a second time, but was stopped by a bullet plunging into his chest. The powerful force toppled him from his horse, and he dropped to the ground.

Bart hadn't missed, and, leaving the injured woman,

he rushed over to Kent. He was still breathing, but was seriously wounded. He then hurried to check on Dream Dancer.

Luke had gently eased her to the ground; her head was resting on his folded arm. Sheila had managed to hold on to the baby and also dismount. She was kneeling beside Luke and Dream Dancer.

"How is she?" Bart asked anxiously.

"She's dead," Luke replied, a sob lodged in his throat. "She saved my life. God! Dear God!"

Sheila's hand flew to her mouth to hold back a scream. Dream Dancer was dead! Although Sergeant Kent had fired the gun, Sheila knew the Dwyers were the real murderers. Now, she despised them even more.

Several riders were approaching, and Bart quickly helped Sheila to her feet and to his horse. Luke eased his arm gently from under Dream Dancer's head, then rushed to the old woman. He was leading her back to the others when the soldiers arrived.

Bart's gaze flew to the mounted troops. He expected to find Charles or Donald leading the group. His eyes widened incredulously; for a moment, he was too stunned to move. Then, as his shock waned, he went over to the soldiers.

The officer in charge dismounted, and the civilian riding at his side leapt down from his horse. He was in his early sixties, but moved with the litheness of a man years younger. He hurried to Bart and embraced him vigorously.

"J.W.!" Bart exclaimed. "My God, what are you doing here?"

"Looking for you, of course!"

The officer with J.W. was Captain Evans. Bart recognized him from Fort Laramie.

"General Pollard is here, too," J.W. told Bart. "He ordered this attack stopped, and is now talking to the Dwyers. This battle will be thoroughly investigated. I've known Pollard for years; he's a good officer." Catching sight of Thomas, J.W. turned to shake his hand. "Luke, thank God you and Bart are all right!"

Bart motioned for Sheila to step forward, and, draping an arm around her shoulders, he introduced her to his grandfather. "Sheila and I are getting married," he added.

J.W. smiled with pleasure. "Miss Langsford, welcome to the family."

"Please call me Sheila."

"I will," he replied. He regarded her with an approving eye, then noticing the child, asked, "Whose baby is that?"

"The child's mother was killed," Sheila explained. "Dream Dancer and I found the baby." As she spoke Dream Dancer's name, the young woman's death hit her with a terrible force. Tears gushed from her eyes, and she turned to Bart, who drew her close.

Bart nodded toward Dream Dancer's body, telling J.W. that Sergeant Kent killed her. He then let the captain know that he had shot the sergeant but that he was still alive.

Evans ordered two soldiers to put Kent on a horse and take him to the doctor.

"J.W.," Luke began. "Do you mind tellin' us just what the hell's goin' on? How did you get here?"

"I found I couldn't sit at home and do nothing but

worry about you and Bart. So I went to Fort Laramie. General Pollard happened to arrive the day after I got there. To make a long story short, he told me I could ride with him to Fort Swafford. We were hoping to find you and Bart there. Colonel Langsford had received a wire from Major Dwyer, saying that Sheila had been found with a party of others. When we got to the fort, we learned that Dwyer had left to attack this village. I had a hunch you and Bart might be involved, so I came along with the soldiers. A scout at Fort Swafford knew the way to this village, and he led us here."

Steadily, the people began trudging back to their lodges. Many discovered they no longer had homes. Bart called to three matronly women who were walking in a huddled group. They came over, and he gave them the baby and asked them to take care of the injured woman.

Luke cast a sad gaze at Dream Dancer's body. "I'll find Yellow Bear."

"God, I hope he's alive!" Bart said.

"He is," Captain Evans replied. "I saw him when we entered the village."

"I feel so sorry for him," Sheila moaned. "He lost so many of his people, including his own wife!"

"Thanks to the Dwyers!" Bart said fiercely. He spoke to Captain Evans. "Will those bastards be court-martialed?"

Evans didn't like the Dwyers, and he would relish their court-martial, but he knew it would never come to that. He shook his head somberly. "Before it's over with, they'll come out of this looking like heroes. Men like the Dwyers always come out ahead!"

481

Bart was worried about Spotted Wing and was relieved to learn that she had fled the village along with a group of women and children. She returned to find that Three Moons was missing and that her sister-in-law was dead. She tried to console Yellow Bear, but he was so heartbroken that he was beyond consolation. She searched for Three Moons among the dead, but couldn't find him. Witnesses claimed he was badly wounded, but none of these people had any idea where he was or what had happened to him.

The soldiers set up a temporary camp within sight of the village. Tents were erected for the officers and the women. Inside General Pollard's quarters, he questioned separately the Dwyers, the soldiers, and the civilians. After a couple of hours he was able to understand everything more clearly. Pollard didn't especially like the Dwyers, but he agreed with their reasons for coming here to arrest Yellow Bear. The Indians had fired first, which had given them the right to defend themselves. He saw no reason to bring charges against the major or the lieutenant.

The general sent for Yellow Bear, and listened to his testimony with an open mind. He talked to the warrior at length, and when their conversation ended, he believed in Yellow Bear's innocence. He promised he would try to have the accusation of murder against him dismissed, but if he couldn't manage it, then Yellow Bear would have to stand trial again. The first trial had obviously been biased. He diplomatically pointed out to Yellow Bear that if he would give his word to keep his people on the reservation, his cooperation would carry much influence with the Army. The white leaders would not be opposed to setting a peaceful chief free.

Yellow Bear gave the general his word that he would keep peace. He was tired of fighting; he knew it was a lost cause. The bluecoats were destined to win, and if he wanted to save his people, then the reservation was the only answer.

Pollard then talked alone with J.W. and assured him that he didn't believe Bart or the others were traitors. He promised him that no charges would be forthcoming, and that Bart was free to return to Texas.

The Dwyers were ordered again to the general's tent, where the man let them know that Bart Chandler would not be arrested. The brothers weren't pleased with Pollard's decision; however, they weren't about to argue with their commanding officer. The general, glad that the unpleasant situation was finally settled, poured glasses of brandy for the two officers, and then with a smile, told them that their transfers to General Custer's command had been approved. The Dwyers were elated, and, along with Pollard, they drank a toast to George Custer and to his ultimate victory over the Indians—a victory in which the Dwyers planned to play a large part!

Sheila left the tent she shared with the other women, went to the river, and walked downstream. She carried a bar of soap and a towel, for she planned to wash. She also had her rifle. She wasn't about to be caught without protection. Night had fallen, but a full moon lit her way. The nearby village was eerily quiet, and such stark silence was unnerving. So many Indians had been killed, yet no sounds of mourning could be heard. It was as though the survivors' hearts and souls had died, and they hadn't the spirit to grieve. Sheila knew they were in shock. In time, the shock would wane. Then they would have to face the tragedy and find a way to accept it.

Finding a secluded spot, Sheila knelt at the river's bank, laid her rifle aside, and washed her face, arms, and hands. She toweled herself dry, then sat down and gazed dreamily up at the stars lighting the vast heavens. Bart had told her that no charges of treason would be brought against them, and the news had lifted a heavy weight from her heart. They also discussed their wedding, and decided to wait and get married at the Triangle-C. They planned to travel to Fort Laramie so she could see her father. Then they would leave for Texas.

Suddenly, sensing another's presence, Sheila turned and looked over her shoulder. Donald had slipped up behind her. She reached for her rifle, but he moved quickly and pinned the gun under his boot.

"I saw you leave the tent, and I decided to follow you," he said, grinning. "You and I have some unfinished business to take care of."

"What do you mean?" she asked, glaring.

"You know what I mean," he replied. "Don't play dumb with me!" It didn't dawn on him that Sheila had no clear memory of that night in his room; he took for granted that she remembered everything. A cruel sneer curled his lips as he continued. "You owe me something, Sheila, and I intend to collect. This time you can't dissuade me by getting drunk and passing out. You were real sly, weren't you? You knew I wouldn't take you if you were in a drunken stupor. I couldn't very well humble and conquer you if you were unconscious. Your plan worked perfectly, didn't it? In fact, it probably worked better than you thought it would. If I hadn't fallen asleep in the stables, believe me, I would have returned and made you pay. But by the time I woke up, it was already morning and I didn't have time.''

Sheila listened raptly, and the missing pieces began to fall into place. No wonder she didn't remember Donald defiling her—it hadn't happened! She was filled with joy, but she needed to know more. Hiding her surprise, she asked evenly, ''Tell me, Donald, did you get drunk, too? I mean, you did drink champagne. You even used both glasses, didn't you?''

''What if I did?'' he questioned, finding her questions absurd.

''That morning when I woke up, you had come back to your room to change clothes.''

A puzzled frown furrowed his brow. ''Hell, yes! My uniform was wrinkled. I had slept in it all night.'' Donald, taken aback, watched as Sheila smiled brightly. He thought she was laughing at him. ''You might as well wipe that grin off your face, you arrogant little bitch! I'm here to collect, and you're going to pay up!''

''Are you completely mad?'' she lashed out. ''You wouldn't dare touch me!''

''Wouldn't I?'' he came back fiercely. ''Are you planning to cry rape? Who would believe you? The whole fort knows you spent the night in my room!''

''You bastard!'' she seethed, trying desperately to wedge her rifle out from under his foot.

Drawing back his arm, Donald swung out and slapped

her powerfully across the face. Then, kicking the rifle out of reach, he dropped to the ground and covered her body with his. He clamped a hand over her mouth to muffle her screams.

Sheila, refusing to surrender, squirmed strongly and somehow found the strength to shove him aside, raise her knee, and jab it into his groin.

Excruciating pain coursed through Donald, and, for an instant, he was paralyzed. Sheila moved swiftly, scrambled to her hands and knees, and crawled to her rifle. She grabbed it, cocked it, and as Donald started to lurch for her, she aimed it at his heart. "Stop, or so help me God, I'll send you to hell where you belong!"

He froze, and stared down at the barrel with wide-open eyes.

She got carefully to her feet, gesturing for him to stand up also. He did so shakily.

She saw Bart and Captain Evans coming toward them, and lowered her rifle. Bart, learning that Sheila had gone off alone, was looking for her. Suspecting he might find her with the lieutenant, he had asked the captain to come with him. He had a score to settle with Donald, and needed the captain as a witness. He planned to beat the hell out of Dwyer, and wanted Evans to verify that he had just cause.

"What's going on?" Bart asked Sheila.

"This poor excuse for a man tried to rape me!" she answered.

"That isn't true!" Donald declared, speaking to the captain.

The slap Dwyer had delivered had cut Sheila's lip, and it was bleeding noticeably. The captain gave her his handkerchief. "If you didn't attack the lady," he said to Donald, "then why is she bleeding?"

Donald couldn't come up with a reason why.

Captain Evans had no use for either Dwyer. He glanced at Bart and nodded his approval. That Chandler was itching to fight the lieutenant was obvious, and Evans was looking forward to watching Donald get the hell beat out of him.

Bart stepped closer to his opponent. "You've had this coming for a long time," he muttered, then, moving with incredible speed, he doubled his hand into a fist and sent it plowing into Donald's face.

Tremendous pain erupted in Dwyer's head, and, stumbling backward, he almost lost his footing. He made an awkward move to defend himself, but before he could, Bart's fist slammed into his stomach, cutting off his breath. Then a vicious upper cut landed across Donald's chin, and the force sent him toppling to the ground.

Standing over him, Bart raged, "Get up, you bastard! I'm not through with you yet!"

"Please!" Donald moaned. "I give up!"

Bart's anger was not appeased. He wanted to kick the man in the ribs, jerk him to his feet, and force him to fight, but he was stopped by Sheila's hand on his arm.

"Bart, leave him alone. He isn't worth it."

Her words mellowed his anger, and he backed away.

Donald got up clumsily. His nose was bleeding and his jaw throbbed terribly. He was about to hurl verbal threats at Bart, but never got the chance. A gunshot suddenly exploded thunderously, and the fired bullet hit its target. A gaping hole was ripped into Donald's chest, and he fell over dead.

Three Moons, who had slipped up undetected, dropped his rifle. He had been injured in the battle, and blood was still oozing from a stomach wound. He dropped to his knees, then slowly sank forward.

Bart hurried over and knelt beside him. He could see that the warrior was a breath away from death.

"Is Dwyer dead?" he asked weakly.

There was no doubt about it. "Yes," Bart answered.

"Good," Three Moons murmured. For hours, he had hid in the shadows, waiting for an opportunity to kill at least one more enemy before dying himself. The warrior coughed feebly, then drew his final breath.

The rifle shot had alerted the camp. Charles and several soldiers came running. As Dwyer rushed to his brother's body, Bart went to Sheila, who was staring at Donald, her face deathly pale.

Bart urged her back toward camp, and Sheila told him what really happened that night in Donald's room. Her relief was palpable. Bart drew her into his arms and kissed her.

Chapter Thirty-Two

Sheila watched her father closely as she waited for his response. She had just finished telling him about the way Donald had treated her. Langsford was sitting in his easy chair, but he wasn't relaxed; his body was taut with anger.

Sheila and the others had arrived at Fort Laramie about an hour ago. Langsford had joyfully welcomed his daughter, then had taken her to his home where they could be alone. There, over steaming cups of coffee, she had filled him in on what had taken place since her abduction. He had listened closely, seldom had he interrupted to ask questions.

As her story unfolded, Langsford felt an intense rage against Lieutenant Dwyer and could hardly believe that he had once held the young officer in such high regard. He also harbored much resentment against Major Dwyer. He considered making a military complaint against the man, but decided it would serve no purpose; the major would undoubtedly emerge untarnished; Sheila, however, would not be as fortunate. She would face public embarrassment, and in the colonel's opinion, Major Dwyer wasn't worth subjecting his daughter to such scandal.

Now, he filled his coffee cup for the second time, took a sip of the hot beverage, and studied Sheila over the rim. He could see that her experience had changed her; she was more mature and had learned a lot about human nature. She was also very much in love, when she spoke about Bart Chandler, adoration shone in her eyes. The colonel was happy for her—Chandler sounded like a honorable man, and would no doubt be a good provider. He had heard of the Triangle-C and was also familiar with J.W.'s reputation. Sheila was obviously becoming part of a good and successful family.

"Sheila," he began, smiling tenderly. "I'm glad that everything has worked out so well. You came out of this ordeal unscathed and are engaged to the man you love."

Unscathed? Sheila wasn't so sure. She knew she would never forget the soldiers' attack on Yellow Bear's village; nor would she forget Dream Dancer. That horrible day would stay with her forever. But she knew it would be useless to talk about it to her father; he wouldn't understand. He still saw Indians as savages who needed to be destroyed or placed on reservations.

"My retirement has been approved," Langsford continued. "I was free to leave days ago, but I wasn't about to do so until you were found. I plan to live in Kentucky, near your aunt and uncle. Someday, I hope to visit you and Bart at the Triangle-C."

A hollow look had come to her father's eyes, and Sheila was sure it was brought on by thinking of his retirement. The man had lived for the Army, and now that driving force had been taken away from him. She found herself feeling sorry for the colonel. "You're more than welcome to visit us anytime you please."

His rheumatism was sending shooting pains down his legs, and he shifted in his chair, hoping a different position would ease his discomfort. It didn't help much. "I haven't been a very good father, have I?"

His question, coming out of nowhere, surprised Sheila. But she answered honestly. "No, not really. But I guess you did the best you could."

"You're very kind, Sheila. So was your mother. You're very much like her."

She left the sofa, sat on the floor beside her father's chair, and took the hand he offered her.

"If I had my life to live over," Langsford murmured with remorse, "I'd be a much better father. I would also have been a more loving husband. But I let my career mean everything to me. I was such a fool."

Her father had never before spoken so intimately to her, and Sheila squeezed his hand with love. "It's never too late. You can visit me often, and, who knows, maybe someday you'll become a doting grandfather."

"And a more considerate father," he added, meaning it sincerely.

Yellow Bear's people were escorted back to the reservation, but Spotted Wing, Lame Crow, and Brave Antelope were given permission to camp outside the fort's gates. Yellow Bear was again locked in the stockade to await a new trial or an acquittal.

Golden Dove, preferring to stay with Spotted Wing, refused a room at the fort's hotel. In any case, she was more comfortable in a tepee. She wondered if she would ever feel at ease in the white man's dwellings. After all, it had been over forty years since she had been inside such a building.

Golden Dove was sitting outside with the others when they saw Bart and Yellow Bear walking through the fort's open gates. They bounded to their feet with wide smiles. Apparently, Yellow Bear had been given his freedom!

Racing to her youngest grandson, Golden Dove embraced him enthusiastically.

"I will not stand trial, Grandmother. The murder accusation has been dropped. But I had to give the bluecoats my word to keep my people on the reservation."

She gently pushed out of his arms. "Yellow Bear, you made the right decision. Our people will survive then."

A tear moistened the corner of his eye, and he quickly brushed it away. "Yes, they will survive," he said with sadness. "But their tribulations have only begun." He moved away to talk to Lame Crow and Brave Antelope.

Golden Dove turned to Bart. "He is right, you know. The people are not treated fairly on the reservations. They often go without enough food or clothing."

"Grandmother, thanks to J.W., I'm a rich man. I intend to help Yellow Bear and his people."

"You are very kind, White Cloud. I am so proud of you."

"We plan to leave in the morning. Sheila and I are

anxious to reach the Triangle-C so we can get married. I'm also eager to show off my home to you."

"White Cloud," she began hesitantly, "I . . . I have decided not to go to Texas with you. I will stay behind with Yellow Bear and Spotted Wing."

"What!" he exclaimed. "You can't mean that!" His disappointment was intense.

"Yellow Bear and Spotted Wing need me more than you do."

"Grandmother, they have had you with them for these past ten years. Why can't you spend time with *me?*"

Golden Dove lowered her gaze, stared at the ground for a moment, then gazed back into Bart's eyes. She intended to be perfectly honest. "White Cloud, I owe it to them to remain. You have always been my favorite grandchild. You and your father were my whole life. It was wrong for me to feel that way. Yellow Bear and Spotted Wing are also my family, and it is only right that I stay with them."

"You're staying out of guilt."

"Yes, but I'm also staying out of love."

"You should leave with White Cloud," Yellow Bear's voice suddenly intruded. He and Spotted Wing had walked up quietly. They had overheard their grandmother's words. "Spotted Wing and I have always known how much you love White Cloud. You do not need to feel guilty. We understand."

"Golden Dove," Spotted Wing said. "You are a good grandmother, but White Cloud is right. Now, you must spend time with him."

"You are a white woman," Yellow Bear added kindly.

493

"Go back to your own world. Our grandfather should never have taken you away."

"Grandmother," Bart pleaded. "I promise we'll visit Yellow Bear and Spotted Wing often. They're my family. Do you think I don't intend to see them again?"

Golden Dove was close to relenting. "But, White Cloud, what about J.W.?"

"What about him?"

"He might not want me in his home."

"He told me you're more than welcome."

"All right, I'll leave with you." But Golden Dove was doubtful. She couldn't quite shake the gnawing feeling that J.W. would resent her living with them. After all, it was her son who stole his daughter!

J.W. had a room at the hotel, and was drinking a brandy when a knock sounded at his door. He was surprised to find that his visitor was Golden Dove. He invited her inside, put his glass on a table, he drew up and asked her to be seated in the small chair.

She perched on the chair's edge, clasped her hands tightly in her lap, and began softly. "Mr. Chandler, my grandson has assured me that I'm welcome at the Triangle-C. However, I think he speaks only for himself. You don't want me there, do you?"

J.W. was astonished. "Why do you think that?"

"You probably blame me in part for your daughter's abduction. I should have forced my son to return her to you."

"I wonder if you could have made your son give her up. How much influence did you have over him?"

"Not nearly as much as his father had. I'm not sure if I could have persuaded him to give Elizabeth back to you."

J.W. drew up a matching chair, and placed it facing Golden Dove. He sat down, and studied her for a long moment. He found her very attractive. He wondered how she would look in a stylish dress with her hair out of braids. He hoped she would eventually decide to discard her Indian apparel, for he was suddenly very anxious to see her as a white woman.

"What was your Christian name?" he asked.

"Margaret Latham."

"Do you mind if I call you Margaret?"

"No, I suppose not. However, after so many years, it sounds strange to my ears."

"Your English impresses me. Why is it you still speak it so flawlessly?"

"I never let myself forget. I also taught it to others, which helped keep it fresh in my mind."

He regarded her speculatively. "You never really became a Sioux. Did you, Margaret Latham?"

She glanced away from his knowing eyes. "No," she whispered. "But I loved my Sioux husband."

"Did Elizabeth love your son?"

"Yes, she did. But she never stopped missing you."

"Why didn't Iron Star let her come see me?"

"He was afraid you wouldn't let her come back to him."

"He was right. I *would* never have allowed it."

"I'm sorry my son took her away from you."

"So am I," he sighed heavily. "But it happened years ago and there's nothing we can do to change it. Margaret,

495

believe me, you are very welcome in my home. I do not hold you responsible for Iron Star's actions. Furthermore, every cloud has a silver lining, even Elizabeth's abduction."

"A silver lining?" she questioned.

"Yes. Bart."

Golden Dove smiled. "You love him very much, don't you?"

"Probably as much as you."

She glazed intently into his gray eyes. They reflected kindness and honesty. She found herself drawn to him; not since High Hawk had she felt such warmth toward a man. As flush rose to her cheeks, and as she got to her feet, her knees felt a little shaky.

"Thank you, Mr. Chandler, for inviting me to stay in your home."

"Please call me J.W."

"Isn't your name James West?"

"Yes," he replied.

"Would you mind if I called you James?"

He smiled expansively. Like Golden Dove, he was feeling a strong attraction. "If you want to call me James, that's fine."

She went to the door. "Amanda and Luke are getting married this afternoon. Will you be there?"

"Yes, I will."

"Then I'll see you later."

He opened the door, and she darted out quickly. She walked outside with light steps; she suddenly felt years younger. Her heart was beating rapidly, but stronger than ever!

* * *

Amanda and Luke were married in the chapel. Amanda made a beautiful bride. Days ago, her cedar chest had arrived from Fort Swafford, and she chose her prettiest gown to wear for the ceremony.

A reception followed at Colonel Langsford's house. The bride and groom remained a couple of hours, then, anxious to be alone, they thanked their host, slipped outside, and hurried to the hotel where Luke had been staying.

A bottle of champagne awaited. They drank a toast to their marriage, then Luke stepped into the hall so Amanda could undress in private.

She was jittery, and her hands trembled as she removed her dress and slipped into her pale-pink nightgown. She went to the dresser and brushed her long golden-brown tresses. Then stepping back, she viewed her full reflection. She tried to see herself through Luke's eyes. Would he find her as desirable as he had twenty years ago? She certainly hoped so!

Suddenly, Luke rapped on the door. "Mrs. Thomas, your husband is growin' mighty impatient!"

"Come in," she called, smiling with anticipation.

He did so at once, locking the door behind him. His gaze swept over her with hungry desire. He moved to her slowly, allowing his eyes to feast upon her beauty.

She went into his arms, and he held her close. "Amanda, I love you so much."

"I know, my darling, and I love you, too. I always have."

He kissed her with urgent passion. Then, lifting her into his arms, he carried her to the bed. The covers were drawn back, and he laid her gently on the freshly washed sheets.

"It's been a long time, Amanda. But you know, I still remember that night we made love. I can recall it like it was yesterday."

"So can I. I remember it vividly."

"We were so much in love." He grinned tenderly. "We still are!"

"Forever," she said.

He kissed her again, and their desire burned fervently as they clung to each other. In time, their passion was blazing, and Luke left the bed to remove his clothes.

Amanda, watching through love-glazed eyes, boldly admired his strong, masculine physique. He was still impressively virile, and just looking at him sent desire coursing through her.

She held out her arms, and he went into them. Lacing her arms around his neck, she urged his lips down to hers, and soon, their bodies came together as one, consummating their marriage and sealing their everlasting love.

Sheila hummed a lively tune as she packed her belongings, and had closed the last piece of luggage when Amanda rapped on the bedroom door and came inside.

"Good morning, Mrs. Thomas," Sheila said, smiling.

Amanda actually glowed. "Mrs. Thomas! What a beautiful name!"

"You've been married now for . . . ." she quickly

counted in her head, "almost sixteen hours. Marriage agrees with you. You look absolutely ravishing!"

"Sheila, must you tease?" Amanda laughed lightly.

She went to her friend and hugged her. "Happiness radiates from you, Amanda!"

"You'll be married yourself soon, and you'll be just as happy as I am."

"Yes, and I can hardly wait!"

"The others will be here any minute. Are you ready to leave?"

Sheila looked about the room to see if she had forgotten anything, but all her belongings were packed. "Yes, I'm ready." A bright smile lit up her face. "I've waited a long time for this day. At last, Bart and I are going home!"

A knock sounded on the door, followed by Colonel Langsford's voice. "Sheila, Mrs. Gilbert is here to see you and Mrs. Thomas."

"Tell her we'll be right there," Sheila told him. She looked at Amanda. "I wonder what Janice wants."

"I suppose she wants to tell us goodbye."

They left the bedroom and went to the parlor, where Janice was waiting. The colonel, saying he would see to Sheila's luggage, left the ladies alone.

Janice was looking exceptionally lovely. Her auburn tresses cascaded radiantly past her shoulders, and emerald earrings sparkled brightly each time she moved her head. She was wearing a stylish summer gown that gracefully emphasized her full breasts and tiny waist. Her eyes swept over Sheila and Amanda. They were both dressed in riding apparel. "Well, I see you're ready to leave. I stopped by to tell you goodbye, and good riddance!"

"Thank you, Janice," Sheila replied. "The feeling is mutual."

She lifted her chin smugly. "Someday, you two will wish you had been nicer to me. Charles and I are getting married tomorrow, and as soon as the Indian situation is under control, Charles plans to leave the Army. We're moving to his home state, where he intends to run for the Senate. He'll win, too, because the people view him as a hero." A childish pout made the corners of her lips droop. "Then you'll be sorry that we aren't friends."

"Why, pray tell, will we be sorry?" Amanda asked.

"Don't act dumb, Amanda! If we were friends, I'd invite you to Washington, where you could hobnob with very important people. But, instead, you'll be living on a dull old ranch, raising cattle and wet-nosed kids!"

"You're pathetic, Janice," Sheila said, feeling almost sorry for her.

"Pathetic, am I?" She laughed nastily. "You'll eat those words when I'm living in the White House!" With that, she brushed past them and headed for the front door. She stopped suddenly, turned back, and said haughtily, "I'm so glad we'll never see each other again!"

"Goodbye, Janice," the women chorused.

She left, slamming the door behind her.

J.W. offered to drive the covered wagon. He invited Golden Dove to ride with him, and was very happy when she agreed to do so. The others preferred to travel horseback.

Sheila bid her father a tearful farewell, extracting his

promise that he wouldn't wait too long before visiting the Triangle-C.

As they headed toward the fort's open gates, Charles and Janice, standing outside his office, watched them leave. For a fleeting moment, Janice actually envied Sheila and Amanda; deep inside she somehow knew she would never experience their kind of happiness—complete, unselfish, and wonderfully rewarding! She quickly wiped such foolishness from her mind. Envy them, indeed! They should envy *her*, for someday she would have the world!

Charles watched them leave with little emotion. He was willing to forget Bart Chandler, as well as Sheila. He had no time to dwell on past grievances; he was too elated over joining General Custer, though his joy was marred by the loss of his brother. Still, riding with the prestigious general would be a feather in his cap, and his name would soon be known across the country. That, of course, would benefit his political career immensely!

Yellow Bear and Spotted Wing were waiting outside the fort's gates. Telling them goodbye was difficult for Bart and Golden Dove. Bart's gaze remained on his sister and brother as they rode away from the fort and caught up to Lame Crow and Brave Antelope, who were waiting in the distance. They turned, waved a final farewell, then headed for the reservation.

Sheila brought her horse alongside Bart's. "We'll see them again," she said, placing a loving hand on his arm.

He smiled wistfully. "Yes, I know."

"Bart!" J.W. yelled from the wagon. "Let's get moving! Aren't you anxious to get home?"

Bart's smile widened into one of joy. "You're damned right I'm anxious!" he called back. His gaze settled on Sheila. "How about you, sweetheart? Are you ready to go home?"

"Oh, yes!" she exclaimed. "Darling, I've never been more anxious to go anywhere!"

He leaned over his horse, kissed her lips softly, then said with an eager grin, "Let's go home!"

Epilogue

THREE MONTHS LATER

Sheila loved the Triangle-C. It was home—and she had never really had a home before. When she lived with her aunt and uncle, they had told her their home was hers, but she had still felt like an intruder. Their elegant house, and their magnificent thoroughbreds, belonged to them and to their children. She didn't truly belong, and never stopped hoping that her father would send for her.

Now, Sheila knew she had finally come home! J.W. was more than ready to hand over the care of his house to Sheila, and with the housekeeper's help, she took over happily. She didn't, however, rearrange the furniture, buy more, or get rid of any of the pieces—she loved the house just the way it was!

The Triangle-C was a mammoth spread, and Sheila

often rode horseback across the wide-open plains. She had always loved to ride, and now she was free to race with the wind anytime she pleased.

Operating the huge ranch occupied a lot of Bart's time, but Sheila didn't mind. His nights always belonged to her! They had now been married almost three months, and their passion was still as demanding as ever. Sheila knew that their love would always burn with wonderful fervor, and this filled her with delight.

Sheila had awakened early this morning, for she had a busy day facing her. She ate breakfast with her husband, then went for her morning ride. An hour or so later, she returned and helped the housekeeper with her chores. Margaret—Golden Dove had taken back her Christian name—had claimed the kitchen as her private domain, and she always prepared sumptuous meals, which were often a cross between her mother's cooking and savory Sioux dishes. At noon, Bart and J.W. returned to the house for lunch; the ladies joined them, then the men went back to work. Sheila had the buggy hitched and rode into town, for she had a very important appointment to keep.

When she returned, she took a long nap, then dressed for dinner. They were expecting guests—Amanda and Luke. Bart came home just as she was finishing. His eyes swept appreciatively over his wife; she was a vision of loveliness. Sheila had chosen one of her nicest gowns; one of sea-green silk trimmed with black lace. It was made to bare her shoulders and temptingly reveal the cleavage between her ample breasts. Her chestnut tresses were unbound, and the dark locks tumbled down her back in shiny waves. She wore a gold locket and a pair of dainty earrings that Bart had given her on their wedding day. The jewelry had belonged to his mother, an inheritance from her paternal grandmother.

"You look very beautiful," he said, desire glowing in his eyes. There was something different about Sheila tonight, but he couldn't quite put his finger on it. She seemed to have a special glow.

"I laid out your clothes," she told him. She gestured toward a filled tub. "And your bath awaits, Mr. Chandler."

"Thank you, Mrs. Chandler." He began to remove his dust-coated duds. "Are we expecting anyone besides Amanda and Luke?"

"No," she replied. "Why?"

His gaze went over her evening gown, and the attire she had picked out for him. "We don't usually dress so formally for Amanda and Luke."

"But tonight is a very special night."

He arched a brow. "Oh? Why is that?"

"Never you mind," she said. "You'll find out when the time is right."

She left him to his bath, and was descending the stairs when their guests knocked on the front door. She let them in and led them into the parlor.

"Where is everyone?" Luke asked.

"Bart is getting ready; he'll be here soon." She was about to say she didn't know about the others when Margaret and J.W. entered the room.

"Did any of you go into town today and hear the news?" Luke asked.

"I went into town, but I didn't hear any news," Sheila said. But then she hadn't mingled. She had kept her appointment then had come straight home.

"What's the news?" J.W. inquired.

"I'll wait for Bart. That way, I don't have to tell it twice."

Drinks were served, and conversation was flowing when Bart arrived. Dressed in a dark jacket, white shirt, and black trousers, he looked very handsome. Sheila's face lit up with pride, as well as desire.

As Bart poured himself a brandy, Luke revealed his news. "I was in town this afternoon and learned that General Custer and his entire cavalry were massacred."

"All of them?" Bart asked, astounded.

"Yep, every last one. They died at a place called the Little Big Horn, wiped out by the Sioux and the Cheyenne. Custer had over two hundred men, and not one of them survived."

"Then that means Major Dwyer is . . . ?" Sheila gasped.

"Dead?" Luke finished. "Exactly."

"Poor Janice," Amanda said. "Instead of being a politician's wife, she's an officer's widow."

"Which isn't much compensation," Luke put in. "Dwyer wasn't rich, and I don't imagine he left much to his widow."

"Women like Janice always survive," Bart said. "She'll find another prey to sink her claws into."

Margaret spoke sadly. "The Sioux will pay dearly for their victory. Now the Army will certainly show them no mercy."

Bart went to his grandmother and placed a consoling hand on her shoulder. "We can be thankful Yellow Bear wasn't involved."

She nodded somberly. "Yes, I am thankful for that."

Margaret, sitting on the front porch, closed her eyes, and listened closely to the music. Bart, inside the parlor, was playing the piano. His talent never failed to amaze her. He played often for his grandmother, and as she watched his fingers fly gracefully across the ivory keys, she found it hard to believe that he had been born in an Indian village. Bart Chandler had nothing left of the fourteen-year-old White Cloud who had been raised as a Sioux.

J.W. was also on the front porch, and he, too, listened as Bart's playing drifted through the open windows, filling the night with beautiful music. Sheila and their guests were in the room with Bart.

"What are you thinking about?" J.W. asked Margaret, his thoughts turning away from the music. He hoped she wasn't still upset over Custer's defeat.

She opened her eyes and looked at him. They were both sitting in pine rockers, which were placed close together. "I was thinking about Bart, and how happy I am that he came here to live with you. If he had remained with the Sioux . . . he would have missed out on so much!"

"He never belonged with the Sioux. He belonged here. I think he knew that from the day he arrived."

"You were very kind to take him in." She smiled

warmly. "And you're very kind to give me a home, too."

"Margaret, these past three months have been wonderful. What I feel for you is much stronger than kindness. But you surely know that."

"Yes, James," she murmured. "I know, and I feel the same way."

He took her hand into his, and held it gently. She was wearing a blue calico gown, and her hair was arranged in a stylish upswept fashion. J.W. thought her very beautiful. "Margaret, are we too old for love?" he asked so softly that she barely heard.

"I don't know about you, but I've never felt younger."

"I've been feeling a lot of vim and vigor myself," he said with a grin. "What do you think Bart and Sheila would say if we told them we were getting married?"

"Is that a marriage proposal?" Her eyes twinkled.

"It certainly is."

"I think Bart and Sheila would wish us happiness."

"Is that a 'yes–' to my proposal?"

"It certainly is."

Elated, he stood, drew her to her feet, and into his arms. Holding her close, he kissed her tenderly and from the depth of his heart. "Shall we go inside and tell the others there's going to be a wedding?"

A bright smile, lit up her eyes and took years off her actual age. "Yes, let's tell the others!" Margaret had never been happier, or more content.

J.W., his happiness as complete as Margaret's, leaned over and whispered in her ear, "They say, my dear, that love is better the second time around."

"Do you believe that?"

"Wholeheartedly."

"So do I." Inviting him to kiss her again, she laced her arms around his neck.

Sheila, wearing her nightgown, sat at the vanity and brushed her hair with long, brisk strokes. Bart was already in bed, impatiently waiting for his wife to join him there.

"Isn't it wonderful about Margaret and J.W.?" she asked. "I'm so happy for them." She looked at her husband. "Aren't you?"

"Of course, I am. But my grandmother marrying my grandfather seems a little strange."

Sheila laughed lightly. "Yes, but they are your grandparents from different sides of the family."

Bart shook his head with amusement. "One never knows how life's gonna turn out." His gaze lingered on Sheila. The saffron glow from the lone lamp was temptingly illuminating her soft curves beneath the sheer gown. "Sheila, you've brushed your hair long enough; come to bed."

"I have only five more strokes, then I will have reached a hundred."

"By the way, you haven't told me why tonight was special. Did you know J.W. was going ask my grandmother to marry him?"

"No, I didn't," she replied. She completed the remaining strokes, then moved to the bed and sat on the edge. Gazing down into Bart's eyes, she smiled radiantly,

"This afternoon I went into town and saw the doctor. Darling, we're going to have a baby. That's why tonight is special."

Bart couldn't have been happier, and drawing her into his arms, he kissed her eagerly. "Does anyone else know?" he asked.

"No, I wanted you to know first. We'll tell Margaret and J.W. in the morning. They'll be overjoyed."

Bart drew back the covers, and she snuggled beside him. "Sheila, I never dreamed I could feel as much happiness as I do at this moment."

"I know what you mean. I feel the same way. A baby! Oh, Bart, I can hardly wait!"

He drew her body close to his, then kissed her gently, but with promise of passion.

"I want you, darling," she purred. "Make love to me."

"Gladly," he whispered, his lips seizing hers. Anxious to possess her, he removed her flimsy gown and pitched it carelessly to the floor. Bart always slept naked, a habit from his boyhood, and he pressed his body against Sheila's.

They surrendered blissfully to their passion; each kiss and touch intensified their desire until it burned like wildfire. Their bodies fused into one, and they soared upward to an ecstatic fulfillment that left them breathless.

"Oh, Bart," Sheila said, her voice tinged with rapture. "Our love keeps getting better and better!"

He chuckled. "If it gets any better than this, I'll think I am in heaven."

She cuddled against him, resting her head on his shoulder. "I love you, White Cloud."

"White Cloud?" He wondered why she had used his Sioux name.

"You were White Cloud when I fell in love with you." She leaned up, gazed into his eyes, and smiled. "My handsome warrior, I adore you with all my heart."

He drew her against his chest and held her protectively close. "I love you, Sheila. I always will."

They discussed the baby for a long time, then, feeling wonderfully content, Sheila fell asleep. She slept soundly, for she was safe in her husband's loving arms.